The
Music
Makers

SHIRLEY RUSSAK WACHTEL

ISBN: 1500785520
ISBN 13: 9781500785529

"Wachtel views her mother's remarkable life, first recounted in *The Story of Blima: A Holocaust Survivor (2005)*, through a creative new lens...Among Wachtel's adroitly rendered scenes of Jewish domestic and communal life, of wartime Poland and 1950s New York, are several small masterpieces; a baby is accidentally dropped and dies, an apple is menacingly peeled in a labor camp, ice melts under a woman's exhausted body in a Polish forest, a father weeps openly over his failure to provide, matzos are broken and challah is dipped. Wachtel entwines the singular and the ordinary with quiet lyricism...An evocative, moveable feast plumbing past and present with equal grace."

—Kirkus Reviews

"*My Mother's Shoes* is an important and significant book which beautifully articulates the joys, the sorrows and challenges that face the "second generation" of Holocaust survivors. As the generation of Holocaust survivors passes from the scene, the Jewish world is beginning to confront the issues that engulf the second generation. Wachtel deals with these issues in a sensitive, creative, yet realistic and factual way. It is not a pleasure to read, but it is important to read. A painful subject beautifully presented to the reader."

—Rabbi Chaim Rogoff, East Brunswick Jewish Center, NJ

"*My Mother's Shoes* represents a significant contribution to the literature of family, of grief, of loss, of the Holocaust and its aftermath for survivors. Wachtel's innovative form encourages the reader to enter the minds and hearts of its main characters and does what Aharon Appelfeld suggests, in *Beyond Despair*, art should do: '… constantly challenge the process by which the individual person is reduced to anonymity.'"

— **Dr. Laura Winters, Chair, English Dept., College of St. Elizabeth, NJ**

"Dr. Wachtel's memoir, *My Mother's Shoes*, addresses the issues of survival and the powerful impact of the bond between a mother and her daughter. Despite the horrors that Betty Russak experienced during the Holocaust, she had a unique perspective on life. Betty saw life as a gift and she transferred these thoughts and feelings to her daughter. This memoir gives us insight into how a mother's inner strength can positively influence her daughter. There was no self-pity in this relationship. This is the story of a mother who taught her daughter to embrace life. It is the story of a daughter's appreciation of her mother's special qualities."

— **Lawrence Danzig Ph.D (Clinical Psychology)**

"I read the excellent *My Mother's Shoes*…I think the story of Blima's survival during the Holocaust would be most appropriate. Incredibly, there are many students out there who have no idea that the Holocaust ever happened!!! Getting this story out to a very wide audience is something I would love to do."

—**John Langan, Publisher, Townsend Press**
(**publisher of** *The Story of Blima—A Holocaust Survivor*).

"The first ten pages made me weep; the following pages simply charmed and fascinated me. I wouldn't change a thing…I am grateful to have read it."

—**Janet Burstein, PhD., Drew University**

"I just finished this book. I'll say more later; I can't stop crying at the moment. I will say now that Wachtel is indeed a wonderful writer, and she has made her mother alive for me. I can see her and feel for her and rejoice with her. Poignant, powerful, mighty writing!"

—**Sallie DelVecchio, Associate Professor, Middlesex County College, NJ**

The Story Of Blima
— A Holocaust Survivor

"Shirley Russak Wachtel does a remarkable job in telling the story of her mother, a survivor of the Holocaust, in the book *The Story of Blima*. The book is an excellent source for upper elementary and middle school students to introduce them to and learn about the Holocaust. The story is written in such a positive and unique manner, that the readers, both adult and student, become quickly associated with her mother, Blima. Involvement by students and educators in the book will assist in meeting the Holocaust/genocide mandate in New Jersey."

—Dr. Paul B.Winkler, Executive Director,
New Jersey Commission on Holocaust Education

"Wow! Shirley Russak Wachtel is a masterful storyteller. Blima is alive, riveting, touching, powerful, deeply haunting, and utterly masterfully told. I am grateful to have read it."

—Yvonne Collioud Sisko, author of *American 24-Karat Gold:*
24 Classic American Short Stories

"I have read it and was very moved by it."

—Roslyn Abt Schindler, Associate Professor and Chair,
Department of Interdisciplinary Studies, Wayne State University, MI

"I just finished this book and I absolutely loved it. I can't wait to read the next book, *My Mother's Shoes*."

—Jennifer Sarhadi, Modesto Junior College, California

For Howie & Jaime, Brad, Charlie

And, of course, Zoey

Acknowledgments

I am deeply grateful to my agent, Ben Camardi, for his continued efforts and faith in my work. I would also like to thank my readers: Marcie Ruderman, Donna Danzig, and Helena Swanicke for their honest critiques and guidance; Jaime Wachtel, Jack and Emily Russak, Lois Zeidner, Susan Strumwasser, Harriet Brown, Renee Price, Iris Ramer, and Donna Barson, family and lifelong friends, for their time and input. I am indebted to my beloved parents, Charles and Betty Russak, whose lives continue to inspire me. Finally, thank you to my children, Howie and Jaime, Brad, and Charlie Wachtel, for their abiding love. Special thanks to my granddaughter, Zoey Wachtel, whom I adore. Finally, I am grateful for Arthur, who stands by me through it all.

"We are the music makers, and we are the dreamers of the dream.
Wandering by lone sea breakers, and sitting by desolate streams. World losers and world forsakers, for whom the pale moon gleams. Yet we are movers and the shakers of the world forever it seems."

—ARTHUR O'SHAUNESSEY

Preface

When I was ten years old, every child in school had to learn to play a musical instrument. Unlike today's students, none of us had a choice as to which instrument we would play. Our fifth grade class under the tutelage of Mrs. Cohn, who was our teacher for everything, and had no musical training herself, had to play the recorder. The recorder, a brown wooden object which is somewhat of a rudimentary flute, can emit a most melodious sound when placed in the proper hands. Sadly, those hands were not mine. It wasn't that I didn't have the desire to play for, certainly, even in those early days, I had felt a stirring of creative energy; it was just that I simply lacked the talent. My fingers, so capable when it came to taking pen in hand and setting words on paper, became stubborn alien objects with a life of their own, unheeding, no matter how much I willed them in the right direction. Most regrettable about all of my attempts to play was what occurred on the day of our big recital, the one with our parents seated, full of pride and expectation, in the school auditorium.

As we sat offstage, nervously awaiting our call to places, one precocious young girl thought it might be a good idea to clean our instruments with a Q-tip which she passed around. I diligently inserted the Q-tip into the mouthpiece and finger holes before passing it on to someone else. And then the concert began. As soon as I placed my lips to the mouthpiece, ready to emit the rising notes of "Yellow Bird," I knew something was wrong. Try as I might, no sound came out, and finally, when it did, it was distorted and harsh. Between songs as the others held their instruments properly at waist height, I was turning my recorder over, inspecting it for stray strands of cotton. In the end, I faked my way through all the selections, pretending to play, bowing deeply to the applause. When my parents joined me after the concert, exuberantly hugging me, I could only feel disappointment. I knew I was nothing but a fraud.

But that was a long time ago, and the old recorder was eventually abandoned for a flute, and then a piano, which still sits silently in the corner of my living room. But my desire to create has not been lost, and as the years passed, I realized I had to listen to the music before I could formulate my own. So I did just that, focusing always on the voices of those around me, those long ago fallen silent, and those whose tunes still sound loud and clear. They are the music makers in my life. And they are the ones who continue to fill my heart, so that, finally, I have found my own notes.

A Rainy Day

The sound of breaking glass. I walk into my father's room. He is seated, as always, in his chair facing east. His back is hunched over, face down as if asleep. But there is something different this time. One of the small ceramic statues—a boy playing the horn—has toppled off the ledge above the desk. My shoe crunches glass and I see the pale green carpet is covered with it. A thousand pieces of boy. I touch my father's shoulder. He turns quickly and I see that he is not asleep at all.

His cheeks, sagging and ashen, bear the marks of tears, and water seeps from his nose.

"I only wanted to fix it," he says.

"I know," I say, "It doesn't matter. We'll sweep it up. It will be fine."

"You don't understand." His voice goes husky. "It can't be fixed."

"No, you're right. But you have others."

I bend to pick up the largest piece. One leg is still intact. It is smooth on one side, coarse at the severed part, just above the knee. I feel its weight in my hand then toss it into the silver wastebasket.

"There was a nick, just a little nick right on the top of the head. So I thought I would use one of the markers there in the drawer to fill in, you know? I took it down, but my hand shakes. I should have just left it alone."

"It's okay," I say again; my foot crunches glass.

"It was from the old country. There were six in all, but there were only three left at the end of the war. The violinist, the mandolin player, and this one. How I wrapped them so carefully in the newspapers! If you only knew how careful I was. Across an ocean, in that city apartment, the house. The nick

was there from the first. Why didn't I just leave it alone?" He swallows then coughs. His body trembles with the coughing for a few minutes until it subsides.

"It could have happened before. It could have happened anyplace," I say, gathering glass, "Besides, you still have the others."

My back is turned when I hear him begin to whimper as a child would when he has just lost his best doll. I turn toward him, and without looking into his eyes, rub his shoulder. It is all I can do. After all, I am my father's son.

He turns again toward the window.

"I should have just left it alone," he says.

Virginia

The first time I see him I am sitting in a large paisley-covered armchair, folding laundry, thinking how big the house is, much too big for one person. A movement in the bushes. I think it is the wind, or a round furry gopher, the neighbor's calico cat. I fold the apricot-colored pillowcase into a neat square, but something compels me to turn again, look outside. It is a child, a little boy. His face is long, pale with an indiscernible sadness. His attire, gray against the dusky shadows, almost as puzzling as his presence. He wears an open gray coat, and underneath, a white buttoned shirt, belted shorts to the knee, a tweed cap askew. I rise. The folded pillowcase still in my hand, I move toward the window. But before I can put my face against the glass, he is gone. Just like that.

I rub my eyes. But once again the day is just that, a day. The lilacs along the perimeter of the picture bay window extending from my bedroom are just beginning to emerge, little bubbles of purple and green, oblivious to the traces of an April chill. The shrubs, newly trimmed, encircle an inviting garden bench which is still wet with yesterday's rain. And the sun, orange and pregnant with heat, has just begun its reluctant dip beneath the budding trees. A quiet moon, though unseen, hangs back reluctantly waiting for the darkness. It is 6 o'clock.

Nothing strange here. In fact, it is just the opposite. Peaceful, I'd say. And I know my mind, once again, has begun to play tricks on me. Long ago, I learned the lesson of not sleeping and yet having that uncanny ability to function with a simple smile and the mask of confidence. It usually works, except that since I have been going through the *change*, those hours of alertness have shortened, sleep becoming more elusive. And sometimes, the dreams which I try so desperately to capture as the first glimmers of sun peek beneath the drawn shades don't come until later, apparitions as I wind my way home from a late night meeting or sit folding laundry. They are visions of the old wooden swing at day camp, the eerie green color of the bathroom walls the morning I realized I was pregnant with my first daughter, the faces of my grandparents. And sometimes, they come in the shape of a boy with a sad face.

I fold the last of the T-shirts and absent-mindedly drop it into the laundry basket. Once again, almost as if in a trance, I find myself leaving the bedroom to turn a corner into the room which these past months has been both my sanctuary and my curse. Instantly, the smell of sawdust infiltrates my nostrils, and I don't have to look down to know exactly where the new Brazilian oak planks meet the old pine which stretches sadly toward the two windows facing the south end of the home. The windows themselves are shielded from the light by simple black out shades. In a corner of the room sits a box where yards of rich copper-colored satin drapes lay waiting, drapes I now have neither the inclination nor strength to hang. My eyes travel upward and I can't help but smile at the two arched towers of shelves which, thankfully, support a wealthy array of books including everything from the Bible to backyard horticulture. At the time, I just didn't have the heart to leave them barren too.

The upstairs office was meant to be a majestic testament to my new status as a tax attorney. But, alas, instead what remained now was a project begun with the best intentions, but never completed. A promise only. I turn around, surveying the rich hue of the mahogany shelves, pools of dust resting in the corners, the exposed beams staring down at me from the ceiling. This room is just like my marriage, I think. Yes, a promise only.

I married Anthony when I was only twenty years old. But, of course, it was what everyone did then, back in the late seventies. It was move-in day at Hofstra University, and I was carrying a garbage bag full of my sweatshirts into the room when a tall lanky boy— what my mother would have called a "tall drink of water" came up behind me and stood with his back against the open door. I hurled the puffy bag onto the unmade bed, the rest of my body propelled along with it onto the mattress. When I looked at him, embarrassed, he was still standing there, armed folded, his lips curling into a crooked smile. And that was it. I don't know if it was the smile, slightly askew, or the way he stood into the door, but at that moment I knew that I could never spend another day without him in my life. No bells, no quickening of the heart, but I knew. Even before I heard the sound of his name.

We were married the day after graduation. My mother sat expressionless in the first pew of our church, wearing a pale blue suit and clutching a small bouquet of pink carnations as my father, touching my elbow slightly, walked me down the aisle. I suppose they were happy to see me married, at least I know my father was glad he didn't have to fund a large wedding like he did for my older sister. He touched his lips to mine as he relinquished me to my new husband. Anthony stood shuffling his feet as we both turned toward the priest. When he kissed me, his lips felt like my father's.

Perhaps that was the first clue, only I didn't know it then. Luncheon in a small cafe, as I sat ensconced at a corner table with my parents, my older sister, Isabel, her husband, Joe, and Anthony's family, his parents, younger brother, Philip. I chatted away as if talking as fast as I could would move me along like a speeding locomotive. "What a sunny day, so perfect for a wedding!" *stop* "What do you think these cutlets were marinated in?" *stop* "I can't wait to see Disney World!" *stop*, and *go*, and *go* and *go*. The trouble was, if I had bothered to pause long enough, I would have noticed that I was the only one doing the talking.

"Anthony, what do you think, should I take out one of those travel booklets for Disney so we can make the most of our time? Well, maybe we should just wing it," I said, answering my own question. "Anthony, oh, they have those miniature cannolis that you like so much. Shall we order some for the table?" Sitting next to me, Anthony turned, and, saying nothing, smiled his crooked smile. I was in heaven.

Years later, those silences which had seemed so mysterious and alluring at first, would crash loudly against my spirit, ultimately, but not irrevocably, breaking it.

It wasn't his fault; after all, he'd been the same as he ever was. I was the one who had changed and, poor man, I suppose he didn't really realize it until it was too late. I tried to tell him, but he was an investment banker. It wasn't *what* he did, truly, it was *who* he was. So when I approached him those years ago, when the girls had barely begun school, he nodded, smiled, dismissed the whole thing as being merely a contrast in personality types. I was Type A, he was Type B. I *yinged* when he *yanged*, that sort of thing. And if that explanation didn't work, well, I was premenstrual, hormonal, wanted another baby. I did want something, all right, but it wasn't another child. I wanted him to *listen*.

I tried again, though, just like I had with my parents. But just as it had been with them, I soon learned never to come to him with my problems. Yet it hadn't always been like that, with my parents I mean.

I guess that in some ways I grew up in what you would call a traditional home. That is, my father went to work and my mother stayed home. It sounds idyllic when you think of it, but, like so many other families during that period in the 1960s, its appearance belied the real state of things. Daddy would put on a suit and hat and leave for the train station before we even got up, and we wouldn't see him until we were ready for bed each evening. We would always hear him before we saw him. The heavy step upon the stair, the crisp click of metal in the lock, the rustle of the newspaper as it disappeared into the trash can. My mother knew it too because her back would ripple slightly, her shoulders straighten as she stood at the sink. Isabel and I looked down into our glasses of milk and sipped slowly until the sound of his voice came floating towards us.

"Hello, girls."

Isabel would lift her chin towards him and smile. She waited for a response, and usually she got one. Sometimes, he pulled her long blond braid in a playful way, and other times he would lift her up so high that she could touch the ceiling with the palms of her hands. Even when he had a bad day and would come home scowling, she could always cajole a smile, earning her an extra Oreo cookie with her milk. He was different with me, though. Only a couple of years earlier, Daddy had lifted me up in the air just in the way he now did with Isabel. I giggled, surveying the world in the playground below me. But then a strange thing happened. The yellows, blues, and reds of the swings and seesaws below merged into one, a spinning kaleidoscope, and I grew scared, forgetting where I was, even who I was. That's when the crisp air suddenly became thinner, and I felt like I was locked in a box, gasping for air. After a few more of these episodes, my parents took me to a doctor who diagnosed me with asthma, a breathing problem. And even though once I entered first grade and that terrible choking feeling ended, Daddy never lifted me into the air again, never came close the way he would when I was younger. It made it much easier for Isabel to become Daddy's girl.

I snapped my cookie in two and chewed it thoughtfully.

"How was school today, Ginny?" he asked, lifting Isabel again into the air.

I shrugged my shoulders.

"Okay, I guess."

"That's good," he said, placing Isabel down gently into the metal seat. He walked over to Mother, who was still standing over the sink, and kissed her on the cheek. Then he said the same thing he did yesterday and the day before that.

"Smells good. What's cookin', good lookin'? I could eat a horse!" And Mother said the same thing she did the Wednesday before.

"Pot roast today."

If it had been Monday, the word would be "steak," Thursday, "roast chicken," and fish was on the menu for Friday. Weekends were a treat because Daddy would walk the two blocks to the pizza parlor and we could have our slice of pizza and orange soda in front of the TV in the living room, just like the people who eat TV dinners. Of course, Sundays Mother made her special stew with pieces of lamb, carrots, and turnips, which we ate early, in time for Sullivan. We all said we liked the stew, but it wasn't until many years later that Isabel would confide that she, in fact, had always hated Mother's special stew, and would spit the pieces into a napkin when no one was looking. I wished I had thought of that, I said, smiling at her with envy.

Daddy removed his hat, washed his hands in the bathroom, and returned to assume the seat at the head of the table. Mother placed a plate in front of him.

"Looks good, hon," he'd say, as always. The clink of the fork against the plate was our cue, and brushing the stray crumbs off our nightgowns, Isabel and I would place our plates and glasses in the sink, and race each other down the hall to our shared bedroom. Then we would jump into our beds, bring our knees up, and strain to listen to our parents' conversation, although usually all we could hear were adult murmurs and the scraping of forks against the plate.

Isabel was nine, and I was a year younger, but we were old enough to understand that even though we all lived in the same house, the adults occupied a world of their own, separate and apart from ours. They sometimes talked for hours into the night sitting at that kitchen table. And then when the first stars appeared deep into the dark skies, we would hear the water run into the sink one last time, and the quiet turn of the knob at their bedroom door. Then the apartment would assume a profound silence, and eventually I could hear the slow metered breathing of my sister under the covers. I couldn't sleep, though, because even at that young age, listening to the silences in the corners of the room, I had the feeling that something was waiting for me in the shadows, something left undone.

During those moments as I lay watching the moon dip slowly beneath the rooftops, I loved my parents more than anything. I closed my eyes tightly and, like any child of eight, wished that if I could just love them enough, maybe they would love me more. Because even if they said all the right things and did all the right things, I still felt a void in their presence. Children just know these things. And the more I wanted to speak the words of my heart, the more I squelched them inside until there was no room left for anything but the emptiness, until the only two words which could ever come out were "okay" and "no, thank you." I knew this taciturn attitude would often frustrate my parents. At first, Daddy would try to cajole me with an occasional word of praise or an extra licorice stick, but when that didn't work, he kind of gave up on me and could focus his attention more on Isabel and, more often, on Mother.

One thing I did know for sure in those dark days. I knew my parents loved each other. I could tell by the way my Daddy would place his hand right over hers when the two would talk at the table, or Mother would stop talking to us in the middle of a sentence the moment he entered the room. Mother's love for Daddy was different, though, because, like all great loves, it was laced with fear. I didn't quite know why at the time, but what I did know was that she passed it like a contagion to her daughters, so that when we bid good night to him, our steps quickened only a fraction, and when we smiled at him, the edges of our lips would quiver. Of course, being only a child, I accepted this as the way of things, assumed all children were just a little bit afraid of their fathers, and would lose myself again in the quiet friendship of books.

There was one time, though. It was a time I shall never forget, even now as I look up at the white wisps of clouds layered like icing across the dimming sky. I must have been five or six when Daddy suggested that we three take a walk to the park where an ice skating rink had just opened. I'm not sure where Isabel was at the time, perhaps at a friend's birthday party, but what I do know was that finally I had my parents all to myself, a family of three. There we were, I, for the first time, wearing my royal blue wool coat with the white fur buttons and a white fur hat to match, all Christmas presents from my parents (Isabel had the same outfit in red), walking between my parents who stood tall. Daddy was wearing his long brown overcoat and hat, and Mother was in her striped black and beige coat with curved bone buttons and a brown leather bag which was in the shape of a bone too. As we strode so regally down the avenue, nodding and smiling to the neighbors, a few even commenting on how sweet I looked or how much I had grown, I felt for the first time ever protected by my two pillars of strength. And for the first time when I smiled at my Daddy, and then at Mother, it was with my heart on my lips. I was so proud!

When we arrived at the rink, we watched the skaters, some swooping across the ice like magnificent birds, others taking tentative steps like toddlers learning how to walk. We stood watching the group for nearly an hour, or so it seemed, until Daddy finally asked if I would like to join them. He would pay the man in the booth for special skates for me. I shook my head from side to side, letting the brim of my fur hat slide toward my eyebrow. It wasn't that I was fearful or anything like that. It was just that skating would mean letting go of their hands, leaving myself unprotected all over again. I shook my head vehemently. I wanted to stand there on that cool bright winter day between my two pillars, like a small blue bud between the leaves. I wanted to stay there forever.

I don't recall a time when I ever felt that way about anyone again—not even at my wedding. But I do know one thing—ever since that day, blue has been my favorite color.

"Oh, shit, Margie, you can't be serious!"

I'll never forget those words. Even though I was only four, I knew that they didn't mean anything good.

"I'm sorry, John. I'm so sorry."

"Well, what happened to the pill, for heaven's sakes?"

"John, you know taking that stuff gets me sick, and besides, you're the one who-"

I had been listening against their bedroom door as soon as I heard Daddy say the bad word. If they opened the door, I knew I'd be in deep trouble, maybe even get a spanking, even though neither of my parents had ever laid a hand on me. But sitting on the cold carpet crouching against the door in my white cotton nightgown, I knew that this conversation was much too important for them to be wondering about me. And I was right.

"Well, what *now*, Marge? What do we fucking do now?" A few gulps, and then I heard Mother say, "I don't know, John."

"Well, I don't know, either. I mean, my God, three kids all under age five. How am I supposed to afford that on a salesman's salary?"

"Couldn't you ask your boss for a few more leads?" Mother sounded small and tired. Silence. An abrupt creak and then I could hear the sound of Daddy's slippers pacing the bedroom floor.

"Margie, I can't make this decision for you, not this time. I'm an insurance salesman, that's all I am, not some lousy billionaire like Howard Hughes."

Mother began to whimper. I gingerly placed my ear against the door, straining.

"I'm going to have this baby, John," I heard her say, finally. The radiator in the living room kicked in and suddenly the apartment walls seemed to shrink. I felt hot and itchy. So that was it! Mother was going to have a baby. A sweet little baby for us to coo at and play with. And, best of all, I would get to be the big sister!

I heard the mattress springs creak heavily this time. Daddy must have sat down. Mother was crying softly.

"John, you know how much you have always wanted a son. Maybe it will be a boy this time. I can feel it, John. Yes, I just know it's a boy."

"That's what you said before Ginny was born, but it wasn't my *son* that time, was it? It was just another girl. Let's face it, Margie, all you give birth to are girls. Besides, I can't afford any more kids."

"That's not true what you said about girls, John. Please, I know that this child will be a son, someone you can play catch with, teach how to fish. He'll follow in your footsteps."

"Marge—"

"Please, John. If I could just have this baby, I know I won't disappoint you this time." Silence. Then Daddy's voice deepened to a low growl.

"Marge," he said, "You know what you have to do."

Mother cried some more for a few minutes, and then silence again. I shivered and slowly made my way back into the bedroom, forgetting the glass of water I had been thirsty for.

As I listened to Isabel's rhythmic breaths, I burrowed deeper under the blanket until it embraced me like a womb. I bit into my bottom lip and tightly squeezed my eyes shut, willing sleep. But I couldn't sleep that night. All I could think about was the disappointment I was to Daddy. And, of course, that meant Mother hated me too since she deferred in all things to him. The anticipation of a new baby diminished suddenly as the cloud of my own inadequacy began to subsume my spirit. It didn't matter anyway, since the little baby never did come to our house, and I knew that I would always remain the little sister. The second girl. My parents never found out that I had listened in on their conversation, but the next day, nevertheless, they reprimanded me harshly. It seems that the night before, I had done a very bad thing. I wet the bed.

Shortly afterward was about the time I began to speak in monosyllables. But all that changed when I moved out and began college. I spoke more; I couldn't stop speaking. But my words, at least those spoken to my parents, were as hollow as my silences had been. They were just words, like a locomotive going nowhere.

There is a voice calling from below. It is not memory this time, but my daughter.

"I'm up here, in the bedroom."

My youngest daughter bounds up the stairs. She has just come from one of her runs, her hair tied hastily in a ponytail, golden brown bangs plastered against her forehead. Her gray sweat shorts hug her thighs beneath a clinging T-shirt displaying UCLA in bold blue letters.

"Isn't that outfit a little skimpy for this time of year?" I say, before I can catch the words.

She ignores the comment, straightening as she places her hands on her hips. Classic battle stance.

"I'm going out with friends. Don't bother to make supper."

I shrug and turn away, making believe I don't care. When I remember something, I turn again to face her, but she is gone.

"Let me know if you'll be past midnight," I say, half to myself. After all, it is a school night. And something else.

"Have you heard from your sister?" I call. But the steady patter of the shower already fills the air, and I return to the window to close the blinds. But then, just before they fall shut, I see a movement like wind and the light of a face in the shadows. It is the boy.

Joshua

I never thought I would end up here. What I mean is I had always assumed that my life would take a different direction. There's just the three of us now, Adam, the old man, and me. A house full of quiet. Nighttime is the worst. I've been unable to sleep again, so I lie in bed watching the shadows of the TV screen dance upon the ceiling, trying to soothe myself with the sounds, pretending they are real people, not just electronic vibrations emanating from a box. And listen like a cat for the grind of the garage door as it opens. But it is already 3 am and the only sound I hear is the occasional whimper of the old man in the next room. When I do hear the *whirr* of the door, finally, followed by the soft squeak of sneakers on the stairs, my body collapses into the bed like cloth on a pool of water.

A door is shut, and then silence. I try to make my mind a blank canvas, not to think of the print shop and the stacks of orders waiting for me the next day. Not to think of how dismal the prospects for the Yankees are this coming season, or the leak in the upstairs bathroom sink whose steady patter has begun to feel like water torture, not to think of my son as he prepares for bed, becoming more and more like a stranger to me, or the old man who believes he has taken up residence in a hospital and not a home. Most of all, I try not to think of history because Alicia is my history, and history is dead.

But, of course, I do think about those things as in my bed I turn toward the white wall, desperate to find a calm center, but

knowing again as I watch the glow of the nightlight, that it will
be another night when sleep escapes me. If only I were outdoors
running, letting the iPod fill my head with music, pushing away
all my thoughts. I check the alarm clock. It is set for 5:30 am,
when I will fasten the laces of my sneakers and push myself into
the early dawn, leaving just enough time to be in the shop at 9
am sharp. I face the wall and close my eyes again. And then I
dream, or perhaps not. Alicia comes to me again, this time sitting in the rocking chair of the nursery back in the apartment
in Brooklyn. She is holding our newborn son, and noticing me
for the first time. She looks up. She smiles. But, of course, that
is impossible. Alicia never sat in that chair, and certainly not
with a newborn. In fact, the only real thing about the dream
is her smile. She smiled at me like that. Feeling my body collapse from under me again, I startle awake. Perhaps this wasn't
a dream at all, and I've been awake the whole time. That happens more often than I'd like to think. I mean Alicia coming
to me as I sit alone at the kitchen table stirring my tea, hand
a package to a customer, or look out the window on a snowy
day. Sometimes, I feel my heart tightening like a vice, as if I'm
about to have a heart attack. I've even seen doctors about it, but
they've assured me that nothing is wrong, I'm in perfect health.
Perfect. I know it not to be true, though. I am damaged goods
at the age of fifty-two. I've been suffering from a tear in the
spirit, but still I am in perfect health. Everyone told me it would
get better. Just give it time, they said. But that was seventeen
years ago, and nothing has changed. Alicia still wears the same
pale green dress I first saw her in on the day we met. Her hands
are small, even for a woman, and when I take one in mine, it
flutters softly, like a bird.

We met at a Dave Brubeck concert in the park. I was a big
fan of jazz, but when my friend suddenly realized that he needed
to write a term paper for the next day, and couldn't go with me,

I shrugged my shoulders and went anyway. As I said, I was a big fan. Alicia came too, but not because she particularly liked jazz, more because she was coerced by her friends, one of whom just happened to be the daughter of Brubeck's accountant. Besides, she later confessed, it gave her a chance to wear the dress she had just found at a flea market, a gauzy sort of thing which fell down to her ankles and had tiny silver-colored spangles at the neck and waist. It reminded me of an Indian sari. As luck would have it, she occupied the seat next to mine.

I thought to myself, sitting in my torn jeans and tie-dyed T-shirt, she's a little weird. But, of course, now I love the dress. Suffice it to say, I didn't at the time. Her spangles shook each time she applauded or moved in her seat; so did the set of narrow silver bangles she had going up her right forearm. It was all quite annoying at the time. But when she took it upon herself to interrupt my enraptured state with inane questions like how long had I been a fan and what other kind of music I liked, my annoyance quickly grew to contempt. Luckily, she didn't notice, and continued to ramble, her spangles clanging, her bangles clinking.

By the time the concert ended, she had all but forgotten her friends and had followed me out of the park and, eventually, home. As we sat next to each other amidst the crush of stone-faced passengers in a subway car, I turned, finally, to look at her face. It was then that I noticed the enormous blueness of her eyes. One could get lost in such blueness. She must have realized, for suddenly she put a hand to the small silver barrette in the shape of a petal, and turned silent. She lifted her hand to brush away a stray hair, one of a mane of thick ash blond hair which she wore, in those days, long and shaggy. Her full lips, pale and shiny with light pink lip gloss, opened slightly. I couldn't take my eyes off of the liquid blue orbs staring at me, until, when the train jerked to a stop, the words suddenly poured from my mouth.

"What's your name?" I said.

Even then I hadn't fallen in love with her. Not that night when we came back to my apartment in the Village and talked for hours drinking Ripple and smoking pot. Not the following week when I took her back to the park and framed her between the trees as I took black and whites with the Minolta. Not when she noticed the photo of me standing in front of an apartment building with my parents in the 1950s and, exchanging histories, realized that her mother had come from the same rural town in Poland as my mother had, where they lost sisters, brothers, parents in the explosion that was the Holocaust. I didn't love her after a month of movies and long walks and intimate suppers in corner cafes, not even then. But it was in the void of her absence, when she disappeared as suddenly as she had entered my life. When I didn't hear the music of her voice, the clatter of the bangles, and everything I saw paled next to the brilliance of her blue eyes.

Finally, after what had seemed like a lifetime, I heard from her.

"Hi, Babe."

"It's you—"

I hoped she couldn't hear the trembling creep into my voice.

"What's up?"

Could she really be so nonchalant or was she putting me on?

"Same old, you know," I said, reining in my fears.

"Israel was great, man. I should take you there sometime."

"Israel? Is that where you've been these past two weeks?"

She laughed her trademark laugh, full and bursting spontaneous, like a bubble.

"Where the hell do you think I've been, man? Didn't I like—tell you? My parents dragged the three of us there, only it turned out to be pretty cool. The Dead Sea, oh my God, Joshua, you just lie on your back and the salt water carries you away into the light. And the Wailing Wall, oh man, you should see it. It's just like a spirit that's in the air. I mean you can feel the presence of *God*,

Joshua. You really can—I even slipped a prayer into one of the niches in the wall."

"What did you pray for?"

She laughed again.

"I can't tell you because you were in it."

I could feel the beats of my heart slow to a normal pace as my fears gradually subsided.

"When can I see you?" I said.

"I'll be over in twenty minutes."

After those two weeks, Alicia and I were never apart again. I confessed my love for her one afternoon as we returned to the park where I snapped shots of her diving into a pile of orange and golden leaves and kicking them up with her feet, like a child splashing in water.

"Hey," I called to her, focusing in on her face, "want to know something?"

"What?"

"I think I'm in love with you."

She smiled then, as I clicked the shutter. It wasn't a smile of surprise, though, and I guess she had realized my feelings before even I had. So typical of Alicia. I still have that black and white photo in the drawer of my night table. Sometimes, I just take it out and stare at that smile. And I close my eyes and wish that I could be transported, through some glitch in the solar system, back to that place, that time. But it never happens.

Two years later, Alicia and I were married under a *chuppah* outdoors in the Negev desert in Israel. As her two younger brothers and friends held the hastily constructed awning, four wooden poles and a sheet constructed of old prayer shawls stretched across the top, I understood what she had meant about Israel because for the first time I had a feeling that this was where I belonged. In this moment. No questions asked.

As my parents escorted me down the aisle, they looked tall again, as they once did when I was a young boy. No longer small and insecure in a land where they never truly did feel quite comfortable, they held onto me and led me forward. I tried, but I couldn't really imagine how they felt as they marched straight ahead with their only child between them. Once again, it was I who was the one who could make up for all their losses during the war. My mother had lost both her parents, two brothers and a sister to the Nazis. The remnants of her family, two older sisters, both unmarried, resided in Jerusalem, and sat on bridge chairs fanning themselves that day. My father lost both of his parents, as well, along with a younger brother to the fires of Auschwitz. Except for his new family, he was alone.

Usually, I resented the heavy burden, the responsibility of having to compensate for them all. When I came home with an "A" in history, you would have thought that the day of salvation had come, with their exuberant shouts of glee, and effervescent hugs. I had no choice but to go to college (not that I didn't want to go, anyway), and when I graduated from City College in New York, well, there was such a disturbance of the peace that I feared the police would be brought in. Neither of my parents had gone beyond a high school education. When I informed them that I was intending on buying a ring for Alicia, a sweet Jewish girl who was also from Brooklyn and, unbelievably, the child of a survivor, there were no shouts of exultation nor dancing throughout the apartment. They simply wept.

Sometimes, I envied Alicia. Only one of her parents was a survivor, and she had two brothers to help her shoulder the responsibility to be the best. But to my parents, I was the world. No-- I was the sun, the moon, the stars. I was their universe.

Sometimes, I can still feel a tightening in my arms where my parents held onto me as they led me forward. And I remember feeling—now, I know it sounds strange—as if their blood was seeping into me—like we were one being. When we came beneath the *chuppah*, my parents each planted a light kiss on my cheeks. My mother, who was only slightly more expressive than my father, wanted to whisper something into my ear.

"Joshua--" she began.

But she couldn't bring herself to finish. I knew what she was going to say, but we were never the kind of family who needed to say those things. I squeezed her hand, and turned to wait for Alicia.

Alicia and I couldn't have children. So we worked. We lived in a four-story apartment building in Borough Park, Brooklyn, only two blocks away from my parents and about ten miles away from her family. In the beginning, to tell you the truth, neither of us was so anxious to start a family. We were intent on our careers. I worked for a graphic arts company which manufactured photo albums; and after working as a typist for a small mail order business, Alicia surprised herself by suddenly having a desire to return to Hunter College for a degree in teaching. She was lucky to find an opening in a fine school district not too far from home, in Sheepshead Bay, where she taught first graders for ten years. They tell me she was a fine teacher, better than fine. She would stoop down to their level when talking to them, never condescending, and patiently explain a concept or answer a question, no matter how many times it was asked. She actually respected the little kids, even in those days when respect for students was not such a popular thing to have. On rare occasions, to this day I still receive a note from former students about how thankful they are to have known Mrs. Goldman. Little by little, she changed in other ways. She gave up the long gauzy skirts for serviceable jumpers with white blouses, and her bangles gave way to pearls. Her straight thick hair, always a cause for concern, was severely tamed into a bun worn in the back of her head. I didn't mind that too much—it only made her eyes shine larger.

I changed too. I decided one day, that I no longer had any joy in my employee status on a 9 to 5 job and, on a whim, became partners in a print shop in upstate New York. Alicia, always one to take a chance, thought it was a great idea, but my parents weren't so enthusiastic. They feared I would lose all my money in the venture, and we spent many evenings locked in heated argument over sponge cake and tea at their house. Eventually, as always, they relented, and my father even provided the capital for the business with the money he had saved from their restitution funds.

"I hope you are not making a mistake, Joshua," he said, handing over the check.

We were lucky, my partner and I. After a year, we were in the black, and after another year, we had doubled the store's profit under the last owner, as a high school and huge shopping center were constructed in the area. Eventually, though, my friend decided to take up another business opportunity in California, and I became the sole owner of the shop.

Life was good. Well, almost. I wasn't home much, what with commuting and working 9 to 6 most days, even on Saturdays. Alicia was stoic; she found herself staying after school to grade papers or assist with special programs. She bought cookbooks and created lavish meals like *coq au vin* and *steak teriyaki*, which I would quickly gobble up, barely tasting the delicate sauces, the savory *ragus*, as I fought sleep each evening. Sundays were our favorite days, though. We always managed to get out of the house on that day. We became film aficionados, and were regulars at the local Chinese restaurant. Sometimes, we would even return to the park, and I'd take pictures.

One Sunday evening when she was sitting on the sofa working on a crossword puzzle, and I was watching my favorite show, *60 Minutes*, she looked up at me.

"What are we doing, Joshua?"

"Huh?"

"What are we doing with our lives? What's it all for?"

"What do you mean?"

"I mean we're here, already here with our careers. Everything is good."

"So?"

"So I want to have a baby."

"Okay."

And that was that. Only it wasn't. She was twenty-five and I was twenty-eight, and it seemed as if everything was perfectly aligned, right to bring a child into the world. We never told anybody of our plans, of course, but quietly liberating ourselves from birth control, enjoyed each other in ways we never had before, the dream always in the back of our mind, but never talked about again. When, after a year without success, we visited a doctor, had both ourselves tested, we were delighted to learn there was nothing wrong. And yet, still we weren't pregnant. I have to admit that both our parents, who were well into their seventies by then, never questioned us, but their eyes lingered when we visited, tittered a bit longer than usual on our faces, as they asked, "What's new?"

Neither Alicia nor I spoke much of our disappointment either during those years. Eventually, out of frustration, I would take up running through the streets with my headphones, an attempt to escape from what seemed my own inadequacies. Alicia, on the other hand, found solace in books, mysteries and romance novels, spent more time with her students, and slowly began to gain pounds as she comforted herself with her creations of thick creamy soups or hot raisin bread. One day, she came home with a puppy. Even though I didn't like the idea at first, I began to feel the first glimmers of affection for Cody, our golden retriever, and after awhile, thanks to our new addition, we began to feel a lightness of spirit again as in the old days. Cody proved lucky in more ways than one. Just after celebrating his first birthday, Alicia and

I were sitting at the breakfast table when she announced that she was pregnant. I was thirty-five and she was thirty-two years old.

We were happy, more than happy really, elated. And our parents, well, they were beyond even that. The pregnancy was uneventful. Sure, Alicia experienced morning sickness, sciatica, and later on she couldn't even wear her shoes anymore because of the swelling. But she weathered it all, because now we had a future. And, for the first time we dared to dream. Boy or girl, it didn't matter. There would be more after this one to make up for all the others, the aunts, uncles, and grandparents who were no longer here. But for now, this child, this one child would be the sun, the moon, the stars. The universe. We painted the extra bedroom. Then we bought a crib and a rocking chair.

During all events in our lives, both great and small, the moment always passes too swiftly. Something like a dream. Perhaps that's the reason that after it is gone, we need to relive it again and again just to make sure it happened. Slow it down, make it real. It was just that way on that day that passed like a dream, a dream which was to haunt me for the rest of my life.

I awakened in the early morning hours. She had begun to bleed, and soon after, the pains came, two weeks early. Driving to the hospital, we might as well have been on a magic carpet. Her bag already packed, Alicia had thrown on a blue and white flowery shift, taking the side of her hair up with a silver pin in the shape of a petal, the same one she had worn on the day we met.

"Just think, Joshua," she said as we sped past the ghost-like shops, the sleepy sanitation workers rattling cans, "in a few hours we will be a real family."

And then it began. Wheeled down the hall. Hooked up. Ice chips. Doctors walking in and out. "How are we doing here?" Doing? Well, great. Sure. Isn't this all supposed to be just a bit painful? I looked at Alicia. Her blue eyes were dancing.

And then something happened. Her face strained and a line the color of violet lightning streaked across her brow. Suddenly, I was pushed aside and the nurse was calling for the doctor. And then there seemed to be doctors everywhere, yelling things, surrounding her. Numbers on a screen and blood pressure and stat and OR stat stat STAT! I looked for some reassurance from Alicia. Her face, her eyes. But her body, tight and straining a moment ago, was relaxed now. And her eyes were closed. They had stopped dancing.

The dream sped up. I was in a waiting room. Waiting, of course. I can't recall if there were others in the room with me or if I was alone. Soon, or maybe later, there was another.

"Mr. Goldman? So sorry...unexpected...a stroke...we couldn't... so sorry."

And then, "You have a boy. A healthy baby."

I replayed the dream again and again and again. How am I to care for a baby? A boy? What lessons do I teach him? Without a mother? With a grandmother who is so ill she may not live to see him? And a grandfather who cries?

The dream keeps me awake at night as my son sleeps undisturbed in his crib. The dream keeps me awake days when I work at my business, when I run. After the running, I come home to the pictures, which is all I have now. And a son. I look at him. Small, big eyes, this son of mine. He will be the sun, the moon, the stars. The universe. He will be everything.

But I keep running, away from the Brooklyn apartment to a house too big, an upstate house, the kind housewives dream of. A house too big for a boy of ten, an old man, and a ghost.

There is a sound. I open my eyes and see the numbers-- 5:30. Slowly, I crawl out of bed, ignoring the weeping of the old man in the next room. Another day has begun and I can't remember if I've slept or spent the night dreaming. I jump out of bed, wide awake.

Christine

Most people don't believe me when I tell them that my favorite meal is breaded chicken cutlets, a baked potato loaded, of course, with sour cream and bacon bits, and maybe a small garden salad splattered with a spicy French dressing. And for dessert, a small bowl of Breyer's butter pecan ice cream, liberally drizzled with hot fudge and a dollop of whipped cream. My mouth is watering just thinking about it! Some people prefer spicy foods like lasagna or New Age stuff like sushi, or the all-American hotdog with fries, but my tastes are relatively simple, even if I am not so simple myself.

Because she knows how much I like it, Ginny makes it for me at least once a week, if she is home early, that is, and if I happen to be. I think she cooks this because it is the only thing she can cook, anyway. She is such a *tool*.

I walk into the kitchen and my sister is already sitting at the granite counter waiting. She is rotating on the stool by pushing herself off with one leg and letting go. I think she is too old for that being she is almost out of high school. But she always was such a baby. Ginny is standing next to the stainless steel oven with the big burners. There is a plate of the raw cutlets in front of her, another plate with some ready-made breadcrumbs, one with a whisked egg, and another one with flour. There is flour all over the place too, on the counter, the backsplash, even on her nose. She looks up when she hears me come into the room.

"Chrissie, I'm so glad you could make it," she says, and drops a dressed cutlet into the pan. The hot oil sizzles and splatters on the stove. I can't tell if she really is happy to see me or if she is just being sarcastic. I'm too tired to worry about her, though. After all, it's already 8 o'clock.

I sit on the stool next to my sister and put my head into my hands so I don't have to talk to her. She doesn't bother me anyway; she is too busy spinning. I hear the sizzle of those cutlets and in a little while I can smell them. Sweet and warm. I walk over to the freezer and take out the gallon of Breyer's butter pecan, which is just for me, since Ginny and my sister only like the chocolate. Dad likes butter pecan too, but he doesn't live here anymore.

The ice cream is frozen over like a rock and there is even a white frost on the outside. I stick the box into the microwave for about a minute as I blow on my frozen wet fingers. While the ice cream is warming, I get the hot fudge from the fridge, which is pretty cold now too, and wait. Then I trade the fudge for the ice cream and wait some more.

I find the scoop, finally, in our "everything" drawer, and cradle it, cold and heavy in my hand, for a moment. I plunge it into the box where it compliantly fills with a white nutty mound, which I drop into a cereal bowl. I squeeze the warm container of fudge, writing my initials on the top. "CHW" in fluid brown script. I plunge the soup spoon into the soft hill and lift it to my mouth. The taste is an odd combination of cold and hot, smooth and crunchy, the rebel ice cream in search of identity. Absolutely orgasmic. But already I am found out.

"Chrissie!"

"What now?"

She turns, sweaty and powder-faced.

"We're about to have dinner. How could you be eating ice cream now?"

I ignore her, but she just keeps talking. That's what she does.

"All right," I say, finally, "I'm gonna eat the stupid chicken cutlets too. When don't I eat them?"

Ginny lets go a sigh, long and loud, then turns and starts moving around the cutlets with the spatula again. My sister stops rotating just for maybe half a second, but then starts spinning again. I think I am really beginning to hate her.

Even though I finish the butter pecan, letters and all, I am still hungry when I sit down to our "family" dinner. Ginny eats one cutlet standing up as she is on a lifetime diet, but fills our plate with three cutlets and a filled baked potato each. I realize the garden salad is missing, so I quickly grab a pack from the fridge and make my own. She gives me the *look*. I try to eat it quickly so I will be faster than her conversation, but I am never fast enough.

"I'm so glad I was able to bring some of my work home so I can spend some time with you girls. And this is so wonderful all being together like this, now that you have graced us with your presence, Chrissie," she says, smiling. I curl my lip at her and take a large swig of my iced tea. She sucks in her long face and narrows her eyes to slits like she is trying to read something in my face. In one minute I think she is going to start melting before my eyes like the Wicked Witch in Oz. I take another bite into the cutlet, letting the juices squirt into my mouth. Thankfully, she turns to my sister.

Then she begins interrogating her about her new chemistry teacher, how many wins they have had on her lacrosse team, and what color dress she will wear to the prom. All that nonsense.

My sister stops right in the middle of eating to answer every single question. She looks at Ginny right in her slit green eyes and tells her how hard she is working in school, how her team is up for a championship, and that she took a minor role in the school play. Oh yes, and the dress will be pink. How fucking sweet.

All of Ginny's attention is on her now, so I guess that lets me off the hook. She likes my sister a lot, which is funny because she looks like Dad, all dark straight hair and chocolate shit-colored eyes, big bubble lips, which would go great with a pot of ruby blush right in the middle of her cheeks. She never even wears makeup or anything, though; she is what you would call a natural. We don't even look like sisters since what I've got is limp straw-colored hair and slit-green eyes. Ginny says that I am like a chameleon, always trying to change what I look like. Well, why would I want to look like *this* anyway?

So you think since I'm the first one born that I'd be the favorite, but it's my sister for sure. Maybe it's because it's like she's her other chance for success or something. A second chance to get it right, just like she did with her job. I mean who dumps a good job as a director of a daycare center to go back to school, get a stupid law degree just so she could work double the hours? That woman will do anything to get out of the house.

To make matters worse, she gets him to buy us this humongous house up in Podunk New York somewhere where you have to take the Jeep all the way down the hill to get your goddamn mail and they close the entire town down whenever there is a drop of snow, which of course makes you a real prisoner in your house. In my opinion, she only bought it to show off, I mean, if anyone looks up in that office of hers, there are already boxes of her diplomas and certificates in frames ready to be banged all over the walls. I think anyone who needs a piece of paper to show off who they are probably doesn't have a good self-image to begin with.

So the house is this little castle of hers with big trees all around it so that you can't even see the front door, and a backyard big enough to fill a stadium, without even a baby pool in it. Makes no sense to me. Of course, once she drags us all up here and has a big housewarming for all her friends (my friends couldn't even find the place), and then about a year later has another bash for her law school graduation—this time outdoors under an enormous tent with waiters and fancy stuffed mushroom caps with celery—she decides she is not happy enough. So what does she do? She tells Dad to get the hell out. Just like that. I mean, he looks at her like she is loony, and then they argue for a couple of weeks before he moves back into the city where we all should have stayed to begin with. She is such a head case.

I have always tried to stay out of things. And I have to admit, that I had done a pretty good job of it until she kicked Dad out. But sometimes a person just has to speak up, and I let her have it. I mean what did Dad ever do except give her everything she wanted? I tried to reason with her about the importance of keeping the family together and that shit. And then I threatened her with moving out since at the time I was about to turn eighteen. When those things didn't work, I did the one thing that I knew would piss her off for sure. I cursed at her, calling her every name in the book. Some of them are even unprintable. But she just scrunched up her face again like Wicked Witch, and took off to some spa in Arizona. For her nerves.

Sometimes, I escaped to my Dad's apartment back in the city. He was pretty cool about it at first, but later I think she would get to him, so he told me it wasn't "feasible" to stay with him all the time like that. Besides, once I turned eighteen, I could move out on my own. Until then, I decided I could make my room, which was about the size of our whole house back in the city, into my place where I don't have to hear my sister's kid music and where I don't have to look at Ginny's old and tired face as she pulls her briefcase up the stairs every night. So I turn my room which has purple walls and a round bed into what you would call a "studio" for my art. My particular field is sculpting, which I have to admit I am very good at. Art has been the only thing in school I was even remotely interested in, and the only thing on my report card which ever got the letter "A." I make mostly heads, nobody special, just nobody people in the streets, like kids and old men. Now, I am not a Leonard DaVinci or anything like that, but some people say I am pretty good. The only problem is that it takes me like forever to finish a piece because the eyelid has to have just the right thickness, and the lines around the mouth mustn't be too straight. I guess Dad saw some kind of talent in me when he went out and bought me a wheel and a kiln to bake the pieces in. He is always telling me how proud he is of me, and that kind of shit. But Ginny, well, she says she likes the stuff, but is always asking what kind of a career could I make out of it. If there is no dollar bill attached, she doesn't want to know it.

So I set up this perfect studio, and put up lime green and lemon yellow curtains on the two windows (out of which I see nothing but trees, by the way), which go with the matching bedspread, all of which I have made myself. Then I buy a long shelf so I can place my heads on it, that is the ones I haven't smashed up because they were crap. But even these I will soon be moving to the apartment. I go out and get some posters for the wall, which are abstract designs with purple in them, and add my friend Laney's pencil sketches because she is a really good artist. On the desk I stick some purple candles which smell like blueberry, and a picture of me, my sister, and Dad when I was ten and she was four and we are standing in front of the Haunted Mansion at Disney World. I find some huge boxes of Snickers and Oreo Cookies along with couple of jumbo bags of Tortilla chips and stick them in my closet which is way too big for even a queen's wardrobe. Next to my bed I have a couple of fancy art books and a Tiffany kind of lamp for reading, and that is about it. My room is what you would call a haven. Too bad I'm hardly ever in there.

I have a bunch of friends in the city. They really are more like family because they accept me for who I am. Ginny hates them all, naturally, because she thinks they are a bad influence. But now that I am twenty-three and can pretty much do whatever I damn please, she realizes that she can't complain too much or I will end up coming home even less than I do now. Laney and Ryan live together in Soho, but it's really Ryan's place since his dad is a multimillionaire CEO in a hedge fund, and a thousand bucks is something like a nickel to him. He gives his son whatever he wants.

Ryan is a lifetime student, I think, who is now studying business at NYU. So Laney is the one that's home most of the time so that she can work on her sketches. I am sure that one day she will have her own exhibit, she is that good.

Nevertheless, Ginny doesn't like my friends, like I care what she thinks. It started with the flower. I have a small one, really no more than an inch, right in the center of my lower back. The petals are emerald green and the center is purple, of course, with a long skinny green stem curving over my left buttock. I showed it to both my parents when they were still together, and my father said "it's not so bad," but Ginny, well, she nearly had a heart attack. She blames Laney for that, since she has got them all over her arms and one over each breast. She sketches each of her designs on paper before she has someone do the actual work, and they are really each quite unique. Sort of like a biography of her life, with grass and buildings and people. Anyway, I bet Ginny wishes she hadn't gone so ballistic over a little butt flower because now I have added to the scenery with some copies of my sculpture faces, one little Asian girl on the upper part of my left arm, and an old black woman of about ninety on my right. Oh, and I put two more purple flowers going up the sides of my neck, just for balance. Now every time I come home with a new one, Ginny doesn't say a thing, she just gives me the slit-eyed look.

My sister doesn't stop talking, but when she finally does take a breath, Ginny sets her sights on me again.

"Chrissie, why don't you slow down when you eat? It really isn't so good for your digestion."

I stab another cutlet off the big platter and push the whole piece into my mouth, just to piss her off. She sighs loudly this time, and folds her arms across her chest. My sister raises her two dark eyebrows and pouts, giving me the sad look. But I am the one who is sad for her because I know she is just waiting for her moment when she can get the hell out of here.

"How is the internship going?" Ginny asks.

"Okay, I guess," I say, shrugging my shoulders.

"Have they brought any new pieces into the museum yet?"

"Just a couple of modern obelisks, nothing special."

"I see…" she hesitates, then adds, "and your work, how is that coming along?"

"I'm working on the same piece that I've been working on for the last two months."

"Oh." She tries to remember, but of course she doesn't.

"It's the umbrella lady who always hangs out in the park."

"Ah, yes. The one with the delicate skin."

"Yea."

"I can't wait to see it." I'm sure she can't.

There is a long pause, and I am starting to feel sick.

"Any chance the museum will have any full time openings?"

There. She said it. I was just waiting.

"I don't really give two shits if there is an opening. I told you I am not interested in becoming a stupid museum curator."

"But I just thought—"

"You just thought. Would you stop bugging me about a job? I am an artist, not some guardian of artifacts in a museum, even though I have been there for six months and I make just enough for what I need. How many times must I tell you?"

She puffs up her cheeks like some blowfish, and I can see a red flash spreading across her face.

"Twenty-three years old, Chrissie, that's how old you are," she is saying under her breath, but loud enough for the neighbors, miles away, to hear, "and out of college for two years, still without a real job. I'm not saying you are not an artist. You know how much I love that first piece you did—you know, the little Chinese girl on the swing? I think you are very talented, really. But you can always have your art, yet you still need to make a living. Why not take some credits in education so you can teach high school?

You were really always so good with young people, so patient, that I think you could be a wonderful teacher. Besides, you could support yourself and have the time you need for your art."

Well, here we go again.

"You just never stop, do you?" I get off the stool, feeling heavy and nauseas.

I toss the empty plate into the sink and hear it clatter. She will go berserk if it breaks because it is one of her fancy ones with the exotic flowers on it.

"This is the reason I hate coming home. You just don't have a clue—"

But I can't finish the sentence. I speed up the stairs, not looking back. As I do, it is not my mother's eyes I feel on my back, but my sister's.

I make a beeline for the guest bath at the end of the hall, the furthest away so they cannot hear me. It is a hateful bathroom because wherever you turn, there are mirrored tiles on every wall. I ignore the white soaking tub that reminds me of a casket, and stop to look at my reflection framed between two tall vases each filled with a single white orchid. I grasp one of the bronze vessel sinks and move in close to examine my face. Long pale porcelain skin with two glassy cat green eyes, an unremarkable nose, and skinny lips. It is not the face of someone I would ever choose to sculpt. It is detestable. It is her face.

I turn on the faucet marked "C" and run my hands through the icy water. I slick back my short red dyed hair, paying careful attention to the purple strands in the middle. The fluorescent light casts a blue deathlike sheen down my face, deepening the dark circles under my eyes. I avoid looking at my body, and take a deep breath. I walk over to the toilet, lift the seat, and bend down. Then, I stick two fingers so far down into my throat, just deep enough until I begin to gag.

Adam

I am in love. It's not so bad once you say it. *In love.* I never thought I would actually feel such a thing, but then again, I've never met anyone quite like Meghan before.

I didn't go looking for it. I mean, who ever does? And besides, I'm pretty much of a jerk when it comes to the boy/girl thing, even though some guys like to brag about that stuff. I've always been kind of a nerd, if you want to know the truth. You know, the kind of kid who would much rather sit in chem lab mixing vials than hanging out with the guys. I suppose that's why it's so amazing that I noticed her in the first place. She was just always there, sitting behind me in English class or a couple of tables away in the cafeteria. For years it was like that. Like the grass under your feet, something you never pay attention to. Until one day, you look down and say to yourself, Hey! This is *grass.* Look at how green each blade is, how silky, with drops of water clinging to it. And isn't that amazing? That's how it was with Meghan. Amazing.

It was something more than natural when she spoke to me for the first time. I think she asked me something about the math homework right before Mrs. Berlin walked into the room. She could have easily asked the same question of Maryann who was examining her nails in the seat next to her, or Robert Jacobs whose big head floated above his open textbook as he sat right in front of her. She could easily have asked either one, especially Robert, who was much smarter in math than I, but instead she chose to turn her body diagonally backwards, fix her saddle brown eyes square in the middle of my face, and ask me. To this day, I don't even remember what it was she asked, but I do remember how the sound of her asking made me feel. Kind of like stepping into a cool shower after you've been walking on hot sand all day. Exhilarating—and a little bit scary.

After awhile, we just fell into it. The talking. First it was only in Mrs. Berlin's math class, the only class we had together, where we would discuss dumb things like my idiotic collection of *Star Wars* figures (she perfectly understood, admitting owning a ridiculous *Hello Kitty* stationery and pencil set herself), and the Yankees, my own personal passion since I turned five. It seems that she knew more about baseball statistics than I did, which was unusual because she wasn't a particular fan of any team, and funny because she was, after all, a girl. After we had endured a few too many "shushes" from Mrs. Berlin, who was usually easygoing, we decided to continue the conversation outdoors after school. We would both get on the bus to her house since the driver never checked the passes anyway. Once we got to the bottom of a hill, which was a couple of blocks from where she lived, we would abruptly turn around and head west toward my place. It was okay at my house I explained when she told me we might run into her mom or sister who would often blow in unexpectedly like leaves in the fall. I reassured her that we would be fine since my dad was never home during the day, and my grandpa, while in his room, wasn't really there in the way you might think. She laughed then, her voice rising up like a bubbling fountain, and shrugged her shoulders. For me, actually the best part of being with Meghan was not getting to our destination, but the walking itself. She mostly asked questions about the kinds of things I liked to do, who I hung out with, my favorite flavor of ice cream. Stuff like that. Before I met Meghan, I never even thought much about myself, much less talked about me. But when I was with her, I *could* talk. And that laugh of hers. She just about laughed at everything I said, like the time she asked me if one day I could go up into space, which planet I would visit first.

"Hmm..." I said, "burned alive on Mercury or frozen to death on Pluto. Tough one."

She started laughing then, short bubbles of laughter bursting out of her like mini volcanoes, until the bubbles came together like a stream of lava until finally she began to hiccup.

"You're so funny, Adam," she said, smiling between the hiccups, "funny and weird."

I looked down at the brown terra cotta tile floor in the kitchen so she wouldn't catch me smiling. I'd been called "weird" plenty of times before, but never funny. And yet, when she said it, I knew it had to be so.

Most afternoons when we would walk under the wide arch into the kitchen, if Papa, my Grandpa David, was sitting at the table drinking tea with Mrs. Ruiz, the lady who looked after him, he would raise his head and smile as if he were about to say something, and then lower his head just as fast, and take a long slow sip from his cup. It was a small porcelain China cup with orange little birds flying on it, which he and Grandma brought over from the Old Country. It looked strange and uncomfortable hugged in his huge bear hands. Mrs. Ruiz, however, would greet us warmly, ask how my day was, and drop another sugar cube into her tea as the smoke rose up her neck, casting gray shadows against her sagging jowls. On those days, Meghan and I would go up to my room and drop our books on the unmade bed. Sometimes, she would ask to see my collection of baseball cards, explaining the meaning of the stats as we went through each one. Other times we would share a couple of the honey granola bars I always kept in a stash under my bed. We would do our math homework and sometimes even mess around some, but that wasn't until a couple of months later.

Most of the time, though, we would place our books on the stainless steel kitchen counter, the one that was never used for any other reason, and I would find some milk, seltzer, and chocolate syrup and make her a real Brooklyn egg cream, just like Papa David taught me to make when I was a kid, and when he still knew enough to remember things. Tall glass with a picture of floppy-eared Goofy my Dad had bought for me on our one trip to Disney World, filled up to Goofy's waist with ice cold milk, a couple of spoons of Fox's U-Bet, and fill the rest to the brim with seltzer water. This became my specialty, and as I stirred first hers, then mine, clanging the sides of the glass with a metal spoon, Meghan became my biggest fan.

When that was done, we would open our math books and begin untangling trig problems that Mrs. Berlin had written on the board earlier that afternoon. Meghan remarked once that the house needed a woman's touch. I didn't care, I said. No one did in this house. But the next day she surprised me with a small bamboo plant stuck in a jar of pebbles which she had kept in her school locker since morning. Two days later, my Dad noticed it on the counter, and I told him everyone got one in bio class. A lame lie, but he bought it anyway.

Meghan would usually begin working first, squinting into the notebook as she bit her lower lip until finally submerging her pencil, making firm determined marks into the paper. It took me longer to get started, though, as when she wasn't looking I could allow my eye to follow the wisp of her dark brown hair as a strand lost its way against her cheek. I could view the motion of her mouth, opening every so often like a tiny rosebud as she sipped egg cream from a paper straw. I could fix on the unexpected freckles which rose like tiny footprints across the bridge of her nose. And finally at the triangle of cool white skin peeking between the collar of her shirt where lay a silver cross, barely noticeable, moving imperceptibly with each breath. Sometimes, she would catch me staring at her, and smile a secret smile then just for me. And I couldn't help but think she knew. She knew I had fallen in love.

David

I have told this story many times before. But, unlike so many others, I do not care if I tell it until the doors of Eternity slam shut. God says we have a duty to learn all of our days, and even still we only understand an infinitesimal part of the universe. And the story I have to teach—well, I admit that still I don't understand too much of it, and I am eighty-four years old already.

I began telling the stories to the little ones sitting at their desks, shuffling their feet waiting for the lunch bell to ring. After about ten minutes, they stopped their uneasiness, and would fix me with their eyes, at first glinting with disbelief, and then the glaze of fear. Even the teacher would stop at her desk to turn her body to me, as if that moment time stood still. And then, when I was done, would be the silence, and I would know that they had heard. The problem was that the stories kept coming even though I did not want them to, the memories marching into my dreams, invading my rest so that sleep became nothing more than an endless battle with memory until, finally, memory won the war so that now I cannot even tell the real from the past. It was and is a constant reliving. And I wonder, is this what it means to be old?

My birthplace, Lodz, Poland, was a town dipped in sorrows. But it wasn't always that way. Today it might have been considered a little town, what we would call a *shtetl*, but for us, it was a wondrous metropolis. Walking out the door onto that first concrete step was like entering into a Purim party, such were the variety of people, the young man with a high black hat and overcoat clutching a *siddur* as he hurried to *shul,* the fair-skinned young woman holding a sack of bread in one hand and a child's tiny fingers in the other as two more tugged at the hem of her coat, the boys in their short pants laughing and pushing each other as the elders brushed past, the old *yid* with a long gray beard huddled against the side of a building for warmth, wiping the wetness from his nose every so often with the back of his hand. Oh, there was so much to see! The buildings served only as scenery for the drama, stoically playing their part in colors of umber and gray, wheezing smoke from their chimneys as the main street conducted its drama. Lodz was a world which never ceased to amaze me, yet I was as comfortable outside my door as I was snuggled into the recesses of my small bed.

Up until the age of eight my life was what some might call idyllic. As the only child, and a son at that, of two struggling dreamers, I was the crown jewel of my parents' wishes. Believe me, it was not because I maintained some extraordinary talent or skill, but just that my parents seemed to confer upon me a certain aura of majesty. If I did possess any sort of ability at all, it was certainly not from my brain, for I had always been shall we say, a less than stellar student in *cheder* where I much preferred practicing the art of making paper airplanes to the rote study of Talmud. No, my abilities lay in my face, normally slender and sweet, but when given the opportunity, could be contorted into the sour smile of my teacher, the wink of our town's old rabbi, or even the haughtiness of the Tsar himself. My knack for these freelance impressions often rescued me from the scolding of our principal when once again I arrived to school after dawdling to stop in at the baker's or have conversation along the way. And, my popularity grew among my peers as I bowed my head and had a little dance for them in cool imitation of Menasche, the town beggar. As for my parents, they would clap their hands and Mama would squeal in delight as I assumed the guise of an opera singer I had once seen in a film. And then, Mama would sit at the shiny black piano under the window and invent a song to accompany me, while Tata would pull his old viola from beneath the bed and run the bow against the strings until they sang too. On rare occasion, my parents would reward me by taking me into the dining room where Tata would open the oak china cabinet with a small silver key. When the double doors opened, I gasped. Before me stood two porcelain figurines, both unheeding my widened eyes. A pianist and a violinist with delicately etched faces right down to their immaculate fingernails, their sculptured brown shoes. To my chagrin, though, I could only stare at their artificial yet lifelike beauty. *No touching, David.* Over time, the small family grew to include a husky drummer, a blonde-haired lady playing the harp, a young boy strumming a mandolin. A king, a newborn baby, a pauper, a baker. I soon learned that these figurines were a collection kept in my parents' hopes of someday opening an antiques shop. Another dream of my dreamer parents. One way or the other, I didn't care why they were there. Imagine the joy when on my third birthday, they even let me place my finger on one. Because, you see, in those days, I could do no wrong. I was, after all, the dream that came true.

But when I turned around four or five, something changed in our household. Mama's face grew tired and sallow, while Tata lost a little bit of the quick step in his heels. And when they watched me perform, it was without that sense of wild abandon I received in earlier days. Only later did Mama confess that it wasn't anything I had done, but rather an emptiness which had begun to seep into their spirit.

"Tata and I prayed so hard," she would say, a few years later, sitting me down opposite her, as she spread her hands, palms open, over her checkered apron as if it were a tablecloth awaiting a meal.

"More for you, my little son than for ourselves, we prayed for a brother or even a sister, a friend to keep with you as you go.

"And now," she said, a smile filling her face like sunshine as she rose and placed a hand upon my head, "*Hashem* has fulfilled our prayers and we are to be a whole family now that the missing piece is to come." She paused then, closing her eyes in romantic reverie.

"Tatala?"

Tatala. Little father. This was the pet name with which she labeled me almost since birth because, as she had indicated many times since then, her father's face was the blueprint for my own.

"Tatala?"

I gazed up at her, with her long lovely brown braid crossing one shoulder, her thick eyebrows shielding the glint in her eyes, and I thought her the most beautiful thing I had ever seen in my young life. Of course, I hadn't a clue as to what she was talking about. I only understood that I was to have a new friend, and that couldn't be such a bad thing, could it?

But a few months later, just before the celebration of the New Year in 1930, I understood. Oh, yes, I understood all too well. That day when I woke up after a night of strange comings and goings and the screams of ghosts, I found Mama in her bedroom cradling a tiny animal in her arms.

"Tatala, come and meet your new brother," she said, shifting the creature so that she could motion to me. Tenuously, I took a few steps forward. The thing had closed slits for eyes centered in a reddish face; a tuft of silvery blonde hair peeked from beneath a cornflower blue blanket.

"He will be named Daniel after your father's father," she said, smiling at my father who stood in the corner, skinny and shrunken like an old broomstick waiting for use. I stepped back quietly and left the room, and since that day it seemed that I was constantly stepping back, making room. Making room for him. A week after his birth, the figurine of a golden-haired boy playing the flute was added to the collection.

It wasn't long before Daniel turned our once warm and loving household into an asylum where frenzy reigned and people either spoke in hurried whispers or voices which had the ring of fear.

"David, come upstairs. The dinner is ready, David!" my beautiful and serene mother would screech out the window as I raced for my life down the street.

Where once our family had been a comforting cocoon with me blossoming at its center, now it had become a storm with my new brother at its eye, and the rest of us running this way and that.

For the first couple of years of his life, Daniel was a sickly child wracked by fits of colic, and later intermittent bouts of asthma. His angelic face belied all that, with pink cheeks and eyes the color of a calm sea. Even his sidelocks remained blonde as he grew, falling against his face in perfect rings, whereas mine hung ragged like a cat's tail. He resembled no one in our family, not even our grandparents.

"Why, he looks just like a little *shaigetz*, Christian boy!" the neighbors would remark as their eyes lingered over his face. Mama would smile, and when they turned away would spit into Daniel's face so that the evil spirits would not harm him. When my brother wasn't crying from pain, he remained sleeping, peaceful in his crib. And even though he had fewer talents than even I possessed, my parents now gazed upon him as if he were a prince, and even though I did my best to entertain them with impressions of Hershel the milkman, no amount of dancing I did could divert their attention from him.

"*Sha*, David, can you not see the baby is ill and crying?" said Tata, or "*Nu*, go study now, David, while the baby sleeps!" admonished Mama. And to my displeasure, she had begun calling me David now that I wore the *halba hoisen*, the half pants, as she liked to say. Even in those sparse moments of harmony when we sat around the dinner table, Mama would repeat, "We may not have ten children, but *Hashem* has blessed us with two wonderful sons. We are a family now." I would sip my potato soup slowly, but the pieces always stuck in my throat.

My brother Daniel grew, but he never grew into the friend Mama had promised. A pest was more like it. Since there was an eight-year age difference between the two of us, interacting as playmates was nearly impossible. When I was playing marbles in the street, he was still nursing at Mama's breast, and by the time he was ready for ball games and games of *hide and go seek*, I was spending my days intoxicated by the scent of ancient scriptures. And when he conjured dreams of goblins and warriors, my thoughts began to turn to girls with flowing skirts and elegant airs. We were brothers, but for the differences between us, we might as well have been foreigners living an ocean apart.

There was one thing that brought us together, though—music. After dinner, once each week, Mama would dust off the seat of the piano, sit down and play from one open book, and even though she knew the Yiddish melodies by heart, she gazed intently at the notes as if seeing them for the first time. Tata accompanied her on the viola handed down to him from his great-grandfather while I worked with my small bow, brushing the strings of the violin which my parents had saved pennies for even before my birth. Admittedly though, my fingers were not as adept as my Papa's, and I soon returned to center stage letting the melodies flow freely from my throat. As for Daniel, my parents made sure that he too possessed an instrument, a flute which he himself had picked out from the music store. And so, immediately after our spoons were placed in the sink, we played the strains of music, the notes binding our family closer than language. Even if it was for only an hour each week.

Daniel was not a good flute player. In fact, he was terrible. He screeched when he should have sung, and he blew stale air when the notes should have been filled with the breath of anticipation. Blended with the harmony of family, the flute was muted, indistinguishable. But alone, the sound chased me down dim alleyways, into the closets of friends, under a drooping willow tree. I would run, sometimes with my closest friends, and other times alone, my oxford shoes slapping hard against the pavement as the flute played—the siren of death. Once, I thought I had finally lost him as I slipped into Morgenstern's pickle store and hid behind one of the cool stoic barrels. I knew Daniel would never have the notion to step into the store with flute in hand, as he would surely recall the week on an errand with Tata when in a moment of childlike exuberance, Daniel had placed the brown wooden flute in his mouth and blew. Morgenstern, who was ladling a pint of sweet red peppers into a clear plastic container, turned an angry eye on the boy, who quickly placed the rebellious object behind his back and held onto it with both hands as if it were a life preserver.

"Who is making such noises in mine store?" growled Morgenstern under his breath leaving the container dangling from his pudgy red hands as he held them like a net over the gray-green brine.

Instinctively, Daniel ran behind Tata's wide black coat and peeked at Morgenstern from behind so that only a set of glassy blue eyes and a ring of golden curls were visible.

"He is but a boy, sir—a four-year-old who is a bit too enthusiastic, I'm afraid," apologized Tata in a tired Yiddish. Morgenstern, who was as wide as he was tall, raised his bushy eyebrows and, opening his mouth, let out such a guffaw that Daniel quivered more than he had a moment ago when fearing the man's anger.

Wiping his wet garlic-stained hands on the white apron, he picked up a pair of long silver tongs which he then swerved in the water until finally, a large green and prickly sour pickle emerged in its teeth.

"For the boy," he said, extending the hand with the dripping pickle," so you have something else besides the noisemaker to put in your mouth." Tata smiled and nodded to his son, who timidly stepped forward and accepted the treat. Morgenstern howled again and turned back to his barrels. Tata grinned and patted Daniel on the head as he crunched the pickle with one hand and held the flute with the other. Only Daniel could turn a potential punishment into a reward. And all he ever had to do was stand there.

But on the day I hid behind the barrel, I hoped my brother's memory had turned into one of Mama's doilies with the little holes throughout so that he could only recall Morgenstern's bearlike features, his bellowing voice, and would stay away. Crouching behind the rough-edged barrel, I tried to slow my breathing, for I had run many blocks down Brzezinska Street in my escape.

"Don't forget to keep an eye on Daniel!" I could still hear my mother's ritualistic warning as I exited the apartment, looking for the first friend who might be tossing a ball into the air or flipping bottle caps against the sidewalk. Before I had taken two steps from the outer door, however, I heard the piercing, unmistakable lilt of the flute, not unlike the sound of a question. It was a reminder that he was close behind me, trying to keep up on his small legs. For the briefest moment, I spied him behind me, silver-colored woolen coat open and flying in the breeze, the flute momentarily silenced, held tightly in his mouth like a pacifier. After walking briskly for several blocks, and to my great dismay, spying not one friend in sight, I pondered my next move. Finally, catching sight of *Feinstein's Sundries* across the street, I found my solution. I stopped so abruptly, I felt Daniel's body slam into mine. He catapulted to the ground, nearly choking on the flute which was wedged in his mouth. Then he got up, brushed himself off, and fastened his round watery blue eyes upon me, as if it were he who had done something wrong. I remained immobile.

"Look, Daniel, I have to go into this store right here to buy Tata some cigarettes. And you know Feinstein does not like little kids in the shop making a nuisance. So you just sit down on this crate to the left like a good *yingala*, a good boy, and I will be right out." Daniel nodded slowly, absorbing my words as if they were sunlight, then silently sat down on the crate and began to examine the holes of the flute. I went inside.

The store was empty, except for Feinstein who was meticulously placing several curls of red licorice into a huge jar. I busied myself at the magazine rack, feigning interest in a glossy journal about the newest cars. After a couple of minutes, though, I again heard the infernal sound of the notes striving to become melody, and my heart quickened with every rise and fall. I peeked out the front window and saw him, patiently practicing as he waited. Without stopping to replace the magazine, I let it drop from my hand, and like a thief shot out of the shop, staying to the left as I pursued the next corner. As I ran, I felt myself lifted in the air, storefronts merging into a kaleidoscope of color and sound. I ran. Shapes of cars, moving figures, ghosts drifting past, clouds. And yet, there was only one thought in my mind, erasing responsibility. Erasing destination. Escape. Escape from my brother. But what I really wanted, although I hadn't realized it at the time, was to escape into the past—a past before Daniel. If only I could.

I could hear the quickening of my heart echo within my ears as I clasped the cool rugged edge of the barrel. Fragments of sound. Morgenstern bantering with a middle-aged housewife, children calling to one another in the street, the cars screeching, humming, the sounds of shoppers on an early afternoon. A slant of light fell across the barrel, warming the top of my head. I peeked. And then I saw it. A flap of silver, a golden curl. And like the voice of a lark slicing through the cacophony, a single pitch, confident and high. I came out from behind my hiding place, then took my brother's hand and headed home.

Virginia

He calls my name. Have I begun to hear things? But then as I reach to place another tomato stem into the ground, coming from behind a full green bush like an errant hummingbird, something calls again.

"Ginny."

My knees creak as I raise myself off the ground and brush the black dirt off my jeans.

I do not stop to remove the cloth gloves, already caked with dirt, and advance toward the shrub as if it were a cougar, ready to pounce.

"Hello?" I say, "Who is this?" While my steps are bold, my voice is not. It is tentative, like a child's. Like my daughter's.

"Hello?" I say again, and venture behind the shrub, looking for the intruder. Yet all I see are some flattened buds, a stone, a chipmunk scurrying into a hole. I straighten up, looking around the yard.

"Hello?"

The sound of birds. A small plane lifting in the distance. I don't know why, but I look up then, as a cloud in the shape of an old woman's face drifts past, and I allow a sudden silvery light to bathe my face in sunshine. A memory of a boy, the one with a long sad face, flashes before me. Ah, but that was a month ago...And my daughter comes to mind. Not the younger one, but Chrissie, the one who calls me Ginny. Perhaps she is in the garden now without my knowing. I wouldn't put anything past her. My heart begins to sink and, standing in the sun's heat, I suddenly feel dizzy. I run into the house, leaving heavy black prints across the beige carpeting. I ignore the blatant tracks, throw off my gloves and sandals, and in one motion reach for the phone as I sink into an armchair. I pray she is there, and only when I hear the reassuring low tone of her voice does my breathing become measured again.

"Hello?"

"Hi, Emma. It's me."

"Ginny! What's going on?"

"Oh, nothing—nothing. It's just that sometimes I think I'm hearing things, people calling my name—when I'm outside working in the yard, that sort of thing."

"I understand," she says. And she does. Emma is my soft place, and so are Celeste, Pam, and Regina. Whenever my fears threaten to converge upon me, invariably I rush to them. Not to my mother, whose own fears crushed her long ago, not to Isabel who lives half a continent away, not even to my daughters, no, certainly not my daughters. Through the years I had gathered these friends like flowers; Celeste, a former roommate from college, Pam, a next-door neighbor when we lived in our first home in Suffolk, Regina, a client whose children once attended my daycare center, and Emma—oh, Emma—our eldest daughters had a short-lived friendship in third grade once. The origins of our friendships were not what mattered, though, the substance was what counted most. The point is each had made me realize that females were not catty creatures, after all. They were there when you needed someone to listen. And soon I came to realize that perhaps I was the neediest of them all. Each precipice I came to, my decision to attend law school, open my home to my elderly father, the divorce, Chrissie's rebelliousness, my friends had been there for me, standing on the other side, clapping when no one else would. Was it no wonder that I turned to Emma now when I felt I was losing my mind?

"You spend too much time alone," she admonished.

"How can you say that? I'm at the office almost all day long, and even some nights. Bart and Sandy are almost always there too."

"I don't mean when you're working. I mean when you're *not* working."

I could hear the disappointment in her voice.

"Sorry, Emma. I'm just not interested in meeting anyone new yet—maybe not ever."

"Oh, Ginny, that's not what I'm getting at."

I sighed, filling the silence. I imagined Emma seated at her computer, maybe sipping a cup of herb tea, counting down the minutes toward her next reality program. She and I were friends, yet we couldn't have been more different. Physically, she was short and round with deep-set eyes and puffy lips which were always painted in a shade of coral, her only adornment. Her wardrobe consisted of a couple of pairs of polyester pants and a few flowered tops out of the sixties. While she shunned personal style, her home remained a model of grace and formality, decorated in country English sofas and heavy oak breakfronts. Orchids and lilies waved gently from each corner of every room, no matter the season. She splurged on one of those flower subscription services which delivers all year round. Emma and her husband of thirty years, Lou, a quiet gray-haired man who owned several bagel businesses in town and never seemed to be home, had two daughters—two perfect daughters, one attending the Wharton Business School, and the other who would be entering Harvard in the fall. Emma herself had never been beyond the boundaries of New York, except for the occasional trip with family to Disney World in Orlando or when visiting her brother and his family in Ohio. When she wasn't buying new throw pillows for her home, she was cooking meals, albeit simple but hearty steaks, fried chicken, and stews. Her main talent, though, lay in baking. Once, long ago, Emma and I had taken a cake decorating class which led to my baking a lopsided devil's food cake with circles of pink and white icing for Chrissie's eighth birthday, an accomplishment which garnished few cheers and was not worthwhile duplicating. Emma, though, soon spun masterworks of sugar and flour, each one in a shape for every occasion—a flag for the Fourth of July, a Raggedy Ann for a new baby, even an ornate red hat on the day Regina turned fifty.

And so, Emma spent her days cooking and decorating her cakes and her home, making appointments at the dentist's, writing letters of complaint when a package failed to arrive on time, watching the latest blockbuster film on a Saturday night. And yet, she was happy. Emma wanted nothing more than what she already had, while I was constantly jumping over hurdles only to be confounded by the next one in the distance. But then, she didn't have anything to prove to a father who never wanted her, a husband who ignored her, and children who disapproved. Although I loved her for her wisdom, her friendship, I envied her contentment. I think what I envied most was the life she had with her daughters. Their IQ's were high but, more importantly, their hearts were loving and gracious. Mother's Day never went by without a bouquet of roses, birthdays never without a phone call, whether from school or when the girls studied abroad. Letters and emails were frequent and studded with private revelations, an affirmation of the closeness between mother and daughter.

"They don't hate you, you know," said Emma softly, once again reading my mind.

"Well, I think Chrissie does. She does, Emma, but for the life of me, I don't know what I've done to inspire that hate." I could almost hear my friend's brain cells firing before she spoke again.

"Why not take her to lunch?"

"What?"

"You know, a girls' luncheon in the city," she continued, and again I could imagine her uncrossing her thick legs and leaning forward as if she could see me on the computer screen.

"Perhaps the two of you could go to a spa, you know, make a day of it."

I laughed.

"Don't get carried away, Emma. That's not quite her style."

"Okay, then. Maybe not the spa, but a quiet lunch in one of those uptown cafes, just the two of you. What do you think, Ginny?"

I considered for a moment.

"I've been so busy lately, I don't know. But…wait, I do have a closing midtown next Thursday, and—"

"Perfect! Why don't you surprise her when she's working at the museum? I'm sure she'd love to see you—really."

Maybe it would be a good idea—if I could just get beyond one more hurdle.

"Okay, Emma," I said, "Okay, I'll try it."

"Good girl. Now do me a favor and go make yourself a cup of chamomile tea, wouldya?"

I hung up the phone, smiling. If my friend had only tried, she could have gotten a PhD in psychology and become a successful therapist. But no, Emma wouldn't have wanted that at all.

The winds were unusually brisk for early May as, stepping off the M4 line, I made my way down Fifth Avenue, exhilarated by the rush of business men and women, and tourists, all eager to be getting to their destination. The black and white pinstriped suit I wore for my meeting felt constricting now, and I wished suddenly I had had the foresight to bring a change of clothes. I secured the wide Pashmina shawl against my shoulders and when I ran my hand against its softness, it reminded me of the time I had held Chrissie close to my body when she was a baby, naked and small. It was no accident that I had chosen to wear the shawl that day. It was purple. Chrissie's favorite color.

The closing had taken longer than expected. The seller's attorney representing an elderly couple who were moving to Arizona for health reasons, was a huge man with a deep tan; his body, straining against a blue and white striped shirt, verged on obesity. Several times during the meeting, he would look down at his sapphire stone set in a broad gold ring, lift his head dramatically to meet my eyes, and apologetically declare a problem. An extra check was needed for transfer of funds from the bank, or a coveted Oriental rug in the living room. I met his gaze, straightened my shoulders, and pretended to brush the lint off of the collar of my pin-striped suit. He isn't going to bluster his way past me, I thought, maintaining my posture. Two hours later, with a grunt, the opposing attorney eased himself out of his leather armchair and extended a sweaty palm as my client, a widow who had raised a family and was eager to resume life in the city, looked on gratefully. I breathed a sigh of relief. At least there was one aspect of my life where I felt in control.

My feet, in black patent leather pumps which no woman over the age of forty should be wearing, ached as I quickened my pace on the sun-dappled sidewalk.

I allow the wind to nudge me forward until, finally, I see the structure looming ahead, waiting peacefully like a giant gray whale. I enter between the tall pair of columns into the spacious marble hall, and a shudder of pride suddenly runs through me. Chrissie works here. My daughter works *here*. For a moment, I am dazzled by the lights overhead, the low chatter of visitors, the towering arches, and I am lost until I look up and see a panel advertising the latest exhibit, "Seated Buddha of the Pyu Period, 8th Century, Burma." She won't care, I think, if I take a little detour. I pay the $20 dollar admission fee and follow the signs, the sound of my heels clicking sharply on the marble floor. I enter the solitude of the gallery where even the air seems reverential.

The Buddha sits, as if waiting for me. I stand directly in front of the statue. My eye traces the smooth gun metal sheen of the sculpture. The intricate netting of the cap, the pensive brow, careful line of the eyes, the broad nose, the balance of the hoop earrings, the mouth—a smile, enigmatic, not unlike that of the Mona Lisa. The legs are crossed Indian fashion, the sole of a foot exposed. The fingers on the left hand are overly long, as if attempting to capture something. And directly below the left shoulder, a break. The arm is missing.

I imagine hands forging the Buddha, delicately shaping the fingers, the serious brow. Born in the Pyu Period, which only a handful can envision today, in a place once called Burma. My eyes voraciously rove over the art work. I share an intensely personal moment with an artist I have never met and could never hope to meet. I know this person, I think. I *understand* you. Without my realizing it, a single tear has dropped from my eye onto the purple Pashmina. I stand back, allowing my eyes to linger over the statue one last time. And then, like a golden light pouring over me, I understand. I understand why Chrissie loves this and what she is trying to say. And suddenly, I cannot wait to tell her. I turn quickly, rushing back into the lobby.

The young girl in the cubicle, though polite, eyes me quizzically behind ebony horn-rimmed spectacles.

"Christine Wernock, you said? I don't recognize the name."

"She's been assisting a Mrs. Parker, I believe. Her interest is in sculpture. The education department, perhaps?"

The flash of a false smile.

"Yes, I know Adela Parker, but there's no one working with her."

Suddenly, the Pashmina seems a living thing, a snake about to tighten around my throat. I attempt a deep breath, but can only manage a thin wisp of oxygen. I feel my mouth opening to speak. A few words spill out of my mouth which has begun to feel like a cup gone dry.

"She isn't expecting me. Chrissie, I mean—it's a surprise, it's--" I stammer.

"I'll go get Mrs. Parker."

As the girl turns, I see my reflection slip like water through her glasses. I try to focus on the colorful banner which hangs from the ceiling, but the words begin to blur, so I close my eyes. I don't know how much time passes until I open my eyes again to a tall, black woman whose statuesque demeanor suggests she herself might have been the model for some of the museum's inhabitants.

"Pleased to meet you, Mrs. Wernock. I'm Adela Parker, one of the curators here. Yes, I know your daughter."

My body begins to relax, but before I can take a full breath, she continues, "Unfortunately, she decided to leave here after only one week. I haven't seen her in several months... Mrs. Wernock, are you feeling all right?"

My mind is racing. Several months. She hadn't seen her in several months. If Chrissie wasn't here, then what had she been doing each day? More importantly, *where* was she?

I hear an echo of a voice calling my name again, and then it feels as if a slab of iron has fallen across my chest. The grand Buddha is holding me down. He is meditating over the loss of his arm. I try to lift the Buddha off of my chest, but I cannot. I try to speak, but I cannot hear my words.

"Water, please."

My feet go numb and I fall out of my patent leather shoes onto marble, as the purple Pashmina loops across my face. Desperately, I try to draw one more cupful of air, but cannot; the thing on my chest is too heavy. Before I close my eyes to a frightening blackness, I hear something. It is not unlike the sound of a flute, rising high-pitched and shrill into the escaping air.

Joshua

Because I cannot look at my son's face, I love to look at his fingers. When he was an infant, they were perfect tiny buds, eternally in motion, grasping objects even when there was nothing there. I loved to hold him as the fingers played around my face, grasping my nose, my chin. As he grew, when we would walk home from the bus stop, sometimes I could feel them like feathers creeping timidly against the back of my hand as they turned to embrace the fingers. At other times I could see them open like a fan at the frosted window as I trudged home after another long day, and I knew that in an instant I would feel them reaching high for my shoulders when I walked in the door. Even when I wasn't with him, I would think about those fingers speedily tapping at the computer or delicately holding a vial filled with a crimson liquid perched above a half-filled beaker. And I wondered what songs would they play one day? Whose hair would they caress? Whose wounds would they heal?

When Adam turned six, the questions that he had been asking from the moment he began to speak turned more substantive. "What happens to the slice of banana when it goes into my stomach?" "Why is that cut bleeding red?" "Where do my hiccups come from?" While these precocious questions demanded complicated responses, Adam's grandparents, who sometimes regarded him as the reincarnation of wise King Solomon, would smile benevolently, pat him on the head, and invent a ridiculous answer like, "A hiccup is just an itch in the belly which can only be scratched by saying the name of someone you love." After shouting, "Daddy!" "Papa David!" "Bubbie Sarah!" and "Bubbie Bea!" and "Papa Irving!"" a few times with no end to the hiccups, even Adam began to doubt his grandparents' credibility. Sometimes, they would simply stare in amazement at Adam, clap their hands in the air, and laugh, "Such questions the boy asks!" But I never laughed. Instead, I went to the hobby and crafts shop in town and bought one of those transparent plastic models of the human body, with all the organs visible in bright shades of red, blue, orange, and green. While the costly item was clearly meant for an older child, Adam was mesmerized by the structure and would spend hours in his room poring through an accompanying booklet which identified each body part. So whenever anyone would casually inquire what he wanted to be when he grew up, Adam would resolutely respond, "I'm going to be a doctor!" in just the way his grandparents had coached him.

Now, when I recall the times when our small apartment was filled the voices of grandparents who hung on each high-pitched word of their energetic, inquisitive young grandchild, I think of those days as, if not happy, a time of contentment. Immediately after his birth, we had hired a practical nurse, and a month later we moved a crib into my parents' apartment followed by Adam himself. When Adam was almost a year old, he was moved out of my old room and into the sunlit nursery Alicia and I had set up for him. Soon afterwards, my parents, both retired, came bringing their prescription medications, chicken soup, and extra blankets. I hired a woman to care for him for the morning hours when my parents reluctantly went back to their apartment. Alicia's parents also visited on weekends, and when together the four of them were not reminiscing about the "old country," they would gaze at Adam when he slept, each immersed in his or her own thoughts, or, when he was awake, smiling, lose themselves in the blueness of their grandson's eyes. When Adam got older, my mother, Bubbie Sarah, would play dominos with him while feeding him spoonfuls of her chicken soup thick with noodles, while Bubby Bea had him stretch out his arms which she covered in light blue wool, knitting him yet another scarf or sweater while regaling him with tales of working on a farm when she was a girl. Meanwhile, the "papas" bonded by a sense of senior bravado, ventured to the Lower East Side, the Brooklyn Botanical Gardens, down the yuppie-filled streets of Park Slope, like two ancient proud birds, the child, Yankee cap securely atop his head, between them.

Sometimes, when I lie awake nights, battered by my dreams of the past, I think of those days. Perhaps I was content then, but those years, in fact, sailed by in a haze of work, accumulating the necessities of day to day living, and more work. In my head, I reasoned that the child, the impossible dream of a pair of lovers, sustained me, but in my heart, well, I knew the dream had vanished the minute my son uttered his first cry. And, although I never voiced the feeling, I knew-- yes, I was certain-- that my own future was just as dead. As for my son, that was another story.

Nourished in the rich cocoon of family, our little man thrived. Adam, waiting his turn on the swings in the playground, would carefully relate how Papa Irving would travel on the train just to see Stengel hit one out of Ebbets Field when the Dodgers were in Brooklyn. Or when munching on a hotdog at the beach in Coney Island, just how it takes *cholent*, a stew made of beef, beans, and potatoes, almost a whole day to cook. When he entered fifth grade and had to choose a musical instrument to play, without a second thought, Adam picked the shiny wooden violin, just like the one once owned by Papa David.

Similarly, the old ones seemed to grow younger in the presence of their grandchild. They found patience as they waited for Adam to button his overcoat, understanding, as he showed them how to fashion origami birds out of paper, and joy in just about everything he did.

Only once did Adam ask about his mother. He was in kindergarten, and the teacher had given the class the standard assignment of making Mother's Day cards, using paper, sparkles, and paste, at their desks. Placing a sheet of yellow construction paper on Adam's desk, she subtly paused and helped him write "GRANDMOTHER" in red crayon at the top. When he finished the card, he quickly made another just like it. When he had finished cutting and pasting, one astute little girl gazed at his project, scratching her head, and asked, "But where is the card for your mommy?" Momentarily stunned, but unperturbed, he only remembered her unusual question once he had presented the cards to his appraising grandmothers, and looked up from the animal jigsaw puzzle he had been working on.

"How come I don't have a card for Mommy?" he innocently asked.

An uncomfortable silence descended upon the room. I glanced quickly around the living room. The eyes of Alicia's parents suddenly welled up with tears. My father gazed intently at the floor, my mother fussing with a thread on her blouse. For once, no one had anything to say. After another minute, Bea helped her husband off the seat of the sofa and the two walked slowly into the kitchen on the pretense of checking the brewing tea. My parents remained mute, waiting for my next move. Finally, I forced myself to look at Adam's eyes. And again, I became lost in the blueness of Alicia's.

"Your mother," I said, weighing my words, "loved you even before you were born. But she became sick, so sick that she could no longer be on this earth. But you have your Papas and Bubbies who love you, and—" I paused, "you have me."

"Oh," he said simply, and turned away, once again intent on putting the pieces of the puzzle carefully in place. Soundless, the room let out a sigh of relief.

The peace of our world was short-lived for, even though I didn't realize it then, in a little while nothing again would ever be the same.

Within a matter of months, Alicia's brothers moved out of the state to pursue job opportunities in the South, taking their wives and expanding families with them. Even though moving to a condominium in Florida would mean leaving their "little prince" behind, Bea and Irving reluctantly packed their bags in search of forgetfulness in Miami. At the airport on that last day, Adam's grandparents took turns squeezing him "one last time," leaving just enough air left for him to ask me if we could stop at Carvel on the way home. As Bea tearfully embraced me, Irving released his carry-on and patted my shoulder.

"Take care. Take care of—" he choked back tears.

"I know," I said, looking down the hall for Adam, who had assumed a position near the long window to look at the planes.

"We'll be okay," I said. When I again took Adam's hand and walked down the sunlit cavern of the airport, I had no idea that in a week's time I would be uttering those same words.

On Thursday mornings my parents would get on the bus to Avenue J and Coney Island Avenue where, whenever the weather was amenable, they would stroll hand in hand past the stores, stopping into a series of shops, the butcher for Mama's nice kosher chicken for the Sabbath, the bakery for a loaf of seedless rye and usually a large "black and white" or sprinkle cookie for Adam, the outdoor fruit market for apples, green grapes, and the occasional melon, the pharmacy for Dad's blood pressure pills, ending up at the delicatessen where the two would splurge on steaming potato knishes and stuffed club sandwiches, lean corned beef for Dad, and turkey with a sour pickle for Mama. Mama would bring along the red netted shopping bag which would be stuffed to capacity with their prizes, carried by Dad, who was always the gentleman, allowing Mama to hold the white paper bag with Adam's cookie and seedless rye which rose like a crown at the top. As the two strolled nodding to acquaintances along the way, a soft rain began to cast an icy sheen over the black tar on the road. The sudden storm introduced a soft haze into the noon light, turning the air a melancholy shade of violet. The two crossed the street and stepped up onto the curb, ducking into the delicatessen for shelter. But then Mama remembered something.

"Oy, the cookie!"

"What is wrong?"

"The cookie. They forgot to give me the cookie for Adam."

"Are you sure?"

"Sure, I am sure, David. Check the bag."

Dad moved the bread aside and peered in, already knowing the answer. Sarah was never wrong.

"Okay, so we will go back after lunch."

"No, they gonna' forget," she says, fastening a plastic rain hat over her head, "You order the sandwiches, and I'm gonna' go get the cookie."

Dad shrugs his shoulders and walks up to the high counter.

"Hurry back," he says.

Corinda Hayes gets behind the wheel, tired and distracted. She has just come from the eye doctor who told her she has glaucoma. Well, what should she expect at age eighty-one? Perfectly natural. Huge drops of water begin to splatter on the sidewalk as her hand quivers and she adjusts the windshield wipers and moves the car forward. She rounds the corner slowly, hand over hand and straight down Avenue J, which is quiet as the rain begins to quicken. But then a black Cadillac suddenly shoots out of a parking space, and Corinda swerves. She does not see the woman in the rain hat crossing the street until it is too late.

Dad is standing at the counter waiting for his order when he hears the screech of brakes outside and a sudden whoosh of voices runs like electricity through the deli. He follows blindly as everyone in the restaurant, even the meat cutter, runs outside. For a moment, he becomes confused. It is the Gestapo, he thinks. They have come for me. So he runs and stops only when he sees the car, a blue Oldsmobile stretched across both lanes, with a woman slumped against the steering wheel. He gasps, but then looks down, and sees something on the wet gutter curled in the fetal position. Slices of rye bread seem to sprout like fungus from the ground as he walks closer. As he falls to the gutter, he drops the red netted bag. The apples, the grapes, the chicken ready for Sabbath, roll swiftly into a puddle as he covers his eyes, screaming.

The hardest thing was telling Adam about his grandmother. At age eight, he already knew too much of death. His mother's death had become like a story in a children's book of endings and new beginnings, but this was different. I told him what happened because he had to know. He listened, his chin in his hands, absorbing every word. And then a strange thing happened. A subtle smile began to curl his lip, and in a matter of minutes, he was suppressing a giggle. He ran to his room. Poor kid, I thought, he laughs because he cannot cry.

My father, on the other hand, cried all the time, unabashedly, wherever he was, while sipping coffee in the morning, stopping for an ice cream cone, walking down Avenue J. It all brought back memories. After all, my parents had known each other for almost their whole lives. Like a child first learning how to speak, Dad learned to make do for himself. Nothing surprised me, not his pain, not the first tenuous steps he took toward independence. He had gone from his parents' home into the abyss of the Holocaust, only to emerge in the arms of my mother. While he "made a living" as an electrician, a skill he had learned during the war, it was she who was his face to the world, *handling*, bargaining, with furniture salesmen, arranging family trips to the Catskills, making sure my school bag was packed and oatmeal warmed my belly each morning. If there was a gift to be bought, advice to be given, we learned to turn to Mama. Oh Mama—why did you leave us? Why *now?*

I didn't allow myself the luxury of crying even though thoughts of Alicia and Mama now battled with each other daily. Although I had never been much of a father, leaving the cuddling and praise to the grandparents, nonetheless, I still had a child to think of. I had Adam.

After two years of hiring one baby sitter after another—a task made more difficult by the fact that I was a male living alone with a child, I packed my bags, helped my father fold his collection of antique figurines, tightly wrapped Adam's plastic body model, and left for a new house in the country, reasoning that I would be within a fifteen minute drive to the print ship, and the elementary school was a good one, only a ten-minute walk for Adam. Once in our new home, Adam thrived, running through the cavernous rooms, hopping on the swings in the backyard, asking questions about the types of trees we had, the names of birds. He was so enthralled with the newness of it all. Even my father found a voice, his mind journeying back to the times before the war, with his parents and younger brother. As the two would sit together mornings having cereal, Adam was transfixed as his grandpa pieced together tales of hiding, the selection, the arduous work of the camps.

"For real, Papa? Did it happen that way for real?"

""Just that way, *boychik,*" said his grandpa, patting Adam's head, as a faint smile flickered across his own lips.

When Adam was in sixth grade, he persuaded his grandpa to visit his class where they were learning about the Second World War. So he came, hesitantly at first, and began to speak, and soon found the children as transfixed as his own grandson had been.

"For real, Mr. Goldman? Did it happen that way for real?"

Within the year, my father, to our astonishment, had become a mini celebrity of sorts. A sudden surge of interest had reawakened the subject of the Holocaust, and my father was soon interviewed by the local newspaper and became a frequent speaker at schools and synagogues. I was even persuaded to join a newly formed group of the "second generation."

"What your Bubbie Sarah and I went through was all so your father, and now you, could have a life, so you should want for nothing. It is through you that we go on," Dad would say as he walked Adam to Hebrew school. Then Adam would turn there in the middle of the street, and hug his grandpa around the waist. He understood.

On the day of Adam's Bar Mitzvah, both grandparents, Bubbie Bea and Papa Irving, now wheelchair bound due to chronic arthritis, came with his aunts, uncles, and three young female cousins. As Adam chanted the Haftorah in the makeshift synagogue which had recently been converted from a firehouse, my father pinched me, pointing to his grandson.

"Quite a *boychick*," he said, dabbing at his eyes.

Adam was a popular boy, and numerous friends surrounded him during the Kiddush luncheon. His blue eyes sparkled as he took another sip of the red wine. His friends, many Christians among the group, jostled him, proclaiming the "good job" he had done. I stood off to the side of the room, a slice of buttered *challah* in my hand, my eyes following the path of a stained glass window which seemed to ascend to the sky. Mama and Alicia are dancing now, I thought.

I run. My feet are as light as a dancer's as they gently touch the earth. The wind, sharp and fresh, smacks against my bare legs, my pumping arms. The music of the sixties which streams into my ears fuels my thoughts and spurs me to run faster, much as a whip to a racing horse. I breathe deeply as a montage of kids on bicycles, towering leafy trees, and swooping blackbirds race past. Everyday, it is a revelation to me, this running, not unlike yoga or Hindu meditation. It is what I do when I am not working, when I am not teaching my son how to drive, or teaching my father, again, how to tie his shoelaces. It is what I do when I want to make sense of things without feeling the need to cry. And to think that I only discovered running five years ago, just as I was stepping into middle age, worried about the journey to old age, worried, as always, about Adam. So I run every chance I get, and as my brain cleanses itself as I move forward, I feel a new serenity and thoughts flood my mind, not of the store, which occupies most of my days, but of my father, of Adam. Just an hour ago, Mrs. Ruiz came to my door, knocking delicately.

"Mr. Goldman, sir, a minute?"

"Certainly, come in," I say, retrieving my sneakers from under the bed, "Is something wrong with my father?"

"Oh, no sir," She pauses and wrings her hands as she stands in the doorway, trying to find the words.

"It is just that your father—well, he soiled himself this morning."

"Oh—Mrs. Ruiz, I am so sorry you had to—"

She shakes her head vigorously, and her ruddy complexion deepens crimson as I walk over to her, patting her shoulder.

"No, no—Mr. Goldman, please, it is not a problem, but well—do you remember what we talked about last month?" I think. I have been so busy at the shop that all I can remember are dates, samples, and orders. New computers, the things I was learning constantly as technology transformed the printing business.

"About your father, sir?" About finding a place for him when—you know?"

Yes, I remember now. She had mentioned something awhile ago. Something about placing Dad in a home an hour's drive away. Placing him when he required more care than we could give. I didn't want to think about it, so I sealed the suggestion away in my mind like a precious nugget, forgotten.

"Well, your father—he is not so good. He sits more than he walks, he cries more than he speaks. Sometimes he even forgets who I am, sir, and now—"

I nod quietly.

"I know, Mrs. Ruiz, it won't get any better. I promise I will think about it," I say, guiding her out the door. I watch as thick shoulders slumping, she shuffles down the hall, opens a bedroom door and quietly goes inside.

As I fly into the flower-scented breeze, my feet tapping ground, I try to consider Mrs. Ruiz's suggestion, but cannot. Last year, as I grew frustrated with his increasing forgetfulness, his hallucinations, I threatened to put him away. He looked up from his office chair, pain etched across his face, his eyes imploring.

"I must go to the camp now again? Maybe I will find my little brother there? Maybe he is waiting for me?" I immediately regret my words and escape the house, my body shaking, thinking perhaps it would be best if I went away instead, and my father stayed. And I think I would have, if not for Adam.

So I run and the thought comes clear like rainwater. I cannot condemn my father into a nursing home, not even the best one. His family, the family I never knew, would not have allowed it. Neither would my mother. Not even Alicia would have approved. I turn the issue aside and bury it again into memory. And then I think of Adam, and my heart swells. As a young child, Adam was taught by his grandparents how to answer the question of what he wanted to be when he grew up. "A doctor!" he would proudly pipe. And as he grew, he voiced that desire on his own. And I too began to believe that one day the son with eyes as blue as Alicia's would be a doctor. But in the past year, Adam had begun to change. The inquisitive child with the ready smile whose questions burst forth sometimes like a geyser, the child whose fingers always sought mine, had undergone a transformation. Physically, he had grown tall and thin like an untamed weed, his curly black hair shielding the questions in his eyes. He was a boy whom many called handsome, and yet he himself was unaware of it, often entering a room bent over, carrying a book, typing, eating with small quick movements. But he changed in other ways too. His constant chatter turned to reticence, and the boy who once had so many questions had begun to wear his silence like a cloak, shutting his door, whispering into his cell phone. I no longer even heard the thump of the basketball in the driveway. And whenever I heard the jingle of car keys and would inquire where he was going, he gave the same curt response, "out," adding that he would be home "whenever." "I'm your father, not the KGB," I say. He smirks. When did he learn to smirk? And I wonder if he has begun to hate me.

I remove my sneakers at the front door, smacking the soles together to loosen the dirt. When I enter the house, it is quiet and hollow, like a museum.

"Adam?"

My voice resonates up the stairs, but there is no answer. Sneakers in one hand, headphones in the other, I make my way up the stairs when I hear a low muffled sound. My feet turn right, toward my father's bedroom when I realize that the sound is not coming from his room at all, but Adam's. I round the corner, sprinting, turn the knob, and burst into the room.

Abruptly, he sits up in bed, his face awash in tears.

"Adam? Why are you crying?"

He looks down at his hands, as if seeing them for the first time, quickly brushes his fingers across his face, leaving long streaks of dirt. Then he looks straight at me.

"Leave me alone!" he growls, his blue eyes flashing.

I don't know what to do, how to respond, so I turn and walk toward the door. He must be upset about his grandfather, I think. Incapable of anger, I try not to be hurt over his outburst. He does not realize that his father, a man who has lost his present, his past, now has only his future. And that future is Adam.

As I turn to close the door, I catch a glimpse of my son curled again like an infant in his crib, softly crying, his beautiful fingers locked together in a child's embrace.

Christine

One day I think she is going to give me a heart attack or something. Just yesterday I get this phone call.

"Are you the daughter of Virginia Wormack?" this strange voice says over the phone.

"Yes," I say, but I am thinking, what *now?*

"She is fine," he says without my asking, "but your mother passed out in the lobby of the Metropolitan Museum about ten minutes ago, and—"

"What?" I say, my heart unable to keep up with his words.

"Oh, she's fine, she's fine," he repeats, "but she was taken by ambulance over to Cornell Medical Center just for tests, so—"

"Okay. I'm on my way," I interrupt, clicking off the phone. Then I think I don't even know where the damn hospital is. So I fly out of Laney's place, not even bothering to wash the clay off of my hands, and get into the first cab I see.

When I get there, I realize that I don't even know where to find her, but I figure the emergency room is a good place to start. She sits up on the table when she sees me, white and confused. This frightens me a little since while I have seen Ginny in a lot of ways, confused has never been one of them. At first, I think she does not recognize me, but then she says, "Chrissie, you didn't have to come." I stop in front of her, relieved to hear her stupid voice.

"What do you mean? Why wouldn't I come when someone calls and says my mother is in the hospital?" I say, running my blotchy fingers through my hair. She holds a straw to her lips and takes a sip of some water in a plastic cup. When her arm moves, I see an IV connected to it. For as long as I can remember, Ginny has never been sick, not even when all the kids in the daycare were blowing snot and coughing. She's never even taken a day off from work.

"I'm sorry," she says for no reason. I shake my head and walk closer. She is really beginning to annoy me.

"What's the matter with you?" I say, finally. Her eyes look at me with softness, and a slight smile plays upon her lips.

"All of a sudden, I couldn't catch my breath. I remember talking to someone at the museum, and—" Then I remembered something.

"What the hell were you doing at the Met?"

"Oh," she says, takes another slow sip of water, then "it was a surprise for you, honey. I thought we could have lunch."

"A surprise?" I can't understand her words. Ginny has never surprised me with anything but nastiness. Who is this woman?

She sighs and motions for one of the nurses to take her cup. I feel like there are pins pricking me on the soles of my feet.

"I had to be in the city for a closing," she continues, "so I thought I would just pop in where you work and take you to lunch, only—"

"Only you didn't find me there."

She is silent.

"What the hell were you doing, checking up on me like that?"

"I only thought we could have some time to talk, Chrissie," she says, her voice rising like a fire, "But then they said you weren't there, that you hadn't been there for months...Oh, Chrissie," and now her voice catches like she is about to cry, "where were you?"

Right about then I can feel the heat spreading to my ears. I have to turn away because this is a hospital. I have to turn away so she will not see the anger in my face. But when I do, I see my sister come flying through the doors like she is on skates.

"Mommy! What happened?" She rushes in breathlessly, and in one movement, homes in on Ginny, hugging her tightly, forgetting about the IV that is sprouting from her arm like a slithery snake.

"Oh, Mommy! I was so worried when they called me."

Ginny's face goes from disappointment to happy surprise in half a second.

"They called you too?" she says. The lines in her face have gone deeper, stretching down from the corners of her mouth. There is an angry cross of tight skin between her eyebrows when she is sad, and it flashes suddenly now. Something in me wishes I could press my thumb against it like clay so that it would disappear.

"I hate to bother you girls. This really is too much, too unnecessary, that you had to make this trip all the way from home," she scolds my sister, pushing her body off of her own. My sister leaves a round patch of wetness on the blue and white hospital gown right at the place where her head was.

"Oh, Mommy," she cries, quickly wiping the tears from her glistening brown eyes, "are you sure you're all right?" Ginny sits up straighter, and is about to speak when a young tall Asian doctor with a shiny stethoscope around his neck walks over to her.

'Your mother," he says after a brief introduction, "will be fine." His hands, touching the stethoscope as he speaks, are like the hands of an artist. His black hair is slicked back over a high forehead. His narrow eyes are a mixture of competence and compassion, and I wonder if I haven't met him before at one of the clubs in Manhattan.

He smiles warmly at us.

"We've discussed this problem with your mother," shifting his eyes toward Ginny, "she is well aware of the problem and she understands what she must do."

A slight shiver is like the feet of a mouse running up my back, and for the first time I begin to take note of the smell of alcohol, which makes me feel dizzy and slightly nauseous. No one notices me, though, as the young doctor whose name I think is Chiu or Liu, continues.

"Although it is not always common, asthma symptoms may have a tendency to return in adulthood. An episode may be provoked by strenuous activity or during stress."

I look at Ginny whose eyes are still pinned on Dr. Chiu/Liu, as the sick feeling comes up my throat. If I don't find a bathroom soon, I think, I am going to barf all over his shiny black stethoscope. But she has been looking at me out of the corner of her eye because she turns her head suddenly and asks, "Honey, are you okay?" then assessing the greenness in my face, turns back to the doctor, "Is there a bathroom close by?" He points to the double doors, and as I run by, I can feel everyone's eyes on me. Everyone's but my sister's.

When I return, my face still stinging from the icy water, I feel my stomach complaining. Barely anything in its contents, my vomit was only a thin stream of oil, and my throat still aches from the soreness. Dr. Chiu/Liu has disappeared, and a nurse is now showing her how to use a special thing which will help her if she has another attack. When she sees me, Ginny looks up but says nothing, and my sister is too busy listening to the instructions to care about me.

"Hello, well, you must be the older sister," says the nurse, her voice soothing like mellow red wine, "My name is Mary." *Grant us health, we pray in Mary and Jesus' name...*I smile, then turn away as she focuses again on Ginny, teaching her how to use the thing which may save her life one day. There is a very old woman moaning on the table next to her, her arms moving haphazardly like wayward vines, and I move away in case one of them snares me. I focus, instead, on a painting of a meadow with pale pink flowers and blue green sky above. The incessant moans and odors of the emergency room recede and become a gentle buzzing of insects as the harsh fluorescent light seems to dim like a sunset. I can feel the spasm in my stomach, like a hardened fist, and resolve that, no matter what, she will never need to use that device—that inhaler— and if she does, it won't be because of me.

"Do you really think Mommy will be all right?" My sister has her legs crossed, picking her toes, as she sits on a tan coach with big sunflower pillows, one of many at Laney's place. She is wearing cropped jeans and a black tank top, partially hiding the cross she always wears. A bright pink headband holds her wispy dark hair in place, and she pauses to stare straight at me, her face white and oval like an egg. She is still not wearing any makeup.

"Nothing is wrong with her, so you don't need to be so dramatic," I say, exasperated, as I push a big pillow with yellow daisies to the side, stand, and stretch.

"I'm sure you're right, of course, you are," she says, trying to convince herself as she returns to picking the toenails.

"Besides," I say, walking over to a bare window and looking down the empty alleyway outside, "she only gets upset on account of me, so I guess I need to put on kid gloves from now on."

"Why didn't you tell her you weren't working in the first place? Didn't you think she would find out?" she admonishes as if I were the little sister and she were the big one. I shrug my shoulders and walk into the kitchen.

Peering into the small fridge, I find some strawberries, peaches, and blueberries which are still good; then I rummage in one of the cabinets until I find the blender. Over the happy whirr of the machine, I listen for the sound of the TV, but hear nothing. Probably nothing on in the middle of a Saturday afternoon, anyway. No DVD noises either, which makes sense since Lany doesn't even have a DVD player. I suppose she is inside flipping through some of the art books, although why she'd be interested in that, I wouldn't know. The blender clicks off neatly and, finding a crystal champagne glass on the window sill, I pour the frothy mixture to the top. I take a long gulp, letting the fruity liquid coat my insides like a spring rain.

It was only last night when my sister had called and said we needed to talk. She planned on taking the bus in, and we'd have a real conversation. I was tired, so I just said okay, fine then, come. In the morning I got up early at 7am, unable to sleep. What did we have to talk about, anyway?

Sometimes, I have to admit that whenever I think about her I feel a deep resentment. She was everything my parents wanted, everything I was not. The good student who obediently goes to every class, who joins the school newspaper, speaks respectfully to her elders, babysits the neighbors' brats, loves to read by the fireplace on cold nights. How Ginny glows every time she tells her friends that her sweet little girl is going to be a teacher! The good girl. As for me, well, I was something else.

I take another quick gulp of the smoothie, licking the icy froth off of my lips then open the door to the pantry. After moving some items aside, I find it in the dark recesses. I pull out the package and bite into the plastic wrapping. Two weeks old, but I was sure the chocolate cupcakes inside were still fresh. My mouth begins to water with anticipation of the whipped milk chocolate fudge and dollop of sugar infused cream. I pop the first one whole into my mouth, but break a second cupcake into two parts, allowing my tongue to taste the cream first, just as I did as a child then letting my teeth sink into the blissful chocolate.

Even though I resent her, I also love my sister. When we were little, she would let me dress her up in Ginny's scarves and hats, then color her lips and cheeks in red, just like a proper lady. We shared a room at the time back in Baldwin, Long Island, and I would prop up our Barbies and stuffed tigers along with my purple Figment doll from Epcot at Disney, and then take out the plastic tea set and arrange our little table. Ginny would give me a liter of apple juice in a glass bottle which I would pour carefully into the tiny vessels, and then fill a small bowl with rainbow jellybeans. I guided my sister's chubby little hands around the small cup as she sat in a tiny rocking chair already too small for me to fit in. I would even try to teach her pig Latin, or something my friends and I called G-Talk, inserting a "g" in front of each syllable of a word. It was our own secret language. On nights when the winds would bang against the shutters or a sudden summer storm would rattle the house lighting the sky with white sheets of rain, I would hear her whimper softly as she climbed into my bed, burying herself into the small of my back. Later, in a larger house, she would cross the hall to my room as our parents' voices rose angrily, rattling against the windows just as the storm did all those years ago.

As we grew, so did the differences between us. It was almost as if I had assumed the role of an only child. But that was only during the daylight hours when I would spend time with my friends figuring out ways to dodge classes. Listening to rock, attending concerts, tanning at the beach, these were the activities which filled my days. But evenings, when the stars stretched peacefully against the sky, the six-year difference between us melted into the night, and my little sister would look up from her Spanish textbook and ask the pronunciation of a word, or wonder aloud how I could eat asparagus even if it was buttered, or, more often, remark on how lifelike one of my sculpture heads looked. Usually, though, we would talk about our parents, the trips they planned for us, the gifts Daddy would bring from one of his trips, and then Ginny's classes, the new job, the growing gulf between them. Sometimes, when Ginny would walk past, she'd peek into the room and smile quietly, and I knew she was thinking about the bond she and her sister once had. I would hug my little sister tighter, knowing the love I had for her would remain dark and hidden, but constant nevertheless, just like the night.

I love my sister, but I confess there are times I wonder if we really are sisters after all. Where she was malleable like the clay beneath my fingers, obeying the rules, following the distinct track Ginny had so carefully etched for her, I was so—so *what?* Indefinable, as different as the colors I sport on my skin. I take a last bite, swallowing the moist chocolate cake as I brush the traces of crumbs off the counter, my chin. I wish I knew who I was. I wish I could mold a *me.*

"Chrissie?"

I look up and see my sister standing at the kitchen door, her eyes filled with condemnation.

"I'm sorry I didn't offer you any," I say, sweeping past her, "Just help yourself to whatever you want." But instead of taking up my suggestion, she follows me out of the kitchen, her arms still folded.

"I didn't come all the way here just to be ignored by you." I am surprised at how brazen her words are, how like our mother she has become. I sit down again on the floor, but this time I place the huge pillow in front of my chest, like a shield. I am too tired to fight.

"Just answer one question for me, please," she says. Towering over me, her face is the face of our father when he first heard Ginny didn't want to be married anymore.

"You can't ignore me, Chrissie. I just want an answer."

I cast the pillow aside and stretch out on the floor as my stomach begins to ache again.

"I don't know," I say, "I don't know why I didn't tell her I quit the job. Is that what you want to hear?"

But she will not back down.

"If you make her sick because of your crazy behavior, Chrissie, I swear, I'll—"

"You will what?" I answer, standing up as my voice rises, "Who are you to tell me what to do? She wanted to hear that I got a job, that I wasn't taking money from Daddy anymore, that I was the good girl who would go back to school, teach, have lunch with her, and live happily ever after. Well, I'm not that girl, I'm afraid. *You* are. But don't worry. I won't blow her image of me. She wants me to work, become a teacher, I'll do that. I'll even move back home, give up my sculpture, if she wants. But for now, just for now, I wish you would get out of this apartment. Just get out of my face." I am yelling, so close to her that I know she can feel the heat of my breath against her pale white skin.

She doesn't move. Instead, she unfolds her arms and places her hands up against her face as an uneasy silence fills the room.

"I worry all the time about her," she murmurs, more to herself than to me, "A child shouldn't have to worry about a parent, should she?" When she looks up again, I see the face of the little girl who had crawled into my bed on those stormy nights. I feel something inside me pulling me towards her, an urge to wrap her in my arms, kiss the top of her soft dark hair and tell her that everything will be all right then watch as her eyelids flutter and close in blissful sleep. But I don't comfort her then, instead I just stand waiting. She takes a long deep breath and walks stiffly toward the door. She stops just as her hand reaches the knob.

"Don't think I don't know what you're doing," she mutters in a low voice which seems to come from someone else outside herself, "stuffing yourself with junk food until you throw up. But don't worry, I won't tell." Then she leaves, slamming the door harshly behind her.

I stand for a moment looking blankly at the closed door, then walk slowly into the bedroom. The bust I was working on, an old woman, stands half-finished, staring at me plaintively. I lift a chisel, just to remove an errant chip on the side of her mouth. But instead, I find myself rushing to the living room window, opening it.

"Meghan!" I call.

But it is too late. She's already gone.

Adam

Soon I will have to tell him. He has seen me cry and soon he will want to know what's wrong. He will ask again and I will have to tell him. How can I tell him I'm leaving home?

When he finds out that I have lied to him, he will be disappointed. Maybe he will get angry, but I don't think so. Anyway, the disappointment is worse. When he looks at me with disappointment in his eyes, it feels like someone is slicing my heart in two pieces. I cannot face his disappointment in me, and I want to leave now, this very minute.

But I resolve to be strong. I am a man now, and I will not back down, no matter what. After all, it is my happiness he wants most of all, isn't it? I take out my cell phone and call her again. It is the third time I have called her within the past hour. When she answers, it is no different from the other times. Her voice is the most beautiful thing I have ever heard. It is the voice I imagine my mother's was like, comforting and wise, yet at the same time it is playful like a kitten purring on my shoulder.

"It's you again!" she laughs, just as excited by the sound of my voice as I am by hers.

"I can't do it, Meghan, I can't do it to him."

Her response is measured, as she weighs each word. She is not one of those girls who is usually given to strong bursts of emotion. Her birth sign is Virgo which means that she is serious and considers things carefully. Perhaps that is why the decision that we had come to so quickly is now so difficult for her.

"Adam, you always say how intelligent your father is, and how he is always willing to listen to both sides of an argument."

I shake my head and close my eyes tightly, almost afraid to think.

"Not when it comes to this, Meghan. This is the one thing that is non-negotiable."

"He's got to understand. We're not doing anything wrong. You always talk about how much he loved your mother...He'll understand," she repeats.

I am silent, feeling a deep sadness stuck in my throat. The sadness of disappointment.

I imagine Meghan lying on her bed, the phone next to her ear. Her dark hair is spread like a fan against the cool pillow, catching glimmers of light from the waning sun. Suddenly, my whole body longs for her again; I feel a magnetic force so strong that it gives me no choice but to submit.

"I have to go," I say, finally. There is a silence, and then I hear, "I love you."

"I love you too," I say.

I turn over and push my face into the pillow, driving all thoughts of my father away. Meghan preoccupies my every thought, my every movement. Whenever I am not with her, I dream of holding her in my arms again, and whenever I am by her side I fear her impending departure. I have tried to analyze what makes her so different. She is pretty, not beautiful. Almost boyish, she has a long fair face with a sprinkle of freckles across her nose, a smile that blossoms like a rose opening, when you least expect it. Her neck is long and white, ready for planting tiny kisses. Her brown eyes are deep and serious, and I often lose myself in their depths. If you passed her on the street, you would find her unremarkable, a simple girl. But for me, she is everything. And yet I wonder if that will be enough in the days ahead.

The annual summer county fair is back, and I decide to go to it. But this time I decide to go there alone. After a short drive to the fairgrounds, I pay the admission and the attendant stamps my hand with the date. I walk towards the blazing array of lights, my hand rolled into a tight fist deep into the pocket of my khaki shorts. Stepping ahead into the cool crisp air, I feel a spark of kinship with my father, the runner, who says there is nothing like a stirring run outdoors to clear his head. I am not a runner, but as I walk weaving between the vendors, the young children who are darting and pointing as they lose their way, the hulking monolith of the Ferris wheel, and the mutts straining at their owners' leashes, I feel my mind slowly begin to clear, my vision becoming distinct.

From the moment Meghan had glanced my way, I felt a change happen in me. At first, we had settled into an easy friendship, working on homework together, sharing common interests. But in the past two years, she had changed, the angles of her body softening, becoming rounder, her smile more confident, and her brown eyes sparkling when they settled on my face. I was changing too. My legs and feet had become very long, unable sometimes to keep up with the rest of my body so that I was always tripping over something. I was awkward, embarrassed, but Meghan would laugh, calling me funny and cute. Funny and cute. I developed a habit of singing to myself. Whenever I was trying to figure out a math problem or write an essay for English class, an Elvis tune would invariably come to my lips. She would sit and watch me for awhile, and before I knew it, both of us would be crooning "Jailhouse Rock." Soon my heart began to race each time she placed a finger on my arm, and I knew something had changed between us, that our bodies weren't the only things that had undergone a transformation. Meghan was the first to say the words which amazed me because they were the same words which had begun to stir like a phantom through my own head.

"I love you."

She loved me because I was funny, weird, and sometimes smart. She loved me for who I was, not what I represented, or what I would be one day. For the first time, someone loved me for me.

Drawn by the sweet aroma of funnel cakes, I stop at a stand and buy one. I take a slow bite, feeling the burn of hot oil against my lips. As I chew, I notice a boy of maybe five or six staring up at me, a large rainbow lollipop held tightly in his hand. I smile at him and he returns the smile briefly then runs back to his parents who are trying to place his squirming baby brother into a stroller. I turn and walk toward the light tinkling music of the merry-go-round. But, as I finish the last of my funnel cake and wipe my hands of its sugary powder, the little boy and the brightly colored lollipop remain in front of my eyes. I think of the few years I already have behind me, and a heat that feels like a melting star settles inside of me. But whenever I think of the multitude of years ahead, all I can see is a blur which hardens into a rock, and again I feel its frightening cold.

Meghan called my father a reasonable man. And he was, except about one thing. Religion. At age eight I was ordained. At least that's the way I see it. That was the year I began Hebrew school and my journey toward becoming a Jewish man. I was trained in Torah, the book of my people, but also presented with my legacy as a descendant of Holocaust survivors. Each time my grandparents would visit, they would talk about their times in the camps, how Bubbie Bea had to hide in the church with the nuns, how Papa David would go looking for cans of soup and blankets when he was in the Lodz Ghetto, how he lost his parents, his brothers, but saved the music figurines in the war. So much loss, they would say.

"But you, Adam, you will be our future. You will grow healthy for all those who could not. Your mind will blossom in a classroom because we never had the chance. Your hands will be healing hands and in so doing will heal us all. For them, I had no choice but to be the best. And when I marry, it will be to a Jewish girl, and our children will be Jewish—we would bear the fruit as we went from strength to strength.

"And that," as my Papa David used to say, "will be our victory."

I walk past a vendor, a middle-aged woman flapping her arms as about a dozen little neon bracelets twirled and lit the night sky. I head for a dark recess in a corner of the fairgrounds, where a solitary beach chair stands next to a cage of bleating lambs. I sit down and watch the sights of the fair spinning before me. I have a deep feeling like a drill grinding in the space above my heart, that life is, essentially, unfair. Not only is it unfair because I had lost my mother before I ever knew her, my grandmother just as I began to know her, it is unfair because I had been the cause of it all. And now I would be the cause of losing my father too, maybe not in the same way, but I would lose him just the same. It is unfair because the only thing that stands in the way of my having the person I love most in this world is the other person I love the most. I put my head into my hands, amidst the dank odor of the animals, the plaintive cries of the lambs, and breathe. As I feel my body shudder, I know that if I breathe again, the tears will come, and this time, they won't stop.

It was Meghan's suggestion as the two of us walked through the park holding hands. A cool spring breeze swirled up through a canopy of leaves carrying the fragrance of lilacs and jasmine along with the promise of rebirth.

"I don't think I can be away from you so long, Adam. There has to be some way that we can go to school together, or at least in the same place," she said, looking down at the rich black earth as she walked, her brown eyes half shaded by long straight lashes. I was hoping to be accepted to Cornell University, early decision on a pre-med track. Since the school was only a fifteen-minute drive from our home in Ithaca, it was decided that I would live at home and so save the fees for room and board. Meanwhile, Meghan was on her way to South Florida State to learn how to become a teacher.

"We've been over this so many times, I just don't see a way out," I say, involuntarily gripping her hand tighter. She pauses then says, "Maybe there is a way." She pulls me down beneath the shelter of a paternal oak where we can face each other holding hands.

"Maybe you could defer for a year, and come with me. At least we could have that time," she offers, her eyes brightening. I shake my head. Cornell had been my father's dream, my first step, he called it. In June, he was planning a graduation party for me in celebration. Meghan sighs.

"Well, I can't stay here, not with things the way they are in my family."

Ah, yes, I think, Meghan's dysfunctional family. The neurotic sister with the crazy tattoos, the mom who is on the verge of a breakdown, and the dad who thinks money is the answer to everything.

"Do you really want me to give up Cornell?"

"Not give up. Oh no, Adam, I'd never ask you to do that. Just a deferral to give us time," she pleads, her eyes softening.

"And what would I do while you were going to school?" I ask, staring at her until her eyes again settle on mine.

"You could help my uncle out in the appliance shop, maybe take some courses that could transfer over," she says, straightening as a sudden chilling wind tousles her hair.

"Where would I live while I was doing this?"

"Oh, I've thought about that too. You could stay at my uncle's place, down in the basement which is fully furnished. He might not charge you any rent, and even if he does, I'm sure it won't be much." I think of the savings I have in the bank, the hours, the years my father spent working in the print shop, the gifts of cash my grandparents showered upon me.

"You'll have enough to live on from the money you make at Uncle Philip's shop," Meghan says, reading my mind.

"And what..," I say, pausing, "what about us?"

"That's the point, Adam, there'll *still* be an us."

"You'll be busy with classes, studying, you won't have time."

"Oh, don't worry about that," she smiles slyly, "for us, I'll make the time."

I turn away, unable to look at her, as I shift uneasily against the tree.

"What are we doing Meghan? I mean, we're taking a big chance doing this. We're going to piss off our parents. A lot of people are going to be angry and hurt."

Tears fill her eyes as I speak, and I have a sudden urge to kiss them away.

"I don't know," she cries, "I don't know any other way we can be together." I hold her in my arms, her body feeling frail and vulnerable.

"Do you think you could ever marry me, I mean, one day?" I whisper. Instead of giving me the answer I want to hear, she lifts her hand and places it gently on the object that has come between us. I look down at her hand and the simple silver cross it holds.

"Do you think that, um, if we do," I say, trying to find the words, "…if we do ever, you know, marry—would you?"

"I don't know, Adam," she says, again lifting her eyes to mine, "I mean it's not that our family is so religious or anything. I go to church twice a year, Christmas and Easter, and the rest of the time I don't really think about it."

"Well, what would our, you know, what about our kids, would they be—?" I press. But then I notice the twinkle in her eye, and the smile which engulfs her face like a river. The feeling is contagious because soon I find myself giggling along with her, the two of us rolling on the petal-strewn ground. And I am reminded of the time we had shared a hotel room in Times Square, on the pretext that I was going to a Young Judea night out, and she was on an overnight trip with her English class.

"Okay," I say, holding her tighter between spasms of laughter, "Okay, we'll work on it."

I get up off the chair, stretch, and look up into a sheet of blackness stretched across the sky. Suspended overhead, the moon, shining like a golden coin, looks full of promise. I ignore the shouting vendors, the smells of buttered corn and cotton candy as I walk. I move steadily toward the outer gates, still open as young revelers continue to pour in. The leather seat in the old gray Mazda is cool and familiar as I start up the engine, forcing my mind to become a blank as I drive home. When I reach the house, it is enfolded by shadows, night birds calling in the distance. I round the driveway smoothly, click the ignition shut, and head towards the front door. When I look up, I see a soft yellow light coming from my father's bedroom. I take a deep breath, remember that I am a man now, and walk inside.

David

I gaze into the bathroom mirror and see the reflection of a tired old man. The eyes, once so full of zest, are now drawn downward, falling into two pools of skin beneath. The cheek once smooth like a lake is now gray and marked with two ragged crevices. What once was hair sprouts like sorry weeds atop the head. I look and I wonder when age came so stealthily upon me.

Was it so long ago that I sat at my mother's table dangling my legs waiting, always waiting for what the next day would bring? If only I had known that the howling Polish winds would bring the sound of marching boots, the end of days as we had known them. But could I have stopped it if I had known? After all these years, the question torments me still. Could I have held back the dark flood which swept away our entire world? After all, I was only a boy.

Sometimes I hear my mother calling me from the window as she did in the old days, her voice rising like a hummingbird into the dank air. Wherever I was, I would turn quickly and run home, Daniel usually at my heels. But there was one day in September that she called us home earlier than usual, when the sun arose high on a Sunday afternoon. As soon as we walked in the door, I felt something different, as if a dark intruder had entered our home and lurked in the corner waiting to strike. My father was stacking canned goods in the narrow pantry with quick, mechanical movements, as my mother hurriedly placed plates and glasses on the table, forgetting the tablecloth and matching napkins. She seemed silently preoccupied, didn't look our way, and when I examined her face for an answer, I saw specks of fear in her eyes.

"Mama, what's wrong?" I asked. She said nothing, only looked at my father who set his face in a grimace and, sitting down, said simply, "Eat your soup." The soup tasted sour and when I went to bed that evening, a hard knot had formed in my belly.

The Nazis came the next day, and in a few hours, Lodz had gone from a vibrant community to a city under siege. It was only a year before I was to be a Bar Mitzvah, and already I had begun studying my portion of the Torah in preparation. But I laid it aside and replaced it with a sturdy iron shovel. The next few days were spent alongside my father and our neighbors digging ditches from which we could defend our city.

"David, you hold that shovel like a girl!" joked Peter, my next-door neighbor as he cut into the packed dirt with the side of the tool. Peter was only a year older than I, but was already nearly six-feet tall and wide of girth. I smiled to myself, but remained silent as I worked beside my father. The work was brutal even though about twenty men and boys shoveled throughout the day. For the most part, our work was quiet, devoid of any conversation which might detract from our task. Mama and the other women would appear above us frequently with meat sandwiches and glasses of cold tea, but few ate anything. We had to work quickly to meet the onslaught of the Germans and whatever else we feared to imagine.

Our efforts didn't matter much, though. What were a few boys who had never fired arms before against the massive tanks? Only seven days after the invasion, the Germans had gained control over the entire city.

"Stay close to home," Mama would warn each time I expressed a curiosity about the activities outside.

"Why?" I asked, "I need to go to school to continue my lessons. I'm not afraid."

"There is no more school!" she shouted abruptly, "You must listen to what I am telling you."

I stamped my foot in the way impetuous young boys do, and glanced at my father who remained mute. My younger brother looked up from his book, his eyes wide with fear. Mama had never yelled at either one of us before.

That same evening, news came that Feinstein's store had been seized. I remembered the rows of long black licorice, the glass jars filled with gumdrops and sourballs, which I now imagined vanished into the air like a cloud. How could they come and take Feinstein's store, I wondered, and for what purpose? Mama's words were heavy with sorrow as she explained that the Nazi invaders didn't much like Jews.

"So just be careful," she admonished again, and turned to wipe down the kitchen table.

It was only the following day that Mama's words took on greater meaning. Papa came home later than usual that evening, his face bloodied. He was cradling his right arm.

"Yehuda!" cried Mama, running to him as my younger brother and I stared in disbelief. Who would do this to Papa?

As Mama delicately swabbed the cuts around his mouth with alcohol and salve, Papa, still dazed, explained that it had happened just as he was closing the store.

"Jew!" someone had shouted from across the street. It was a word which Papa knew well, yet this time the sound of it was coated with venom.

"Jew!" again, and then the sound of boots clicking sharply, approaching him. He looked up to see the pale cold eyes of two young Gestapo soldiers staring straight at him.

"Do you not know your name, Jew?"

"Yes, sir. It is Goldman, sir."

The one who had spoken, a tall, ruddy-complexioned youth with bright red hair, suddenly let out a guffaw, and turned to his partner, a darker version of not more than twenty.

"Do you hear that, Franz? This Jew does not even know his name."

His partner smiled in assent, clutching a truncheon between his hands. The other soldier, the nameless one, turned back to Papa, an inexplicable fierceness in his pale eyes.

"Your name is Jew, you idiot!" he yelled, startling my poor Papa so that he instinctively lifted his hands to his ears.

"Is this your shop, Jew?" the red-headed one persisted, this time prodding my Papa in the chest with his truncheon.

"Y-yes, sir," stammered Papa, "it is just for children, dolls and such, decorations. Worthless things."

"I see...yes, worthless things," said the soldier, standing back as if looking for something on the ground in front of the store, "And is this how you care for your shop of worthless things, by letting garbage accumulate in the streets?"

Papa looked down at the sidewalk, but saw nothing, only the black scuff marks of the invaders, and uncannily, a skinny flower emerging between the blocks of pavement. Had he understood what this soldier was saying? He had rattled the words off quickly, and Papa's knowledge of German was halting at best.

"The paper, you vermin Jew! Pick up that paper that is there on the ground in front of you!" Papa, startled, looked around the sidewalk for the slip of paper, but saw nothing. He bent down to reach the tiny flower when he felt the swift kick of a boot slam into his arm.

"Stupid Jew!" the redhead exploded, "you'd best be a garbage collector than a shop owner of worthless things."

As Papa clutched his injured arm, the soldier swung his truncheon, hitting Papa so harshly across the mouth and face that he felt his brains rattle.

"Just for good measure, Mr. Jew, so that next time you remember to clean up the front of your shop," he added, as the two walked off, laughing. Papa, his head throbbing, slowly eased his body off the ground. As he did, he searched for the piece of paper in front of his store, yet saw nothing but a now flattened flower. As he stood to full height, he tried to take a deep cleansing breath, but could only cough up blood. He remembered Mama and his family then, and turned, allowing his legs to carry him home. It was the first time in the eight years since he had owned the store that he left the door unlocked.

As Mama carefully checked his arm for breaks, under her breath she said how fortunate we all were.

"Could have been worse, God forbid," she murmured, patting the arm, satisfied.

"We will have much to be thankful for this Rosh Hashanah."

But we soon found out that any thanks or prayers would have to be made quietly as the Nazis ordered all services canceled for the High Holy Days, and all synagogues shut. Heeding the proclamations of the invading force, Jews throughout Lodz went to work instead. I began to wonder if I would become a Bar Mitzvah at all.

"Hurry up!" said my friend, Peter, over his shoulder as he threw my pants onto the bed. I knew that I was taking my time, but it was only because I wanted to prolong leaving. Less than an hour earlier, the Nazi invaders had announced that all the Jews were to be moved immediately to the north of Litzmannstadt, which is what they now called our city. It didn't matter much to me that they had changed the name of my home since Lodz no longer resembled the home I knew anyway. So what if it was named after some German general I never heard of?

I folded my summer shorts neatly into my small suitcase, making sure to leave my winter coat and cap out for the cold journey ahead.

"Thank you for helping me with this. Mama is too busy helping Daniel to pack."

Peter shrugged his shoulders.

"What else have I to do?" he answered.

My eyes stayed on my friend's broad back as he moved methodically, examining each article of clothing before deciding if it should be placed in the suitcase. Peter and his family wouldn't be going anywhere like the rest of us.

He is lucky, I thought, as I glanced down at the band with the yellow Star of David wrapped securely around my arm. He and his family had tried to put a good face on the departure on that last day, noting that at last we would be free of the terror which permeated the streets like an insidious virus these last few months, so that we would be able to govern ourselves and do as we please. I listened, but remained doubtful. I had heard rumors that the Jews would be forced from their homes, but also that the place where we were going was rampant with infectious diseases. I had also overheard the Polish gentiles on the street air their relief at not being exported to so foul a place.

I shut the suitcase and carried it into the living room where Mama was covering our shiny black piano with an old sheet. My little brother, now seven, clung to her skirt with one hand and held the ubiquitous flute in the other. Since Papa's beating, Daniel had become like a button on Mama's clothes, never daring to be apart from her.

Mama's fingers lingered for a moment on the ivory keys which had issued no sound in many months, before covering them too. Then she sat on the piano bench, as if to catch her breath. The piano which had given our family years of joy and precious memories, was too big to take with us, and would remain mute until our return. Papa had discarded the violin case and wrapped the instrument in Mama's soft cotton robe. Daniel, of course, held onto the small wooden flute, while my own instrument stayed locked within my throat. And I began to think that perhaps never again would it be raised in song.

"Put the suitcase down, David, and come over here."

My Papa's stern voice set me in motion, and I followed him into my parents' bedroom as he closed the door behind us. "Help me with this," he said, first grabbing a corner of the mahogany dresser, and once that was moved, the mirror resting on it framed in pine. Behind it into the wall was a cutout in the shape of a box; a blue cloth sack rested at the bottom. Who had done this, I wondered. Papa pointed to the sack.

"You see that, my son? Those are the figurines your Mama and I collected over the years. They are now worth little more than a few cents, but someday they will be quite valuable."

"But why are--?"

"Shh! I wanted you to know where they are hidden so that if one day something should happen to us, you and your brother can return for them. I doubt that the Gestapo will bother moving this old mirror once they have riffled through all the drawers. So I wanted you to know where these things are."

"But Papa, why wouldn't you and Mama come back for these yourselves?" I asked, feeling the pulsing of tears behind my eyes, "You could come *with* us, Papa."

"Of course we will come back, we will all come back. This is just so you should know," he responded, growing angry, "Now come help me move this dresser and mirror back."

On the train north as I sat next to my father, his eyes closed in exhaustion, I thought of the lonely antique bowls, clocks, and figurines on the shelves in his store, the store he never returned to after the beating, and tried to imagine their destiny in the hands of foreigners. But my mind, most of all, kept returning to the little horn player, the yellow-haired violinist, the hefty drummer, and all the other little "boys" in exile within the old cloth. They are just like us, I thought, as the train rocked me gently past the icy trees toward my new home.

I'm not sure what I expected to see once we reached our destination. Perhaps a room where I would have a soft fluffy bed to myself, even a couple of shelves for books. I hoped the new oven would have several burners on it so that Mama could make a large pot of *cholent*, a slow-burning stew of meat, potatoes, and beans, alongside some carrots, and her warm sweet-tasting compote when apples and pears were in season. But, then, I worried too about the matter of the diseases I had heard about, although Mama often said that any bacteria could be killed with enough boiling water.

Once we arrived, I found to my relief that the talk of diseases had been, in fact, just rumor. As for my other expectations, well, let's just say that my new habitation was somewhat less than I had hoped for. Ascending a long narrow staircase as we each, even Daniel, carried our bundles, we had to turn sideways through a slim door which opened upon a single room with four cots which posed as beds, a small freezer, and single burner for a stove. One curtainless window cast a thin ray of light into the musty room as Mama placed her bags down, surveyed the room, and sighed.

"It will be fine," she said, not looking at anyone in particular. Relinquishing my dreams of a fluffy bed and steaming bowls of thick *cholent*, I placed my suitcase on my bed and began to unpack.

In a matter of months, approximately 230, 000 Jews living throughout Lodz had been transferred to an area of only 4.3 square kilometers. Some saw this as a good thing, though, proclaiming that now we Jews could all work together and help each other without the cloud of fear of being beaten and even murdered on the streets. As I looked around our meager room, I wasn't so sure. After a couple of months, I began to miss my old friend, Peter, and his scathing, but lovable jokes, the tart smell of brine in

Mendelsohn's cool dark store, and even the smooth feel of the *yad* pointer in my hand as I began to study Torah.

Papa's wounds had begun to heal, and he soon was inquiring about jobs, anything just to make a *groshen*, a coin or two, and put food on the table. Owning a shop like the one he had was out of the question since he had neither the capital for such a venture nor was there much of a market for knickknacks and such when most were striving merely to put clothes on their backs. As fortune would have it, our next door neighbor, Jonas Greenblatt, who was an electrician by trade, mentioned that a helper was needed at a munitions factory which had just opened on Kopernik Street at the outskirts of the ghetto, which is what our new neighborhood, securely fenced in, was now called. Although Papa had never so much as screwed in a light bulb without difficulty, he jumped at the chance, promising Greenblatt that he would be a fast learner.

He was true to his word, for since the day he had begun, Papa was never without a job during all his days in the ghetto. While the hours were long, and he would often return after nightfall, he always left the apartment with a spring in his step. It was good to have work, he said, and as the days went by, Papa began to take a certain pride and pleasure in the fact that by placing two wires together he could bring light into the darkness.

Mama too found work, as a seamstress, fulfilling the increasing demand for clothing. Papa had purchased a sewing machine and thread from a neighbor who, lacking a talent with needle and thread, preferred to eat rather than hold onto a family heirloom. As she sat by the light of our solitary window, her fingers quickly moving the fabric along, her foot pressing the pedal, Mama would often wonder aloud if Mrs. Kitzman or Mrs. Hemmelstein would have enough money to pay her this time, or if they would even have enough canned beans to offer as fair exchange. And, as I watched her fingers expertly guide the fabric, I knew that she still ached for the touch of the old black piano beneath the dusty coverlet.

As for myself, I too profited from Greenblatt's generosity when he procured for me a job assembling rifles in the very same factory with my father.

"Come here, *boychick*," he said, turning me around and straightening my shoulders, "Walk with your head high and your shoulders back like so, and you can easily pass for a boy of fifteen." And why not, I thought to myself, as I pushed back my shoulders, I was already tall for my age, and Mama always said I had the wisdom of a grown man. So I set a sternness into my brow, and within the week was working besides boys of sixteen and seventeen years of age. Even Daniel was forced to set aside his books and, burying his wooden flute in the pocket of his coat, sat a few hours each day splitting thin sheets of mica.

One would think that with each family member at work, our earnings would be more than sufficient to meet our needs. Even before obtaining these jobs, we had just enough in Rumkies, the ghetto currency imprinted with the signature of our Judenälteste, our Elder Jew leader, Mordechai Chaim Rumkowski, to buy some potatoes and pay for the sewage. But our self-sufficiency was short-lived, for as soon as our hands were set in motion for the Nazis, Rumkowski arranged for our payment to be made in food only. And we soon realized, as the pain of hunger began to gnaw at our bodies, that even this would not be enough.

Rationing had become a way of life. Only the office workers received a couple of loaves of brown bread more than we, yet this too was barely enough to sustain them.

Things got so bad that one day after five grueling hours working in the steamy heat of the factory, the boy next to me suddenly collapsed.

"Morris!" I cried, attempting to pick up the strapping boy, my heart beating wildly. Some of the other workers saw what had occurred, and within minutes, had lifted the raven-haired youth outdoors, and began dousing him with bucketfuls of water until, finally, he revived. He looked around bewildered at first, and then pushed the others away.

"I am fine," he said, his voice growing in assertion. Within minutes he was back standing in his usual spot, screwing metal to metal. As I watched him warily, I thought if this could happen to Morris Lipinski, a boy easily twice my size, how much longer would it be until I succumbed to our situation which seemed to be worsening each day?

The next morning, a factory worker named Tovich approached me with a proposal. The boy, already eighteen years of age, had a sly eye and quick tongue, and his craftiness had served him well for, after only a month, he had been promoted to foreman.

"So, Goldman, all is well with you?" he said, twisting a toothpick around his mouth as he spoke.

I shrugged my shoulders, not knowing what to make of the question.

Tovich smiled, revealing a single gold tooth.

"Just a friendly question. Your father, he is working hard outside, perhaps too hard?" he asked, tilting his head toward the exit where Papa was positioning some pole lights outdoors. Without waiting for me to answer, he placed a hand on my shoulder and, his mouth to my ear, whispered, "Your father, he is old, and you— you are just a boy no bigger than a corn stalk. How long will it be before you fall like Lipinski, with your skinny arms and knobby knees? How long before the Nazi swine scoop you up for dog fodder?" Summoning an inner strength, I turned to find a surprising note of kindness in his narrow eyes.

"What choice do I have? None of us have choices here."

A smile slowly widened, filling Tovich's face.

"Are you hungry, *boychick*? So many are hungry these days. But there are those of us who are helping our brothers with cans of beans, potatoes, even cigarettes. A young one like you can be of use to us if you use your feet as well as you use your head. There is food to be had if you are willing to help other Jews such as you. Give this some thought, Goldman, times are hard," he winked, and walked off.

I had heard of the black market operating beneath the noses of the Nazis. Boys as young as eight were often used to procure necessities, even luxuries like cashmere blankets, in exchange for similar items. I looked across at Lipinski whose once-thick arms struggled to lift a box of lug nuts to the counter, and resolved to speak with Mama later that week.

The month was December when I celebrated my thirteenth birthday that was to have been the day of my Bar Mitzvah. Instead of celebrating the day I was to assume manhood as a Jew, my parents were lamenting yet another change to their circumstances, which had undergone more upheaval within the year than had been endured in my lifetime. Papa arrived home earlier than usual that day and, as a result, supper that night was one of the rare times we could eat together as a family. As Mama placed a bowl of barley soup with tiny bits of barley floating atop, I noticed some fine lines had begun to appear beneath her eyes. Her oversized pink shift fluttered lightly as she placed the biggest bowl of soup in front of Papa who, as the largest among us, accepted it silently, but would often place spoonfuls of the liquid into the bowls of his children when Mama turned her back. The processed meat on our plates looked like a brownish red mound of gelatin, yet we were grateful even for this as most days the Nazi rations arrived spoiled or cut in half. It is surprising how easily religious restrictions and an appetite for decent food can be relinquished when one is hungry.

I watched my parents chew their food solemnly, and I felt a mixture of sorrow and yearning tug at my spirit. I wondered where my Bohemian parents who never cared about the next day, who never worried about work, and would instead take time for the family to play our instruments together, whose laughter permeated each corner of our household, had disappeared to. I wondered who these ghosts were now sitting at our family table who had robbed me of my fun-loving parents. Mama, as usual, was the first to speak the unspoken.

"How much longer will it be, Yehuda? How much longer until there is so little to eat that we are starving?" she asked matter-of-factly.

Papa took a small bite of the meat and held it in his mouth for awhile.

'I can understand your silence if it were only us two, but the children, Yehuda. Daniel cries from hunger each night and I can no longer bear his tears."

Papa looked up from his plate.

"And what would you have me do, Natalia? Go out with my guns like a cowboy in a Western movie?"

Mama grew increasingly frustrated.

"Who is Rumkowshi, after all? He and his conspirators fatten themselves at the expense of the rest of us! Perhaps this man, this Judenalteste with his regal white hair and his aristocratic ways is not a Jew at all! And yet we sit here like lambs to the slaughter, without so much as raising our pinky. Look at your friend, Bodner, our old neighbor; he is not afraid to join the others. To speak up for what is right, to—"

Papa slammed his fork on the table with such force that it rattled the plate.

"Bodner! Must I hear that name once again? Let him complain, let them all complain, but I tell you, Natalia, I will bide my time. The Gestapo is behind every door, and if Rumkowski is in their pocket, then there is nothing for it. I have learned that lesson too soon."

Then he turned and walked out, slamming the door with one arm and then quickly clutching the other which still continued to plague him. Mama, grim-faced, busied herself at the sink while Daniel, on the verge of tears, found solace in his customary place in the closet beneath the hangers of clothing. I continued to sit at the table sucking the dessert, a reddish frozen water which passed for beets.

After a few minutes of angry silence, a light melodic sound like the song of a lark cut through the stagnant air.

Mama didn't hesitate. She walked purposefully to the closet door which she yanked open, reached down for Daniel and, pulling him up by one arm, slapped him swiftly across the face.

I sat riveted in my chair as Mama returned to the dishes while Daniel's sobs shook the small room. After awhile, even the memory of the flute song faded into stillness.

I didn't know it then, but I had become a man that evening, yet in a different way than I had expected, for I had learned an important lesson. Hunger not only affects people's stomachs, but their hearts as well. I also knew something else. I knew that I couldn't ask Mama about working in the black market that day. And so I put it out of my mind.

The next day, we found out that Papa's words had been prophetic, for that morning, Bodner had been deported along with the other dissenters, all labeled as traitors to the cause. By the fall of 1941, 20,000 more Jews had entered the already overcrowded ghetto, with approximately one thousand individuals arriving daily. Even Roma, the Gypsies, flooded the ghetto, only to be met by a backlash of those who refused to be fenced in with arsonists and thieves. Soon enough, though, they were ousted to begin the work in Polish farms—at least, that's what we were informed.

As more entered the ghetto, we soon came to realize that we had worried about the wrong thing. It wasn't those coming in that would send a tremble down our spines, but the thousands who had now begun to leave to who knows where each day. Each day too brought a smaller ration of food, and we began to yearn for the days when we first arrived within the ghetto's confines, and hunger had been only a fleeting ache, like the breath of a child, not the constant pain in the belly it had become. Our bodies now dictated our needs, and we thought only of two things--food and warmth. As coal was in short supply, our skinny bodies shivered during the icy winters and we worried that they would one day snap like twigs on the branch of a willow tree.

During the winter of 1942, fear, like a living soul, had moved into our household. It stalked us as we went about our business each day, and hovered overhead as we turned in our beds at night. But greater than the fear of starvation or disease was the thing in our hearts and on our breaths, but which no one could speak—the fear that we would be separated. Lists had been drawn up and "wedding invitations" sent out for thousands by the day. Some people even went willingly to a camp called Chelmno, with the promise of a good meal dangled before them like a mirage. I was skeptical, having already witnessed the treachery of the Nazis and their promises for a better life. I looked to my parents, trying to catch a glimpse of the old determination in their eyes, and prayed that they too would not concede.

One evening in January had me convinced that they would. As Papa dragged himself into the bed, his arm throbbing and his head feeling dizzy from hours of factory work, I lay in bed, eyes wide open, hunger a constant alarm precluding sleep. But then in the frosty silence came a low moan, something like a dying animal from a dark corner of the room. It was Mama. She was hunched over, clutching her stomach, a thin green liquid streaming from her mouth onto the floor.

"Mama, what is wrong?" I cried, running over to her.

"David, go back to bed. I will be fine," she muttered, her face contorted in pain. She moaned again, and another puddle appeared on the wooden floor. This time Papa awoke.

"Natalia, you are sick!" he said, approaching her quickly and placing both arms around her shoulders as if to stem the next upheaval.

"No!" she cried, releasing herself from his arms as the vomit surged from her body almost endlessly. Papa opened the door and ran downstairs without even his slippers. When he returned, he carried white snow as a gift in his hands which he offered to Mama.

"Take this, for your strength," he said, in a soft voice as if speaking to a child. Mama's eyes rose to meet his briefly and then gobbled the snow hastily as if it were manna from heaven.

"Slow," said Papa, holding steady as the whiteness melted into her mouth until all that was left were Papa's wet red fingers. He held her tightly and placed her back onto the bed until the color returned to her cheeks.

"Does Mama have the sickness?" I ventured, daring to speak at last. The illness, of course, was dysentery, an affliction which sapped the remaining strength of its victims, and was often the cause for exportation.

"No," Papa said emphatically, his eyes never leaving Mama's face, "She only ate something that does not sit well in her belly. Is that not so, Natalia?"

Mama, too weak to answer, only closed her eyes wearily and nodded her assent.

Nevertheless, tears began to fill my eyes, and suddenly I was frozen with fear.

"Truly, Mama, you won't let them take you?" I whimpered, "If you are sick, they will take you, but you promised, promised they would not."

Papa helped Mama ease her head onto the small pillow and then walked over to where I stood erect, hands behind my back against the wall. He put one hand on the top of my head.

"No, David, do not worry. We will never let that happen."

And then in the icy stillness of that January night came a sound rising as if on the wings of an angel. No one had noticed the swift flash of golden curls, and now from the darkness of the closet, a flute sang. And this time, no one stopped it.

Papa was true to his word, but only until September that same year, when our wedding invitations arrived. While Mama had revived from that first illness, it had left her too sick to work. But in the past month, after enduring a batch of spoiled meat, her condition worsened once more and, this time, the demon inside her wouldn't let go. As for Papa, he hadn't worked in the past month, his arm having finally betrayed him. He described the pain as a ghost sitting within his bones, just below the elbow, twisting a dagger slowly. And yet, the pain had not clouded his mind, for in the waning days while he was still able to work in the factory, he would call me aside, teaching me too how to bring light to the darkness.

Daniel stood next to me clutching his wooden flute, the one thing that reminded him that he was alive, as our parents, suitcases in hand, kissed us goodbye. They tried to convince us of the Nazi line, that Chelmno was a kind of spa which would nourish them and restore their health. But as they spoke, I thought that the only ones they were convincing were themselves.

Mama, her eyes brimming, kissed each one of Daniel's golden locks and held him so tightly I thought he would easily be squashed like a peach. When she came to me, her eyes lingered on my face and for a moment seemed to bore into my soul. She said only, "My son," and in that instant I felt the heat of hot tears sear my cheeks. I couldn't speak, but I had heard. I nodded my head slowly. Then it was Papa's turn. He kissed my brother only once on each cheek, pointed to the flute still held tightly in my brother's hand, then put a finger to his own lips and smiled as Daniel stood mute. When he hugged me, he formed words into my ear, "Do not forget what we spoke of in the old home."

"I won't, Papa," I said, feeling his heart beating as he held me close.

"Look after your brother," Mama admonished as my parents walked out of the apartment for the last time. As they descended the stairs, I could already hear Mama's cries pierce the air like lightning.

I closed my mind to my own terror and looked down at my little brother. At age nine, he looked no more than six years old, a delicate emaciated child whose mischievous smile was now no more than a memory. I thought of all my parents had said before they left, and also what they didn't say. Mama and Papa weren't the only ones who had received wedding invitations. Daniel too had received one. But, even though my parents had left with their heads held high, they were determined that their child should not endure the same fate. And that meant that I was to be both mother and father to my little brother. That I needed to swallow my fears, hide him, protect him, until the day our parents would return.

"Come, Daniel," I said, placing my arm around him, "let's sit on the bed and play some cards."

When the Gestapo banged on the door, Daniel was hiding in the closet. I opened the door willingly, but they threw me against the wall as they stormed in. It wasn't me they were looking for. A German shepherd strained at the leash as it barked high-pitched warnings, its jowls leaking venom. I held my breath as they ransacked the few possessions we had, turning over tables and beds, barking orders in German. When the closet door flew open, the animal putting its nose to the floor, I felt my heart jump to my mouth, but remained silent as clothing and pillows spilled onto the floor. I prayed that Daniel would remain still high on the shelf crouched down behind an old giant stuffed dog. Surely they could see that no child could be small enough to fit into such a compressed space. The closet door slammed shut and I felt a gust of air stream from my nose. As the blonde-haired soldiers brandishing their truncheons towered over me, threatening, blasting their hideous words until my eardrums shook, I remained stoic, remembering what had happened to Papa, as I clenched and unclenched my fists behind my back. Within mere minutes, they were gone, with only the echoes of the terror below reverberating in the apartment.

Swiftly, I ran to the closet door and flung it open. I jumped up and flung the cloth dog onto the floor. My brother, flute nestled between his hands, sat pale-faced, his chest heaving. "They are gone, Daniel," I said, pasting a smile on my face, "Come, give me your hand." But my brother remained riveted to the spot, as if he hadn't heard me at all.

"Come, Daniel," I said again, raising my voice as I extended my hand. But instead of giving me his hand, Daniel opened his eyes suddenly into large orbs, the color draining from his face. A door slammed, the sound of barking, angry voices, as the Gestapo pushed me aside fiercely, pushing me harder into the wall, and with one movement grabbed my brother by his golden locks, the same ones my mother had kissed, and pulled him off the shelf. There was no time for me to react, the words trapped in my chest, as Daniel's shrieks blew like an endless siren down the stairs.

I sat stunned for no more than a minute, feeling the ache in the back of my head. And then I felt hands at my back and a voice.

"Look after your brother."

I ran blindly down the stairs, into the chaos of the streets where mothers were pulling at their hair, screaming. Howling toddlers were torn from the arms of their fathers, wives separated harshly from their husbands, daughters fainting on the arms of their captors. Panting, I looked down the street, desperate to catch a glimpse of my brother. The dim gray sky shimmered with flashes of Nazi bayonets, as victims became mud beneath their feet. I looked to the right and left, my eyes straining, my heart beating so hard I thought it would escape from my chest. And then a sound. Clear like a bell, like a flute. I ran toward it.

"Daniel!" I screamed, catching sight of the bouncing golden curls. Ignoring the insistent ache in my head, I willed my legs to fly until I reached him. His arm was in the vice of one of the steel-faced blonde soldiers who moved purposefully, pulling my brother along. The flute was in his mouth, calling me.

The words came to my mouth without thought.

"Leave him! He's just a boy. You have no need of a boy!" I shouted, flinging myself in front of the soldier, punching his chest. My fists had no more effect than a fly beating against a screen door. The soldier's reaction was one of annoyance.

Calmly, he removed a pistol from its holster and aimed the gun at my head.

I froze in that instant, time standing still. A light sound floated into the air. The officer turned, looked down at Daniel, and shot him between the eyes. Then, throwing him on the ground like an old jacket, turned on his heels and walked away.

Feeling my legs collapse beneath me, I fell upon my young brother and wrapped my arms around him in an attempt to protect him as the circle of red in the middle of his forehead grew larger. A sob erupted from deep within me as I cradled his head. No one seemed to hear it, though, as bullets flew and dozens screamed in our beloved Lodz, a city gone mad. Yet in that madness only one thought came to me, clear as the sound of a flute. I was alone now. For the first time in my life, I was alone.

Virginia

My head is pounding. Back in the office, I suddenly felt as if the walls were closing in on me. Just as I breathed a sigh of relief having completed two closings, another property contract had come in. The media is constantly whining about an economic slump, yet from my vantage point, I don't see it. Usually, I thrive on being busy; I mean it takes my mind off of Chrissie, wondering why she insists on resisting me at every turn. What's wrong with that girl, anyway? I needed air. I grabbed a batch of papers and headed for the refuge of home.

It is one of those hot August days when merely the thought of movement meets a tired resistance. I choose the spot closest to the garden where I can view the face of the sun between two tall cypress trees. I notice with pleasure that the black-eyed Susans and purple coneflowers are already in full bloom, sprinkled with soft white heath aster. The prairie dock with its large yellow leaves open fully to welcome the warm light. I sit down and raise the back of a lounger with large burnt orange pillows, and open my laptop. I pull up the latest contract, but after awhile the words seem to blend together. I rub the bone between my eyes. The fear of mounting papers, confusing rates, and deadlines slips slowly from my brain and allows sleep to infiltrate its recesses. I close my eyes to the bright sunlight; a curtain falls.

The sleep which overtakes me is deep and cleansing, but when I again open my eyes, a haze appears before me, and the flowers shimmer as if sleepwalking in the mid-afternoon heat. The laptop presses on my bare knees as, disoriented, I look down at a carpet of neatly clipped grass interrupted, strangely, by a shadow in the shape of a child. I look up, confused, and as my eyes clear, I see him—again—before me.

He is no more than four feet tall, a child of perhaps six years of age. Curly locks of hair capture the light of the sun framing his pale translucent skin. He stands at a distance of only a couple of feet, neither smiling nor frowning. In his hand is an object which looks like a plain brown stick. And, most unusual of all, he wears a heavy woolen coat.

His eyes meet mine, unafraid, shining like sapphire blue marbles. And I think—am I dreaming? After a moment, I find my voice.

"Hello. Can—can I help you?" The blues remain steady on my face. I try again.

"Do you live here? Are you lost?"

Still no response. The boy is calm, almost serene. I think maybe he does not understand English. But something about him tells me that his is a language I do not know.

"Are you lost?" I repeat.

A rustle in the bushes, and he turns suddenly, startled, as a tiny brown chipmunk skitters across the grass. I reach out.

"It's okay," I say.

A thought comes to me, resting like a pebble on a tranquil sea. I have seen this child before. But how can that be? And then I remember. Years earlier when Chrissie was in fourth grade, there had been a visitor to school—an older man with gentle eyes who spoke of the war. He spoke of his family as well, of their dreams for a better life, and how those dreams were crushed. There was something about this boy, but what was it? I make a mental note to research the period on my computer. But, of course, right now, I am confronted with this child, perhaps a child of immigrant parents, who are more than likely frantically searching for him.

I don't recall anyone new moving into the neighborhood, but I admit that I've been so absorbed in my own life lately that I haven't had much of an opportunity to open my front doors and look out. Besides, the nearest house is several yards away. But what am I to do about the child?

Calmly, I move off of my chair, walk over to him, extend my hand.

He pulls back, like a scared bird.

"No—I'm not going to hurt you." I freeze in place and consider.

"You must be warm," I say, "Would you like something to drink? Maybe some iced tea?"

He looks at me, wary, as I pantomime drinking from a cup. The boy offers no response, but his eyes remain calm.

"Fine," I say, "I'll just go inside and get you something cold to drink. You stay right here."

I back away, still fixing my eyes on him. He is as he first appeared standing still as a sentinel in the midst of greenery, his long gray coat catching the light, the stick firm in his grip. I turn quickly and run inside.

My hand shakes as I hold the pitcher of iced tea and pour it into a tall glass. I run through all the possibilities of the identity of this child. Perhaps he is someone visiting a relative. Or maybe he's with friends, just playing a game. Could it be he's part of a roving band of gypsies trying to scam me? Do gypsies even exist outside of Europe? I decide that he is not malicious after all, just an innocent child. I grab a chocolate chip cookie from the pantry and, with snack and drink in hand, walk outside.

Somehow, I know even before I lift my eyes to the landscape. He is gone. No sense in looking for him either. I sit down on the side of the lounge chair, and take a sip of the iced tea. Everything is the same as when I left, the sun suspended high in the sky in a direct line above the chair, crocuses trembling in the distance. All the same except for one thing. The shadow is gone now, and so is the boy.

I place what is left of the tea along with the cookie on a small side table and stretch out on the lounge. I examine my legs, long, white, covered with freckles. I hate them, but there is not much about myself I like these days. A sense of unease returns to me as it has over the last few weeks and, with it, an increasing feeling of urgency. I'm not sure of its source, though. Perhaps it is because Meghan wants to leave home and live with Anthony's brother in Florida, perhaps it's Chrissie who has grown eerily quiet, more distant over the last few weeks, or maybe it is just my mother—again.

My mother died young. If fifty-three is considered young, that is. One morning in early spring she was on her way to the superette for a bottle of milk for Daddy's coffee. As she hurried down the block on that pale gray day, she stopped suddenly, looked up to check the sky for rain, and took a step forward. Mrs. Rasmussen had just left the dry cleaner's when she saw her, her body contorted into a fetal position on the sidewalk there in her thin green jacket, as if she were in a deep sleep. Only she wasn't. The doctors said it was her heart, a genetic defect perhaps, or just one of those inexplicable twists of fate. It was the last thing anyone expected, least of all Daddy who, sitting at the kitchen table in suit and tie, waited patiently for the milk which never came.

I was a young bride, married only a few months when I got the phone call.

"Mother's gone," came the low voice.

"Daddy? Is that you?"

I had just stepped out of a hot shower and was patting my hair down with a towel.

"Mother's gone," he repeated. After that, he didn't say much more, and as time went by and he moved in with my sister and her husband, he said even less. It was as if the father I had known, once confident, headstrong, had crumpled in on himself, shrinking like a disintegrating flower until—finally—he disappeared altogether. We didn't talk much in the intervening years between my mother's death and his own, in a nursing home at age ninety-three. Although I would take the trip to my sister's home in Canada, visiting often, sometimes with the girls, I could never really get him to talk about those early years or the succession that followed.

"Daddy, I've opened my own business, a day care center at home," I telephoned one day.

"Fine," he said, adding, "I haven't slept all night."

And another time.

"We've moved, Daddy. A beautiful five-bedroom home with a courtyard and tons of windows to let in the light."

"Probably a waste of money," he murmured, and handed the phone to my sister.

Even after I brought him into our home, when he had a room all to himself where the girls came in to greet him with coffee in the morning, and to rub his feet at night, he had few kind words. Oh, it wasn't that he didn't love them. Little lights danced in his crystal blue eyes whenever Chrissie would bring him her latest sculpture. Once, at their urging, he got up off his worn leather chair and proceeded to show the girls how to do a jaunty fox trot, just like in the old days. But when they began to compliment him on his spry movements, his gallant turn of the head, he loosened his grip on Meghan and fell back into his chair.

"I'm tired," he said, and closed his eyes.

Sometimes, when he slept like that in his chair, I would slip into his bedroom and simply look at him. The cool breeze that sneaked past the open window filtered through the strands of his thick white hair pushing them up and down again like cresting waves. His usually grim mouth, relaxed now, gave him an almost benevolent demeanor, and once more I marveled how a man approaching ninety could so easily be mistaken for a sixty-year-old. My heart would quicken then, in the old way, and for a brief moment I became that eight-year-old girl eager to crawl inside the protection of her father's heart. But then, he would open his eyes suddenly, appearing cloudy, disoriented. Quickly, I moved out of the room, closing the door behind me, not waiting for the anger to return.

"Daddy," I said, some years later, my spirit alight with anticipation, my eyes brimming with tears, "I've been accepted to Fordham Law School. I'm going to be a lawyer, Daddy." He looked up at me as he sat in his wheelchair in the lobby of the nursing home.

"Got any more of those red jellybeans?" he said.

After that, I gave up trying, and two years later, Daddy died peacefully in his sleep.

It should have ended then, this yearning to please my father. But it didn't. If anything, I became more driven, racing through law school in competition with those young men and women unencumbered by teenagers and the accompanying angst, or marriages where years of bitterness had forged an impenetrable wedge. Their futures stretched before them like an open plain, while mine appeared increasingly murky. Some time between the beginning and end of law school in my quietest moments when the statutes and laws, the cases and rulings no longer competed with each other in my head, a singular image would alight like a ghost on a blank sheet of computer paper. Not my father, but my mother this time. And I remember her as she was, sitting at the kitchen table, cradling a mug of hot tea in her long fingers. I had just returned from my honeymoon for our first visit, both now as married women. It was a rare moment, just the two of us together. Daddy wouldn't be home for another hour; neither would Isabel, who was already living in Florida and dealing with a one-year-old. How I envied her then, her sense of blasé contentment.

"How have you been, Ma?" I said, pasting a smile on my newly tanned face.

"Oh, you know. I'm fine, I'm always fine," she said, placing her mug down on the table and reaching out to examine the shiny gold ring on my left hand.

"How was the honeymoon?" she asked, letting my fingers slip like rain from hers.

"Oh, wonderful. The weather was perfect and, well, we both enjoyed ourselves so much. Disney World is fun no matter what age you are."

"I should think," she replied, looking into my eyes, then, "Anthony's a good man."

I nodded, biting into the still warm slice of homemade marble cake she had placed on a plate in front of me.

"He's a very good man," she repeated, stirring her tea absent-mindedly.

I stared at Mother for a minute or so, trying to find her beneath the heavy lashes, the dark eyes. For the first time possibly in my existence, I saw my mother's life apart from mine, and the realiza-tion, as I spoke, made my heart beat faster within my chest.

"How about you, Ma? Do you and Daddy have any plans for a vacation this summer?"

"Vacation?" she said, coming out of her reverie, and looking around the large kitchen my sister and I had grown up in as if she could find an answer in the old orange and yellow flecked wallpa-per.

"Well, I suppose we'll go up to the Catskills for a week or so, as usual."

"How many years has it been, Ma?" I asked, leaning forward, "You and Daddy have been going to the same place since Isabel and I were teenagers. Don't you think it's time for a change?"

Mother giggled, as if this were the most absurd idea she had ever heard.

"Don't be silly, Ginny. Where would I go?"

"Why, anywhere. You two certainly have enough money saved, and it's about time you treated yourselves. You could go to Ireland, Ma, and visit those cousins you always talk about. Or maybe you could take a cruise."

Mother laughed. I hadn't heard her laugh like that in a long time.

"I don't think so, Ginny," she said, wiping a tear from the corner of her eye, "Your father wouldn't like the idea of all that packing, not to mention the travel expenses which are so high these days."

"But what about you, Ma? I mean with Isabel and I grown up, married and away from home, it's your time to do for yourself now."

Mother glanced around the room again. What was she looking for, anyway?

"Children grow up so quickly," she said, almost to herself.

I decided to drop the subject, and walked into the living room. I stood before the air conditioning unit and let the fan blow cool air across my body. Mother followed me inside, sat down on the upholstered couch, and stared at me appraisingly.

"Marriage agrees with you, Ginny."

I smiled at her. Mother sunk into the soft place on the cushion. Hands folded, she looked small and pale. Her light brown hair was immobile, sprayed firmly in the shape of a flip. She still wore the same blue and white cotton shift I remembered, the hem of which lifted slightly with each soft exhalation of the whirring fan.

I walked around the immaculate living room. It was exactly as I remembered it from my childhood days except for the addition of two 8 by 10's of her daughters with their respective spouses on our wedding day. Plastic apples and grapes shone in an antique bowl which sat upon a white doily, which in turn rested on the round glass coffee table angled between the beige and brown striped sofas. A chestnut étagère held Daddy's collection of shot glasses which sparkled now from their daily wiping of Windex. A small round table in the corner of the room proudly displayed a series of miniature black and whites of my grandparents, all stilted poses with faces reflecting the formality of the times. I stopped in front of one of the two watercolor paintings which hung between the long sealed windows with their Dacron drapes concealing the street four flights below us.

"They are so beautiful," I said, in spite of myself.

"What's that?"

"The paintings," I said, letting my eyes linger past the line of feathered clouds, the blend of pastel blues of the sky which seamlessly met the calm grayish green of a rolling sea.

"They're really quite good."

"Oh those," said Mother, dismissing the pictures with a flick of the hand, "that was so many years ago."

I turned my eyes to the other painting, this one of a house at the shore. Resting on a hill, it looked clean and white, the kind of house one might happily spend a lifetime in, with its sienna-toned roof, and red chimney extending into the soft grays of dawn. Mother wanted to be an artist once. She even had begun studying art in college, and hired a private mentor. But then she met Daddy, got married, had children, and ultimately released her aspirations without thought, letting them dissipate along with the soapy water of the dishes she scrubbed each evening.

"You should take it up again."

Mother laughed, laughter like the clinking of crystal wine glasses after someone makes a toast. It was good to hear again, twice in the same day.

"Ginny, sometimes you say the silliest things."

"I mean it, Ma. Just look at the lovely colors on these landscapes, the attention to detail. Didn't you paint these on your honeymoon up in Cape Cod? If I'm not mistaken, you and Daddy took us up there once when Isabel and I were little. In fact, that white house with the red chimney looks familiar."

"It should. It was your great-uncle Patrick's home. He died a couple of years after your younger sister was born. We had a garden out back which I thought was all my own. It was only a few feet round, but to me it seemed endless. It was filled with gerbera daisies of every color; pink, blue, purple, yellow, orange, with round black eyes in the center. I used to sit right in the middle of that garden and lift my face to the sun, thinking nothing could harm me. Oh, Ginny, I wish you could remember it! My, we had some wonderful times in that place," she sighed, letting her eyelids flutter, her memory travel back to a time, a time when her parents, her older brother, Oliver, a younger sister, Sue, were alive, a memory forever locked to me.

"Paint again, Ma," I said, calling her back, "You have the time now, and I'm sure you still have the talent."

"Oh, Ginny, I'm sure I wouldn't know where to begin, and besides, there's so much to do in the apartment. I have the cleaning, my baking." I look at my mother, so determined, so sure of her life, and a sense of urgency returns to mine.

"And no children to care for," I interrupt, "now that Isabel and I are out of the house. Come on, Ma, I'll go with you to the art supply store and we'll get you an easel which you could set up right in the kitchen. What do you say?"

Her eyes stared up at me, and for a moment I thought I saw a flicker of the old hope return. But then she lifted a hand to push back an imaginary stray hair. Her flip didn't move as she shook her head vigorously and got up.

"Come," she said, "help me clear the table."

Two weeks later, Mother was dead. So I never did find out if she still had any talent, but now, whenever I look at the two seaside paintings which hang on the walls of my dining room, I like to think she did.

I had never seen Anthony so angry. His hands were latched onto the back of the Chippendale chair so tightly that I thought it would snap in two. Instead of breaking it, he simply sank to the floor, expended. If I wasn't so irate myself, I would have gone to him, touched his yellow gray hair, placed my cheek next to his, cold, tear-streaked, and said, "I'm sorry." But I didn't place my cheek next to his, didn't do any of that. I stood firm, arms folded sternly across my chest, afraid to release the torrent of emotions I was feeling inside.

Anthony couldn't understand why I wanted the separation. Frankly, I wasn't so sure myself. I only knew that if I didn't free myself then, I never would.

A conversation which had begun reasonably had escalated within a matter of minutes until now Anthony stood at the entrance of our sun-filled white mica kitchen, purple with his anger, and shaking a trembling finger at me.

"One more chance, Ginny. One more chance to save this. To save our marriage, to save the sanity of our girls," he shouted, his voice already hoarse from yelling, his eyes still ablaze with anger, confusion.

"Don't make this mistake, Ginny, not after everything I've given you, not after I let you open our home to all those kids, let you go to law school on a whim. And now that you're onto a new job, I guess you don't need me around anymore, do you, Ginny?"

"You *let* me? Is that what you think you did? You *let* me do these things? Well, thanks, Anthony, thanks for *letting* me become my own person," I shot back angrily, feeling the heat rise up my neck to my ears.

Frustrated, he shook his finger at me again, but this time lowered his voice.

"Once I go out that door, I'm not coming back," he said, and then, "Are you sure, Ginny, that this is the way you want it?"

I looked at his face, the same sculptured cheekbones which had first attracted me, the slumping narrow shoulders, the eyes like acorns under straight dark lashes. He was right. He had done nothing wrong. As I felt myself slipping again, I turned quickly away.

"I can't do it," I said.

I heard the side door slam, felt its reverberations, and walked stiffly out of the kitchen, past the dining room with its two water-color paintings, upstairs into the yet unpainted master bedroom. Then I fell on my knees and, alone in my massive new two-story colonial house, began to cry.

The sun is waning now as I rub my eyes. I pick up my laptop and books, and pull open the back sliders. I know that the next few hours will be spent in my office, researching, hurriedly typing contracts, trying to make up for an afternoon wasted in sleep. I will drink several shots of espresso and eventually replace the black cartridge in the printer. I will think of nothing but work because, after all, it is the thing I love to do. I will not think of the boy, I resolve, shutting the blinds. And that night, I do forget. But then, sometimes, like a shadow in a garden of sunlight, the dream keeps coming back.

Joshua

"Come in," I say, at the soft tap on my bedroom door. Adam enters wearing a blue T-shirt, khaki shorts and flip flops. He stands at the door for a moment, looking down. I assess the broad shoulders, the lock of curly hair which falls across his forehead, and again my heart swells with pride. But in an instant that pride changes to concern as I notice large teardrops falling from his eyes onto the polished wooden floor.

"Adam, what's wrong?"

He shakes his head, still looking down. The words stick in his throat. I click off the baseball game, now in extra innings, walk over to my son and wrap my arms around him. But he is concrete, immobile, and soon I move back. The sadness in his face has been replaced by determination, a quality I have not yet seen in my young son.

"Adam, what's the matter with you?" I ask, feeling an icy tremor climb up my back.

"Dad, I need to tell you something," he says, still averting my eyes.

I paste a smile on my face and sit down at the foot of the bed.

"Ask away."

He takes a deep breath.

"I know you're not going to like what I have to say."

Then I say, "Adam, you know you can talk to me about anything." But I am thinking, I've only got one boy and he's seventeen years old. What do I know about raising kids? What will I say when he tells me?

But he doesn't tell me anything. Instead, he just stands there looking down at the planks in the floor. And then, just like that, I know.

"Is it Meghan?"

He nods, imperceptibly, walks over to me and puts his head on my shoulder. He is sobbing unabashedly now, now that the words can no longer come. How I love this boy!

I turn into him, comfort him, kiss his forehead wet with sweat.

"It's okay, Adam. It's okay if you like her."

He picks his head up, looks directly at me.

"Like her? Dad, I'm in love with her."

I hold my breath, hoping he can't see the color drain from my face.

"You're only seventeen," I say.

"Did you hear what I said, Dad? I love her. I love Meghan and I want to be with her."

"Okay. Fine, you are with her. I understand about first girl-friends. But you're young, Adam, and you have a crush."

He pulls away suddenly, almost pushing me into the dresser.

"She's not a crush, Dad. She's my girlfriend, not just my first *girl* friend, either. We want to spend the rest of our lives together, don't you understand? I love her and she's not Jewish, but that doesn't matter to me. I love her, Dad!"

He is screaming, holding his head in his hands.

"Adam—"

"No! I don't care what you say. You have no right to tell me what to do, who I can see. I know, I know how I feel, and that's enough."

He pounds the top of the dresser with his fist, so hard the wedding picture of Alicia and me falls, breaking the glass.

I stand back. Suddenly, I don't recognize this person, this irate person. This is not my son. This is not Alicia's son.

"Adam, please calm down," I say, trying to keep my voice steady. He begins to pace. The words are no longer stuck in his throat. They come like torrents.

"I know you want me to go to Cornell, but I don't really want to go there. I'm not going there. If I'm going to become a doctor--and I will, by the way, become a doctor, then I can learn how to be a doctor at any school. In Florida, the schools are—"

"Whoa! Florida? Since when are you going to Florida?"

"Meghan's going to be at Miami State, and I'm going with her. I can go to the community college there for a semester, only until I get accepted to the university. I won't need any money from you, either. I can maybe get a job working for Meghan's uncle, and live in a room over at his place. We won't even be living together, Meghan and I, but I can visit her up at the dorm."

I turn away so that Adam cannot see the smile on my face. I understand now why they say comedy and tragedy are close sisters.

"You've got it all figured it out," I say.

I hear the sound of his fist again, this time slamming into the bedroom door. I turn to face him.

"You can't tell me what to do. You can't tell me who to love!" he bellows.

"I never tried," I say. Who is this person? What has happened to my son?

"I'm going to marry her, Dad. I'm going to when I turn eighteen, and you can't say anything that is going to stop me. I know Meghan is not Jewish, and you always told me I needed to marry a Jewish girl. But it doesn't matter because we can't help who we fall in love with, and Meghan is great, she's beautiful, probably smarter than I am, and she gets me, Dad. Remember how you used to talk about my mother and how she made you feel, how you knew from

the moment you met that you were right for each other? It's like
that between Meghan and me."

I release the rage which has been boiling inside of me, and
grab his arm fiercely.

My voice is low, restrained, threatening.

"Don't you dare mention your mother in the same breath with
that *shiksa*, your Gentile girlfriend."

Adam shakes loose of my grip and storms out of the room.
Seconds later, I hear the sharp slam of the front door and then the
growl of the engine as he leaves. He is probably going to her house,
I guess, willing my rational mind to overcome the hurt, the anger,
the memories. But I am unsuccessful. Because in minutes I feel
my stomach turn over as I run to the bathroom and vomit, pushing
away the last ten minutes, the nightmare my son has placed me in,
until I am empty of any feeling at all.

Lying alone in bed as I wait for the sound of the garage door
cranking open, I try to remember Meghan. I have only seen her a
few times sitting in the kitchen with Adam on days when I would
return early from work, at the high school games, the plays. She
was a pretty dark-haired little girl with the slender nimble body
of an athlete. She was polite, and would smile shyly whenever we
met, before returning to whispered conversation with my son.
Occasionally, she would giggle at things he said, a sweet sound
like water rolling down a hill. I never bothered to notice how he
looked at her. After all, he'd told me they were friends.

What had she done, this girl, to bewitch him? I smirked at the
thought. At their age, all a girl had to do was look at a kid, laugh
at his jokes, touch him on the arm, and he was hooked. Stupid
kid. I thought he knew better than that, thought he had what my
father used to call *"sychel,"* the Yiddish word for good common
sense. But I suppose I was deluding myself. What makes my kid
different from all the others? Dad used to call it thinking with

what's between your legs rather than what was above your neck. Had Adam really lost his mind? And yet, he had seemed so determined, so sure of himself.

I have a need which fast becomes a yearning to talk to my father, to make sense, *sychel*, of all this. What would he tell me? Would he say not to worry, that it's just a phase, that Adam was just thinking with what was between his legs? Would he call Adam into his room and shut the door, explain to him, reason with him? Or would he tell me to cut him off altogether, show him who the parent was? But even though my father is just down the hall sleeping soundly, I'll never know what advice he would give me. I'm the one who has to come up with the answers now. The trouble is I don't have any.

I get out of bed and sit numb at the foot of my queen-sized mattress and watch as a single golden stream of moonlight filters into the room, casting a nostalgic glow on the floor, Adam's baby pictures on the wall. The stream of light slowly disappears into darkness when I hear the motor of the garage door, footsteps on the stairs, a door quietly close. Before I climb into bed, I bend down and carefully pick up the shattered glass, the photo of me and Alicia on our wedding day.

During the next few days, an icy silence descends over the house. Adam has decided that I am the enemy, and so, while we occupy the same home, we live apart, coming and going without so much as a nod of the head. I tell him one morning, as he is getting ready for his job as a day camp counselor, that it's okay if he hates me; after all, I can't control his feelings, not his feelings for me and not his feelings for the girl either. It's what we *do* about these feelings, I advise, that we can control, though. He shrugs his shoulders and moves past me.

"Anyway, I still love you," I say, more to myself than to him. But already he is outside and doesn't hear. My heart feels heavy as I get into the old station wagon and head for work.

"You're late," says Dom with a smile as he stands at the counter filling out some forms. My assistant for the past fourteen years is approaching seventy, and except for the youthful twinkle in his eyes, looks it. Although he has more than enough in savings from his former job as a carpenter to retire comfortably, whenever I broach the subject, Dom dismisses the idea.

"What would I do with myself, go to gay *Paree*?" he laughs, exposing the deep crags in his swarthy face.

"The shop is only a hop away from where I live, so it's no hassle for me getting here," he says, adding, "besides, this place isn't worth a dime without me." There is some truth in that, I think, since over the years Dom has stepped in whenever I had to attend one of Adam's softball games, meet with his teachers, or take Dad to the doctor. Dom never married, so he didn't even consider it an imposition to fill in for his boss, and besides, the customers all knew him and loved him, Dom was that congenial.

I suppose if a guy was to have a best friend, Dom would be mine. Although he'd never been invited to my house, he liked to hear all about Adam, his achievements at school, his science projects, his homeruns. He also understood when my mother died, respected my silences, listened on the rare occasions I wanted to talk, even attended her funeral. Dom was a good listener, the kind of guy you'd like to take out for a beer, and on many occasions, after we closed the shop I did just that.

"I'm sorry, Dom," I say, opening the glass door to my office and placing my attaché case on the large wooden desk where stacks of work orders waited, along with a tall cup of Starbucks, black. Dom never forgets. I decide to confide in him later, after work. But, of course, I can't tell him everything.

"Wow, these kids today," Dom sighs, rubbing his balding pate with one hand while cradling a cold one with the other. We are seated at the counter of a dark bar nestled between a dry cleaners and Chinese restaurant. We are the only two at the bar since it's Wednesday and still before 7pm. The establishment, open for as long as I can remember, is a convenient escape since it's only a couple of blocks from my print shop, which Dom and I have just locked up for the night. The bar's owner, a guy known only to me by the indelicate name of Guzzler, tends bar himself that evening, and after serving us two brews, resumes watching the ball game which is projected in fuzzy tones from a small TV screen up in the corner of the ceiling. The white haze of cigarette smoke from a middle-aged couple seated at one of the tables wafts across the room.

"Well, I say you should let him go," continues Dom, who takes another swig, then wipes his mouth.

"What do you mean? I should let him go without money, without a real plan? I should just let him go like that?"

"Look, I don't have any kids myself, and God knows, I'm no expert, but I was a kid once myself. And nothing—I mean nothing-- would make up my mind more than when my old man said I couldn't do it. How do you think I ended up here? Just hitched a ride from the Bronx and learned the hard way. My old man was plenty mad, but I wasn't about to give him the satisfaction."

He takes another gulp, smacks his lips.

"Adam's not like that, Dom. He thought this all out and he's going, no matter if I tell him to or not."

"So let him."

"And what about my deposit at Cornell?"

"Collateral damage."

I nearly choke on my beer.

"Gee, Dom, that's a lot of money we're talking about."

"Look," he says, leaning forward, "if the kid is that determined, I think you have to write the thing off as a loss, like it or not. Can he go back there if—I mean *when* he changes his mind?"

"A deferral? Well, I suppose."

"Okay, then," he interrupts, "it's settled. Let him flap his wings a bit, he'll come flying home." He sits back, motions to Guzzler, who sets up another one.

I gaze down at the bubbles floating golden in my half mug, recalling the distinguished campus at Cornell, the green ivy hugging the staid brick buildings. An image of Adam comes to mind, round glasses secured on the bridge of his nose, book bag casually flung over his shoulder as he walks briskly across campus. The first leg of his journey toward becoming a doctor. He still wants to be a doctor, he had said so. Not at Cornell, though, at least not for now.

"I guess you're right, Dom," is all I can say, still picturing the serene image of academia. We had both loved the school.

"Earth to Joshua."

I look up as Dom prods me gently on the side of my arm.

"You were zoning out again, pal," and then, beckoning Guzzler away from his game again, "How about another one for my friend here? I think he needs it more than I do."

A few minutes later I push both mugs, one still full, across the counter. Dom means well, I think, and I suppose what he says makes sense, but none of it really helps. Because the real problem isn't Cornell at all, but something I can never let Dom, my good friend, in on.

The car ride home seems longer than usual that evening. These past few days I am in no hurry to get home, even if Mrs. Ruiz is already looking impatiently at her watch. For the first time in my life I am not eager to see Adam, at least not the Adam who has been occupying my house lately. The Adam who lives with me does his own laundry, takes his meals out, grunts when he leaves the house. I want desperately to break through this shield he has created, find my child, mellow and loving, and rescue him from the demon who has taken possession of him. But I do none of that. When I walk in the door, he is standing at the kitchen sink drinking a glass of milk. His eye catches mine before he turns stonily away. I walk upstairs.

"Mrs. Ruiz?" I tap gently on the door to my father's room. He is seated in his chair looking up at the wooden shelf and its collection of miniature musicians. Again, I wonder what he is thinking, remembering, as he stares, his eyes fixed upward. Perhaps it is as I fear, that his mind has become nothing but a blank, not thinking anything at all. And as I walk over, kiss him on the top of his scant gray head, I again feel a sense of panic that the decision I will need to make is drawing near. Like Adam, he does not acknowledge me.

"How was everything today, Mrs. Ruiz?" She fixes a blue plaid sweater across my father's shoulders and gathers her things.

"Oh, about the same, Mr. Goldman, no better, no worse. He took a little more oatmeal today, though. And he seemed to recognize your son, I think."

Adam was in here? Well, why shouldn't he be? He wasn't mad at his grandfather; it was me he couldn't stand.

"Mr. Goldman? Is everything all right?"

I smile automatically.

"Sure. What do you mean?"

"Well, Mr. Goldman, sir, if you don't mind my saying, is something wrong between you and your son? Some problem?"

"Why, no," I say, fighting to keep from swallowing my words.

"Nothing, really. Just that both of you seem angry, not as friendly as usual. I hope you don't blame me for some problem, with your father, I mean."

"Oh, no, Mrs. Ruiz. Certainly not. We're pleased with you. It's just with Adam graduating next year and starting a new school next fall," I swallow here, "I guess we are both a bit tense."

I walk over to the door, hold it open for her as she pats my father's hand, sighs, and makes a slow heavy exit.

"Goodbye, Mr. David. Be good for your son," she says with a wave of the hand, "See you tomorrow."

"Tomorrow, Mrs. Ruiz," I say before taking a deep breath. I think about this house and the secrets we all keep from one another. But, of course, I can never share any of this with Mrs. Ruiz. Just like Dom, she just wouldn't understand.

Dad is compliant, like an infant, as I delicately put him to bed. Almost immediately, he is snoring, and as I watch him before leaving the room, I see glimmers of the man who raised me, in the curve of his cheek, the worry which was a part of him for as long as I have known him etched into the lines of his brow. I kiss his head again; the soft gray hairs flutter momentarily, and I leave, shutting the door softly behind me.

Large fluorescent lights cast lonely shadows down the wide aisles of the A&P as I join the handful of night shoppers seeking a forgotten loaf of bread or a satisfying pint of cookie dough ice cream at the end of a long day. They are not like me, though, since as I saunter down the beverage aisle, I can't think of one item I might need.

I made the five-minute drive for one reason only, and that was to escape the silences of the house, the closed doors which challenge me, the sorry walls with their collage of family photos, the dreary clink of the wind chimes whose lilting melodies recall happier days. As I walk past the cans of Bud Light on sale, I think of Dom, who lives a life of perfect contentment, loving no one, needing no one, happy to just be. Do I envy him? Perhaps. But would I give it all up for his life of contentment? Adam? My parents and the legacy so long ago instilled in me? Alicia? Again, I wish for my darling beside me, to feel the touch of her slender fingers in mine, to see the violet sparkle in her raven hair, to hear the sweet tinkle of her long silver earrings as she bends over me as I work at my desk. No, I reason, I wouldn't want Dom's life at all. Not even now.

I felt only a small amount of guilt as I confided my troubles to Dom back at the bar. How could I tell him everything? While raised Roman Catholic, he is not what they call a "practicing" Catholic, didn't even think about religion at all.

Once, several years ago, Dom took pity on my lonely state, and tried to fix me up with a single cousin of his. "A real looker" he called her. When I politely declined, he shrugged his shoulders and asked no questions. But a couple of years later, he informed me that she married one of his old construction buddies and had moved to Wisconsin. They have twins, I hear.

Even though I'm not an observant Jew, only attending syna- gogue once a year on the High Holy Days in the fall, I always knew that being Jewish was the essence of who I was, who Alicia was. As a single parent I thought I had done my best to instill the same feeling in my son. And, I thought I had been successful up until a couple of weeks ago. But it was more than just being Jewish, identi- fying with one's culture and race. I was the son of Holocaust survi- vors who grew up with a table of empty settings, too young then to miss what I never had, grandparents, an uncle. As a child, lying in bed alone when the fears of the night closed in, I often wondered if I had been born then, lived there, could I have survived? Could Adam? I knew one thing, though, as well as I knew my own name, Joshua, after my mother's father, Yussel, who died in the camps, and that was my obligation. I would never marry outside of my religion; no, I would not be the one to sever the link. I thought Adam felt the same way too, but I suppose he didn't.

As I step over some shards of a broken jar of tomato juice, I think that I must be losing my mind. Adam is seventeen and surely he will have plenty of girlfriends before he makes the commitment to settle down. And yet, he seemed so sure.

I turn into the produce aisle, stopping in front of the bins of carrots and celery being doused by the automatic sprayer. At the end of the aisle, a tall slender woman with hair the shade of dull copper catches my eye. She is examining some peaches before placing them in a plastic bag, but feeling my eyes upon her, she looks up briefly and smiles. I smile back, pick up a couple of red MacIntosh apples. It is only after I pay for my purchase that I realize that the woman is someone I recognize from college preparatory seminars at the high school. She is Meghan's mother. Bag in hand, I stop, frozen for a minute at the front doors of the supermarket. Surely, I think, she knows of her daughter's plans and can't approve. Maybe if I speak with her, we could join forces, reason with them. I stand there in front of the doors, letting the cool misty dew of summer fall on my bare arms. I want to go, to talk with this woman, but I can't. Because if I do, Adam will hate me forever. I open the car door, place the bag of apples beside me, and drive out of the parking lot.

The morning is clear and refreshing, the sky a bright shade of aqua as I step outdoors. It is early with an infant sun still cradled low in the sky on a Saturday, and the streets lined with their manicured hedges and pine saplings are free of joggers and distracted workers eager to get on the highway before the morning rush. I do a few stretches before beginning my run, adjust my iPod, breathe deeply. I gaze up at the house, blinds tightly shut on two rows of windows, like sleeping eyes. The bricks painted a pale yellow are welcoming, yet the front of the home is not bordered by flowers, but, instead, white and yellow pavers which seem cold and distant now. It is one of the few homes in the neighborhood devoid of grass and completely surrounded by concrete. Buying the house seemed like a good idea at the time for a single father with a young boy. With no expansive lawn to mow or plants to water and fertilize, it looked like it would make life easier. But it wasn't long before I came to regret my decision. On warm spring days when the daily responsibilities had become, at times, too much for one man to bear, it might have been nice to look out at the flowering shrubs, to smell the hopeful perfume of colorful blossoms. And so, securing the laces on my sneakers, I again resolve to break up the concrete, put in a lawn. Next year, for sure.

I move forward steadily, allowing the harmonic tones of my favorite band, Chicago, to fill my mind. I am only two blocks away from home, and look both ways before proceeding at the curb. Seeing my way clear, I step down when suddenly a red sports car appears rounding the corner. I pull back quickly, but my foot reacts too late and slams into the ground. It is a misstep, a fluke. I hear my ankle snap, and then another sound pierces the pale morning sky as I fall, crying out in pain.

At the hospital, my son, who was woken from a deep sleep, rushes in, his hair an unruly mass of curls, his wrinkled T-shirt and gray sweatpants testament to the fast exit. There is something else too. I see flecks of fear in his large blue eyes.

"What the hell did you do?" he says, coming alongside the medical table.

"I'm okay," I say. I point to the heavy white cast, "A stupid misstep is all."

He shakes his head slowly, looking down on the tiled floor, saying nothing.

"Adam, I'll be okay."

"Good," he says, raising his eyes to meet mine.

I smile, hopeful.

But what Adam does next scares me, more than the pain of having to send my father away, more than a broken ankle. Because without so much as a wave of the hand, Adam turns and walks away.

Christine

Sometimes, on cloudy days, I climb up the back stairs of the apartment building, open the steel door, and walk outside. I walk to the center of the roof and lie down on the cool hard asphalt. Then I become a spectator, watching the clouds sail slowly past the sun. I am mesmerized by the parade of characters as they ease across the blue gray sky merging and separating as they metamorphose into the grand ladies with pompadours, silly court jesters, hags with long noses and sharp ears. After about a half hour of the silent parade, I picture myself rushing down the stairs to the eighth floor, eager to plunge my hand in clay, to bring life to the images of clouds which are now held like fragile blossoms in my brain. But instead, I lie on the asphalt long after the clouds vanish into the sky, banished by the angry eye of the sun. I wearily get up, stretch, and run down the stairs, my mind satiated with images.

I hurry into the coolness of my room at Laney's, open the large square box and remove the block of gray modeling clay, my fingers already feeling the energy of the life to come. My fingers tingle as I plunge them into the oil-based clay, again feeling the orgasmic rush as I form the embryo of my design. Long ago, I rejected plaster sculpture with its strict armature, the drudgery of mixing plaster of Paris, the tedious work of dipping the cloth and building, for the more organic feel of shaping life amidst the smooth pliant clay. Slowly, I add form and dimension to the clouds in my head. I stretch the slender torso to appropriate height, curve the shoulders, shape the bowed head like an egg, push in clay, pull out the book laden with pages. I scoop more clay for the hair, spreading coils at the protrusion of the forehead, on the sides of the cylindrical neck, rounding more for the fullness of the beard. From the clay block, I cut a slice which looks like a sampling of brie, and delicately shape it into the form of a heart which I divide in two, cutting inroads into these, add ears to the side of the head. I don't bother with eyes, but instead create the lids with flaps of thin clay. There. He is reading. I use a coil with a ball for the bridge and end of the nose, which is long and slightly crooked, creating the ala, or bulging membrane around the opening of each nostril. I add more coils for the lips, use the stick for the philtrum between nostrils and upper lip. I shape more coils into the form of cascading water for the heavy shawl which covers the head downward, ending in carefully etched tassels on both sides. Under my hand, the pages of the book materialize; age is etched into the haggard face in the form of wrinkles. I stand back to realize my creation, where the clouds have led me.

"It is a rabbi, a rabbi praying," I say to myself, surprised. I am always surprised by these inspired works of art, just as a mother may be surprised by the sex of a newborn, its temperament, personality. With an artist's eye, I examine the unfinished sculpture, the flat cheeks, the lack of detail in the fingers spread compliantly beneath the heavy book. But it is already late in the afternoon, and I am spent, so I resolve to continue the work tomorrow. Nevertheless, I have to admit, I am pretty proud of my creation; art, mine or anyone else's, always makes me smile. It's probably the only thing that does these days. I don't know if I'll ever have a kid in my lifetime, but it's no big deal since I already know what it's like to give birth. When I lie down, finally, on my bed and close my eyes, I fall into a deep sleep, dreaming of clouds.

It isn't long before the phone shocks me awake.

"Hello?"

"Hey, Chris, did I wake you?"

"Umm. Laney? I was just taking a nap. What's up?"

"Well, you better get up because I think I might have some good news for you. You know Alan Morris, the guy I work for at the pr agency? Well, it seems a friend of his has a nephew who is a sculptor. He makes these metal abstract pieces that no one can figure out. Well, anyway, he's from Nebraska and needs someone to help him set up a studio in the city. Well, and oh, to make a long story short, I brought up your name and told him you might be interested. So, what do you think, Chris?"

I hesitate. I've had too many offers like this before to get too excited.

"Who is this guy, Laney? I mean, how do I know that I won't work my ass off and he'll say 'bye, bye' after a week? Or maybe he'll decide he isn't coming to New York at all, and wants to set up in LA, or maybe he's some kind of freak who—"

"Hold on!" Laney interrupts, "I forgot the best part. He's got some kind of sponsor, so he's willing to pay, about six hundred a week. The guy is looking for an intern, someone who has 'a good eye' he said, and is willing to learn. And, I think he's legit, even been written up in some art journals. Google him if you don't believe me. So, what do you say, Chris?"

I shrug my shoulders. Despite the gut feeling I have that I am heading for another disappointment, I think six hundred dollars a week is better than nothing.

"Okay, Laney," I say, "give him my number."

Peter Krasdale's apartment is located above a bustling fabric shop in the heart of Chinatown. By the time I finish walking up the dimly lit winding staircase, I am almost out of breath, the purple strands of my hair slicked against my forehead. He is waiting at the top of the stairs, arms folded, wearing neatly pressed khaki pants and a white long-sleeved shirt, buttons open at the neck. He is prematurely bald, but in a handsome way, I think. Overall, he looks as if he has just stepped out of a spa, as he extends his hand, a wry smile playing on his face.

"Hello, I'm Peter," he says, showing me in, "I'm sorry about the stairs. I know they're a killer, but I'm actually staying with a friend, so I didn't have much choice in the matter."

He leads me into a cramped room which is occupied by a small couch, one old leather armchair, several unpacked suitcases, and, along two walls, the most fascinating metalwork sculptures I have ever seen.

I open my mouth, but the only words that come out are, "These! These are—" and I know I'm making an ass of myself again.

But Peter (did he tell me to call him that?) doesn't seem to mind. He smiles again, his green eyes twinkling. He looks no more than thirty years old.

"Thanks. Yes, they're mine."

"Sorry," I say, feeling flustered, "it's just that these are all so--so beautiful."

"Thanks," he says again, removing some books from a chair "please have a seat.

"I only got off the plane from Omaha yesterday, so things are kind of all over the place," he says, apologizing again.

"No, really, it's fine," I answer, sitting down and placing my large brown leather portfolio next to me on the floor. Sweat still clings to my brow, and I remove a tissue from a small Vera Bradley change purse and wipe my face.

"Sorry," he says a third time, "Can I get you something to drink? A glass of water or--?"

"Oh, no. I'm fine, really."

"Good," he laughs, removing a laptop from the leather recliner, "Because I haven't a clue where anything in this place is anyway." He laughs. His laughter is smooth, self-deprecating.

"Your work?" he says, pointing to the portfolio.

"Oh, oh yes," I say, lifting it up as he takes the portfolio from my hands.

"Photos of my sculptures. Mostly clay, just portrait work, nothing like your stuff here, I mean your art." Suddenly I feel like an idiot, sitting in my pink cotton peasant blouse, long black skirt and sandals, twisting a used tissue in my hands. But Peter doesn't seem to be paying any attention as he slowly turns the pages.

He stops midway, though, and says more to himself, "Nice bust."

I feel the blush rush to my face and, biting my lip, will myself to keep quiet. I am such an idiot!

He closes the portfolio.

"Not bad," he says, "Your pieces are well-detailed. You work a great deal in clay like Voulkos and Takaezu, only not in the abstract. Nevertheless, these show a lot of promise."

I shrug my shoulders, not knowing what to say. I can't stop looking at his green eyes. Cat's eyes, they sparkle.

"I started working in this organic clay-type sculpture, but somehow drifted into iron and other metals. Somewhat more durable, I think," he says, laughing at himself again.

My eye is drawn to the sculptures against the wall and, without asking, I walk over to a large piece, perhaps 8 feet by 4 feet. It is a series of vertical lines angled at what looks like rooftops, as if photographed from a high altitude.

"I call that one 'Cityscapes'," he says, coming up behind me.

I take a few steps to the side to get a better view of all its angles. The gleaming black lines of the sculpture crisscross as they approach the base, suggesting the frenetic energy of a metropolis. It is evident from the intricate design of the piece that it took careful preparation and skill to frame, not to mention a giant dollop of imagination.

"Brilliant," I say, on impulse.

"Not really, but some people seem to like it."

"I'll bet! I don't think I could ever do anything like this."

"Sure you can," he says, sitting back down on the chair, stretching his legs forward as he clasps both hands behind his oval bald head, "You've just got a different style, that's all."

"I don't know," I say, shaking my head, still mesmerized by the piece.

"Let's take a look at your resume," he says, snapping me to attention. I can't believe what a jerk I am, insulting my own work. Why would anyone hire someone like me?

I retrieve the resume from a manila envelope inside my portfolio and hand it to him. I sit back down, legs together, hands clasped in my lap, waiting. Well, I think, I am here to learn. No one should expect perfection from an intern.

"Not much formal training," I hear him murmur to himself, but when he looks up, he is smiling.

"When can you start?"

"Really?" I say, standing impulsively as the jerk I am, and then, "I can start anytime you like, Mr. Krasdale."

"How's tomorrow, then?" he says, adding, "and please call me Peter."

I feel as if I am flying down the stairs. When I open the door to the street, the bustling crowds seem to have dispersed, the muggy air now replaced by a light cleansing rain. The portfolio secured under my arm, I walk briskly to the corner where, under the protection of a flimsy awning in front of a tobacco shop, I remove my cell phone from my bag. There is only one person I need to talk to now and, confidently, I click the number.

"Chrissie! It's so good to hear from you, calling in the middle of the day," and then, "is anything wrong, honey?"

"Don't be stupid," I say, lowering my voice, making it more subdued, "Just thought you might like to know that I got a job, and I start tomorrow."

"Are you kidding? Oh, honey, tell me all about it. Is it in the city? At a museum or an office?" Ginny's voice has reached such a high decibel that it is starting to annoy me. But I don't tell her that. Instead, I tell her all about the job, Peter Krasdale, and, of course, the money. I can't get the words out fast enough.

"That's wonderful, Chrissy," she says, but I can tell from the sound of her voice that she is not thinking it so wonderful at all.

"What's wrong?" I say, biting the nail on my pinky.

"Oh, nothing really," she says in that coy way of hers, "I mean are you quite sure that this sort of job will lead to something better? Are you sure this guy is on the up and up, that he won't disappear after a week? Now, don't get me wrong, I'm happy you have a regular salary, but don't forget it's still far from enough to rent an apartment in Manhattan. If I were you, I would definitely keep this job, though, while you look into teaching just so you have a steady income."

There she goes again with teaching, I think, squeezing the phone tighter in my hand.

"Thanks, Ginny. Thanks for the encouragement," I say, pressing the 'off' button and heading down the street.

I have ordered a whole pizza pie along with a pitcher of Diet Coke. As I shake the Italian seasoning onto my hot slice and watch the pieces of pepper, basil, and oregano fall like confetti, I think of Peter's green eyes. Shiny marble eyes. I bite into the first slice, slightly burning my tongue, as I allow the oily cheese to slide down the corners of my chin. The pizzeria might not be quite as good as Joe's Pizza, but it was the first one I came to in Little Italy and, besides, I was pretty certain I wouldn't run into anyone I knew there. My eyes focus on the dark red paint which extends to the ceiling, the black and white photos of Sicily lining the walls, as I take another bite, and then another, feeling the burnt taste of the thin crust on my tongue. After finishing a couple of slices, I pour the soda into my paper cup, its ice cubes clicking against the plastic pitcher. I take a big gulp and allow the cool sweetness to saturate my throat, fill my chest. After I finish the last slice, I take a couple of napkins from the tin dispenser and dab the oil from my lips. The rain has stopped by the time I step outside, and I walk quickly down the block until I find what I am looking for.

The bag of zeppoli, warm balls of dough covered with powdered sugar, feels warm in my hand, its aroma drifting up to my nostrils. I have bought a half dozen to share with Laney and Ryan. But by the time I arrive at the front doors of the apartment building, I have already eaten all but one. The white bag is already damp with the spongy heat of the zeppoli as, walking into the elevator, I pop the last one into my mouth.

The next few days are filled with anxious, hectic, but joyous activity. I scan the real estate section of the newspaper until I find the perfect space for Peter to work, a downtown loft, unfurnished, with huge windows, and plenty of floor space to work on his sculptures. There are forms to be filled out, agreements with suppliers, galleries. Most of the time, Peter isn't even around, so I stand in for him. And when he is there, I observe him working. His process is different from mine, slower, with short spurts of energy. The work is large, loud, more construction than art, and I am fascinated. I do not think he looks at clouds.

I know Peter likes me. I mean as a worker, of course. He tells me so all the time.

"Another one out of the hat," he'll quip when I find some box he's been looking for, or "The Purple Comet does it again," when, referring to the purple in my hair, he marvels when I run out fast to pick up his dry cleaning. He has all kinds of nicknames for me, which I guess shows how much he likes me. More than that, he needs me. In fact, no one has made me feel so needed in my entire life.

Days breeze into weeks, weeks into months, and like one of Peter's sculptures, I become transformed under his steady hand. It is as if a magical door has opened for me in that loft, and I am inside one of the skyscrapers in "Cityscapes," looking out at the rest of the world, and thumbing my nose.

"Holy shit!" says Ryan as he nearly trips over some of Peter's tools on the floor. Laney claps her hands and turns kind of like a ballerina.

"You weren't kidding about this place, Chris." She scratches her knee at the place where her jeans are torn, flings her hot pink mohair sweater over a bronze sculpture, and flops down in the massive orange tweed bucket chair. Meanwhile, Ryan is strutting around the perimeter of the space intermittently poking between the bars of a long narrow sculpture called "Quest," peering inside the depths of what looks like a bronze copper baseball glove which is labeled "The Secret."

I stand, hands behind my back, as the two take in the room. I can tell they are proud of me, especially Ryan, who normally doesn't say much unless he is pissed off about something. He puts one skinny arm around a six foot tall unfinished piece made of iron that kind of looks like a sad scarecrow.

"Hey, Ryan, it looks like you could be that guy's twin brother," chirps Laney from her nest in the bucket chair.

Ryan throws her a smirk then wraps himself around the scarecrow thing just to prove her point. All of us laugh. Tall and thin with a mop of dark hair, Ryan is always dressed in black. If he stood there for a couple of hours like that, he could be a part of the piece. Who could tell the difference, after all?

"Want a drink or something?" I say, trying to play the perfect host, "I think there's some beer in the fridge." They both say no, as they are on their way for some Chinese anyway. They ask if I can join them, but with Peter still in Nebraska, I have to sort through the supplies that came in today, and check the mail. Ryan slowly unwinds himself from the scarecrow and extends his hand to help Laney from the bucket chair. Whenever my friends stand together, they kind of look like flipped out comic book characters, a Mutt and Jeff, as Ginny would call it, what with Ryan being super tall, sort of a Jeff Goldblum type, and Laney's being short, fuller up front and across the hips. Ryan has a kind of black uniform on all the time, ratty old jeans and a smelly sweatshirt or T-shirt, while Laney is partial to colors and vintage, boas especially when the weather gets cold. Truthfully, I have to suppress a laugh most times when I see the two of them together but, hey, what's that thing they say about opposites attracting? Must be the case here, since I hardly ever see them fighting.

"Cool job," says Ryan as he slithers past me, but then seems to forget something, comes back and picks up my arm like it is a noodle. With the other hand, he uses his thumb and presses the spot on my upper arm, just below the old woman tattoo.

"Ouch!"

"Sorry. It's still there, isn't it?"

I jerk back my arm, pull down the sleeve of my white cotton polo, and turn away. Doesn't he already know I'm not into blaming anyone? But he never stops.

"Look, Chicken Bones, I'd get that checked out by a doctor if I were you. How long has it been, a month?"

I ignore him and pick up one of the cardboard boxes that serves as a file cabinet. He's right, it probably was a month ago that we were all at a club dancing. Kind of wild, all moving like a large crazy monster. So Ryan slams into me with his pointy elbow. I go to the floor, my arm turns a new shade of purple, a black and blue, I think they call it. But I get up right away. I am a slow healer. No big deal.

"Chicken Bones?"

"It's okay, man, I'm on it."

Ryan shrugs and Laney looks at me kind of apologetically. Then they leave.

I have been working for Peter for three months now. Most of the time he is not even at the loft, but he still relies on me to hold everything together. The funny thing is, I've been so busy working that there has been no time for my own sculptures. I haven't even finished the old rabbi on the window sill, but just the same, I am learning. I get to work early and leave late. When Peter is around, I stay even later, watching him at work, the sinews of his muscular back moving rhythmically as he wields his mallet. Sometimes, I even hand him stuff. He usually tells me to go home if he works too late. But I tell him I have time, all the time in the world. And he appreciates that. I can tell by looking at his marble green eyes.

One morning, I get to the loft later than usual. When I walk inside, though, right away I can tell something. First, a couple of the sculptures are missing, including "Cityscapes." A few empty beer cans are scattered on the wood floors, which is unusual because Peter is so neat. And then there is the note. Held with a piece of tape right on the stainless refrigerator, it is addressed to me. It isn't very long. It says that his sponsor, the guy with the money, has left the country, and so the gallery exhibit planned for next week has been cancelled. Close up the apartment, it says. He'll be in touch again soon. He signs it "Peter." Not even a thank you.

I pick up the empty beer cans and toss them in the garbage. I find some sheets of plastic and cover the sculptures that are left. I pick up all the cardboard file boxes and line them up against the wall in the bedroom. Then I lock the door.

As I get into the elevator, I am thinking that Peter is probably wrong. He will not get in touch.

I step outside of the building, walk down the block, and suddenly realize that I haven't eaten breakfast yet. I stop in front of the bakery at the corner and stare for a few minutes at the devil's food cake in the window. Then, with a quick glance up at the cloudless sky, I go inside.

Adam

I am swimming in cotton. I know where I have to go, but everything is so blurry, muted. I just want to get out.

I am at the steering wheel of my car, driving to the only place which makes any sense. Meghan is already waiting on the front porch when I arrive. She is seated on the top step, a green and yellow plaid scarf wrapped around her mouth; a matching hat covers her head and ears. She hugs herself and shivers, it is that cold. Even for Ithaca, winter's sharp sting has been relentless. But when she sees my car turn into the driveway, she lights up, letting her arms fall back as she stands. She is my lighthouse in winter's cold gray sea, leading me home.

Meghan gets into the car, not bothering to look back.

"Let's go," she says.

We drive for awhile in silence. A frozen stillness stretches ahead as I keep a slow steady push on the gas pedal. The residential neighborhoods with their sleek patches of ice and tired tree limbs which seem resigned to their nakedness finally give way to the open road lit by a white sun and a comfortable stillness.

"Want an apple?" she says, unwinding the scarf and removing an apple from her pouch as the heat from the radiator settles around us.

"No, no thanks."

"Do you believe it, Adam? Do you believe we actually got away with it?"

She smiles then takes a bite out of the apple whose redness matches her cheeks.

"I know," I say. It is all I can say. I want to keep my eyes on the road and not on Meghan.

"What did you tell your dad?"

I clasp the wheel tighter, say nothing. Truthfully, I can't even remember the lie I told him. It is like cotton.

Meghan takes another bite out of the apple, savors its sweetness.

"I told my mom I was going to visit a friend from camp. She knows you're coming along, but she's cool with that too. What she doesn't know is that Nicole isn't."

She laughs. "I already called Nicole, of course, and she'll back me up. She knows what it's all about. She's got a boyfriend too."

Boyfriend. I suppose that's what I am. But the word sounds foreign to me, like a different language. I will have to learn this boyfriend thing. Meghan doesn't notice my unease, though, and, finishing the apple, throws it into a plastic bag and sits quietly for awhile.

I continue driving into the cold. The silence brings a renewed warmth into the car, the air around us. For some reason, the image of my mother, the image of her photograph, comes to mind. She and my father riding in a car. I concentrate on the road.

Silence rides as a third passenger in the car. It is not like the silence at home, the poison in the air that makes me want to cry. I have not really spoken to my father since that time in the summer. When we do speak, our language is mechanical, all business. Even when I got the letter from Cornell, where I had applied for Early Decision, I told him the news like I was telling him it looks like rain or something. He smiles then laughs. It is the first time I have heard him laugh in months. And then, of course, the tears start to come. When I felt the choking in my own throat, I turned away. I turned away again when he tried to hug me.

"I'm not going," I said simply, and ran upstairs without looking back. I knew he'd be mad about the lost money, mad that things would be difficult with the deferral and all, but I didn't care. I also knew he would be standing there with a long face, the tears still in his eyes.

Meghan's voice cuts through the silence like a hot laser.

"I wish we could stay away forever."

"What's that?"

"Adam, I don't think I can wait until we graduate. I need to get out now."

The road, fresh with wet black soil, curves upward, and I maneuver the car deftly up the hill. The wheel feels secure in my hands as I focus on my destination.

"Adam?"

"Meghan, I can't talk about this now. I need to concentrate on the road, can't you see that?" My voice rises higher than I intended. I don't want to hurt her feelings, but I can't do this. Think about *now*.

She sits back, closes her eyes. For the rest of the trip we sit together winding up the hill until we reach the top and can no longer hear the melancholy music of the cold wind as it whistles through the treetops. As we round a final corner, suddenly there is a gray-white stillness in the air, the icy lace in the row of winter branches parts, and our cabin waits shining like a lantern in the clearing.

The car comes to an uneasy stop underneath the bramble. Meghan unfolds herself from the seat and quietly moves outside. She stands for awhile, staring.

"Isn't it beautiful?" she asks.

I look at the cabin. It is just that, a cabin. Bare in the dim light with fractured shingles and streaked glass, it seems to shiver like an old woman who knows, at last, her days are numbered.

"No," I say, "it's not beautiful at all. It's a cabin."

I grab my overnight bag from the back seat and walk up to the front door. Finding it unlocked, I venture inside. Meghan remains standing, still staring at the cabin, as a light snow begins to fall.

The cabin is empty except for a cinnamon-colored velvet sofa, a couple of chairs, and a fireplace which has made a home for a dusty nest of spiders. There is a kitchen with a stove, empty refrigerator, a few plastic utensils, and a can opener. The bedroom is empty save for a nightlight, a huge brown stuffed teddy bear in the corner, and a monstrous bed, or rather, mattress, with a rococo headboard. I check the closet and find one old navy woolen blanket and a vacuum cleaner. The bathroom has a sink and a working toilet. I put down the bags and take a leak, relieved that Meghan thought of bringing sleeping bags and some food. I gaze through the small bathroom window and see her outside, looking up at the new moon, letting the snow coat her nose, dust her hair. She looks happy.

Not wanting to disturb her, I unpack the sleeping bags, place them on the floor, remove my toothbrush and toothpaste from the overnight bag, set these on the sink counter in the bathroom. I remove the package of kosher franks and carton of wine coolers and put them into the small white refrigerator which, to my surprise, still works. I glance at the sad fireplace and quickly decide to hunt for the thermostat, which I find next to the front door. The heat kicks in with a loud grunt, and soon a dank but warm odor permeates the air. I remove my coat, scarf, and sneakers, plug in the small vacuum cleaner, and work it over the thin beige carpet. After awhile, I hear the soft creak of the front door. I click off the vacuum.

Meghan takes off her boots, sheds the heavy yellow parka like a second skin, emerging slender and fragile like a twig, with matching brown thermal polo and corduroys. She is so beautiful in her plainness, and again my heart quickens at the sight of her.

"You've been vacuuming!"

"Do you want to sleep in an inch of dust? I don't."

I turn the vacuum back on. It coughs, then emits a low purr as she steps into a corner of the living room, sits down in the spot I haven't yet vacuumed, and watches me. I don't know why she does that, but I think there are many things I still don't know about her.

I finish the vacuuming, take a deep breath, and look around. The place still doesn't look so good, but at least there's no more dust on the floor, except for where Meghan is sitting, of course. Her eyes follow me as I come to her, sit down on the floor, and twine my arm around hers. This is the most comfortable I have felt in months, and I tell her that.

"Me too," she says, leaning her head on my shoulder.

"How long has your uncle owned this place?"

"It's not my uncle's anymore. He sold it three years ago to a friend who can't get rid of it, so he doesn't mind if we come up here and turn on the heat in winter, open the windows in the summertime. My sister came up here, swam in the lake a few months ago. No TV, no computer, but it's not too bad, you know, the whole nature thing."

She brightens for a moment. "My mother once told me about a place she and her family used to go to up in Cape Cod. She tells me that I used to dance for my grandparents there right on the front porch. But I don't remember it. The way she told it, the summer home seemed a lot more, well, furnished than this place, with a real piano, and pictures on the walls. If I close my eyes, sometimes I think I can imagine it. I can imagine it here at this very moment. Can you, Adam?"

"I guess," I say, feeling good, good that I don't have to put the barriers up, like I do at home. Good that I don't have to think about my father judging me, being ashamed. Or my Zayde, stuck in the room like a prisoner, a prisoner of his own body.

"Adam, I'm so unhappy."

"Why?"

"I'm not sure. Sometimes I think I know, but other times, I—" Her voice trails off.

I feel her quiver beneath my arm, and I hold her tighter.

"I wish we were in Florida, Adam. I wish we were there right now."

I sense she is upset with her mother, and I don't want to get into it—God knows, I have my own problems. But because she wants to talk, I have to ask.

"Is it your mom? Is she hassling you again? I mean, is she mad about your going to Florida—with me?"

"Yes—I mean no. I don't know. I don't really think she cares as far as you're concerned. It's just that she thinks it might be a good idea if I went local, so I'd be close by. So I could be with her for-ever, and ever, and EVER!" Here she squirms out of my embrace.

She turns away, but when she looks at me again, her face is awash in tears. Seeing her like this makes me afraid. There is something in me that wishes I hadn't come here, had never left my house. I don't show her my fear, though. Instead, my voice is calm.

"Why are you crying?" This seems to be the wrong thing to say because as soon as the words come out of my mouth, she takes the jumbo bag of Fritos off the counter and flings it straight at me.

"Hey!"

She paces the room, back and forth, back and forth in her sweat socks. She won't talk, but seems to be conducting some inner dia-logue with herself. I sit there, still wanting to get out of this place. It seems I am always wanting to get away from where I am. Maybe what I really want is to get away from myself. I remain on the floor, place my head between my legs, and wait.

After what seems like hours, she finally stops and looks down at me.

"I'm sorry, Adam. It's not you, really. It's me. I'm the most messed up person you could ever hope to meet. Honestly, you'd better get out while you can."

I say nothing.

"My mother just doesn't get me. I mean she doesn't really get anybody. My mother, I guess I love her. No, I *know* I love her. The thing is I think she loves me and my sister too much."

I pull her down next to me, hold her close.

"My mom, she's okay. Only she thinks she's superwoman or something. First, she ran a daycare center, and then a few years ago, she decided to become a lawyer. You would think she would be too busy to worry about me, but that's not the case. It seems she's got it all figured out for me, Ithaca College first then I'm to be a teacher for the next thirty years of my life. I don't mind these things, really I don't, only I'm so confused now. I want to leave, to set things straight in my mind, but I'm afraid. She won't like it. She yells, she screams, she gets so, so *hyper.*"

I think of my father, his quiet ways, the tender silences which have turned to poison.

"But she'll let you go to Florida, won't she?"

"Let me go? Adam, I *have* to go. But I'm afraid to leave. I'm afraid to leave and I'm afraid to stay home." She laughs.

"Why?"

"Because she needs me."

I remember then about her mother, her breathing problems.

"You can't be with her forever, Meghan."

"I know," she says, quietly.

"You have a sister who's around," I add, wondering again what it must be like to have a sibling, to not be the only one.

But suddenly, Meghan shakes herself loose of me, stands, as if a spider has just fallen on her, and says, "I'm hungry. How about some supper?"

As the steady snow covers the small cabin with a dome of white, I make the decision not to chance the fireplace and, instead, cook the hotdogs in an old pot on the top of the stove while Meghan sets the table. In the absence of plates, she places sheets of paper towels in two spots on the table. She takes a handful of Fritos and places some on the corner of each sheet, sets the strawberry wine cooler which she found in the fridge at her house, on the table. I pour the pot of boiling water into the sink, feeling the heat rise into the pores of my face, then retrieve each frank from the pot, tuck it comfortably into a bun, and place our meal on the table.

"Wait," she says, and runs over to her backpack, which is on the floor next to the door. She removes a round clear glass which holds a single brown candle. Taking a matchbook from her pocket, she lights it.

"It's called 'apple pie,'" she says softly, then sits back down. I bite into the hotdog, wishing I had some mustard to go with it, take a sip of the overly-sweet wine cooler. We sit for several minutes eating quietly. We are the picture of domestic tranquility.

After awhile, we begin talking. We talk about friends, girls who gossip too much, guys who are either cool or uncool, what it will be like living in Florida, what it will be like when she is a teacher and I am a doctor. These are the things real couples talk about. I think it is not so bad.

After we are full and I have burped at the table, making her laugh, we clean up, being sure to throw away the empty bag of Fritos, the paper towels so the bugs will not get to them. We wipe everything down good, wash the old pot, put it back on the stove. Then we share a package of Twinkies. By 9 o'clock we are playing the travel Scrabble game I have brought along. No one, I think, can call us irresponsible.

I am lying on the floor on my side, already tired, bored by the game. Meghan's brown eyes are filtered by her long lashes as she concentrates on the tiles. Her face is simple, open, and I am learning not to be so afraid of it. I think, though, you have to be a little afraid of someone to love that person, to keep it mysterious. I am just a little bit afraid of Meghan, but I am more afraid of what the future holds for us.

"Adam, I think you win."

"Huh?"

"The game. I can't think of any more words I can put out. Not with these letters."

"Are you sure?"

She nods, stretches her legs in front of her, throws back her head, and yawns.

"Okay, then," I say. I close up the game. Meghan looks relaxed and, for a brief moment, I envy her. She has not lied to her mother.

The snow has stopped falling and a faraway feeling settles over the little cabin, pulling us to a different place. It is as if we have landed on an alien planet, and the feeling opens up the tight knot of fear which has been coiled like a snake in my chest for the past few months. I take another wine cooler from the fridge, drink half the bottle in one gulp, let the tart carbonation rise inside my chest. I sit in the corner, my hands together, as if I am praying. Meghan comes to me slowly, extending one leg at a time like a dancer. She reaches down and parts my hands.

"You never talk about it."

I look up at her. She has the face of an angel, an angel with black hair, bangs, and a crooked smile.

"What's there to talk about?" I say. I am only being honest. There is nothing to talk about. My father will never accept her.

It is as if she is sensing my thoughts.

"Your dad is a nice guy. Besides, you're his only son. He'd never do anything to stand in your way."

"You don't understand, Meghan. You don't really know him. He won't accept you as my girlfriend, certainly not as my wife. It is, as he says, 'non-negotiable.'"

"Maybe if I talk to him?"

"No!" I shout. I spring up, tipping over what is left of the wine cooler. The liquid makes a winding trail halfway across the frayed carpeting, into the kitchen. It looks like blood.

"Promise me you won't say anything to him. It will just be worse. I need to handle it."

"Okay," she answers. Her voice is meek, tinged with fear.

My hands shake as I tear off some more paper towels, dampen them, wipe the carpet, the floor.

"It's because I'm the only kid he has that makes this so impossible. Everything is on me, don't you see? My grandparents were Holocaust survivors, singled out because they were Jewish. My great-grandparents were gassed in the camps, my uncle shot through the head by Nazis when he was just a little boy. I have the burden of being the future, the one who continues that legacy, as my dad has reminded me so *many* times. Meghan, you're not Jewish, not one of the Chosen People, not part of the plan. Perhaps if my mother had lived, she would have been more understanding. But she didn't, and this is the way things are."

"Oh," she says. And that is all. She is seated at the table, nervously twisting a few strands of her hair. I look at her until her eyes meet mine.

"But I don't care what he wants," I continue, "He can't make all my decisions for me, tell me what school to go to, how to live my life. He can't tell me who to love."

"But I want you to be happy, Adam. I'm not that religious. If you want me to convert, or raise our children as Jewish, I could."

I shake my head vigorously

"It wouldn't matter. In our religion, babies are automatically Jewish if they are born from a Jewish mother. Besides, I wouldn't want you to convert. It wouldn't help."

"Your grandfather seems to like me," she offers.

I recall the childlike smiles of my Zayde when he would sit at the kitchen table with Mrs. Ruiz, the sweet kiss on the cheek for Meghan when she extended her hand. My dad used to be polite to her too until he learned who she was. Now his looks are daggers.

"My grandpa's a good guy," I say, "Maybe he would have understood this once. But now it's my dad who is the problem. Meghan, could we not talk about this anymore?"

She nods silently. I go into the bathroom, brush my teeth, and peek into the small bedroom consumed by the double bed. There is only a mattress on it, no linens or pillows. It looks foreboding, foreign, and I walk out, past Meghan into the living room where the two sleeping bags are already on the floor.

I shut my cell phone without glancing at the time. I decide then that I want to stay on this planet a little longer. I retrieve the 'apple pie' candle from the table and place it on the window sill near my head. I remove my jeans, sweater, underwear, folding them, making sure to place the jeans with the condom in the back pocket on top. Then I open my dark green sleeping bag. It feels cold against my skin as I crawl inside. I try to remember the first time, at the beach, but I can't. It was the first time for us both, and while it was awkward, energetic, exciting, it wasn't very memorable. But this time will be different.

I hear the bathroom door click shut, the sound of Meghan's bare feet delicately scraping the carpet. She stands by the window for a moment, her lithe dancer's body in shadow against a stream of moonlight. She pushes her sleeping bag aside, and moves into mine, her body warm and fluid. The cotton in my brain dissolves, replaced by the clear light of the moon. As I reach up to blow out the candle, I am thinking this is mine, not my father's, not my grandfather's. This is mine.

David

Someone kisses the top of my head and tucks me into bed. The kiss is not tender like my mother's kiss; the hands are rough, not soft, but they will do. Again, I yearn for her, like I did those many days in the apartment, sitting alone, rocking myself to sleep as the wolves of the night prowled unceasingly. Every day of my life I long to see the light in her eyes as she kisses my face, the loving voice as she whispers, "Tatala, it is time to sleep." Sometimes in the middle of the night, I startle awake, thinking I have heard her calling me, the melodic notes of the piano in the distance. But it is just the hoot of a night owl or the rasp of the telephone in one of the rooms. I tell myself not to dwell in the past; it is all I can do to understand the present. And yet I still listen for her voice. I wonder if I will ever stop listening for it.

After they scooped my brother off the streets, the life still seeping from him, I remained on the sidewalk as the chaos slowly dissipated. I had only one thought as Daniel's blood dried brown on the palms of my hand. What was I to tell Mama and Tata? That I hadn't protected their baby, had relaxed my vigilance and given him up for the Nazis? These questions raced through my head until I felt it would erupt. Like someone who had suffered a life shattering stroke, I became incapable of movement. Finally, as the orange sun loosened its hold on Lodz, I felt strong hands lift me up, carry me indoors, place me down beneath soft covers. There was the murmur of voices, but I couldn't make out what they

were saying. I fully expected the night, serene and peaceful, would
envelope me in death's compassionate arms. And, at age fifteen, I
welcomed the prospect.

To my dismay, the sun rose brightly the next morning, and I
was still alive. I found myself in an apartment other than my own,
occupied by a young married couple, Lazar and Sonya. It was
Lazar who had found me sitting dazed in the street, Lazar who had
carried me for several blocks, up a flight of stairs to an apartment
which appeared just as bare as our own.

"So you have awoken from your rest, I see."

I looked up, trying to adjust my eyes to the stinging rays of the
sun.

"You seemed in a bad way back there on the street. I thought
maybe you needed some help, a little soup, a place to sleep before
you were trampled under the feet of those monsters. Just a place
to come to yourself again."

I close my eyes, rub my head, trying to wipe away the memories.
But I see only the golden curls, the trusting smile before me.

"I'm not well," I say, but nothing more because I can already
feel a sob compressed in my chest. I can only murmur my name,
hardly above a whisper, when they inquire.

A young blonde woman, pretty, tall, and, of course, thin like
the rest of us, rushes to me with a glass of hot tea.

"Here," she says, touching the glass to my lips, "Drink."

The tea is soothing, and I finish it as quickly as I can in spite of
the heat which scorches my insides almost immediately.

"I'll boil some more water," she says, and hurries out again.

Lazar introduces himself and his wife, who is now in the
kitchen, and in turn, I tell him my name. He informs me that they
are from a family of farmers living in the rural outskirts. Less than
a year earlier, as deportees to the area, they had expected better
living conditions, only to find themselves trapped in the basement
of humanity, with only a couple of blankets to keep them warm,

and meager rationings for sustenance. And yet, with the little they possessed, they had enough to offer a drink of tea, a slice of bread to a stranger.

"Where do you make your home, David?"

Home? I hadn't thought about home in a long time. Surely the bare vermin-infested rooms my family had occupied over the past two years could not be considered home. So I say nothing.

"It's fine. You do not have to speak now. Take your time." He hesitates for a moment, moves awkwardly in front of the bedroom dresser where, looking in the mirror on the wall, he adjusts his suspenders, buckles his leather belt tightly over loose-fitting pants. From the bed, I see his reflection in the dusty mirror, a high brow above a sturdy nose, a full-lipped mouth which seems like it should always be laughing. He is perhaps only five years older than I. But it is the mirror itself which catches my attention. It is like the one we had at home in my parents' bedroom. The one which holds a secret. The reflection winks at me now; the lips smile.

"I'm afraid I have to go off to work now, David. Although I would much prefer to sit and chat here with you awhile longer. Brick laying isn't the easiest of jobs. But as long as I have strength to lift with these scrawny arms, there will be food on the table. Thank goodness we only have two mouths to feed here, not like some others."

I look at Lazar's arms raised to the top of his head, adjusting a cap. I recall the arms that held me securely only yesterday, the arms which returned me to this world, and I think here is a man whose family will never starve.

"I work too."

He turns to me, cap off to the side of his head, looking like a rogue.

"So the mute speaks at last," he says, "And what sort of work does a boy your age do?"

I swallow.

"Electrical. I am an electrician," I answer, immediately promoting myself to my father's position.

"Well," he says, "that's quite a skill for a boy so young."

"I'm fifteen--well, almost."

"Are you? Sorry. Ah, I suppose all children here look younger, and the elders seem older than their years. After all, what can grow strong and healthy on dry soil?" He turns to leave the room just as the sound of a shrill whistle ascends in the air. I sit up as if a bullet has shot through my back.

"David, what's wrong?"

I listen like a hunter stalking his prey. The whistle emits one more plaintive cry and stops abruptly.

"It's the kettle, David. Only the kettle."

But the sound has already sliced through the confusion in my brain so that I can see everything clearly. Finding movement again in my legs, I jump out of the bed and run past the tiny kitchen where a stunned Sonya stands pouring hot water into a glass. I look for the door, find it, and turn the knob. Now I must look for something else.

I stumble down the flight of stairs and out the apartment building. I look first one way, then the other. All seems the same, with workers wrapped and hurrying to their jobs, soldiers bantering, laughing as they patrol the streets. No one would know. One day after the world falls apart, everything is still the same.

I see a familiar shoe repair shop, now closed, a tailor shop, closed as well, and I realize that I am only three blocks away from my own apartment, then two more blocks from the place which has been forever burned into my memory. I turn left and run.

I keep running. No one bothers to turn a head as they grimly walk toward work; they are moving away from their fears, while I am running towards mine. My breath forms droplets in the thin cold air, but I do not stop until, finally, I reach my destination.

The sidewalk in front of the rundown four-story apartment building has dried now, revealing brown splatters across its face. It looks now like one of those sad paintings by Picasso, suggesting a story within a story. But I do not stop to untangle its web since I am too busy searching. My eyes dart back and forth over the abstract, seeking the object which is too small to be carried off in a rain puddle, too large to be mistaken for a trampled cigar. Frantically, I retrace the steps back to the apartment. But no, I think he had it in his hands. Who would take such a thing? I run back outside, my coat open, flying behind. Once again, I stop at the place, fearing at any minute I will look up and see the stern face of the Gestapo leering down at me. The people, all young men and women with solemn faces, walk briskly past. The world, not only my own, has changed in these past few weeks, for it is now almost devoid of the middle-aged and elderly, as well as the children. With both the cautionary wisdom of our parents and the hopeful, carefree laughter of the children gone, we have only ourselves to rely on.

I search for nearly an hour, circling the spot where my brother died. I would never see my brother again, I knew that. But now I also realized that I would no longer hear his voice either, the sweet innocent sound of the flute. I walk back to the apartment.

I don't know how many days I spent sitting alone in the apartment. At first, I lit a candle for Daniel, thinking that with no proper burial or gravesite, it is what my parents would have wanted to do, had they been there. Without a *minyan*, the quorum necessary to conduct a proper service, I said the words of *Kaddish*, the prayer for the dead. A few hours later, the flame of the candle goes out and I too go to sleep.

I can't recall much about those dark days. It seemed as if I was all alone in my black solitude, and I resigned myself into a sort of forever sleep, wishing I too would die. Of course, I didn't eat, had only some yellow water from the sink. But just as one who lives in the midst of a stable full of manure becomes incapable of smelling the odor, the lack of food no longer perturbed me; I had become accustomed to the constant ache in the belly. My hunger did have one effect on me, though. My mind, so long devoid of nutrition, entered into a kind of delirium, and I began talking to myself. To be more specific, I conversed daily with the rather large stuffed dog which had been pulled from the top shelf of the closet on that tragic day. The discourse, or I should say, monologue, consisted of theories on how to lift our treacherous economic situation, or how to dissemble ourselves, appear inconspicuous, should a soldier pass by. Sometimes, I even recited my entire *Haftarah*, the incantation of scripture, which I had prepared but never presented for my Bar Mitzvah. But then there were times when I placed my head between the broad paws of the animal and cried. I wondered when Mama and Tata would be coming home.

I don't know if I spent days or weeks by myself in that apartment; the time seemed to be as endless as the night sky. One morning, however, as I woke to a pale gray dawn, I thought I heard someone calling me.

"Tatala, wake up. Wake up, Tatala."

I looked up into the sky, which held but a single star which I took as a sign that I must, at last, get up. I walked into the bathroom where I splashed cool water on my face, as I got ready for work.

There was something different at the factory when I returned. An energy was missing, and the workers' movements appeared almost as mechanical as that of the machines. The feeling of camaraderie had been replaced by a dull sense of resignation as each worker went about his job. No one commented as I took my father's place among the electricians, and only Greenblatt turned to pat me lightly on the back. I wondered if he had heard about my parents and Daniel, but I acknowledged my friend only with a nod of the head. It didn't take me long to learn the intricacies of each task, for my Tata had taught me well. I found the steady work taxing, but also experienced an exhilaration I had not felt before. As I concentrated on each task, twisting the wires together, bringing light to the darkness as my father had done, I felt an odd sense of peace. Thoughts of my parents, regrets over my actions after they were gone, and old fears receded into the background as the work of my hands progressed. Best of all, the work entitled me to rations once again. It was not until later that evening as I sat alone at the table with my small loaf of bread which was to last the week, that I realized just how hungry I had been. I consumed the hard bread with relish, drank a potful of water, and lay down next to my stuffed companion. As my bones sunk into the thin mattress, I let the day's exhaustion sweep over my body. I slept that night, and for the first time since Daniel's loss, my sleep was uninterrupted, deep. But the nightmares, as always, remained.

The next morning, I had not been at work more than ten minutes when Tovich confronted me.

"I have had word that you have fallen on some hard times, *boychik*. Sorry to hear it." Tovich, with his short black curly beard and one raised eyebrow, did not look as if he was too sorry for my troubles; just the same, I nodded in assent.

"Each one of us needs to struggle for ourselves. We can use young strong boys, boys who are fast and quick, boys like yourself. Otherwise, we submit to the swine who, well, let's just say we have alternatives here."

I remembered the first time Tovich had made this offer, the uncertainty I had felt, the fear of telling my parents. This time I didn't hesitate. That evening, I became a runner for the black market.

After only a few days, I found that I excelled at this task, becoming even more adept as an agent of subterfuge than I was as a factory electrician. Under the cloak of night, I would procure liquor, cigarettes, even the occasional treasure, but mostly bread and endless provisions which served to sustain me. Sometimes, I rode the rails to reach my destination; at other times, I sneaked through alleyways, stuffing the pockets of my thin woolen coat. The locals I dealt with were grateful for my help, some even embracing me with tears in their eyes as I handed them a couple of potatoes. They would pat my cheek and call me an angel who had the power to resurrect them from the dead. They marveled at my youth, the glint which was still in my eyes, my hands which did not shake. I was one of them, they maintained, not an outsider like those Austrian Jews who bargained for each filthy seed. Some asked questions. Where did I obtain these provisions, these gems? Was Rumkowski behind this too, just as he was the one who decided which of us, the elderly, the infirm, those who opposed him, were to be transported? I had no answers for any of these questions. Truthfully, I did not care. Or perhaps I was just too afraid to seek the answers.

I lived this life, or rather existed, as a worker by day and underground runner by night, for nearly two years. I was just coming into my manhood, and yet I already felt the weariness of a man whose years far outnumbered my own. Somehow, I always found myself running, to work, to the train, through the streets, meeting strangers I never knew existed before the war. In my haste, I did not stop to look at their faces lest I was reminded of my own dear parents. And yet, whenever an apartment door creaked open or I turned the corner of a foreign street, my heart quickened in the hope that once again their faces would come before me. But mostly, I tried not to think.

In June of 1944, the order came down from Heinrich Himmler himself that Lodz, the land of my birth which had slowly become a prison, was to be liquidated. Only we didn't know it then. We only knew what Rumkowski had told us, that we were to be sent to

Germany to repair the damages caused by the Allied air raids. My nightly trips had ended by then, and even our days in the factory had petered down to a few hours. In the end, I had found a way to stay alive. But alive for what? That question remained.

I mostly stayed in the two-room apartment, shades drawn, with only the ghosts of my family to sustain me. Just as I had nibbled on my last bit of stale bread, sucked the last pebbles of barley from the soup, the speakers down the street blared, sending a cold jolt through my body. I grabbed all I needed, my small satchel of winter clothes, a family photo, another of my mother standing before the piano as a young girl. And, hugging my beloved dog whose fur still glistened wet with tears, I shut the door and went downstairs.

The streets outside were chaotic, with young men and women, skin already sagging on their bones, clinging to each other like lost hens.

"David!"

I turned and caught sight of Lazar and Sonya holding onto each other in the throng. Lazar's firm arm reached out, pulling me to them as he had once before, making me one of their own.

"We are all going on a journey, then," he said with a wink, although a deep sadness glimmered within his eyes. Sonya, her blonde hair secured in a loose bun, a thin light blue frock clinging to her pale skin, kissed me on the cheek and squeezed my arm. Neither of them asked why I had left their home so abruptly, why I had been frozen to the sidewalk in the first place. And so, as we were pushed along in the growing crowds, my affection for these two strangers grew.

"Do not be afraid, David," Lazar said as we neared the gates of the huge railway station, surrounded by Nazi soldiers with powerful black guns, salivating dogs barking at their feet.

"I'm not afraid," I said, stepping forward as I noticed the row of cattle cars ahead. And, in fact, I was not afraid, but anxious to leave Lodz, the place I could no longer call home, eager too to see my parents again.

As the steamy vapors of the sidewalk rose in the early August heat, along with my new friends, I stepped up into the car, ready to embark on a new adventure, for what could be worse than what I had already endured?

I soon realized that our frail, emaciated bodies had served the Nazis well as dozens upon dozens poured into each car. Thankfully, no one screamed. Each sat in silence with his or her own worries, self-recriminations, and choking fears as the train forged ahead. No one knew the length of our journey and, as we were merely humans, after awhile, an individual was forced to push himself into a corner and urinate while others huddled against a high open window to lift someone, pants below the waist, so that person could be relieved of a churning stomach. And, when the stench became unbearable, a number of us grew sick, some sending vomit spiraling into the already filthy air.

As Lazar helped Sonya to her feet after she experienced a sudden surge of illness, he turned to me, confiding that she was with child. This time when he spoke, it was not followed by a wink.

At last, the train churned to a stop, and as the doors rattled open, the Jews rushed off the train, gulping air. A few of my fellow passengers began to fret about having been separated from their luggage, others complained harshly about the watches and rings which had been ripped from them, but I was not amongst them. Noticing families cling to one another, I counted myself lucky that I was responsible for none other than myself.

As I watched Lazar and Sonya being jostled ahead into the crowd as he held her arm tightly, I remembered the new wrinkles which had appeared in the young woman's face, the hollowness beneath her eyes, and, without knowing why, I began to mourn the unborn child within her.

Somewhere, only moments later, the men were separated from the women, as a rumor rose up in the crowd. This was not Chelmno, where my parents had been taken, at all, but Birkenau, the portal to Auschwitz.

All of our eyes were directed upwards as we walked, some already dragging their useless bodies forward. A cloud of ominous smoke hung in the purple sky, the foul odor of the cars having been replaced by something far worse. Gazing upwards, I accidentally tripped into someone in front of me and fell to the ground. Almost immediately, I felt my side ache as blood poured from my chin. In another instant, I felt the sharp pain of a soldier's truncheon at my back. As the soldier ordered me to my feet, I did not look at him, but got up and, hobbling, blended into the crowd of men. For some reason, I thought of my father.

As I looked at the stern face of the man with the stethoscope around his neck, I did not know that I was staring into the eyes of the Angel of Death, the infamous Dr. Josef Mengele. In a corner of my mind, I wondered about the oath all doctors take, the oath to aid humanity. And I thought perhaps even Satan can come in the guise of a healer. Quickly, he surveyed my bent back, my injured chin, and without even asking my age, pointed to the line on the left.

It was a sorry line, indeed, for it consisted mostly of once virile males, homeowners, businessmen, even young boys like myself who, these last few years, had all been turned into decrepit old men. As I made my way toward the line, I caught sight of a familiar face.

Greenblatt grasped my arm and hugged me as if his life depended on it.

"You too? Ah, what is this world coming to?" he cried as he held me close.

"Greenblatt, what is this all about? Where are they taking us?"

"Listen," he said, his mouth next to my ear, "It is for nothing good, I can tell you that. I want you to do something, but you must listen carefully. Stand here in front of me, and when I tap your shoulder, I want you to run like hell over to that other line on the right. You will be safe there." He then added, "I know about your activities at night. Why, who do you think told Tovich to single you out? I know you are a fast one too, so you will succeed. After you are safe on the line, when the bastards have turned away, I will follow. Are we agreed?"

I gulped and nodded as the line inched forward. I wondered if I would, in my condition, be ready for one more task.

The tap on my shoulder, and I ran, like a light beaming, merging into the right line. I looked for Greenblatt's reaction, but could see no change in expression as he moved forward. And then, like a cat, he was running towards me. Instantly, a shot rang out, catching him in the leg. He was sobbing as a couple of the men lifted and carried him back to the line on the left. Poor Greenblatt. He had saved both my father and me, and yet I could not return the favor.

Once I had lived in a massive home; it wasn't really, but as a child, for me, it seemed so at the time. Then we were forced to move to smaller quarters, and now, once more, I had changed habitats once again. My living space was smaller than ever, a bunk of straw, my partners sleeping above and below. Soon I feared I would be compressed into a space no greater than a mouse hole, and what would become of me then?

They are nice enough, my roommates, but of course, we've no time for idle chatter, each keeping secrets well hidden within the heart. The one above me, Dombrowski, is the son of a butcher, though you wouldn't think of it to look at him. His face is clean-shaven like a baby's; he is slender as a weed, his movements like a robot. He tells us simply that he has been abandoned by his parents and three younger sisters who were transported from the ghetto two years earlier. "Dead," he said simply, his face like stone. But how, I asked, how could he know such a thing? His cold eyes stared at me. He knew.

The one below, a broad-shouldered youth who spoke with a stutter, was named Feinstein. Yes, the very same name as my purveyor of sweets, the old shop owner of my youth. I soon learned that he was, in fact, the nephew of my friend, as well as a jeweler who had lived with his new wife in the suburbs. He was tall, thin, stooped, and quiet, even quieter than most here, and spent many of his nights on the straw lamenting the loss of his wife whose hand had slipped from his as they awaited the train. "Lost through my fingers like water, just like water," I would hear him moan each night. And I never knew if the words came from his sleep or otherwise.

Life here, yes, even here, can fall into the ordinary, the mundane. The methodical call of the roll, the walk to our jobs, heads down, the daybreak to dusk fitting sockets and fuses under the hot sun, the clipped march of boots, the snap of whips, the occasional blast of a pistol, and always, always, the sour smell of burning flesh. It is amazing, I think, how the human body can become accustomed to even this chaos.

But then there are the interruptions. A month after my arrival, as I return from a day's work, clutching my aching side, I see a tumult as I enter the barracks. Conquered by my curiosity, I make my way toward a small crowd where I find some ten to fifteen prisoners beating someone relentlessly with all the slim power left in their bare hands. Shouts of "Murderer!", "Traitor!", "Hitlerite!" fill the air. A soldier shoots his pistol into the sky, and the crowd parts revealing, to my surprise, an older man with billowy white hair, holding his head and crouched against the wall. The faces of the prisoners become dark as they shuffle off in their large striped uniforms. In the low murmur I hear someone say, "Rumkowski."

Other times, there is even a glimmer of light in the camp. I was working on a generator with a couple of the others when suddenly I heard someone call my name. At first, I feared it was one of the overseers who clung like fungus to our every move. But, I soon remembered that to them I had no identity, was only a number.

In the next moment I felt myself being embraced by a short stocky man with thinning gray hair.

"David! It cannot be! Is it true then that God really exists in this dungeon of misery?"

After he had released his hold on me, I looked closely at his face, which yielded no clue to his identity.

"Do you not remember me? I'm Zuckerman, the shoemaker. Why, you saved my life, the lives of my wife, my children with those provisions. And all for a silly clock!"

Every so often I would endure these encounters, words of gratitude, joy for the job I had done those many nights back in Lodz. I smiled thinly, thanked them for their praise, and would go about my business. I was happy to have helped them, but my actions had brought me no solace. They didn't bring back my parents.

We worked steadily under the watchful eye of the Nazis, and then one day we didn't. No roll call, no march to the factory, and eventually, no more food. When my head wasn't hurting from deprivation, I slept, dreaming of our daily ration of weak bean soup and rubbery bread as if it were a banquet. Disease, hunger's evil twin, and foul conditions became rampant. Caught in the throes of dysentery, many of even the youngest, welcomed death.

As I sat on the straw tracing the bold numbers emblazoned on my forearm, I felt my fears slowly recede. The implacable faces of our captors evaporated from my mind, their relentless domination replaced by uncertainty, and even worry as the Allied forces drew closer. And then one day after weeks, or perhaps months, as I lay on the straw trying to recall the words to my *Haftarah*, there was a great swelling of voices in the camp. I followed the others who were not yet incapacitated outdoors into the dense purifying snow. All around were ruddy-complexioned soldiers, Russians waving from tanks, shouting words which only later we understood. They were telling us we were free.

Five months. That was the span of time I endured buried in the black hole that was known as Auschwitz, and four years in the ghetto under the harsh foot of the Nazis. And yet it felt as if I had already spent several lifetimes in the nether world. Emerging to my freedom meant a rebirth of sorts. Almost two million departed the fires of Auschwitz, but many more did not. Of those who survived, the majority, if not all, were too weary and despondent to seek vengeance, but, like infants, required only nourishment, a warm bed at night. And once they had that, most remained somewhat dazed, not quite knowing what to do with their newfound freedom.

Soon after we were settled in our new homes, former military barracks, but with warm blankets, wedges of thick brown bread, soup with abundant vegetables, and chocolate, even sweeter than the bars in Feinstein's shop, as much as our stomachs craved, all supplied by the miracle of a society called the Red Cross. Yes, we still wander inside the confines of the barbed wire, but now we are free men. Free men!

We may be free, but we have yet to be free of illness, for I have heard of hundreds grown sick, dying beneath the violent grasp of dysentery. Others, more than I would like to count, succumb to a more insidious enemy, as insanity and depression take up residence in the camp. I witnessed more than one mother standing, staring dumbfounded at the new list of survivors from Auschwitz, Bergen-Belsen, Buchenwald, and the other killing factories. After a minute's time, they would begin tearing their hair, screaming to the heavens. Or a father or brother who keeps returning to the list of names, only to turn away crushed and ashen-faced. I too surveyed each list, each name, searching for the two who were dearest to me. But my premonitions proved correct; I never found them. Chelmno, as I had feared, had not been a resort at all, but a place where the evil ones could continue their grim business.

I never cried for my parents, never mourned them during the war's aftermath. My fears and grief had already evaporated with the endless tears I shed for Daniel during those long nights I spent alone in the apartment. I became more reticent even as others resumed their lives, as the realization that this time I was alone, really alone, sunk like a stone within my heart.

One morning as I awoke, stretching my new muscles as a newborn might, I noticed a great fanfare outdoors. A group of men were marching with joyous expressions on their faces. In the midst of this rejoicing, I could see something held aloft. What was my surprise when I realized it was a Torah, God's laws for the Jewish people. Quickly, slipping on trousers and coat, I joined the throng. And that evening, in front of not one, but a dozen *minyans*, with tears in my eyes, I read my *Haftarah*. At age seventeen, I had become a Bar Mitzvah.

The Allies and the Red Cross volunteers were compassionate, treating us delicately, as if we had suffered some terrible burn, and why not? We had become living skeletons. But time and the gentle hand of friendship began to restore our health, brought color back to our cheeks, and helped us face the uncertain future. One day, I decided to leave. I needed to get past the wires, live inside a real home where I could come and go as I pleased. That very day I saw someone whose face I feared had been long lost among the rubble.

"Lazar!" I called, nearly toppling my chair at the table where I had been playing cards outdoors with two other boys. He turned his head, confused for a moment.

"David. Once again," he said, staring at my face just to make sure it was me.

Lazar was no longer the robust, hardy man I knew. He approached me with a definite stoop, his face covered by a scraggly yellow beard. Lazar looked haggard; his eyes had lost their gleam.

I tried not to show my amazement.

"After these many months, Lazar, how wonderful to see you, alive!"

He looked at me, curious, as if to question if, indeed, he was alive and walking.

"Yes," he said slowly after a moment, "I believe I am alive. But why, David, for what reason?"

I couldn't respond. I was overcome by the sight of a man I once thought could taunt the heavens come so low, so despondent. He sat for awhile looking down at his fingernails as the rest of us continued to play. Finally, he spoke.

"They are gone," he said, still looking down.

"I know," I replied, playing my card.

"My Sonya," he said after another pause, adding, "my child."

I nod. What words can I say? There are no words.

Lazar sits, watching the game for the next hour. He does not share in the chick peas or ginger ale we have before us. He does not pat me on the back.

When someone wins, when the game ends, we push our chairs back. I turn again to Lazar.

"You made a home for me once. Now I will find one for you."

Locating a place to live is not as difficult as I imagined. In order to not submit us to further frustration, the new order has mandated that Germans open their homes to survivors.

Exaggerations aside, our first home was a palace. A three-level brownstone with chocolate-colored bricks and clean white trim, it sat in the heart of Munich or *Munchen* as it was then known, on a street where, unbelievably, tall trees with bright green leaves stood proudly, and children, actual children, played. And we, the new tenants, began to learn to smile again.

The owners of the home were a married couple. The Klingers, both in their sixties, were the parents of four sons who had served in various capacities for the Reich. The first sight to greet us as Lazar and I entered the ostentatious parlor was a large oil painting which hung over the mantel, dominating the room. There, shining in a brown uniform with a bright red insignia on his armband was a likeness of their oldest son, Leo, who had been killed in an early battle. Suddenly, overcome by a sense of repulsion, I pointed to the hideous portrait, and shouted, "Get this shit out of my sight!" The couple startled at first, looked at each other. Within minutes, the husband was on a step stool reaching up for the painting which he quickly rushed to the basement. That night as I lay in the bedroom Lazar and I shared, I slept well. Better than I had in the last few months, better than I had as a boy resting in the warm cocoon of family.

There were others sharing the home as well. With us was a family of three, including a son, Jakob, who was about my age. They were from Lodz as well, and had escaped the devastation of the ghetto intact. On the floor above us lived two sisters, Malka and Sarah who were originally from Vienna, and after surviving in a series of camps, ultimately worked as cooks for the Nazi officers in Auschwitz. They still had a hope of finding their widowed mother on the list. Malka, about twenty, with thick black hair which she wore in a long braid down her back, was by far the more attractive one. She loved to talk, tell stories of her childhood, speaking animatedly and smiling often with her full red lips. But it was Sarah, the younger sister whose hands were like soft white doves, who captured my attention. At age fifteen, she spoke little, and only above a whisper when questioned. Small of stature, with short light brown curly hair, she was more solemn than her vivacious older sister, so that it was somewhat of a challenge to see what her pale face with eyes as blue and deep as the ocean might look like with a smile upon it.

Once I asked her how many times as she prepared a nourishing meal for her captors did she spit in the soup when they weren't looking. It was then I saw the bud of a smile begin to blossom, which she quickly covered with her fingers spread like a fan. I reached for that small hand, held it between my own. It was delicate, soft like the hands of my mother who held me as a child. So perfect.

"About a hundred."

"What's that?"

"You asked how many times I had spit into their bowls. About a hundred."

"I see," I said, holding her hand a while longer.

Four months later, we had learned to become a household of sorts. The sisters worked, voluntarily this time, as cooks for some of the neighbors. Jakob and his father found work assisting a dealer in furs, while I resumed odd jobs as an electrician. Lazar too found work as an apprentice to a local carpenter, and eventually even formed some friendships with other survivors.

As for our hosts, after time, they learned to respect and even like us. Frau Klinger prepared spicy meals for us from her native Hungary, while weekends her husband taught Jakob, the sisters, and I how to tend garden. One gray afternoon as the heavens opened and a cold rain pounded the earth, Sarah, bored and emboldened by our friendship with the Klingers, sat down at a black baby grand piano which rested in the corner of the same room where the oil painting had hung. Brushing her fingers tentatively against the keys, she sounded the notes so familiar to me from my childhood. And then, like magic, she began to play. The music of the piano swam throughout the room, bringing a joy to us that we had never hoped again to feel. The melody was also a spark, a reminder of my hesitations, of what I still needed to do.

A week later, I announced that I was going home, back to Lodz. Perhaps I would return and, depending on what I found there, perhaps not. I asked Sarah to come with me.

As was her way, she didn't respond, but simply extended her hand. I felt a slight tremor as I took her slender hand in mine, knowing that this would change everything.

Virginia

It began as a good day. I had closed no less than two deals in the same week, and this time, Barton noticed.

Barton Barr had given up a lucrative partnership in one of the top ten law firms in Manhattan to open up his own firm here in the "boonies," his endearing, if not condescending, term for Ithaca. At age sixty, Barr had one of his glorified "premonitions" that money, and a lot of it, was to be made there. A year later, he had another premonition when I walked into the three-room office suite in the heart of town. Bart noted that he liked to gamble on a sure thing, but some thought he had taken too much of a chance on a woman in her mid-forties who had already undergone several career changes, and had just barely slipped past the golden doors of law school, diploma in hand. So I worked hard to maintain his faith in me, coming in early, as early as 6 AM, and leaving as late as midnight. Many times, most times actually, I found myself bringing work home, just to prove Barton Barr right. Just to show he did not make the biggest mistake in his career hiring a middle-aged washed up former daycare center director. And it didn't matter if I neglected the cooking, the cleaning, the half-finished bookshelves, the virgin soil in the backyard waiting patiently for the gardener's hoe. It didn't matter that I had one daughter about to graduate high school who couldn't wait to escape from home, another who had escaped, but not, according to her, gone far enough. And a husband who was already gone, but whose presence, thanks to his daughters, still scorched the air like the putrid emissions of a skunk. None of that mattered to me as I single-mindedly forged ahead, proving once again to Barton that no, he had not made a mistake.

And today, finally, Barton Barr affirmed that he had been right all along. He actually complimented me. Well, almost. He walked in this morning, at 8AM, wearing his usual pinstripe navy blue suit, white shirt and, this time, a red and blue striped tie. His black hair had just the faintest touch of gray, and was slicked down away from his brow to cover a growing bald spot. Even though he hadn't smoked cigars in years, his voice reflected the gravelly texture of a smoker, low and uneven. As usual, he walked briskly, cradling a cup of Starbucks, black, in one hand, the *New York Times* in the other. I looked up from the computer screen, a bit dazed as numbers still floated before my eyes. I had already been at work for over an hour.

"Virginia, you've had a busy couple of weeks, I hear," he said, stopping to set the coffee down on my desk.

"Bart--" I startled at the sound of a voice I had barely heard since my initial job interview, "yes, I suppose so."

"Well, you're doing a really good job for us here," he said, smacking the desk with the newspaper for emphasis. He smiled, just the slightest upward curve of the mouth, deepening the dimples in his deeply tanned face. Only his eyes which were the palest of greens, with thick pouches beneath, revealed his age. I should consider myself lucky, I thought, as Barton Barr's trim torso moved gracefully into his office. But I didn't.

Worry still drifted like a fog circling my mind, an unwelcome stranger. I was free of the stress of exams, a husband, even, to a large extent, my children. And yet I still felt just as trapped as my mother had been.

When my colleagues arrived in the office at precisely 9AM, Bart's door was still closed. All in their twenties and early thirties, they were an eager group, ready to prove themselves and move on to a more prestigious firm in Manhattan or another metropolis, if need be. Sandy, a freshly minted young attorney, reminded me somewhat of my own daughter, Chrissie, if she had reached her potential, that is. A tall, reed thin strawberry blonde with skin so pale it looked as if it had been powdered, she wasn't shy about voicing her resentment at being a player in the Barr Group, Attorneys at Law. Sandy had cultivated an interest in women's rights, but because she was, as she often lamented, a "poor test taker," only gained admission into a lackluster law school. Since she had received less than stellar grades, and failed to be anointed on law review, Sandy was forced to seek a job on her own in the very place she had been born and raised. She was known to stand at the water cooler when Bart was out of town, and mutter under breath the words, "real estate law sucks." The rest of us would snicker, nodding our heads, though none was brave enough to offer a verbal affirmation.

Then there were Prentice and Paul, or the "P" boys as I like to think of them. Prentice, with straight light brown hair and pouty lips, was a stocky quiet type from the Philippines, and had worked as a car salesman before making the decision to attend law school. He wasn't too interested in real estate law either or, for that matter, didn't seem to care for any kind of law at all. He was polite and pleasant enough, I suppose, but had little else to recommend him.

Paul, also thirty-something, was the peanut butter to Prentice's jelly, some might say. He had also undergone a career change, leaving a secure position as a middle-school teacher of social studies, and had passed the bar exam after five years of attending law school at night. Paul was tall in an awkward sort of way, and took great pleasure in laughing at his own jokes. He was the one at the end of the day who would scratch his balding head and suggest going out for drinks at Casey's as if the thought had just occurred to him, as if he hadn't been thinking about it at all.

Chad was different, though. Besides me, Chad was the only one who had graduated from a well- known law school. Heck, the best. It was Harvard. So you might wonder how someone like him, whose IQ was known to be off the charts, and could charm a snake out of a basket in dead silence, would be working for a small firm in upstate New York? The answer was simple, really. Chad, with his perfectly coiffed auburn hair and gleaming white teeth, was lazy. And besides, Bart was his uncle.

And then there's me. Besides being considerably older than my colleagues, I was the only one who saw my position as an end rather than a means to a goal. No aspirations, no top law firm for me. I no longer had anything to prove. Since I didn't pose a threat to the others, I was welcomed wholeheartedly into their circle; they even began to affectionately call me "Mama," not a term I particularly appreciated, not when my own daughter referred to me as "Ginny."

As the others slowly began dripping in, as if being wrung from a worn washcloth, the office resumed its familiar pace. Watching the sun crawl across the papers on my desk until they were covered in a white glow, I began to feel a lightness of spirit. I had to concede that I was, finally, in a good place in my life. On a whim, I turned to Sandy, who was typing a document as if her life depended on it, while simultaneously blowing an errant strand of blonde hair off her forehead.

"I was thinking."

"What's that?" she says, not bothering to look up.

"I was thinking that maybe our group could go out for a drink or even dinner tonight."

She stops typing, gives me a quizzical look.

"I mean it. I think it would do all of us good to escape for awhile. What do you think?"

Sandy arches her back, stretches her long white neck, and for a moment she resembles a crane.

"Okay," she says before resuming her typing, "I'm in."

Panda, a dimly-lit Thai restaurant on the outskirts of town, is deserted except for a few over solicitous waiters and a solitary bartender who is cleaning glasses behind the counter when we walk in. Chad and the P's go for some beer as soon as their eyes fall on the long sleek bar, while Sandy and I head for a comfortable booth which, as we slide in, envelopes us in deep burgundy tones. I resist the urge to apologize for the choice of restaurant, understanding that the group, more accustomed to raucous bars like Casey's after a full day in the office, had merely acquiesced to my suggestion.

"Nice place," offers Sandy, surveying the 75-gallon fish tank with its array of gold, black, and white salt water fish floating nonchalantly through sprays of algae. Next to the tank, a stone fountain pour streams of water continuously on an array of plastic coleus, providing a soothing backdrop for the muffled conversation of the boys at the bar.

"I've been here a couple of times before with my daughters," I say stupidly, then bite my tongue. Not tonight, Ginny, I tell myself.

Ignoring me, Sandy goes on.

"Well, whatever they're cooking, it certainly smells good."

She grabs a large black leather-bound menu with ornate gold lettering, and opens it. She lets her index finger slide down the parchment, focusing her eyes intensely, just the way she examines a contract.

"Umm, this is interesting," she says, more to herself than to me, "Neptune's Nest with shrimp, scallops, and lobster with vegetables." Sounds yummy!"

When she looks up at me, her face lit by a broad smile, round eyes ingenuous, she has the air of a child of perhaps ten years of age. My heart clinches suddenly; she is Chrissie. Chrissie opening her presents on Christmas Day.

"So, what do you think?" she asks, wiping an eyelash off her cheek.

"Sounds fine to me. Everything's good here, but don't you think we'd better wait for the others?"

"I guess," she says but, like Chrissie, she has already tuned me out and is back to reading the menu.

I adjust the skirt of my lilac suit, and take up my glass, letting the cold water glide generously down my throat. After awhile, the silence between us begins to feel awkward, and I turn my head again toward the bar.

"So, Sandy, tell me about yourself."

She looks up as if I've just slapped her in the face.

"What?"

"Why don't you tell me something about yourself?" I say slowly, deliberately, as if I am speaking to a very young child.

Fortunately, she doesn't appear to be offended by my tone, but shrugs. She puts down the menu, letting it fall like a bridge between us.

"I hope you don't mind, Sandy. It's just that we've been working at the same place for almost a year now, and besides what school you've attended, I hardly know anything about you."

Sandy's eyes move up and down my face, surveying me as she did the menu just a moment ago.

"Nothing much to tell, really."

I move forward, clasp my hands together on the table.

"Well, for instance, have you lived here in Ithaca all your life?"

She smiles to herself.

"Sometimes it seems like I've lived many lives here. Daughter, student, worker, yep, it's all been right here." She laughs hollowly. A wisp of sadness appears like a cloud over her eyes then vanishes.

"And your parents, are they from these parts too?" The words come out too fast, and I realize I'm playing the "mommy." I bite my tongue again.

"It's all kind of boring. My Dad has a big family up in Albany, and my Mom was from up here too, that is, until the divorce."

"Oh, I'm so sorry," I say, feeling a sudden affinity for this woman I do not know, "Where is you mother living now?"

Sandy casts her eyes upward.

"I like to think she's in heaven." There is no trace of sarcasm in her voice.

"The plane she was on crashed on 9/11."

I reach forward and grasp her hand, which feels cold and limp. The image of a kind woman I do not know dissipates then bursts like a bubble from a fountain stream.

"I'm sorry," I say again.

She looks at me and smiles. I think it is the first time she has ever smiled directly at me.

"It must have been awful for you."

"It was—it *is*. She was on her way to California to visit her best friend from college who, at age fifty, was getting married for the first time. The funny thing was, Mom had never been on an airplane in her life before that day. She was so excited..." Her voice trails off and she pauses, looks down, wipes an imaginary crumb off the table.

My hand tightens around hers, and I am suddenly drawn to this girl who reminds me of my daughter.

"She was a good person, a decent mother, I suppose. Now me, I wasn't the best of daughters. If I had been, I'd have stayed home, helped on the farm, married—done all the things she wanted me to, lived the life she lived. But that wasn't me. If she told me to wear the yellow dress, I'd put on the red, or maybe wear pants instead. If she told me to date the boy next door, I'd run away, stay away...and she did, you know. There really was a boy next door. His name was Gil Adams, a likeable fellow who actually did marry the girl three houses over who had no qualms about becoming a farmer's wife. And when Mom couldn't understand the purpose of college for a girl like me, I made sure that I won a scholarship, went on to college, and then law school.

"My mother was a broad-faced, church-going woman with a ready smile who worked next to my father in the fields and sold produce on weekends. Her idea of fun was canning preserves, which she also sold. My dad is the sort of guy who went about his business grim-faced, quiet. If I asked him for money for school, he'd give it to me, no questions asked. Mom was the talker, and would just say 'still waters run deep' when dad wouldn't say a word as he tilled the soil, or sat at the dinner table, sometimes not even talking for days. After she died, he still didn't talk, but he cried. She had left him a couple of years earlier, but—well--he just about cried everyday." She pauses, unfolds the green cloth napkin at her plate, folds it again.

"I just wish—I wish I had had a little more time with her. To show her that I really *did* come out okay. Even if I was still here in Ithaca, even if I wasn't her."

"I'm sure she would have been very proud of you." I keep my hands tightly clenched in my lap now, repressing the urge to tell her about Chrissie.

A nostalgic silence fills the vacuum between us as the boys return from the bar, laughing boisterously, and settle into the circular booth. Chad, red-faced, eyes already glazed, falls into his seat, spilling some of the beer onto the burgundy leather, as the others follow suit.

Sandy quickly regains her composure, and with the ease of a veteran actor, launches into a story about mistakenly picking up someone else's cell phone, who turned out to be the cousin of some reality show participant I had never heard of.

I sit back, a voyeur now, and quietly watch my young colleagues as a scientist might observe a lab experiment. As I sip my Mai Tai, the bubbles of the water rising in the fountain softly accompany the sounds of whispered conversation, spurts of laughter, as the black, white, and gold fish, oblivious, swim by in a haze. Neptune's Nest is as good as it sounds and, that night, no one calls me Mama.

When I arrive home much later, after 10 o'clock, Meghan is already sitting at the bottom of the stairs.

"What's wrong?" I ask after turning, quietly clicking the locks into place.

She pouts, pursing her lips, relaxing them. She fingers her necklace nervously. I know my daughter well enough to understand that something is bothering her; she's just trying to think of the best way to say it.

"Out with it, Meghan," I say, exasperated, as I kick off my shoes, place my attaché case and purse on the console. By the time I have gone through the mail, mostly solicitations destined for the trash, she still has not spoken. I turn to look at her. Meghan's black hair is hastily pulled back, her face flushed with tiny beads of water forming on her forehead. I can tell she has been running up and down the stairs, counting "fifty bottles of beer on the wall, fifty bottles of beer, if one of those bottles just happen to fall...", a little ditty I sang to her years ago when teaching her how to count, which she adapted to her indoor exercises. Exercising—something else Meghan does when she's nervous.

"Meghan!" I am tired, and the bed is just a short flight up.

"Okay, Mom, don't get excited, where have you been so late, anyway?"

"Since when do I have a curfew, Meghan? If you need to know, I was out with a few of the others from work. I'm entitled to get out once in awhile too, aren't I?"

A cloud of disbelief passes across Meghan's eyes, but she continues, calmly, "Don't get yourself excited, Mom. It's just a question."

"Look, Meghan, it's been a long day, and I have to be up early tomorrow, so if you've got something to say, I wish you'd say it."

She takes a deep breath, pushes the wet bangs from her forehead.

"Well, it's about college. I know that I've already been accepted to Florida State, and all, but I—well, do you think I'm ready?

Wouldn't it be better if I stayed here at home, went to the community college for a couple of years before moving on?"

I stare at my daughter in disbelief. The ticking of the grandfather clock in the hallway resounds in my ears now like a clamorous echo, the beating of a hollow tin drum.

"Meghan," I say her name slowly, try to find the words, "we've been all over this. You were the one who wanted to go away, start again in a new environment, study to become a teacher. And now, all of a sudden, you're not sure anymore? What's really the problem?"

She looks down again, fingers the necklace. I sit down next to her on the bottom step. And then, of course, I know.

"It's the boy, isn't it? What's his name? Andrew?"

"Adam."

"Yes, Adam." I remember a tall skinny kid with a mop of curly hair, the two of them standing in front of the house one evening last summer, a rushed greeting, the pink blush spreading like fire across my daughter's cheeks.

"What's the issue, Meghan?"

She looks down, shakes her head, and swallows.

"He got accepted to Cornell, but he wants to come out to Florida to be with me."

"Cornell? Why, that's Ivy League. It's a wonderful school. Whose idea was this, anyway?"

"His—ours, I mean. He plans to defer from Cornell, and get there eventually. Adam's really smart, Mom, going to be a doctor. Nothing will change that."

"Oh, honey, I know four years sounds like forever, but it's only a short time to be away from each other. You'll see one another during breaks, summers, anyway. And besides," and here I catch myself, the echoes of my mother's voice ringing in my ears, "you have the rest of your lives to be together."

Meghan turns to me, her pale face awash in tears.

"It's more than that, Mom. It's his dad. He hates me."

A dim memory comes to me, of a stoop-shouldered tall middle-aged man standing in the produce aisle of the supermarket staring at me. As if he wanted to say something.

"What do you mean?"

"Just what I said. He hates me because he thinks I'm taking his only son away from him, and because I'm not Jewish."

I feel my arm tightening reflexively on hers.

"That's ridiculous."

"I think he's afraid I'm going to convert Adam or something. His grandfather is a Holocaust survivor, and Adam has an obligation to continue the line, and blah, blah, blah." She is crying hard now, her face in her hands.

I let her sob into my chest, relieved that one of my daughters, at least, still needs me. I try to remember that day, years ago, when a sweet elderly gentleman visited Chrissie's seventh grade class. An image comes to mind, an open shirt, tweed jacket, sparse gray hair, the soft voice tinged with a slight accent. I couldn't recall the stories, but know with a certainly that there was a boy. Someone dressed in a gray wool coat, holding a flute in his hands.

"Meghan," I say, my voice low, a mixture of exhaustion and tenderness, "his dad doesn't hate you. How could anyone hate you? He just doesn't want his son to give up an opportunity, and I can understand that.

"Anyway, you're the one I'm worried about. And, what I do know is that no one should change her life for a boy. You have your dreams, he has his, and (here again I sound like my mother), what's meant to be will be. Meghan, he's just the first of many." She grimaces, her body tightens.

"I'm not saying I want you to leave home, but I think that going away is what *you* really want. Haven't you been convincing me of that the last few months?"

She nods sullenly, wipes her tears with the back of her hand. She's exhausted too.

"We'll talk more about it in the morning, okay?"

She nods, lifts herself to her feet, and I follow up the stairs. As I shut the door, Bart's morning compliment, the success at work, suddenly seem irrelevant. A soft tap before I get into bed.

"Mom?"

"Yes, Meghan?"

"Don't worry," she says.

I don't sleep well. So when I hear the tired churning of the garage door, the scraping sound on the stairs, I jump up like a cat, listening at the bedroom door. A bright light filters beneath the door, and, later, a low growl again from the garage, the sudden whoosh of a bathtub faucet. Barefoot, I tiptoe across the carpet, glancing quickly at the bright white numbers on the clock—4 AM. I breathe slowly. It can only be one person at this hour.

I pad down the hall, the shag carpet feeling prickly beneath my feet, as I try to quiet the bold staccato of my heart. I am drawn by the high-pitched singing, like a soprano practicing her notes. Only when I get closer, I realize it isn't someone singing at all, but a soft sorrowful wail. I place my hand on the half-opened door, peek inside. What I see sends me falling backwards.

Chrissie is seated on the toilet. She is shivering, wringing wet, and naked except for the coat of moonlight which covers her in an eerie white. She is facing the bathroom window which, for some reason, she has opened. She embraces herself, rocking like an old woman, sending her sad song into the air like a siren, the kind of warning they used to sound during air raid shelter drills in the sixties.

I move closer and look. She is too absorbed to see me there staring at her back, the line of bones framed beneath a thin skin, translucent in the moonlight. Like someone whose life is slowly ebbing before your eyes—someone in the throes of an unseen war. Suddenly, the air is stifling, putrid. I swallow the bile rising up my throat and rush back to my bedroom.

As I pull the covers over my head, the bed embraces me like a cave, shielding me in a chilling darkness. I wish I could wrap my mind too, stop it from worrying, thinking, and then an image flashes into my head. I am with my sister. We are together at night, wearing our white cotton nightgowns, and listening by the door of our parents' bedroom. We're afraid, not so much that we will be found out, but of what will happen next. After awhile, I open my eyes, in my own home now, still afraid, but this time alone.

The light in the bathroom has been shut, the whooshing of water turned off. Why do I hear it still? It is like the tide rolling morosely back and forth. Oh, Chrissie! How can I help you? My mind becomes as tumultuous as the sea, a churning whirlpool, with Chrissie at the center. I try to catch her, but she emerges, only to be gone in the next minute. Of course, I can't save her. After all, how does one catch a wave?

I glance over at the clock. Already a half hour has passed. Exhaustion presses heavily against my eyelids.

He is standing on a corner not far from where I live. I don't see him until he is almost directly in front of me, but he doesn't move, won't let me pass.

"Get out of my way, you! I have to get to school or I'll be late."

He smiles, not unkindly, but still doesn't move. In his hand is an instrument which he places, eye still on me, to his lips. The music is beautiful, not like the cacophonous fumbling of a child, not a siren, but heavenly. Yes, like something from heaven. I wake up, rub the sleep from my eyes. But I can't believe what I see. The boy is still there, standing directly across from the bed, in his old wool coat, a stick in his hand.

I am incapable of speech, but somehow, miraculously, words fill the air between us.

"Are you lost?"

He looks at me, confused. And for the first time, he speaks.

"No," he says quietly, though distinctly, "are you?"

Our eyes meet. There is something familiar about this child, I think, with his gray wool coat hanging limply from his body, the golden ringlets of hair escaping from beneath the cap. His eyes, a deep glimmering blue, belie the youthful face. There are stories in those eyes, I think. One could swim in those eyes.

"How did you get here? Why are you here?" I ask, unafraid. It is impossible to fear such a boy.

He mouths the words slowly. Then, a sound.

"Don't you know?" he asks.

"Know? I don't know anything. I don't even know how to be a parent anymore."

"You are a parent, Virginia. Let it be."

"What? I don't understand. Who are you? Are you even real?"

"Let it be, Virginia. Leave her in the closet. She'll come out when the dogs have gone."

Chrissie? Emaciated, bones protruding beneath the skin.

The boy takes a step closer and I see his face, not white, but gray, hollows beneath the eyes. He holds a stick in his hand. No, it is a flute. Heavenly music.

"I'm not lost, Virginia. I'm right where I should be."

Suddenly, I can't stand the talking. I am tired; I want to go back to sleep. If only he would play again, play a lullaby.

"What do you want, Virginia?" he asks, speaking without moving his lips, the words suspended in air, "What do you really want?"

I close my eyes and I am back in Cape Cod, the house on a hill, a house even my memory cannot reach. And yet, I see it all clearly now. My mother on the porch, painting.

"A field full of daisies," I say "Gerbera daisies in every color."

He nods, then turns around and is gone.

I put my head down on the pillow just as early streaks of sunlight fall laser-like across the bed. For the first time in months, it seems, I sleep undisturbed. My sleep is dreamless, pure, and deep. Deep like the eyes of a child.

Joshua

Daytime folds so neatly into the night that after awhile, time has accumulated like an undifferentiated stack of paper sitting on the counter of my shop. I suppose this is a good thing, this lack of a curve, not even a ripple in time. But it gives me no comfort, this endless stretch of days, because my time, once filled with a simmering sense of anticipation, seems drained now. I have become an automaton, going through the motions—waking early for work, tending to the miniscule concerns of the print shop, then back, the blaring silences of the home, the escape as I shoot out the door, running.

It was only last month that Dom told me the news. He had been diagnosed with pancreatic cancer.

My hand fell to the side of the counter and held on as I felt myself going weak at the knees.

"I—I don't know what to say."

Dom shrugs his shoulders.

"Nothing much to say," he says, turning away just as a customer walks into the store.

We were busier than usual for the next couple of hours, spending time with the customers, faxing, entering orders on the computer, and when our eyes would accidentally meet, we withdrew just as quickly. But Dom's news stayed with me throughout that afternoon, hovering like an angry cloud. Finally, there is a lull and, as Dom wipes his ink-stained fingers on a paper towel, I walk up next to him, place a hand on his shoulder.

"Look, Dom, the doctors, are they—"

"They're sure, if that's what you mean, boss. I had every test they could invent. At first, I thought it was maybe indigestion, an ulcer. A couple of pills and I'd be fixed up okay, but then after the tests and more tests—well, you just know."

"But maybe if we get you into Manhattan. I know a few doctors there who are top-notch. If there's anything, Dom, anything I can do..."

Dom smiles, touched. His gravelly voice calm, reassuring, just as it was on the day he first walked into my shop. But there is something new, different in the pupils of his eyes. And I soon realize what it is. He is afraid.

"Don't bother. They're sure. And listen," he adds, molding the paper towel into a ball, tossing it into the empty metal trash basket where, hitting bottom, it makes a dull thud, "don't get any ideas about making it easy for me around here. I want to work. I want to work for as long as I can." He turns abruptly, walks down to the end of the aisle, and begins stacking some work orders. Discussion ended.

I never bring the subject up again, and neither does he. I drive home that night wishing my commute was longer. It is February, and already the days are getting longer, with the sun pausing higher in the gray sky and, when the frost parts, it opens to the briefest promise of spring. The days when one can breathe again without the sharp sting of cold, a time of year I usually looked forward to. Now, though, spring signals the time when my friend, my only friend, and my son, estranged, but my son nonetheless, would both begin to leave me. The days that brought rebirth and renewal now only heralded the fact that soon I would be alone. I remember days as a child when I fervently anticipated the end of school and lazy afternoons swimming in the lake upstate with my friends. Now as I drove home, I prayed for time to stand still.

At first it was difficult for me to believe that Dom had been sick at all. He approached customers with confident strides, his body retaining its robust, quick movements. Nor did he shy away from arguing with anyone stupid enough to take him on, whether the subject was his beloved Patriots or how to rid the world of terrorism ("bomb 'em all"). Even when he began a round of radiation treatments which turned his face into a bright pink candle, and, despite his protests, forced him to take a day off from work practically every week, he compensated for it by insisting on lifting the heavy cartons containing reams of blank paper. And, whenever someone told a joke, Dom would still have that same laugh. Like a train rolling right over you.

But after a couple of months, there were signs. Dom's debilitation was something I had stopped noticing, or, more accurately, chose to ignore. A weariness had settled into his muscles so that his gait as he walked through the door in the morning had slowed. Every so often as he stepped onto the stool at the counter, I would hear a resigned sigh, and on a couple of occasions, as Dom would reach up to a shelf for a calculator, I even caught him wincing in pain. And on a couple of mornings, I watched, biting my lips, as Dom would emerge from the bathroom, stooped and shaken. While the chemo had no effect on an already hairless head, it had nevertheless sapped him of his vigor, robbing him of the cheerful glint in his eyes, silencing his once-invulnerable voice.

And still, I barely took note of any of it until one day when again I wanted to take my time getting home, I persuaded Dom to come out with me for a couple of drinks. Besides, I reasoned, I had heard that they had just refurbished the place with a new 52-inch flat screen TV.

As Dom poured one glass after another of plain tap water down his throat, Guzzler bent low across the counter and whispered, "What's wrong with your friend?" I turned to look at Dom who was seated at a nearby table, crouched over two empty glasses.

"What do you mean?"

"He looks terrible. Is he sick or something?"

I shifted to look at my friend again, this time letting my eyes linger across his ashen face, his trembling hands. How old was Dom now, seventy? In his current state, he could easily have been taken for a ninety-year-old.

"Yeah," I say, moving toward Dom, feeling the mug of brown beer frozen, stuck to my hands, "he's sick."

I wasn't a good friend to Dom. Not even when his eyes rolled toward me like a lost mongrel, pleading for the help he couldn't and wouldn't voice on his own. Not even when I'd see him push himself down the aisle to meet a customer or, on one occasion, as about to answer the phone, he doubled over in pain. And when he went into the hospital, then I was the worst friend of all. I couldn't even bring myself to visit him.

The funny thing was, I didn't even feel guilty. As I sat behind the steering wheel on my way home or took the first tenuous steps outdoors after my injury, I had only one thought. I needed to escape.

I am talking to Alicia now. Really talking. In the past, Alicia was there, always there, but as a shadow, a darkness cast upon my every move. Every joy would be accompanied by "what would Alicia think?", every difficulty, the acknowledgement, "if only Alicia were here now, she'd know what to do." But now things are different. The shadow has taken form and I see her always behind the dresser, or at the stove, and I find myself pleading, "Ah, Alicia, my life is falling apart. I've failed our son, and—what else is there? I've failed our son." But Alicia doesn't answer. She never does. She just gives me a sympathetic smile, twirls her silver earrings, and disappears.

Only once did someone catch me talking to her.

"Yes, sir? Is there something you need, sir?"

Mrs. Ruiz stood by the front door, her hand tentatively on the knob. I had been sitting at the bottom of the staircase musing, assuming she had left for the night. But I failed to take into account the time the caretaker needed just to make her way out the door. When stepping outside, she had been shocked by a blast of arctic air, and lingered indoors fastening her crocheted hat, her gloves, wrapping the long mohair shawl with the fringes around her torso.

I stared at her, wiped the image of Alicia from my eyes.

"Drive safely," I said. She nodded and stepped out, quickly enveloped by a sudden whirlwind of snow.

I spend time in the kitchen, more than usual, since the accident. I wonder if it is the kind of kitchen most women would like. Anyway, that's what the realtor told me before I moved in. Stainless steel appliances and counter, cherry hardwood floors, glossy white cabinets. The kitchen's cold sharp edges reminded me more of a laboratory than a family gathering place, but I was in no condition to object at the time. In the fifteen years since Adam and I, and later my father, moved in, it hasn't changed much. The burners, unaccustomed to use, remain pristine, the oven cleaned to a shine by various housekeepers, stands ready to serve, even the refrigerator is underutilized, yielding little except for the occasional carton of orange juice or milk. The room, except for Adam's plant which sprouts full green leaves, is only a reminder of a promise unfulfilled.

I sit at the kitchen table now, watching the purple sun sneak through half-closed blinds. Soon it will be dark, and Adam is still not home. But this time I am not worried about him. Instead, I will myself to return to the list I have been formulating all day long in my mind. In the gathering darkness, my hand finds an unused memo pad sporting nothing but the shop's pristine red and blue logo in the shape of a globe on each page, and a pen next to it on the counter by the telephone. In small, precise handwriting, I put the thoughts on paper, imbuing them with a new power. I review my list, adding or subtracting a word here and there. Satisfied with the list, the reasons for my decision, I commit all to memory, then tear off the sheet, fold it twice, and place it into the front pocket of my pants. Before I can act upon my decision, though, there is something else I must do.

Papa, fully dressed, is seated in the tattered recliner and is staring out the window. I stand by the door, silent, watching the back of his head, his white billowy hair, fine like a baby's, his wide hands clutching the arms of the brown leather chair as if he were in a plane about to take off for unknown skies. He doesn't see me or hear me, but seems to be listening to the tunes in his head, bobbing to the silent beat, his right foot tapping rhythmically. Off to his right, the china figurines that remain from those he saved, are clean, free from dust, aligned on a high shelf, and waiting. At least that's the way they always look to me, watching Dad in his chair, ready and waiting. I wonder what they could be waiting for, but then the thought comes to me like a warm steady breeze. Of course, they are waiting to play their music.

Often I catch my father staring at them as well, he and the musicians watching each other. I have often wondered about him too, the rush of memories clouding his mind. But I never ask. I am too afraid of the answer.

Suddenly, he has felt my presence in the room. He turns, looking over his shoulder, his eyes sparkling with recognition.

"Joshua," he says, a smile lighting his face like a memento of happier days.

"Yes, Dad. I thought you'd be in bed already." I move forward, stand in front of the window, filling his view.

"Ah, well. Not yet. I thought I would just sit here and look out the window for awhile. The view is so beautiful, don't you think?" I look briefly out the glass, seeing nothing but the murky gray of impending night. There are no flowers in the backyard, and the concrete is as quiet as a corpse.

"Dad, it's almost night time. Nothing much to see out there now."

He raises his eyebrows in a knowing way, smiles again.

"Ah, sometimes I think the darkness is more comfortable, more beautiful than the light. Don't you think so, Joshua?"

I find myself smiling back. He is his old self again. I shut the blinds, move forward, and kneel at his chair. My hand, on top of his now, stops the tapping of his fingers.

His eyes, withered pupils set in a basket of wrinkles, are clear now. He looks at me, smiles again. He is here now, this is my father, I think.

"I was just thinking about you, Joshua."

"You were?"

"Yes, I was thinking about when you were a baby, no more than two years old. One day, just at the beginning of spring, a day like it is today when everyone wanted to be outdoors, when just to smell the air made you happy, your mother and I took you to the Lower East Side. Ah, I remember like it was yesterday! So sweet you were in your little blue hat and sweater, moving like a drunken sailor each time we set you on your feet. And you cried, oh how you would howl, when I placed you down in the stroller. Yes, you knew your mind even then, squirming out, eager to place your shoes, whose soles were still so white and clean, onto the ground. Your Mama, oh, she was so worried that you would fall, but I said, 'Sarah, let the child go!' So we are walking down the street keeping our eyes on you the whole time, and where do you lead us? Well, right into Moishe's Pickle Shop, do you recall? And Moishe gave you such a pickle, why—" here Dad giggles, placing the palm of his hand over his mouth, like a child, "at first you didn't know if you should eat it or stick it in your ear. And when you did take that little bite, well, you frightened yourself, yes, you did, with the water spraying out from its center all over the place, into your lovely eyes." He pauses again, recalling—his mind seems very far away as he grins to himself, "How we all laughed then, your Mama and I, even Moishe. I had not laughed so much in years! Do you recall it?"

I look at my father, a warmth seeping straight though my body, numbing the sadness like hot wine. How long had it been since I heard him laugh like that? Five years? Ten?

His eyes struggle to open wide. He remembers something.

"And then you ran away. Playing a game of hide and seek behind the pickle barrels. Your fat little legs like bulging salamis pushing themselves away from us into one corner and that. How worried I was! So worried that something would happen. I ran after you circling around and around that shop, getting dizzy from the smell of brine. 'Daniel! Daniel!' I called, but you didn't answer. It was making me mad, like a *meshuganah* I was chasing after you. But then, from the sky it seemed, like a thunder bolt, I heard you. Your eyes were big with fear when I picked you up out into the cool air, away from everyone. Why did you run like that, Daniel? Why?"

My father looked at me, helpless, much like a child himself. Already his eyes had clouded, the clarity gone, and with it, the laughter. Once again he was trapped in the maze of his memories. Downstairs, a door opened and shut.

"Dad, I have to take care of something," I say, turning him around in his chair. I take the *Forward*, the Jewish newspaper, still folded as when I brought it into his room that morning, and place it on his lap. My mind stumbles again, as I wish I could recall the Yiddish words of my childhood, but they are a tangle, and I feel helpless to reach him.

"I'll be back shortly to help you change into your nightclothes."

He looks up at me, his eyes imploring, the veil firmly in place.

"I'll be right back," I say. I close the door to his room, push my hand into my pocket, touch the folded paper, and head downstairs.

Adam is looking into the open refrigerator, his body showered in cold white light. I stand at the door unnoticed, foolishly wishing to slice this scene, like a piece of honey cake, this idyllic peaceful *ordinary* moment, wrap it carefully, and place it into the pocket of my pants, keeping it forever. But, instead, the list is in my pocket and the image of my son, which is before me, his face flooded by light, will soon dissipate like a ragged strip of paper carried off by an angry wind. I hesitate before finding the words.

"Adam," I repeat, gathering my nerve, "it's important."

He slams the door so forcefully I can hear the jars rattling inside.

"What?" he says, coming at me, his face contorted with malice, "what is it *now?*"

"It's about college, son. We can't go on avoiding this discussion."

"Discussion? Since when do you discuss anything? No, you tell me what to do—and I listen, just like a private in the Army. You'd like that, wouldn't you, Dad? Because you like to control people. Hey, maybe that would be a good idea. Maybe I could enlist in the Army to save you the worry of trying to control me. You would know just where I was at all times." Adam's slender face is puffed with his anger now as, inches in front of me, he glowers menacingly.

"Adam, you're just talking nonsense now."

"Okay, fine. Everything I say is nonsense to you, anyway. Is there any sense in our having a conversation when you are always right anyway?" He stands in front of me, hyperventilating, using all two inches of height difference to his advantage. I gaze into his flashing eyes, trying to find my son. Taking a deep breath, I lower my voice.

"Calm down, Adam."

He stares at me for another second, opens his mouth, then thinks better of it. He turns sharply and bounds up the stairs, taking them two at a time. But I am on his heels. I cannot let my resolution falter. Not now.

The door slams in my face. I open it.

"Adam, I need to talk with you."

His back is toward me, but I see something in his hand, his fingers frantically texting someone. Who? The girl? Suddenly, I hate all kids, and the technology that has forged a chasm between the new generation and the one that holds me now firmly in its grasp.

"Adam, if I could have your attention, your *complete* attention for only a few minutes." Suddenly, he turns, looks at me, then at the object in his hand, dropping it on the floor as if it were a burning ember. Careless, I think, after all, how much would it cost to replace such a thing? But the sound of his voice acts like a whip, snapping my mind back to the present.

"Talk!" he commands.

I tap my pocket again, sit down on Adam's carefully made bed. It, like everything else in the room, is well-organized, neat. I clasp my hands together and begin speaking in a tone which is reasonable, adult.

"No matter what you think of me right now, I hope that you have considered your future. Adam, you must know how special you are. Your wish to become a doctor, why that's—that's great, so commendable. You must know how smart, how talented you are, how proud I am of you, how proud your mother would have been had she lived." My voice trails off on the last words, heavy with emotion.

But Adam snickers, as if to say he's heard it all before. I can already feel my stomach turning, but I continue.

"One day, I believe—no, I know this—one day you are going to do miraculous things. I don't know how exactly, but your hands will *heal* people, make them well. And, oh, Adam, that's such a gift."

Adam begins pacing, picks up a soccer trophy, replaces it on the dresser. He is exasperated.

"Get to the point," he says.

"Well, the point is that I am proud of you, and as your father, I want the best for you, so," I look down at my hands, "I've sent in that deposit. You can't turn this down, can't take a chance that you might not go there at all, give up your dream for—for a girl. Adam, you're going to Cornell in the fall."

Adam stops dead in his tracks. Stares at me, daggers flying, targeting me in the air between us. He looks down at his hands as if he is seeing them for the first time, plunges his fingers into his mass of curly dark hair as if he is about to pull the strands out by the roots, then looks desperately around for something, anything to grab. He lifts the soccer trophy, holds it in midair, and for the first time in my life I am scared, frightened of my own son. His eyes pause briefly on my face, holding me in his vision, but he suddenly turns, pulls back, and hurls the trophy like a shot-put at the mirror above the dresser, which abruptly shatters, sending an ear-splitting screech into the muted air. He turns again, pulls at the blue plaid comforter, attempts to fling that too across the room, but only succeeds in brushing it across the shards of glass which catapult into the air like pieces of a rainbow. In one motion, then, he grabs his notebooks, textbooks off the desk and hurls them atop the mountain of rubbish on the dresser. He looks around again, begins to walk toward me, when he is stopped by the phone underfoot. He picks it up, points it at me like a weapon.

"This is bullshit," he screams, "and you know it. This isn't about me, how smart, how brilliant I am. It's about what you want, Dad. You want me to stop seeing her because she's not in your plan for me. But she's not just some girl, some *shiksa*, Dad. She has a name, and it's Meghan. And if she isn't the image of what you think is right for me, well, that's too bad. I love her and I am never going to give her up, not for you, not for grandpa, not for my fucking legacy. So I would advise you to get your money back from Cornell because I am going to be in Florida with Meghan."

I stand up, trying to control the involuntary trembling in my legs. The paper in my pocket feels hot, burning into my skin. I make a futile attempt at a laugh.

"You don't understand. The deposit can't—"

Adam's face is now next to mine, the phone held tightly in his grasp. His lip curls venomously.

"Do you know that if I had a gun I could kill you now?"

His sharp words cast a fire, branding my cheek. Before I can react, he is in the hall, pushing past a shadowy mass huddled against the door.

My father's terrified screams send a chill through my body.

"What is to become of us?" he cries, crawling toward me, his hands bloodied by the pieces of glass, "They are going to kill us all. Oh, Daniel, you must hide. Don't be afraid now because I'm going to get you. I'll take care of everything now. Please, please, you mustn't be afraid."

I close my eyes and wait until the shaking which has spread now into my limbs, fingers and toes, has stopped. Then I step over the glass, moving toward my father and, lifting him into my arms in the same way I once held Adam, carry him back to his room.

It is after 9 PM when I am finished. In an odd way, I am almost grateful for the mess Adam has created. Sweeping up the hundreds of pieces of glass, making the bed, cleaning the slight wounds on my father's legs and the palms of his hands, had filled the last couple of hours, the activity providing a reason not to confront my fears, the worst of which was the realization that my only son did, in fact, hate me. And in his hate, he had resolved to reject who he was, the man he someday could be. I sit at the stark kitchen table surrounded by cold metal, making a feeble attempt at reading an old yet unread mystery novel. As the heat from the mug of tea cradled in my hands slowly cools, I try repeatedly to make sense of Adam's words. Did he mean what he said? Could my son really kill his own father? No, the whole idea was absurd. This wasn't Adam, not the Adam I knew, not the child I raised, the child of his mother's dreams. No, I decide finally, this was not my Adam. I walk over to the sink, pour the tasteless tea into the drain, and watch as the teabag reluctantly follows and is churned up angrily by the garbage disposal. The sound is so loud that I almost don't hear the familiar chime of the doorbell. As I sprint into the foyer, the thought occurs to me that something must have happened to the car. Why else would Adam not be coming in through the garage? As I reach for the doorknob, I feel my heart quickening in anticipation of Adam, remorseful, apologies pulsing at his lips.

But when I open the door, I realize that it is not my son. Standing before me is a tall woman with reddish hair. Her pale long face is serene, untroubled except for her mouth which is set in a tight straight line. I hadn't seen her in months, and yet I knew her instantly. I know her because she is the girl's mother, the woman from the produce aisle at the supermarket.

Christine

Why is it so impossible to get warm? I've already dragged an old Army blanket and a down comforter up from the basement, and I'm still shivering just like grandpa used to when he lived with us, right before he was sent to the old folk's home. That was only a few months before he died. Am I dying too?

I push myself up, wrapped tightly in a padded cocoon on the round bed, and press my forehead against the window pane which still bears the coating of an early morning frost, even at this time of year. The window, expansive, is framed with silk drapes in bright swirls of yellow and purple which remind me of an exotic bird about to fly off for parts unknown. I close my eyes tightly, wishing only that I could strap myself to the back of that bird, ascending higher into the whiteness of the sky, only to disappear where no one can ever find me again. The dream seems so real that I soon realize the hint of wetness against my chin and also on the old beige comforter, which from the looks of the wrapping I had found it in, had just come back from the cleaners. I don't care about ruining it with my tears and snot, though. In fact, I'm glad.

My eyes fully open, and I take in the oddest scene. In the creamy haze of daybreak, an army of jet black birds has swooped down from the still-barren trees in the backyard. In one motion, they sweep over the stiff pale yellow grass which has only just begun to thaw from last season's cold. In the same way that night sabotages the daylight when you aren't paying attention, that's the way it is with these birds. They cover the entire lawn, not even leaving an inch of grass visible. They dominate the backyard like soldiers on a mission; in their frenzy, they are oblivious to my spying on them. They are an omen. I am sure of it.

My shivering doesn't stop. With the nail of my forefinger, I tap once, twice against the pane. And then, as if one has swiftly removed a dirty tablecloth, they move upward, back onto the patient limbs of the trees, back into the pink clouds, until I wonder if I had imagined the whole thing. A thin ray of sunlight finds its way from beneath the mask of clouds, casting a single ray, like a laser, onto the grass, just now awakening to day. I move away from the window. My forehead has left an impression on the glass. It looks like a whale.

She has seen me. I could feel her eyes on my back last night when I came in. I wanted to turn around, tell her she has some hell of a nerve invading a person's privacy in the bathroom like that, but I wasn't in the mood. Just too tired.

I don't care what she was thinking, either. Probably that I was drunk. But I wasn't. Not even a beer. I was just full, I mean my stomach was about to burst from the hotdogs and fries. Oh yeah, and the onion rings dipped in white horseradish. They were good, though. But, man, was I sick afterward.

I never intended on coming home. I had had dinner with Dad that night. I called him on a whim and even suggested that we get together. I could almost see him smiling right through the phone, it was that easy. He'd rather cut his wrists than say no to me. But these days, what was I to do? I don't have much money of my own, and I don't want to be a total pig, mooching off of Laney and Ryan all the time. Wondering how far I could take this thing, I sweetly suggested going for Mexican.

"Oh, Chrissie, you know all that stuff gives me heartburn," he said.

"Oh, well...I only suggested it because this new Mexican place is just a block away from where I'm staying, and since I have to get back early to meet my friends, well…Maybe we could do it another time then?"

"No, Chrissie. It'll be fine. I suppose I could find *something* to eat. How does 6 o'clock sound?" Like I said, it was just that easy.

The fajitas were terrific. And so were the chicken tacos, the rice and beans, and the chips with extra hot salsa we had beforehand. The fried ice cream cooled me off pretty nicely, I'd say. Why, if I close my eyes I can taste the blend of vanilla and cinnamon right now. Dad was feeling good too, contented with a couple of chicken cutlets and plain white rice. By the time I left *The Hacienda*, I had a full stomach and 300 dollars in my pocket.

The sprint up the stairs to the apartment was more like a trudge, and by the time I had reached the fifth floor, rivulets of sweat were dripping down my forehead. When I opened the door, the apartment seemed different somehow. Silence hummed in the corners as the musky scent of incense settled in the rooms like a sleeping tabby. Before I could switch on the light, a moan, long and languorous, was exhaled from the direction of the sofa, startling me. It was only then that I remembered. But it was too late. The light clicked on like a bomb, exploding with such ferocity that it sent a sudden jolt through the couple on the coach.

Laney and Ryan slowly untwisted themselves from the pretzel they had become. Ryan's bony ass glistened with sweat as he reluctantly turned to face me, covering his dick with one of the soggy orange pillows. Laney didn't even bother covering up, turning her pendulous breasts to face me, as she planted a reproving scowl on her scarlet face.

"What the--?"

"Oh, Laney, I forgot," I said, shrinking back against the wall.

Even Ryan, whose demeanor usually bore an expression of benign amusement, seemed less than happy with me. I recovered before their eyes could adjust to the harsh light and Ryan could lose his hard on, swiftly shutting the door behind me. Damn. Their five-year anniversary. "Alone time" Laney had called it. Only after I ran down the stairs and walked some four or five blocks, I can't quite remember how many, did I slowly begin to emerge from the fog which had held my brain captive the moment I switched on the light. I had promised her that I would stay away—how could I have forgotten?

When I looked around, I was standing in the middle of a crowd of people on the corner of 27th and Park, waiting for the light to change. The people all kind of looked alike to me, like high tech urbanites in their flamboyant scarves and scuffed boots, blackberries screwed to their ear, and all on their way, it seemed, to the same destination. I wasn't one of them, though. So I crossed onto a side street, and before I knew it, I found myself at East Houston and Ludlow, standing in front of Katz's Deli. Right where I was supposed to be.

The middle-aged guy behind the counter looked at me kind of funny when I placed the order, but shrugged his shoulders, wiped his fleshy palms on his stained white apron, and wrapped up three blistering franks while simultaneously barking the order for one portion of fries, another for onion rings. As I stripped off a twenty from the wad of bills Dad had given me, I could already begin to feel my stomach contract hungrily. I surveyed the restaurant quickly and, noting that the place was already teeming with evening diners submitting to the sudden urge for "real" food before resuming their Monday morning diets, I walked outside, letting the warmth of the wrapping paper seep into my hands, which had already begun to shake with anticipation. I walked for only a couple of blocks before finding a vacant spot on the curb on a block occupied by some freight trucks and a couple of cars whose drivers were lucky enough to secure free late night parking. I couldn't eat the food fast enough. I found myself pushing the franks into my mouth, slicing the oily red meat, skin and all, past my teeth, down my throat, followed by quick bites of the fries and slippery

white-coated onion rings, washing all down with the cool efferves-
cence of the cream soda. As I ate, for some reason, the image of a
pencil sharpener came to mind. I suppose the occasional pedes-
trian owners of the shoes and sneakers which briskly whisked past,
briefly wondered at the strange girl with the purple streak in her
hair who was sitting on a dirty curb wolfing down hotdogs. I didn't
care, though. It all tasted so good!

I don't know how long I sat on the curb, but after awhile I began
to feel sick. I stood up, a bit wobbly at first, intoxicated by the
gas fumes of the passing cars. I walked aimlessly until I noticed
the harsh lights bouncing off the white chandeliers whose crystals
trembled softly in the window. I must have been in the Bowery.
The street was isolated, except for me and my bloated reflection,
an audience of two entertained by a show of lights. I wasn't looking at the glimmering spectacle anymore, but the round figure
with the puffy face, circles forming two half-moons beneath her
eyes, just like a clown. A pathetic clown. I turned around and
caught the first cab I saw.

I blew all the cash I had left on the trip upstate. I didn't care.
I was pretty sick by that time and made the driver stop twice just so
I could get out and barf. I slept most of the way, I think; anyway,
by the time we pulled up in front of the house, it was already past
midnight and just by the shadows forming against the windows,
I could tell Meghan and Ginny were already asleep. Taking off
my shoes, I climbed the stairs as quietly as I could and made my
way, by the light of one dim nightlight, down the hall and into the
bathroom.

I knew she saw me. I could feel the little blonde hairs on the
nape of my neck rising up as a chill spread throughout my body.
But I didn't move. Before the realization of her presence sunk
completely into my brain, she was gone.

The burnt orange of the frankfurters, the chopped meat and
salsa, the starchy whiteness of potato, along with scattered flecks

of crimson blood formed a collage as the mixture became a whirl-pool swirling down the toilet bowl. I was still shaking, and it took me a few minutes before I could stand upright.

I still wasn't feeling very well, not the way I usually do after purging, not in control. I pinched the doughy skin beneath my ribs, squeezing the flesh between my fingers. I never weigh myself, but I knew. I had ballooned into this—this thing that I no longer recognized. It was no wonder I couldn't hold a job or even find a boyfriend. I was totally unlovable.

I couldn't do it anymore. The air around me had become constricting, the light above the long mirror over the sink, too harsh. Something balled up in my throat and I spit a wad of pink mucus into the sink. There was nothing left in me anymore. Exhausted, I clicked off the light and stumbled into my bedroom.

A soft padding down the hall, like petals falling. I sit up, fix my eyes on the rectangular center panels of the door to my room, and wait. Inevitably, there would be the recriminations, the shouting, the bitter stares slicing me from head to toe. The muscles in my arms and legs tense. I am a warrior about to engage in battle.

But when the door opens slowly, the slip of a round white face, pale blue pajamas, edges through the door.

"Meghan. I thought you were Ginny."

"I'll bet," she says, climbing up next to me on the bed. She sits on top of the heavy beige comforter, curls her legs, tucking the fluffy matching blue rabbit slippers behind her. She looks into my eyes, examines my face.

"You look awful."

"Thanks a lot. You don't look so hot yourself," I say, shielding my face as I pretend to rub the sleep from my eyes.

"Why are you home, Chrissie?"

"What do you mean?"

"I mean there's a reason. There's always a reason when you come back home."

I open my hands, peer out at Meghan and, in spite of myself, feel a sisterly pride sweep over me. She isn't a kid anymore, I observe, marking the intelligence behind her brown eyes, the lines of concern at the forehead.

"I sort of got kicked out of Laney's for the night," I admit, "She and Ryan were having a moment."

"Oh," she says, allowing herself the hint of a smile, then settles her head onto the edge of my pillow.

Slowly, I begin to feel the tension seep from my shoulders and down my arms and legs.

"I really did think you were Ginny, you know." Meghan makes a face as if I had just force fed her a lemon, and twists her straight hair up off the nape of her neck.

"I wish you wouldn't call her that."

"What?"

"You know, Ginny. She's your mother. Mom."

I turn away from her, face the window. The sun is full and orange now, consuming the fledgling background below. The blackbirds have all disappeared.

"Where is she, anyway? I thought she would have paid me a visit by now."

"Well, she did peek in on you yesterday."

"Yesterday? I only got here last night," I say, remembering the long noxious cab ride, my rumbling belly.

"Chrissie, you slept all day yesterday. I knocked on the door a couple of times, but you were dead to the world. What's wrong with you?"

I rub my eyes. Am I dreaming? I was tired, but had I really lost the whole day sleeping?

"Chrissie?"

"I'm okay," I answer, turning back to face her, "I guess I was just really exhausted, that's all."

She pauses, silently taking in my face, my body, her deep eyes pinning me to the bed.

"Your hands," she says, "they're shaking." She picks up my right hand, holds onto it. "Chrissie, it's so cold." I pull away from her, push off the heavy covers with the snot still on them.

"I have to go. I need to get back into the city now."

"I don't think you should go now, Chrissie," her eyes examining me, boring into my body. I try to summon laughter from the pit of my stomach, but can only emit a disgruntled gurgling sound.

"Chrissie, you look terrible," she says again, "I mean sick, like you're really sick. Your lips are blue, you've got some yucky crust around your mouth, your eyes are sunken in. And you're so—so skinny I can actually see your ribs under the nightgown. Please, Chrissie." She chokes back tears, her voice heavy with emotion, "Please, you need to see a doctor."

I jump out of the bed, pulling off the bed sheet, wrapping it around my body. I am indignant.

"Are you crazy?" I bellow, or at least I think I am screaming, but my words seem not to have made an impression on Meghan, who is still staring at me, her pupils swamped by her hurt, her dismay.

"You need help," she says again, adding this time, "and you've got to stop blaming Mom."

Something rises up in me. I am a cougar ready to pounce.

"Blaming her? Are you out of your mind?"

Meghan stands up on the bed in her blue furry slippers looking out of her role, paradoxical. She is the four-year-old leading a battalion. I fashion a stern grimace on my face to mask an emerging smile.

"That's your problem," she continues, summoning all the power in her billowing cheeks, "you blame everyone because you can't find a job—yeah, yeah, you say you're an artist, I know. And then there's the boyfriend thing—you claim Mom never liked them either. But did you bring home anyone who ever remotely resembled a human being--who didn't have a dozen rings through his nose, or lightning strikes across his forehead? You're always complaining about having no money, playing Mom and Dad against each other, when you insist on living out in the city away from this hell hole, as you call it. Just look at yourself. You look like some kind of clown—I'm sorry to say it, Chrissie—but you really do, with all those fancy doodles all over your arms and body. Who are you trying to get away from? Yourself? Chrissie, do you really hate yourself that much?"

Finishing her rampage, Meghan collapses on the bed, burying her head in her lap, deflated.

I am standing next to the bed, unable to respond, to even move one leg in front of the other. Meghan's words have plunged me into the depths of icy waters. I feel myself drifting, confused. In my muddled brain only one thought emerges, crystallized, as a signpost in the distance. Meghan hates me. Like everyone else, she hates me too.

I arrive at the apartment just as the tops of the gray buildings are becoming tinged with a violet dusk. I get there more by instinct than careful planning, having found some money in a sock drawer in my room, and taken a local cab (fairly cheap) to a bus bound for Penn Station. The apartment is empty, baring none of the messy residue of that night's scattered pillows, yellow stains, the scars of raucous lovemaking. Even the vanilla incense has dissipated, replaced by the moldy odor of half-bitten apples left on the kitchen table. I head straight for my bedroom. I stand staring at myself in the dusty full length mirror which hangs on the narrow door of the closet. I examine the lines etched vertically down my cheeks, impressions created by two nights of sleeping. The eyes— empty save for a green flash of anger in the corners--, the bluish tinge of the thin lips, the imperfect nose. The body, dumpy in my sister's old gray sweatshirt hastily assumed as I hurried out the door. Meghan was right. I am ridiculous.

Of course, I am out of money again. I try all the usual places—my shoebox of art supplies under the bed, the back pockets of my jeans, a childhood glazed ceramic piggy bank which actually resembles Porky Pig—*That's all folks*—inscribed on its rotund pink belly. In the middle of my search, Peter Krasdale comes floating across my mind, baldheaded, smiling. For the third time this day, I check the messages on my cell phone. Nothing. Where *was* Ginny anyway? Meghan had said that she tapped on my bedroom door a night earlier. And this morning she wasn't even in her room. I move from kitchen to bedroom to bathroom, my thoughts firing randomly. Above it all, I hear Meghan's voice, childlike still, cutting through the mélange of sounds in my head. No job. No friends. A clown. A fuck-up. Just a fuck-up.

I need air. I open the window, and delicately climb out onto the fire escape where a brisk wind scrapes against my cheeks. Quickly, I run down the metal stairs which ring morosely with each step. The smooth metal of the banister is cold against my palm. It is a mother's hand, strong, secure, leading me through the city streets on an afternoon of Christmas shopping. It was the one wonderful time I can remember having with her. Meghan was only two, too little to come along, and had to stay back at home with Dad, so it was just the two of us. We lived in Brooklyn then, only a short ride on the subway to 34th Street. As we sprinted up the stairs into the open air, Mother holding me close so I wouldn't catch any of the germs collected on the concrete walls or clinging to the homeless guys who sauntered aimlessly nearby, we emerged into the brightest sunlight I had ever seen in my life. And the people—*so many people*—carrying huge bags overflowing with boldly wrapped gifts, smiled as we passed by them so that I think they almost envied the mother, confident, forging ahead, and her young daughter, flying behind like the tail of a magnificent kite.

I don't know how many blocks we walked when something touched me lightly on the head, coating my nose, my cheeks. I looked up to see white petals falling from the sky. I stuck out my tongue to taste one, feeling the sensation of cold rainwater. This wasn't like any kind of snow I'd seen before in our own neighborhood, the kind which rested quietly hugging the sidewalk in large gray mounds, or threatened underfoot, a soupy mixture of watery curls. The snow that covered me in a lacey veil of white seemed like pieces of heaven then, a confirmation that, yes, there *is* beauty in the world.

And suddenly we were there. Jostled to the very surface of Macy's front window, so close you could see the little clouds of our breath like tiny doilies pressed against the pane. Despite the crowd pushing against us to get a better view, Mother carefully pointed out the major players in the manger scene, as my eyes bounced from one sparkling star to the next. It was almost too much for me to take it all in. I think that was the moment too when I had made my decision, only I didn't know it at the time. How wonderful would it be to capture those faces forever—to make them live again so that everyone could just stand there staring, wondering what was behind the eyes, just like looking through the glass of Macy's window.

We were hurried inside amid the clanging bells of the Salvation Army volunteers with their long blue coats and brass buttons. Mother held onto my hand tightly as we entered the general din of the store, but it was more than a store, really. It was a glittering wonderland of stacked gifts wrapped in red and gold foil, ladies in fancy scarves spraying perfume on little white cards as you passed by, and the alluring aroma of gingerbread from the café which beckoned us to stop and sit awhile. But we didn't stop. Instead,

Mother kept on, her eyes glowing like radar, intent on her destination.

Hangers clicked against each other as she swiftly surveyed the argyle sweaters for Dad until, finding just the right one in navy blue and gray, she flung it on the counter, as if it were a medallion of victory. Next, it was on to the toy department where she instructed me to find one educational toy and a baby doll for Meghan. Remembering my sister's love of all animals, finding the educational toy was easy enough, and I quickly chose a circular device with photos of farm animals which made the appropriate *baa* or *meow* when you pulled the string. Locating the baby doll was much harder though, as I inspected aisle after aisle, carefully considering each innocent plastic face. Finally, my eye lit on a rosy cheeked sleeping cherub whose golden brown eyes snapped open when I picked her up. Running my finger through her silky black hair, I turned to Mother, who, taking the doll from me, proclaimed that she did, in fact, look just like Meghan, as the two of us marched our prize toward the long line of exasperated parents attempting to rein in their fidgety toddlers as they sneaked out of strollers, their hands perpetually grasping at the stacks of toys which appeared at every turn. After we had paid for our purchase, Mother asked where I would like to go next. I glanced over at the seated Santa Claus, ringed by children while he maintained an artificial look of merriment, and shrugged my shoulders, secretly hoping for a better alternative. Mother grinned at me conspiratorially and then, thankfully, headed back toward the escalators. Down two flights. Girls' clothing department.

"Here we are," she announced, letting go of my hand.

"What's over here?" I asked, stranded in a sea of ruffled skirts and sweater sets.

"Pick something," she said, nudging me forward. For a moment, I stood dumbfounded, but soon proceeded down each aisle, tentatively touching the boldly striped woolen vests, the jeans with their elaborate embroidery on the pockets, the metallic-colored silk blouses. We found ourselves in the coat department when, putting her hand on my shoulder, Mother directed me toward a rear wall.

"There. Over by the mirror."

A mannequin, only a little taller than I, wore a winter coat made of white rabbit fur with large buttons, and a matching fur hat.

I circled the mannequin a couple of times, thinking the coat was, just had to be, a million dollars.

"It's nice," I said, finally.

"Try one on."

Already, she was burying her hand amidst the fur coats, ultimately extracting one in my size.

I put it on, feeling the caress of the silk underlining against my skin, the luxurious softness of the fur as Mother buttoned me into it.

"What do you think?" she asked, standing back.

I looked at myself in the mirror, feeling my tongue glued to the bottom of my mouth.

"It—it's beautiful," I stammered.

"Yes, yes it is."

I stared at myself looking like a princess stepped out of a castle in a movie. I had never felt so beautiful, so *perfect*.

"Well, then, it's yours," I heard her say, as if from a distance.

I looked at her quizzically. She came up behind me, placed her hands on my shoulders, so that the mirror captured the two of us, mother and daughter, in its compliant face.

"I had a favorite coat when I was a little girl, too. A blue one. I think every girl should have a favorite coat of her own, don't you?"

She leaned in close, placing her lips next to my ear.

"Dad likes you girls to be surprised, so we'll just have them wrap the coat up, and you can open it on Christmas morning." Leaning in closer, she added, "It'll be our secret."

I nodded at the two faces in the mirror, entranced. Our secret, she had said. Just mine and hers.

After leaving the girls' department, we had one more stop to make—the linen shop downstairs where Mother treated herself to new cotton bed sheets with little pink flower buds on them, along with the last minute addition of a furry blanket for me—in purple, of course.

The snow had stopped falling by the time we left Macy's and walked, still at a brisk pace, down the fog-filled sidewalks. Avoiding the abyss of the dimly-lit subways, Mother led me through the maze of shoppers, finally stopping at a small diner on the corner of Fifth Avenue, where, taking off our coats, we slid into a booth. She ordered coffee and a cheese Danish for herself, and I had two large sugar cookies complemented with red and green sprinkles for the season, and a steaming cup of raspberry-flavored tea.

It seemed like we sat for an hour, maybe longer, in that booth, as I watched my mother sipping coffee, looking tall and self-assured. As for me, I blew on my tea and chewed my cookies slowly, even picking a few errant crumbs off my turtleneck. I wanted the day to last. I wanted it to last forever.

The streets look bleak now as I brush past a group of Korean teenagers busily chatting as they hover over a map. I don't know how long I have been walking, but I know where I'm going. By the time I arrive, though, I discover that the diner is gone, replaced by a dry cleaner's. Somehow, I knew it wouldn't be there.

The white rabbit fur coat remained my favorite that winter and the following year, warming me even as blossoms appeared on the majestic trees in front of the brownstone. By the time I turned ten, though, I had outgrown the coat, and I later found out that Mother had sent it to a rummage sale. Meghan didn't need it; she owned her own coat by then.

This time, I pull back the heavy double glass doors, walk inside, and climb the stairs slowly. The air in the vestibule is musty, smelling of orange peels and stale cigarettes still clinging to the open incinerator chute on the third floor. I take a few shallow breaths and unlock the door.

It is all I can do to drag myself over to the bed. I fall on my back, closing my eyes to a peaceful darkness. I desperately want to sleep, to open the floodgates to those memories, to be carried away by my dreams. And to float forever in this sea of dreams. To never get up.

But, of course, I cannot sleep, and find myself, bones still aching, trapped immobile in this hideous room in the city, surrounded by faces. They stare at me now, white and lifeless. The old black woman, fleshy lips slightly parted, flared nostrils, half-closed eyes, the hint of wisdom. An Asian girl with long flowing hair, head tilted, eager—for what?—something...They are unfinished, deformed, the works of an amateur, a dreamer. What ever made me think I was an artist, anyway?

I ease myself up on my elbow, feeling a thousand years old, and stare into their blank eyes. I look for the character, the statement I was trying to make—*something*. Yet all I see is the reflection of myself. Untalented, unloved, ugly. Ugly.

I move off the bed and open the window to a steel gray dusk. I look down, past the gaps in the fire escape, to the isolated street below. I pick up one of the busts, the face of the young girl, filling my arms with it, and delicately step outside, placing it on the landing. Then, carefully, I bring out the others, placing them in a row as spectators to the circus below. Picking up the girl again, I feel the weight of her against the palms of my hands. I look down once at the courtyard yawning below, which is empty save for a couple of early shrubs on the periphery, shivering tenuously in the cool breeze. I turn the head toward me, shielding her expressionless eyes from what is to come.

"Ginny never liked this junk, anyway," I say to no one in particular. Then, holding her aloft, I slowly loosen my grip. As the bust hits the ground, it shatters. The white pieces sail upward into the sky then drift down again. Just like petals of snow, I think, as I reach for the next one.

Adam

The scent of freshly toasted English muffins greets me as I walk into Meghan's house, reminding me of mornings spent with Bubbie Sara and Zayde David when I was a kid.

Meghan is standing at the counter, still wearing her pale blue pajamas and these ridiculous slippers with fur, even though it is almost noon.

"It'll just be a second," she says, catching the small circle of dough, crisped brown at the edges, as they pop up with a snap. She lifts them, still steaming, between thumb and forefinger, then gingerly drops them on a paper plate next to another set, already toasted. She opens the refrigerator and reaches in for a few small jars of jam, and places them next to the muffins on the kitchen table. Meghan turns to me before pouring two mugs of hot chocolate which she has boiled in a pot on the stove.

"Want some cream cheese or butter? There's plenty in the fridge."

"No," I answer, sitting down at the table, running my hand through my hair, "No, I'm fine."

She flashes me a smile, and brings over the two mugs. Her flannel pajamas make a swooshing sound as she brushes past, then, almost as an afterthought, bends down and tilts her face, kissing me full on the lips.

"You look cute in those," I say, pointing at her feet, tasting her mint toothpaste in my mouth, "Did you sleep late this morning?"

She frowns, sits down, and reaches for half a muffin before blowing on her mug of hot chocolate and taking a sip. She looks just like a petulant three-year-old, I think, and again I resist the temptation to take her in my arms.

"Actually, I've been up since about seven," she says, shaking her head, "Chrissie was here."

I reach for the grape jam, spread a generous dollop on both halves. *With creamy peanut butter on white bread for lunch at Bubbie's apartment.*

"How come? You said you hardly see her at all anymore."

Meghan settles in her chair, crossing her legs as, picking off a burnt end, she nibbles her muffin.

"You know what? I'm not really sure why she ended up here. She said something about her roommates needing alone time. I don't know if that was bullshit or they just kicked her out. She probably just ran out of money, is all. That's the only reason she ever graces us with her presence. Most of the time, anyway." Meghan grows pensive, picks up her mug, warming her hands against the red ceramic.

"And that's it?"

She looks at me as her soft brown eyes meet mine then grins slyly.

"Well, I kind of told her off."

I raise my eyebrows and take another bite, feeling the juices slide happily down my throat.

"Okay. I really told her off. About everything, how she's just a user, taking advantage of others just to satisfy her own needs. Especially Mom. I can't decide if she's mad because she thinks my parents split because of her, or if she's just jealous that Mom is happy—because clearly Chrissie is anything but."

Ignoring the paper napkin as she wipes her mouth with the sleeve of her pajamas, Meghan ponders this last statement. She murmurs a few words, which fall silently into her lap.

"What is it, Meghan?"

She looks up at me, her brown eyes large, afraid.

"She's sick. Adam, something has to be wrong with her, seriously wrong. I've caught her throwing up in the bathroom, and I have a feeling since she's been out of the house, it's gotten worse. She always wears these big tops that look like sacks so that you can't see her body. But, when I was next to her on the bed this morning-- oh, Adam, she's so thin!"

I finish the hot drink and the chocolate morsels cling to my tongue, turning bitter.

"Did you tell her? Did you tell her what you just said?"

Meghan shakes her head, bites her bottom lip.

"I told her. I told her that and more. Adam, I was horrible to her. I told her she was running away from herself, and that she looked like a clown."

The image comes to mind, and I fight to suppress a smile. I had only met Meghan's sister a couple of times, but with the bright streak in her hair, the silly tattoos, I had to admit the label was an apt one.

"Adam, are you laughing?"

I look at Meghan, my face blank. I can't tell her I barely remember her sister, that my heart is just too full of its own problems at the moment. I just don't care.

"I'm sure she appreciated your advice," I say, hoping my voice registers concern.

"What?" she says, turning to me as I feel a flush creeping up my face, "Are you even listening? She doesn't appreciate anything I say to her, don't you get that? She doesn't listen to me, she doesn't listen to Mom. She doesn't listen to anyone, Adam." Her lower lip is quivering, and I rush to her, hoping to stem the tide of tears I feel certain is about to come. But she wrests herself from my embrace, so that I cannot see the film of tears which sparkle hotly in her eyes. She moves her limbs mechanically, tossing her plate into the garbage can beneath the sink, then stands watching as her full cup of hot chocolate swirls obediently down the drain. She turns the faucet on full force until the brown water runs colorless then shuts it. For a few seconds, Meghan seems to watch the drain intently as if waiting for a solution to bubble up in front of her.

"No one understands."

"Meghan? I could talk to your sister, if you want," I say, standing next to her, arms at my sides, feeling helpless.

"It's not that. Chrissie's not even here, anymore. She left a couple of hours ago. It's me, Adam. It's all about me."

I fall back into my chair, struck by a fear which has just now begun to circulate through my body.

"You mean you don't love me anymore."

She looks up, then, quizzically, and I breathe air out. No, that's not it. We're okay.

In spite of the chairs and stools all around, Meghan takes a few steps back, wedging herself into a corner next to the pantry. She looks so vulnerable then that I want to scoop her into the pocket of my jeans and zoom out the back door, high into the thin air where the still white-capped mountains shimmer like flag posts in the distance. I am sitting in the chair, immobile, my jaws locked, my thoughts still racing over the events of the night before last.

At last, hesitantly at first, Meghan begins to speak.

"It isn't fair, you know. I'm not even eighteen years old, and I shouldn't be responsible for all this—this shit. I don't only mean the stuff about Chrissie, but everything, especially my Mom. I worry about her being alone, even though she's at work most of the time, anyway. I worry about her getting sick—you know the breathing problem she had last year? And I worry about her worrying about Chrissie. Even when she doesn't show it, I can still tell. And she depends on me to be there for her. I mean sometimes it's like I'm the mother and she's the kid. She calls me her "rock." Can you believe that? I'm her rock! If she looked a little closer, she'd find this rock is made of foam rubber, nothing to it. But that's not the worst part even. She confided something in me the other day. 'Meghan, I'm having visions,' she said. Visions. What kind, I asked her, gently, like I was a therapist or something. Just a boy, she tells me. No one she knows or has ever seen before. I press her for more information, what does he look like, does he ever say anything? But she shuts up. 'It's nothing, Meghan,' she says, then, 'I shouldn't have mentioned it at all.' 'Okay, Mom, I answer her, 'You're probably just tired, is all.' I am calm when I say it, too. Oh, Adam, you would have been so proud of me, I was that calm. But do you know what I really felt like doing? What I really wanted to do was hop on top of the railing upstairs in the hall and throw myself straight down onto our shiny white marble floors. That's what I felt like doing. Don't look at me like that, Adam. I'm not that stupid. But sometimes I just feel so trapped, between my mother and my sister, both depending on me. Sometimes, I just need air, you know?"

She pauses. The silence in the room screams so that I can hardly take it.

"A couple of days ago, I saw a strange thing, at least strange for this time of year. I was lying on the couch in the living room reading when I felt something tickle my leg. I look down and there was the sweetest little ladybug. It was black and bright orange, and its round wings were halfway up, poised like it was ready to fly. I lay perfectly still for awhile, feeling tiny shivers as it made its way up my leg. Then I turned slightly to put down *King Lear*, who was right in the middle of his big speech, bent carefully over the little bug and, before it knows what's happening, cup it between my hands. I could feel the soft fluttering against my skin as it tried to escape. But this isn't for long because soon I am opening the sliding door at the back with my elbow, and freeing it. It only took a second, I swear, and the thing seems to melt into the air, it was that small.

It made me feel good to see that, and sad too, you know? I mean none of God's creatures should be trapped like that. Not even a bug. Not even an eighteen-year-old girl."

I slowly stand up, collect the matching jars of jam, and place them inside the refrigerator. I allow myself to linger in the icy vacuum, take one deep breath, and shut the door. I look at Meghan, still curled into the narrow space, hugging herself, head between her legs. I bend down, touching her shoulder with the tip of my finger. Like a lazy earthworm, she uncoils instantly, stretches, and falls into my arms. The delicate touch of her flannel pajamas, the subtle scent of lemons in her hair, her vulnerability—it all ennobles me.

"It'll be okay, Meghan," I say, feeling the smallness of her in my arms as I embrace her closer, "We'll get out of here, and it'll be okay."

She twists away, looks at me, perplexed.

"It won't be that soon. And it won't be forever. Your Dad—"

And then the guilt lodged for two days in my brain like a throbbing tooth, emerges again and so does the pain. Yet the facts of that night are muddled still. The stubbornness of my father, and then chaos. I threw things, said—what did I say?—confusion beneath the throbbing in my brain. Unlike the way it is with Meghan, I was the one who felt vulnerable, weakened, incapable of action, trapped. I remember throwing things, wanting to create chaos out of the order of my life, to break free. I wanted, at that moment, as my father stood iron-jawed in front of me, the only thing blocking me from what I wanted—I wanted to *kill* him. Instead, I ran out, drove the car three blocks, counting the lights of the streetlamps until I realized I didn't even have my cell phone, couldn't call anyone. And then, as the lights began to flicker, I grew afraid that I would get lost, lose my way, blinded by the tears forming puddles in my eyes. And so, I stopped the car on a tree-lined cul-de-sac where the houses were already gray with sleep, and listened to the Knicks game on the radio. Then, when it was over, I went home.

"Adam?"

A small voice.

"Hmm...?"

"Adam? This isn't going to happen, is it?"

"What are you talking about?"

"Us. I mean, I just don't see it happening. I'll probably end up just staying here, going to the community college, until—you know, things get better with my Mom and Chrissie. Then, I'll go away, get my degree, teach. As for you, well, you can't turn down Cornell. Besides, your father—"

"I can handle my father," I blurt out, feeling the muscles work explosively through my jaw.

"I can handle him," I repeat, lower this time, releasing Meghan, as I look out the small window over the sink where a robin tentatively alights on the bare branch of a willow tree, and begins making its way across sideways like a tightrope walker.

"Besides," I continue, "my father can't control my life any longer. He's not me."

Meghan rubs the sleep from her left foot and eases her way out of the corner until she is standing behind me, and when she speaks, I can feel the breath of her words against my neck.

"Your father—even if he did approve your delaying Cornell, he won't ever agree to us being together—maybe if I were someone else. If I were Jewish, maybe he would understand, accept the way we feel about each other. Maybe."

Tension rises up my spine like a sudden blast of wind. I find myself whirling with the force of it, directly facing Meghan.

"Shut up!" I scream, "You don't know what you're saying."

Meghan's shoulders crumple and she takes a step back, her face a mask of white. The look in her eyes is the same I saw in my father's just two nights ago.

I work to stem my increasing rage. And as I do, I block my father from my mind, replacing him with Zayde David's benign smile. *Zayde holding onto the back of my bike as I swerve down the street.*

"It was my grandfather who was in the Holocaust, Meghan, not my father. He was the one, he and my other grandparents who suffered for being a Jew. Not my father, he's American, born in Brooklyn. You can't get more American than that."

Meghan relaxes. Concern returning to her soft brown eyes, she sits down again at the kitchen table, now empty, and begins tracing imaginary circles on the wood with her finger as she listens.

"My Zayde David, he's the one who really counts. My Dad's smart, I'll give him that, but Zayde David, he's way smarter. And I don't mean in the ways people usually think of being smart. He came to America not knowing a word of English, and when he was older than me, he was in school learning how to write 'I see the dog' and baby things like that. He even has the notebooks to prove it, and once he even let me look at them. Pages of paragraphs about my Dad when he was a little kid learning how to swim, stuff like that. I tell you, it freaked me out a little bit, looking at the pages which had begun to turn an antique yellow, with all the precise marks of a blue fountain pen. You could just tell how long it took him to make the 'k' stand proud, to loop the 'l' just so. I think you have to admire a man like that.

"The thing about my Zayde David that makes him so cool is that he's a story teller. When I was little, probably about three or four years old, I would sit on the floor of my grandparents' apartment playing with my Star Wars figures—I think I may still even have a few of them in the bottom of my closet—anyway, while Bubbie Sarah would be watching her soap operas, Zayde would sometimes look up from his *Forward*—that's the newspaper that was written in the Jewish language, wink at me, and say, 'come here, boychik'. Then he'd fold the newspaper neatly, place it at the side of his chair, and sit me on his lap. 'Star Wars you like? Darth Vader, a villain?' he'd say, 'ahh, that stuff is all made up. Let me tell you a real story.' And then he would. I mean even though I was just a little kid, he told me all of it. Sometimes, my Bubbie would catch him talking to me about the Nazis and killings, and blood in the streets, you know? And she'd just stand there outside the kitchen looking in, eyes getting bigger with each word, and say something in Yiddish about the 'kend', which was me, the *child*. I didn't need to know the words. I knew she didn't like that he filled my ears with such things. So Zayde would always stop in the middle of a story, lift me off his lap and set me carefully down like I was glass or something, making an *'oy'* kind of sigh as he did. 'So,' he'd say then, 'see what Bubbie has for you in the kitchen.' But the minute my Grandma would turn around, our eyes would meet again, and he would nod and give me a smile, as if to say, 'I'll tell you more later.' I would follow Bubbie into the kitchen for a black and white cookie and a glass of cold milk, but I couldn't wait to climb back onto Zayde's lap to hear more about how he hid his little brother up in the closet so that the Nazis wouldn't find him, or the days he would stay in the apartment all by himself watching and waiting like a soldier, after his parents were gone, after his little brother, Daniel, was shot. Did you know they shot him in the head right in the middle of the street? Sometimes I wonder how my Zayde could talk about those things, let alone live with them.

"I'll tell you one thing, my Grandma was actually right all along. I *was* too young to hear about such things. For years, I would get up in the middle of the night screaming because of the nightmares, and yet I always wanted to hear more. Some of the stories weren't so bad, like the times before war broke out, how he used to make music with his family. My Zayde would sing, and Daniel, his little brother, played the flute. I once asked him why he doesn't sing anymore, and he just shrugged his shoulders and laughed, saying it was impossible for him to carry melody. Of course, he supposed his voice was still adequate, he said, but he never had the desire to raise it in song. I think he was afraid that if he did sing, it just wouldn't sound the same anymore.

I think of all his stories, I liked the ones about Daniel best. Maybe because I always wondered what it would be like to have a little brother. He'd say he was a pest, always following him around, but then sometimes in the middle of these memories, I would see tears come to his eyes, and he couldn't talk anymore. Then he'd change the story to how he met Grandma and the two of them went to Prague where they married.

Zayde David had no pictures of anyone in his family, but he had something almost as good. One afternoon before I had begun school, and my Dad was at work, Zayde took me to the playground at the park, just the two of us, leaving Bubbie back at the apartment. Sitting on a bench as he tied the loosened lace of my sneaker, he suddenly seemed to remember something. He removed the light jacket he had on, and rolled up the sleeve of his shirt, exposing the skin. There on his forearm were numbers, a tattoo. I asked him where he got that from. He said it was a gift, a gift from the Nazis to the Jewish people in the camps, so that they wouldn't forget. And then, his mood seemed to change, and he rolled down his sleeve and told me to go play on the swings. No more questions.

I played on the swings, but I didn't forget. The following week, I came up to him as he was reading his paper, and held up my arm to his face. With my new set of markers, in bright blue I had written my telephone number. I thought he would be pleased. After all, almost anything I did made him happy. But this time, he only sat staring at my arm and then his eyes met mine with a coldness I had never seen in them before. He got up, grabbed my arm fiercely, and marched me into the bathroom where he scrubbed the markings off so roughly that it left a reddened patch on my skin. He said nothing as he did this, and I too remained mute, stunned by his reaction. As he dried off my arm with a terrycloth towel, he spoke to me in a low steady voice. 'You are never to do this again.

Not you. You are a Jew, Adam, a free Jew living in a free country. I did not come here for you to be a number. Here you are a free Jew'. I didn't really understand what he meant, why he could have a tattoo and I couldn't. I just stayed away from him for about a week after that, but soon everything was all right again.

I think I loved to listen to Zayde's stories so much because I needed to hear about where I came from. I mean Dad never told me anything about my own mother except that she was beautiful. Each time I would ask about her, he'd start to cry, so eventually I just stopped asking. But Zayde, he always liked to talk, not about my mother either, but the old days. Even if they were sad."

"I know. I think he spoke to my sister's class."

I look at Meghan. For awhile, I had forgotten she was there. But here she is, in her flannel pajamas and fluffy slippers, brown hair falling into her eyes. I touch the strands, move them to the side of her brow.

"My Zayde would have loved you. I know he would."

"But your Dad--?"

"My Dad—my Dad is wrong about some things. He just wants to control my life so I won't leave him, so he won't have to be alone."

"He has your grandpa around."

I shake my head sadly.

"No. Zayde's not the same anymore. *I'm tired, boychik. Close the door and let me sleep.* Dad's been talking about putting him away, into some kind of home." I pause. When I glance out the small window, the sun is full against it, spraying it with orange shards of light.

"If he were here, though, he wouldn't care if you were Jewish or Catholic or Hindu. He wouldn't care if you were black or white or yellow. And he certainly wouldn't care about my legacy. He knows the past is just history, something we read in our history books at school. People aren't like that anymore. What I mean is there are no more Nazis. People accept each other now."

Meghan listens silently, touching the silver cross at her neck. And again, she looks so small, so childlike. At the same time, though, there is something in the curve of her brow, a wisdom like that of a person much older, like Zayde.

At that moment, I love her so much that my mind becomes distracted, my thoughts, my fears, all camouflaged by Meghan. Meghan everywhere. I run my tongue against my gums, tasting a sticky sweetness. I hold her closer and I can feel a strength, the power of Zeus in my arms. Then, without thinking, I whisper the words.

"Meghan, will you marry me?"

I feel her melt into me, and my heart surges like a rock bathed in orange light.

David

I was right. Once I met Sarah, my life did change. She awakened something in me which I had never experienced before, something only a man could experience. Now, of course, I was a man, not by virtue of my paltry eighteen years on earth, but because of the lifetimes which had swept through me these last few years. Since losing my younger brother on the streets of Poland, I had survived through a single will—the will to save myself. But after meeting Sarah, everything did change. I had someone else I needed, someone I needed to live for.

Our stay in Lodz was short-lived, for the sunlit charming town whose neighborly streets I skipped through as a child had been transformed into a dank tomb where the few stragglers who returned there trod delicately on the blood-drenched sidewalks, and people still spoke in respectful whispers. The two men who stood smoking cigarettes in front of the apartment building on Palacowa Street where I had spent the first thirteen years of my life looked middle-aged, but were probably only a few years older than I. Survivors were all of an age in those days, and the very old, the very young loitered only as ghosts in the air.

We were lucky, Sarah and I realized as our footsteps echoed morosely up the five flights of stairs to the small apartment on the right. Outside the building, a banister lay in the middle of the street, concrete and broken furniture and mortally wounded appliances in a monstrous pile along with it. The apartments of my old building were all vacant, waiting like patient sentinels for their occupants to return. The rooms were as grim as we had left them that last day as we hurried out, Nazi rifles at our backs. Only now there was a tragic sense of bleakness in the drawn shades, the sagging couch, the closets yawning open like mouths screaming. I did not remember my home, a place of warmth and music, this way and, almost immediately, I wanted to leave.

The bed which had once held my parents as they talked and slept was now nothing more than a wooden frame and the mattress a rusty bunch of coils, the antique scrolled headboard now absent, no doubt the work of postwar scavengers. I hesitated only a moment and, ignoring the thick blanket of dust on the surface, I placed my hands on the mahogany dresser. An urgency flooded my muscles, and after one strong thrust, the dresser and the cloudy mirror atop it were moved forward. There, just as my father had predicted, was the blue bag embraced now by a filmy spider's web. I reached through the thin threads and slowly eased the bag out of its hiding place. Carefully, I retrieved each figurine from its womb. Of the violinist, the pianist, the serious child with a horn, the joyful mandolin player, the sturdy drummer, the pale-skinned girl at her harp, only the mandolin player, horn player, and violinist remained intact. The others were the victims, with cracked torsos and broken arms, no doubt having suffered irrevocably by drawers jostled and abruptly opened. Remarkably, each retained its glossy veneer just as I remembered when they were ensconced on the shelves of Tata's antique shop. In that moment, but only for a moment, life took form again in the old apartment. The three of us in symphony, Mama at her piano, Papa on violin, and me singing, voice raised to the angels.

Sarah stood silently next to me, and placed her hand on my shoulder. Even then she was wise, letting me bask in the sunshine of my memories, even if it was only for a little while.

"See?" I said, taking in the elegant row of musicians with a sweep of the hand, "My father had a whole shop full of these, and cuckoo clocks, and Dresden bowls, the finest china. And now, only these remain."

She touched the violinist's cap with the tip of her finger.

"Survivors."

"Yes," I replied, smiling back at her, "just like us."

I replaced each intact little soldier in the blue silk bag as she watched. Sarah never said another thing about them, never ventured a guess as to their worth. And for that and the wonderful fortune of meeting her after all that had happened, a secret joy entered my heart, and once more I began to feel hope. We left the bedroom, not bothering to return the dresser and mirror to their former positions or peek into my own little bedroom which had inspired many happy dreams. Before closing the apartment door for the last time, I took a quick glance around the living room. Living room. Such a suitable name once, but now inappropriate for a cell which contained two large grimy windows, a torn and sagging sofa, a patch of white on the wall against which a piano stood. Sarah followed as I rushed down the stairs, still chased by the song of the flute.

Now that I had convinced myself of the impossibility of returning to Lodz, I could begin planning my future. The Klingers were, to my astonishment, bereft when I told them that Sarah, her sister, Malka, and I had decided to leave for Prague, where the sisters had cousins who were living with a Gentile family.

"The government of the Czechs is yet unstable, and is sure to fall under the heavy hand of the Communists," pleaded Herr Klinger, "Here you have work, a place under the bed for your shoes, the garden."

I shook my head slowly but adamantly, and thanked him and his wife for their kindness in taking us into their home. My words oozed gratitude, but as I packed clothes into my one leather suitcase, I couldn't help but think how much I wanted to leave this country, these Germans. It was different with Lazar, though. Water sprang to his eyes instantly when we told him, but no amount of coaxing could get him to join us, for his grief for Sonya had sunk like a stone in his heart, rooting him to the earth, so that he desired only to be close to his love.

"Lazar, there is nothing here for you now," I begged, "You can come with us to Prague. Sarah's cousins assure us they can make room for you. No problem at all."

Lazar sighed, long and deep.

"David, my friend, you have your youth still, but as for me—"

"Lazar, you are only thirty-four years old. You are not heading for the coffin yet."

Lazar shot me a stern look then muttered to himself, "You are a child, my friend." Anger fueled by impatience erupted in me. Who was he calling a child? Surely, I had left my childhood back in the Lodz apartment with the broken figurines.

"Sorry for that," said Lazar, suddenly remorseful. He came over and squeezed my shoulder, a hint of the playful friend I once knew teasing at his lips.

"I would like to join you, really. And perhaps one day I will, but for now, well—I am not ready to leave this place to which I have grown accustomed. Not ready to part from the air my Sonya once breathed."

I thought of my parents then, and the lists of names which surfaced daily. Each morning for weeks I would read, pupils trembling, the names of survivors issued by the Red Cross. And each morning I would return to the displacement camp, dejected. Until one day the lists stopped coming and I had to lie down in my bed, as I had done as a boy alone in the apartment, awaiting their return. But soon the tears dried, and as I wiped my clouded eyes, I did not see the darkness. Instead, I saw Sarah. And so, a new chapter of my life had begun.

Sitting next to Sarah on the train heading west, I swallowed bile which stuck in my throat as the motor growled, a death rattle beneath our feet. Sleep did not help much either, for whenever I closed my eyes, the ghosts of the men, women, and children piled against each other, skin against skin as they advanced toward their deaths, sprang behind my closed lids. As usual, Sarah sat quietly next to me as her sister, Malka, prattled on in an attempt to dissipate the tension.

"Do you think Ava and Estella live in a mansion? I think they must, from the description in their letters, don't you? Our two cousins are such master bakers! What a feast we shall have, don't you think?" Malka went on and on, answering her own questions, as the train chugged lazily ahead, past old farmhouses, rolling plains, and windmills standing silently at attention. I spent most of the ride staring at the shifting landscape, my forehead plastered against the frosty window. When we eventually reached our stop, and the doors to the platform opened, we each pulled our single suitcase from the overhead berth, lugging them outside where, we took note with some bliss, we were utterly ignored by the travelers, all eager to get to their own destinations. Led by Malka, who walked with broad strides, her thick black braid flying like a broom behind her, we ascended the stairs. Malka remained undeterred in her running monologue as she spoke of the modest roof of the *Altenschul* in the ghetto, the silvery wetness of the cobblestones when the cousins shopped on a rainy day, the stately chime of the clock in Town Square. Such were the details of the cousins' letters.

Finally, we emerged to a brisk wind and a sidewalk bordered by a grim field on one side and a road where cars battled each other for a space on the other. I wondered at this "Golden City" I had heard Malka speak of, for to me it looked no different from the provinces of the homeland I had so abruptly departed.

The two sisters were seated on a bench directly facing the station, and upon noticing us, arose as one piece. Before they could take a step forward, though, Malka descended upon the two.

"God is good, is He not? After all that we have been through, my dears, to see you alive and well. It is—well—just a miracle!"

The sisters complied, letting themselves be engulfed by Malka's exuberance. Soon, Sarah too was in the fold, the four chattering in a Slavic tongue yet foreign to me. I hung back, feeling the chill of the March air race through my corpuscles.

"David, come meet our cousins, Ava and Estella, the premier bakers in all of Prague!" called Malka, while Sarah delicately extricated herself from the circle. She came to me, taking my hand as the group turned to face me.

"Ava and Estella, this is our David," she said, a flush of pink rising to her cheeks.

The sisters' eyes rose to meet mine, as they murmured something indiscernible.

"Please," said Sarah, "Yiddish only."

"So sorry for our rudeness," said the taller one, her voice rising, as she nodded in greeting.

"Welcome," echoed the other.

"Thank you," I responded, finding my voice, "It is an honor to meet the two cousins I have heard so much about. I am indebted to you for your hospitality."

Ava, the taller one, whispered something into her sister's ear, as the other half-smiled at me in embarrassment.

"Come," commanded Ava, turning toward the line of cars in the street, "the auto is just a few steps away." As the cousins paired off with the newcomers, I was able to assess the appearance of our hosts. I concluded that physically, at least, little separated the two except for their height, Ava being a good three inches taller than her counterpart who, I soon noticed, walked with a rather pronounced limp, which I later learned was the result of a bout with polio when she was just a toddler. Both sported thin frames, rather small breasts, and dark blond frizzy hair pulled into a bun which only served to accentuate their birdlike features. Their movements were stiff, almost robotic, as if they gave great concentration to each task. Their legs, as they walked, were held close together, leaving little room for any man to bridge the space. In all, they were the kind of girls, at thirty-eight and forty-two, whom one might consider destined for the convent, had they not been Jewish, of course. So it came as no surprise twelve years later they still occupied the same home as spinsters.

After an hour's drive, we entered the three-bedroom walk-up over the bakery whose sweet aromas instantly curled around us. I glanced quickly at Sarah, and noticed her eyes had become downcast. I understood then that this was not the place she had envisioned from the cousins' letters. Malka's reaction, though, was more blunt.

"Why, cousins, surely this is not the Rosko bakery home? The one where our mother drank cold milk and played with the Persian cats when she was a child?"

The cousins exchanged curious looks with one another, but Sarah soon interceded.

"Our imaginations play tricks on us, Malka, do they not? Things always appear on a grander scale when we read through the lines. Anyway, this place is surely better than what we were accustomed to at the camps, no?" she cajoled her sister, "Now, cousins, if you will show us our sleeping quarters?"

As I unpacked my bag in the bedroom on the right side of the parlor, a good distance away from the pairs of sisters on the left, I had to admit to myself that Malka was not entirely wrong in her assessment of our new habitation. I acknowledged that I had little to compare it to when I remembered the opulence of the Klingers' home in Germany, and the apartment in which I grew up, with its two bedrooms and small bath, which seemed now even more spacious than my new surroundings.

The apartment seemed pleasant enough, though, with fanciful female touches which set a man's mind and his rugged tendencies at ease. Lace doilies were scattered upon each end table supporting sentimental Tiffany lamps for nighttime reading. There were tiny sets of saucers and cups sprouting designs of pink buds which, all resting on shelves next to two huge silver urns, reminded me of the antiques which abounded in my father's shop. A prim sofa and loveseat of plush green velvet which could support no more than one man of girth, added a sense of order and warmth to the place. An old standing oak cabinet which housed a radio that actually worked indicated the new era in Prague.

As for my bedroom, the mattress was passable, the one chest of drawers adequate for my belongings. These sparse furnishings, along with clean sheets, a pillow, and a warm woolen blanket convinced me that the decision to move from the Klingers' had been a good one. And, if I ever became hungry for intellectual stimulation, there was a volume of Kafka's works on the night table to serve my appetite.

After a few days living over the bakery, I had become accustomed to the scent of apple strudel warm from the oven, the fruity aroma of fresh-baked Linzer tarts, and the comforting heat of thick black bread. There were other things I became used to, like the cousins, Ava and Estella, who, in spite of their rigid posturing, were as guileless and open as young children. It was, no doubt, this innocent nature which saved them from succumbing to despair as the Nazis swept through Prague. Ava, somewhat more outspoken than her sister, was not shy about revealing the turmoil of the early years. The first morning as we sat around the kitchen table eating Mrs. Rosko's honey cake and sipping mugs of black coffee, Ava turned her head, birdlike, in my direction.

"Good cake, David, no?" and, as I nodded, "Well, I have always like it," she added. She took another small bite, wiping the crumbs onto her napkin.

"I suppose you are wondering how Estella and I got so lucky. I mean, with the Nazi problem, and all. Mama, may she rest in peace, had befriended Miriam Rosko, in the *gimnasium* when they were quite young, no more than six years of age, I think. And, the girls, being alike in temperament, had enjoyed swimming together, even in the town pool indoors during winter. Did you know our mother once had aspirations of becoming an Olympian, although neither Estella nor I took to the sport as much. Well, um, I digress. As the girls grew, they became the best of friends, like sisters really, and this despite the fact that mother was a Jewess, and Miriam hailed from a rather devout family of Roman Catholics. Mama used to say she spent more time in her friend's home than in her own, for you see, her family was so cordial and besides, who would not like to spend time within the walls of a bakeshop? Warming to the memory, Ava smiled at her sister then, who nodded silently in assent. Noting that my mouth had opened just a touch in surprise, she continued, "Yes, David, it was in these very rooms, I can tell you, that Mama and Miriam spent many a happy day playing games of tag, hide-and-go-seek, or creating plays with Miriam's two older brothers and baby sister. So, you see, that this home, the parlor, this kitchen, had become much like Mama's own, more so really. It wasn't until Miriam married and, unable to have children of her own, she and her husband assumed ownership of the bakery from her parents who were quite old and infirm by then. As the eldest girl who had learned how to knead dough when she was no higher than her mother's knee, it was quite natural for her to eventually become the town's master baker and, besides, what a clamor would there have been if the townsmen no longer had their poppy seed cakes and prune Danish! Even when she married, she thought it wise to retain her native surname for this reason."

Estella squelched a laugh at this, and quickly placed the palm of her hand over her mouth as her sister resumed.

"But even as the two friends who were separated when they were eight or nine, after Mama's parents, along with her younger brother, Malka and Sarah's father, moved to Poland, the friends kept in touch, and Mama was allowed to spend summers with Miriam here in Prague. Well, as you know, when young men and women are in close proximity with one another, and they are of an age, well, the flirting and reddened cheeks when they are together—oh, I am sure I do not have to tell you of such things," she added, casting a mischievous grin in Sarah's direction who, for her part, gazed down at the floor as Estella giggled again, adjusting her lame leg as she sat so it extended in front of her.

"So, oh well, one thing led to another and Miriam's older brother, Stefan, and our mother became enamored, and, as Mama tells it, it was all quite a scandal. The two had to marry in secret." At the last words, Malka, who was seated next to me, let out such scream that I felt the heat of her words scathe my cheek.

"No! Oh my, my!" she shrieked, "Well, then, this means that you both are Christians? Is that how you were able to avoid the camps?"

Ava rotated her tiny head in Malka's direction, unperturbed; her only indication of annoyance were her pale cornflower blue eyes, which grew larger than usual.

"No, we are Jews, I can assure you. Stefan, our father, was so bewitched by his bride that he acquiesced to all of her demands, and the only one that she made was that all their children be raised in the Jewish faith. Of course, we all know that it is the womb which determines the faith of the children, anyway. And so, yes, we were raised in the Jewish faith. Did you not receive our letters about the *Altenschul*, the festivities of Purim?" Ava was so convincing that even Malka had to admit that the sisters were no less Jews than they.

"Of course, our mother's family was quite distraught about the whole thing, their daughter marrying a gentile and living so far away from home like that. But then, well, with the Nazi siege, they had bigger things to worry about, I think. And after awhile, our situation even began to put your grandparents and father's mind at ease, cousins, for as Roskos, it was but a light thing for Estella and I to claim our Christian heritage. And, we did in 1939 when Slovakia declared her independence from Prague, and Nazis filled the streets. Papa moved us from the small apartment building down the street to his childhood home here above the bakery, where Miriam took us in.

"Those were hard days, cousins, I can tell you. Estella and I even took to wearing Miriam's elaborate gold crosses with the dying Jesus on our necks, even though everyone told us we had the appearance of true Aryans, you know, our silvery hair and blue eyes. Nevertheless, we refrained from the Yiddish language we had learned at home, wore the crosses for all to see. What did it matter what we wore on our chests, after all? In our hearts we knew what we were. Each day as Tanta Miriam taught us the language of the ovens and sharpened our eyes for measuring the flour and sugar just so, the Nazis in their stilted boots and starched uniforms would sweep the streets of Jews, and each day it seemed another of our friends would suddenly vanish, never to be heard from again. What happened to old man Goldman, we'd ask one day. Or Rosa Livingston, the seamstress, the next. After awhile, we stopped asking. We didn't want to know. Tanta Miriam kept us busy in the bakery, though, even if the sugar had been confiscated and vermin had gotten into the flour. Sometimes, we had no business for weeks, except for the occasional scowling Nazi who demanded what he could without payment. But in spite of it all,

Tanta Miriam enlivened our spirits with tales of her girlhood, and drew the shades tightly whenever there was a furor in the streets."

Malka raised her head suddenly after being lulled by Ava's tale.

"Wait—Tanta Miriam, do you mean Mrs. Rosko, the baker?"

Here, Estella intercedes, adjusting her leg once more with a knowing smile, "The dear lady whose lemon cookies you tasted just now, the one who resides in the room downstairs, is our father's sister. We still call her *frau*, even though her husband, Leo Posova, succumbed to a sudden heart attack after only two years of married life."

Malka drops back in her chair, for once, speechless. Even Sarah is wide-eyed.

"If our religion allowed a belief in saints," Ava goes on, "I would be quite confident that Tanta Miriam would qualify. She cared for us as her very own after—" here she hesitates, "after our parents were taken."

My curiosity bested me at this point, and I inquired, "But if your mother was married to a Christian, was that not a guarantee--?"

Ava emits a throaty laugh.

"Guarantee? With the Nazis there is only one guarantee, and that is there are no guarantees. It was a whim, I think, on the day they were taken, for by 1941 our vanquishers looked for any excuse to satisfy their sadistic needs, and one day my father gave them just that. He was standing in front of the shop smoking a cigarette when across the street, he noticed two Nazis patrolling the neighborhood. Only a couple of steps ahead was a middle-aged gentleman who, perhaps due to a broken leg, was walking with crutches as he carried a bag of warm rye bread he had just purchased from our shop. Instead of walking around him, the two soldiers began to taunt the man, and soon were beating him over the head with their truncheons."

I winced, then, recalling the beating my Tata had received in front of his own shop.

"My father was a peaceful man with the heart of a lamb. But I think it was because of Estella that he was spurred to action, you know, he couldn't bear to see anyone abused, least of all someone with an affliction. He ran toward them, pleading with the Nazi swine. But instead of halting their attack, one of the soldiers grabbed Papa by the arm, as the other sent the man on crutches reeling with one last death clout. As a trail of dark blood poured into the gutter, my mother, hearing the commotion, ran outdoors calling my father's name. Well, they grabbed her too, like a kitten by the scruff of the neck. Tanta Miriam saw it all right downstairs from the window of the shop, but when she emerged screaming, begging the larger one holding my mother with one paw, he put his hand on Tanta's face, throwing her to the ground. Thanks to God, they did not beat her to death too. After all, the town needed a baker.

"And where were the two of you while all this was occurring?" I asked.

"Scouring the neighborhood for grain only a few blocks away," Estella offered, "For had we been there, well, we would have met the same fate as our parents."

"And that fate was--?" I asked impetuously.

"Terezinstadt. They were sent to the camp at Terezin." This time it was my Sarah who spoke. "We learned of this only recently from our cousins' letters."

"Yes," said Ava, dropping her voice an octave, "deportation to Terezin was as good as a death sentence. It didn't matter that Papa was not a Jew; he was a dissident. In spite of our name, our crosses, we feared that we were nevertheless under suspicion. There was talk that we spoke Yiddish in our home. Being labeled a traitor was easy for a poor man then." Ava exchanges a knowing glance with her sister and falls silent.

I knew, of course, of Terezin. A number of my fellow inmates in Auschwitz had arrived from the camp with incredible tales of terror and deception. Originally built as a fortress by Joseph II, it resembled a small village and, in later years, was used as a prison for dissidents, including Gavrilo Princip, responsible for the assassination of Archduke Franz Ferdinand, heir to the Austro-Hungarian throne, an act which triggered the First World War. Under Hitler, the camp became a theater of the absurd, where children and adults alike engaged in communal activities including soccer and other sports as a spectacle for the visiting Red Cross. Although the fires of the ovens which so proliferated in the more eastern countries did not light up the night sky at Terezin, only 9000 of the 30,000 Jewish men, women, and children survived Terezin, either felled by starvation or disease, or like the majority, transported to Auschwitz and other camps, where they met their demise. The sisters later indicated that this had been the fate of their dear parents, for word had come that they had been transported to Treblinka shortly after they had arrived in the "utopia" of Terezin.

After Ava's words, silence fell like a shroud over the room; even Malka was suddenly struck dumb by the news, whether from the epiphany that the bakery and its housing were not as glorious as she imagined or the knowledge that her cousins were only half-Jewish.

Finally, I stood up, placed a hand on Ava's shoulder, and looked into her eyes. It is what we Jews, we survivors do, for, indeed, everyone has a story to tell.

During the next few months, just as a young bird first tentatively stretches its wings before flying, I learned the ways of a free man. I spent my days walking the streets of Prague in heavy black rubber boots and brown wool coat. I looked in the windows of the jewelry stores where anxious shop owners were again setting up their display of garnets. Hourly, I stood in the middle of the square listening to the music of the Astronomical clock,

welcoming the change of time again. Once, I even treated Sarah
to lunch at a small dark café where we feasted on goulash made
with fatty chunks of beef and hearty potatoes, accompanied
by a stein of rich black beer. Often, I would walk past Ava and
Estella's *Altenschul*, the oldest of all the synagogues in Europe,
and admired the tall white spires of the *Maisel Shul*, also in the
ghetto, where our beloved Torahs, wine cups, and relics rested
undisturbed. The Nazis had meticulously accumulated these
for a future "museum" dedicated to the memory of the "extinct"
Jewish race. I never stopped inside, never visited Kafka's grave,
which was only kilometers away in the new cemetery, for the
Communists, though not such vile perpetrators of terror as the
Nazis, were, nonetheless, not too fond of us Jews.

Prague, like other cities of this nature, is a world, as they say,
consisting of "little worlds," so it wasn't before long that residents
learned of my skill as an electrician. And before I could aptly
settle into my new abode, I was working for several hours each day.
Like my neighbors in Poland and Germany, the citizens of Prague
considered electricians akin to magicians, and who was I to argue?
Once again, each time I screwed in a light bulb, I remembered to
say a silent thank you to old Greenblatt.

Neither did Sarah and Malka remain idle. One evening as we
sat at the kitchen table with Sarah and Malka, old Mrs. Rosko who,
despite her life of travails, possessed a mind as sharp as the knives
at the local butcher's, turned to her nieces and said something in
a thick Slavic accent which, even though I listened intently, I could
not comprehend. Ava translated.

"Tanta is enjoying the soup very much. She thinks maybe it is
good enough to sell."

Malka and Sarah exchanged glances, and immediately broke
out in laughter, which they did seldom, and it was so good to hear,
so cleansing and refreshing was it. After collecting herself, Malka
spoke first, dabbing her eyes with a napkin.

"This soup? Why we have been making it with more or less potatoes and barley since we were little girls. It was our Bubba who showed us how. Who would ever want to buy it?" But Tanta, needing no translation, pointed toward the back door which led downstairs to the street below.

"*Alla! Met ala koyfen,*" she pronounced in Yiddish. Everybody would buy such a soup!

And so the idea of a new business was born, where Malka and Sarah would cook the same soup they made for the Nazis, only without the extra "flavoring," and serve it downstairs at the bakery counter alongside the sweet *kuchen* and *mandel brot*.

Despite the sisters' thriving enterprise and my steady work as an electrician, and despite the fact that after six months, I had already come to know the streets of Prague as well as those of Lodz, I still felt as if I were a stranger, an intruder. The Communists, or course, proved to be less than hospitable hosts once they had ousted the provisional government and taken power, and had even begun to cut access to Jewish synagogues and cemeteries.

I knew there was one thing, though, that I could do to make myself feel less of an outsider. And so, in April, 1948, just over a year after our arrival, Sarah and I were married, having a modest ceremony and dinner at a restaurant which was not too many kilometers from the shop. The cousins, dressed in their best royal blue and purple frocks, beamed, and tears streamed from Malka's eyes as Sarah and I embraced under the canopy, our makeshift *chuppah*. That same evening, Sarah moved her belongings into my room. Thus, we truly began our lives as husband and wife.

I woke up screaming. Through the fog of sleep I could see Sarah's white hand on my arm, feel its cool gentle touch.

"Another dream, my darling?"

I nod, wiping the sweat from my brow.

"The same as before? Is it the same?"

Yes, I tell her, feeling the beats of my heart slowing steadily to a normal rate. Always it is the same dream. The sound of a flute, and then searching in the darkness until I run following the streets, so many blocks, the sound getting louder as I run. And then, just as I see them, my legs collapse beneath me. I try, but I can't get up. The music seems farther and farther away now, but I am fixed, paralyzed on the ground. And then silence, a river of blood. I wake up screaming, drenched in sweat, with only Sarah's maternal touch to calm me, return me to the world of the living.

It is a dream I will have for the rest of my life, and I accept it. It is my penance.

Malka has found a gentleman friend. He is a longtime customer of the bakery with a particular fondness for its savory potato soup. Igor is a strapping thirty-five-year-old who managed to hide in the forests of Slovakia during the Nazi surge. An easy-going fellow, he is a suitable match for Malka's fiery nature. Best of all, he has but a single purpose, to immigrate to Israel where he will farm the land of this nascent nation. Fortunately, the Communists, eager to be rid of us Jews, support this idea, and before long, Malka and Igor are planning their new life together as man and wife in a free land.

While Sarah and I are gladdened by this news, we are also anxious. What will become of us now that our places of worship, books, even our music have been indefinitely banned? Can the world continue to exist with yet another Holocaust of our people? Are we to be cut down like an infant taking its first breath, snuffed out at the very beginning of our lives? The questions gnawed at me daily.

There are so many reasons I believe in God. On a Monday in February, 1949, a letter from a cousin, Mayer Stern, arrived, providing me with one more reason to believe. Until its arrival from America, I never even knew I had a cousin, but Mayer certainly knew of us. The only child of my mother's brother who had perished in Treblinka in the early years of the war, Mayer had somehow traced me to Prague. And now, this stranger whose blood lines I was somehow connected to, was making me an offer. America. He offered to become my sponsor so that I could move to America. And the only thing he asked in return was to finally have a family.

So once again we took leave of a home that was never really a home at all. Ava and Estella smiled thin-lipped, promising that one day we would all see each other again. I tried to believe them as I hugged each one in turn, thinking that in spite of their rigid appearance, they were among the kindest people I had ever met. In the taxi on the way to the airport, Sarah and I shared one last slice of Mrs. Rosko's honey cake, wondering if we would ever find anything as sweet in our new home.

We arrived in Borough Park, Brooklyn after a week's sojourn in Jerusalem, where we witnessed the wedding of Malka and Igor, and helped settle them in their communal home. The first thing I did upon our arrival in Brooklyn was send a letter to my old friend, Lazar. Again, I extended him an invitation to join us, this time across the ocean in America. But, as before, I had little hope that he would accept. His home, he had explained, would always be close to his Sonya.

Mayer Stern was a bear of a man, in every sense of the word. A rotund figure with a wide smile and not an inch of his body, it seemed, which was free of coarse black hair, he bore no resemblance to any of my family members, who had always been fair-complexioned. Yet, he was cousin enough to not only sponsor our journey and arrival, but provide shelter for us in the two-bedroom apartment which he and his affable wife, Mina, shared.

"So, cousins, how do you feel now that you are newcomers, *greenhorns* here in this America?" asked Mayer, wiping his mouth brusquely with a napkin, as we all sat down to a dinner of Mina's *cholent* which, as customary, had cooked for eight hours on the stove.

I looked at Sarah, who was blowing on a forkful of steaming beef, "I'm not quite sure, to tell you the truth. Brooklyn seems quite different from Poland, and even Prague, for that matter."

Mayer nodded.

"Well, I would say so. But you will find people here most accommodating, and while money does not grow on trees, as they say, I'm quite sure that with your skills, you will have no problem finding work."

"It is almost implausible to realize that, finally, we can live and pray among Jews again, without fear of having our books banned, our businesses locked up, our lives taken, God forbid."

"This is true," said Mayer, helping himself to another portion of the thick bean, potato, and gravy stew, "Just the same, it is best not to be too free with your words. What I mean is, here people do not want to hear anymore of the sorrows in Europe. For Americans, the war is over, done."

I considered Mayer's words. How could a war be over for those who were never really in it? Of course, soldiers fought, and sacrifices were made, but these Americans could never understand the inferno, both literal and figurative, which we had endured, the bruises on the souls of those who managed to outlive all the others. Nevertheless, heeding Mayer's warning, I promised myself not to speak of my ordeal for all the days I would remain in America.

Just as in Prague, I spent several of my early weeks as a newcomer wandering the streets of my new city. As I walked beneath a verdant canopy on an afternoon where, warmed by a luminous blue sky, shoppers and sojourners strolled along Sixteenth Avenue, there were numerous sights to remind me of home. Children playing tag in the street, smiling *greenhorns* with aprons standing in front of their shops, beckoning young mothers to come taste their wares, even a candy store filled with chocolates, black licorice, and sourballs all the colors of the rainbow. Here and there, Yiddish phrases could be heard along with Italian and Spanish, as women

pulled along tired children. *"Mendele, kim ahaya!"* Come along!
Or, at one furniture store, the man who after determining *"viful"*,
how much the cost of a table, makes a show of stomping out of the
store only to return again as his ermine-collared wife looked on.
Before long, I concluded that there would be plenty of business
here for working hands, and plenty of children for—well, we would
have to see what the future brings.

But we didn't have to wait long. Within a month after our welcome, Sarah announced that she was with child. The announce-
ment, while the occasion for much joy, also put a fire in me. If I
was to be a family man, I could no longer be a boarder, but needed
to have a place of my own. So I set about finding an apartment,
and with fortune against my back, I was able to secure one on 58th
Street, only two blocks away from my generous cousins. The apartment consisted of a small foyer leading to a living room on the
right and a large kitchen which looked onto a sunlit courtyard on
the left. The two bedrooms were separated by a narrow bathroom.
One of the rooms could easily accommodate the king-sized bed
which Sarah had always dreamed of, and the other bedroom had
room enough for bigger dreams—one, maybe two children.

We thanked our hosts, knowing that this time we would be seeing them again soon as frequent visitors to our home. And so, by
the time Sarah's belly had become almost as round as Mayer's,
we had painted the walls white, set up a mezuzah at every door-
post, and moved into apartment 6B. I had already begun working steadily for Leon Schneirer, an American Jew who advised me
of the necessity of learning English, obtaining my citizenship as
well as a union card. Focusing on these goals left me little time
to worry about Lazar's letters which had stopped coming once I
reached America, or the song of the flute which still flooded my
dreams. No, I didn't have much time at all, for on a sunny morning
in December, our son was born. Yehuda. Yehuda—named after
our fathers, but here in America he would be known as Joshua.

Joshua, a free Jew whose future was as limitless as the sky. As I held my newborn son in my arms, I felt just as I had the day I met Sarah--this was the happiest day of my life. I kissed Sarah and the baby and left the hospital as if dancing on a cloud. When I arrived home, I removed the musicians from the blue silk bag which hung in the back of the closet. Then I approached a narrow standing bookcase and, one by one, carefully placed each on the top shelf.

Virginia

He has kind eyes. The brown of the iris is steady, confident, but at the edges there is a sadness which reminds me of the puppy which my parents once bought us for Christmas, the one that, after only two weeks, we could no longer keep.

If Joshua Goldman is surprised to see me, his eyes don't register it. He is taller than I remembered, and when he stands against the door, inviting me in, he is slightly bent over, almost as if he is somewhat embarrassed by his height. There is an indiscernible warmth to the high-ceilinged spacious foyer, perhaps from the single yellow light which emanates from a room to the side of the staircase.

"Come in, Mrs. Womack," he says in a voice which is just at soothing as his eyes. Then, not stopping to ask for my jacket, he leads me into the room with the light, the kitchen.

"Please," he says, just as natural as if I had been there yesterday, "sit down." I take the chair across from him at the table which like everything else in the room is stark, metal.

"So you remember me, then?"

"Why, yes," he says, easing himself slowly, almost laboriously into a chair opposite me, "I think we know the same people." A half-smile.

"The same people? Oh, you must mean my daughter, Meghan."

"Yes. Isn't that why you're here? My son, your daughter?"

I open the buttons on my jacket and release a long breath. I had not expected this.

"Well, no. Actually, I'm not here about Meghan at all."

Concern flickers across his eyes.

"Well, if you're not here because of your daughter—I don't mean to be rude, but why are you here?"

I bite my lip. All of a sudden, I feel silly, childish.

"Mr. Goldman, I know you must be thinking me slightly insane at this moment. But if you'll just indulge me, I think I can explain."

He looks nervously toward the foyer, turns to me.

"Okay. Can I offer you some tea or coffee? I'm sorry we don't have much else."

"Oh, no. No, thank you. Mr. Goldman?"

"Joshua, please."

"Joshua, thank you. I'm here today because I think you're the only one who can help me."

"Well, uh, sure. But is this about my printing business? You're always welcome to come down to the store." He hesitates. "But that's not what this is all about, is it?"

"No, you're right. But I think you can help me, or perhaps your father?"

He shifts uneasily in his chair, looks toward the foyer again.

"No, I don't think so. My father is asleep upstairs."

I look at my watch. It is only just past 8, but he's an old man, and I, well, I'm just not thinking.

"I'm sorry. Perhaps I can come back another time."

"Mrs. Womack—"

"Ginny."

"Yes, Ginny. I really don't think any time would be good for my father. He's—well-- his mind isn't quite right these days."

"Oh, I'm sorry." I feel my heart slowing as a feeling of light-headedness sweeps over me. I grasp the edge of the table for support.

"Mrs. Womack? Are you all right?"

"Yes." I allow the feeling to drift through me, like a wave of air. Suddenly, a glass of water appears on the table. I take a sip, finding it cold.

"Thank you. I haven't eaten much today. I'm sure that's the problem." He watches my face intently for a moment before speaking.

"If it's about my father, perhaps I can help you. I am his son, you know." Another half-smile.

I try to return the smile but only manage to do something funny with my mouth. I decide not to look at him at all, but focus instead on a large green stalk which emerges from a small ceramic vase on the counter.

"Okay. For the past year, I've been having dreams, only they're not really dreams since they come when I'm wide awake sometimes. Often at night when I'm in bed, but at other times when I'm outside in the backyard working or resting."

He leans forward.

"What's the nature of these visions?"

I turn to meet his eyes.

"Why, it's a boy. A young boy, maybe five or six years old. He has a sweet face, very fair, with deep blue eyes. His eyes. I remember them so well because they were large for his face, and wise. You know, not exactly the eyes of a six-year-old. But what is really odd was how he is dressed. What I mean is he seemed like an anachronism, out of his time, you know, in an old gray wool coat and cap. At first, he seemed so real that I actually asked him if he was lost. But, of course, he wasn't. Looking like that, how could he be? He just stood there staring at me, holding a flute."

"What?"

"He didn't say anything."

"What did you say he was holding?"

"A flute."

A cloud floats over his eyes, and he looks up at the ceiling. He is a kind man, I think. He understands.

"Your father—he had a younger brother. I just thought—"

"Is this some kind of joke?" He is looking at me now, the softness around his eyes splintering into anger.

"Why no, I—"

"I mean if this is your way of gaining favor for your daughter, I can assure you, Mrs. Womack, it is not going to work."

I feel a flush of heat rush to my face, but I am afraid to stand up, afraid my legs will wobble and collapse beneath me. Just as suddenly as it began, the flash of hatred disappears from his eyes, which he buries now in the palms of his hands until the weight of silence in the room becomes unbearable. Finally, after what seems like several minutes, he moves his hands, his face emerging like moonlight beneath the clouds.

"I'm sorry. I've been under a great deal of stress lately. Please, please forget what I just said."

"It's okay," I say, forcing a laugh, "Stress is something I know a little bit about too, now more than ever, I think."

He sits up and tilts his head toward the stove.

"I could use some tea now. Are you sure you won't join me, Mrs. Womack?"

"Well, yes. On second thought, I think I will. And please, call me Ginny."

"Ah, yes," he says, unfolding a spindly body which is not unlike that of an aging athlete, as he gets out of the chair.

I blow on the unsweetened tea which, I notice, swirls in a mug labeled "Cornell." On his cup is the inscription "#1 Dad." After these amenities, he is the first to speak.

"You were right. My father did have a brother. He was killed by Nazi soldiers during the war. I remember something about his playing the flute. His constant playing used to bother my father when the two were younger. But how would you know about that?"

I nod, take another sip of the tea.

"I'm not sure myself. Maybe I just remembered your father talking about him."

Joshua's eyes sparkle as he recalls.

"Yes, of course. Dad spoke quite a lot about those days before and during the war. He volunteered at schools, libraries, synagogues, even churches. He was quite a speaker."

"Yes," I say, "Yes, he was." But I am lying. I don't remember what kind of a speaker he was, or what he said about the war. Only the boy.

"Where did you hear him speak?"

"I'm not exactly sure. I know he spoke in front of Chrissie's class, that's my older daughter. But I must have heard him someplace else too. Otherwise, how could I envision the child in such detail?"

Joshua nods, says nothing.

"Well, anyway, I'm sure I must have. It's just that the boy seems so real, right down to the tarnished buttons on his coat, the soft almost white hairs of his eyebrows. And I can't understand why this is happening. Sometimes I feel like I'm losing my mind."

He considers this then asks, "This boy—has he ever spoken to you?"

I try to remember. The dream, like an old photograph, comes shimmering before me.

"It was last night. Only to ask if I was lost."

"He asked you that?"

"Yes—it was strange. I mean for him to ask that. But it was only a dream. What do you think?"

If he thinks my confession at all bizarre, his face makes no note of it, his features remaining serene, contemplative.

"I don't know. Dad used to think about Daniel all the time. He said he would come to him in his dreams, asking to be saved again and again. So instead of trying to forget, because he couldn't forget, he decided to tell everyone about him. So he could release himself. But he never could, not really."

"What does this all have to do with me, Joshua?"

He shrugs.

"I don't know. I don't really know anything about you."

"He knew my name. And he spoke only once in a dream. But what I recall most is the music."

"Music?"

"The music of the flute, an old sad kind of a song, but beautiful at the same time. That song, I can't get it out of my head. When I saw you that evening in the supermarket something clicked and I remembered about your father and the boy. I thought if I came to you I could get some insight into the child and why I can't get him out of my mind."

Joshua looks down, then towards the foyer again. At least he doesn't think me crazy. Even if I am.

"Ginny, I wish I knew why. But I don't. My father had a lot of guilt about outliving his little brother, I know that. But I barely know you. I wish I could help."

There is a sound. At first, I think it is the siren of the kettle again, but I soon realize it is something different. A keening, the low moan of an animal. Someone is crying.

"Don't worry about that. It's my father upstairs."

"But—how?"

"He cries at night sometimes. I think he still misses my Mom. I think it's everything."

"Should you go to him?"

"It'll stop. But as I was saying, I wish I could help you. Perhaps you should see somebody to, you know, work it out."

Another sound. And then Joshua is no longer looking at me, but someone else. Adam is standing, car keys still in hand, at the entrance to the kitchen.

"Hello, Adam," I say, smiling. But he doesn't answer, just stands staring at the two of us. The room goes cold.

"Adam?"

Now it is Joshua who speaks, but in a tone less friendly than my own. A darkness settles into the boy's eyes such as I've never seen before, not even in Chrissie. If I didn't know better, I would have called it evil.

He turns around quickly, and upstairs the sound of a door slamming reverberates through the house. Then silence. Even the crying has stopped.

"I apologize for my son's rudeness, Mrs. Womack." Joshua stands up, his shoulders sagging again.

"No apology necessary. I know how temperamental these young people can be." I stand up, buttoning my jacket quickly.

"Thank you," I say, standing at the door. His handshake is tentative, his eyes sadder somehow than when we met. As I settle into the cool familiar leather of my car seat, I think about the three of them, Joshua, his father, and Adam. But I have no answers. Only more questions.

The next few weeks roll into months which are quickly filled with the minutiae of work, leaving me little time to contemplate or dream. The dreams have not returned, and neither has the boy. I have become The Barr Group's top earner and the most respected attorney at the firm. Even my co-workers regard me with a sort of deference; after all, as a middle-aged mother of two, I pose no threat to their own aspirations. In another five years, I'll still be there, still respected at The Barr, while they will have moved on to more prestigious positions in corporate law in the city, or jobs working for the government in Washington, DC. Even the usually apathetic Chad has shown signs of an itch, particularly when he and his uncle have words, an event becoming more frequent of late. Chad is always quick to remind him of the legal wolves just waiting to tear him away.

I rarely bring home work anymore, preferring the clinical confines of the office to home, which recently has become too big for one person, too quiet. The early frenzy of the first few months when I tried to complete the home office, the backyard, has gone, and today the books remain on the shiny new wooden floor, the fresh soil in the backyard unplanted, all reminders of a life half-finished, still incomplete.

My friends, who have always called often, have begun to drift, through no fault of their own. Parents die, children marry, and they find them themselves trapped in the web of their own lives. I can't blame them; after all, there is so little time for any of us. Only Emma remains a lifeline. Emma, whose voice on the phone conjures up the image of my mother, patient and loving. She will ask me about myself, the girls. And, unlike most friends, she will really listen to my answers. I've stopped complaining these last few months, become mum about the visions which have gone, intently pursuing conversations about work instead. I prefer to hear of Emma's daughters' accomplishments, one engaged to marry, already working for NASA, the other garnering awards at her Ivy League college. It actually comforts me to hear that. Like a salve.

Emma is my guardian angel, and I have become Sandy's confidante. In the midst of reviewing a file, I will sometimes feel the slightest tap on my shoulder.

"Ginny, do you have a minute?"

"Of course."

Occasionally she speaks of a case she is wrestling with, or her dissatisfaction with the job, the echo of her father in her ear, still calling her back to the heartland, to home. But mostly, Sandy talks about her dreams.

"Do you ever wish you could just escape from everything, Ginny?" she will say, adding quickly, "No, not you. You're probably the most contented person I've ever met, happy just where you are."

I stop in the midst of a line I am typing and turn to look up at her. The statement is so absurd that I really want to laugh, but instead I simply say, "Not exactly."

"Well, you sure seem to be. I mean you are always so intent on the details. And the clients sure love you. You're the one they all want to deal with."

"You mean they like to deal with the more mature one, don't you?"

"Don't sell yourself short, Ginny. You're damn good at what you do. When I get to be your age I hope that I have it all together the way you do. I really admire you, Ginny."

I smile and shake my head. If she only knew.

"Ginny?"

"Yes?"

"Can I tell you something?"

"Sure," I say, turning away from my work as I get ready to listen to another tale of "the one that got away."

"I think I might be leaving the firm."

The expression on her face changes, reflecting my own astonishment.

"I've had an offer. It doesn't pay much, even less than what I'm getting here at Barr, and they specialize in women's rights. Working there, I think I could really make a difference."

I swivel around in my seat, and take both of her hands in mine. "You know what I think? I think you'd be a fool not to take it."

She smiles, the kind of smile that hurts as it stretches your face.

"Thanks, Ginny. I needed the affirmation."

She takes a deep breath, wipes the tears which have appeared in the corner of her eye, and I know she is thinking of her father and, perhaps, her mother too. I should have let it go, gone back to my work, but I couldn't.

"You just told me how much you admire me. Well, if that's true, you have to know that the only way I got to where I am is by following what I know to be right. By giving up everything for what I know to be right."

Sandy falls into her chair, her long black silk skirt collapsing like a parachute around her.

"You can't let him continue to dictate your life. Your mother was okay with it. She was living her dream, I think. But you're not her."

A wind blows into the room. Odd, I wonder, the windows aren't open. Nevertheless, I shiver. My mother comes to me then, paintbrush in hand. She steps lightly across my heart.

"You must always follow your dreams."

Sandy smiles at me.

"This place isn't so bad, you know. After all, I met you here." She turns back to the papers on her desk, her white sleeveless blouse shimmers purple beneath the fluorescent overhead light. The slope of her back reminds me of Chrissie.

It is June in the mountains of Ithaca, a reminder of why we came here in the first place. The grass grows tall, unconfined, and the scent of wildflowers driven by warm breezes is everywhere. On days like this, with the promise of a new season, golden sun-filled days and cooling nights, Ithaca, I think, seems at the top of the world.

Meghan has become a phantom, her life a whirlwind of final exams, senior awards, and a zillion farewells. The car is now a ticket to her independence and freedom. Soon enough I realize she is tethered to me only by the cell phone which she uses daily to "check in," and the kiss she hurriedly plants on my cheek before running out the door. It is preparation, I realize, for her final exit to Florida from which, my heart tells me, she will never return.

The boyfriend, Adam, seems to be around whenever she is. Nice boy, I think, forcing myself to forget the menacing look in his eyes that evening in his father's house. She doesn't talk much about him anymore, though. Doesn't ask my opinion. But instead of feeling neglected, I can only feel relieved. Soon enough, he will be at Cornell, and she will be following her own dreams to become a teacher.

The streets so long deserted during the icy winter season are alive with activity once again. The people I pass in the center of town on the way to the cleaner's or the market are relieved to be embraced by the sun once more, smiling easily as they mutter a friendly greeting. As for me, I am anticipating still another change, for Meghan is graduating and leaving for Florida in two days. After the graduation, her father and I, per her request, are taking her out to dinner at her favorite restaurant and since we have an extra ticket (Chrissie is ill again), Meghan has asked that Sandy join us. Generally, I am happiest when planning, and I would be, lighthearted even, if not for the pit which sticks in my chest each time I want to inhale. Like an unhappy stone, Chrissie sits inside of me, a reminder that for me, contentment is still elusive.

After the procession and the ensuing jubilation, parents reunite with daughters and sons in a crowd filled with flowers and balloons in the gold and white colors of the school. Encircling us, they sparkle like little suns. Anthony, Sandy, and I stand off to the side as the graduates make tearful last goodbyes. Looking past the groups taking pictures, I see Adam's father standing against the building with an older man, probably an uncle. The two are sullen, oblivious to the hubbub. A few feet away, just before the path veers into the rear parking lot, Meghan and Adam are deep in conversation. She is leaning against the building, fingering her necklace in the way she does when she is nervous, while he is looming over her, palm against the brick wall. He is doing all the talking, it seems, as she listens, nodding occasionally. From my vantage point, I am unable to see her face directly, but something tells me that there are tears in her eyes. It is, after all, a first love.

My perceptions appear right because as Meghan makes her way toward us, she quickly wipes her cheeks with her hand, plasters a smile on her face.

"Where's dinner?"

I hand her the small bouquet of white carnations I purchased for her that morning, hugging her again.

"It's a surprise," says Anthony, kissing her still shiny cheek.

"Okay, let's go, "she says, linking her arms through each of ours, just as if we were really a family the way she always wished we could be.

"I love family style, don't you?" Meghan exclaims, reaching for a thick slice of fried zucchini.

"What a waste of all those leftovers, though," adds Sandy, dipping into the marinara sauce.

"Just like my father used to say, 'Eat up, people are starving in Europe,'" I remark, passing the garlic bread to Anthony who is too busy eating to comment.

"I don't get it," Meghan says, and Sandy looks on, puzzled.

"Never mind. It was a 50's thing." I look at the two of them, my daughter and my young friend, and think they could almost be sisters. And I feel like a traitor.

The conversation throughout dinner is casual, easy, with Sandy describing college life, the excitement of sororities and dormitories, in detail, as Meghan listens, enthralled. Meghan tells her about the new laptop she received from Anthony, and proudly displays the new Movado watch from me. Anthony is busily savoring the mushroom ravioli. And I am, instead, savoring the moment, like so many small moments that make a life. I could be happy today, I am thinking. But the stone sits there, waiting, in my heart.

"Tell her you're coming, Mom."

"I don't know, Meghan. I just don't want to get into all that with her again."

"I'm leaving on Sunday. Gone. I'd like to know that you two are at least talking again."

I sigh. There is no use in arguing anymore. I can't alienate both my children.

"Okay, Meghan. I'll call her."

Chrissie wasn't available, so I left a message. She didn't return my call, so the next day I decided to go see her. But I didn't do it because of Meghan. I did it because of Sandy.

I decided to walk the several blocks from the Port Authority just so I could have more time to think. I circled the bustling pedestrians, buildings and shops, losing my way momentarily in the overcast neighborhoods. Once I arrived at her building, I made sure to take the five flights slowly, stopping at each landing to catch my breath. At the fifth landing, I take an extra breath before knocking on the door.

It takes several minutes before Chrissie answers. She looks somewhat disheveled in gray sweatpants and plain white T-shirt, as if I had just woken her up. After unlocking the door, she turns away, and I can see she is heading toward the bedroom, as if she had expected me all along or perhaps she didn't know me at all, I couldn't decide which. I had seen enough of her face to notice that her skin had become almost the shade of her sweatpants, reflecting a gray translucency. Her eyes seem larger than I remember. I follow her into the bedroom.

I had only seen the apartment once before, the day she moved in. She hadn't changed much since then, her possessions few, the same touches of purple in the quilt, the *Figment* doll we had purchased for her from Epcot when she was five. The room is now in sharp contrast to the communal living area which is dotted with the detritus of youth, a scattering of DVD's, chunky candles, movie posters, and a basket of rotting bananas on the coffee table. After a quick survey of my daughter's room as she slips into the bed, I notice some items missing.

"Chrissie, where are your sculptures?"

She says nothing, merely points a finger toward the window. I walk over and look down past the fire escape at the courtyard below. And then I understand.

"Oh, no, no. You didn't break them?"

She shrugs her shoulders, burying her head further into the pillow.

"Every one of them?"

She turns to face me, with only the slightest upturn of the eyebrows.

"The little Chinese girl too?"

Silence.

Chrissie's face is immobile, her cheeks sunken in like an old woman. Recalling that evening in the bathroom, I try not to imagine the body underneath the cloth. My daughter seems so waif-like, so lost, I fight to resist the temptation to wrap her tightly in my arms.

"Why did you do it, Chrissie?"

She looks straight at me, her eyes like saucers.

"Why? Because, Ginny, because they were crap, that's why!"

"Oh, baby," I say, trying to find the words, "they were beautiful. I just wish you hadn't."

Chrissie sits up, perplexed.

I take another deep breath, try not to look at her.

"I just don't understand why you would ruin them when I know the time you spent on each one.

"They were beautiful," I say again.

"They were a waste of time. I could never make a career doing that. You said so yourself."

I look directly at Chrissie. Chrissie with the eyes of a child.

"I was wrong. Honey, you are talented. Really talented. The other day, I was talking to someone at work who is quite a lot like you, now that I think of it. She's not an artist, but she does have a passion. She asked my advice about changing her job, so I told her the truth, the same thing I told my own mother many years ago. Follow your dreams, no matter what it takes. That's the way I've always tried to live my life. I don't know why I couldn't say that to my own daughter."

"Because you want to control me."

I stare at her eyes, so helpless a moment ago, and see flecks of fire in them. The withered tattoo, a stem against her neck, is throbbing.

"I suppose so. But it wasn't because I didn't love you. I just thought I knew what was best for you, a steady secure career like teaching. I don't know why I thought so, since I've never stayed with one thing very long, not even my marriage."

The tenseness around her mouth softens at this admission. She sits up, considering her words before speaking.

"I don't think I can."

"If you just—"

"I don't think I can do it all again. I had a job, but the guy left and never came back. Besides, I need supplies, money. Dad's been great, but—"

"I'll take care of that, Chrissie. You just get back to work. One thing at a time."

She leans forward, scratches the top of her head, and looks around the room as if she is expecting someone. For once, she does not know what to say. Finally, she utters one word.

"Okay."

I want to hug her, more than I ever have before. But instead, I rummage through my purse until I find what I am looking for. I place five one hundred dollar bills on the dresser then turn toward Chrissie who is still sitting on the bed.

"One more thing. Don't tell your father about this. It'll be our secret."

Chrissie's face is expressionless, except for her bottom lip, which is trembling. And then I do not kiss her, I do not embrace her. I just leave.

A sharp wind-driven rain has begun to fall. Umbrellas are snapping open, plastic crackles as the vendors hurriedly cover their wares, waterlogged shoes squish down the sidewalk. The music of the streets.

I continue walking, trying to keep up with the crowds, and this time I do not lose my way. The air is thick now; the clouds are rolling purple in the sky. I try not to think of Chrissie, or of Meghan who will be leaving tomorrow. Maybe I'll put some more books on the shelves or buy some bulbs for the garden.

The water is cold when I step into it, all the way up to the ankle. My pale and freckled ankle. When I was a girl I tried bleaching away the freckles once. My mother yelled at me when she found out, but she never told my father. My sister, though, didn't have freckles. She never had to worry.

I am tired and the icy cold has begun to press against my neck. I decide to hail a cab, but I am invisible, it seems, and so I keep walking, pushed ahead by the rush hour surge, the rain.

The music of the street grows louder. A familiar song, like a flute, boring into my brain. It fills my head, making me dizzy. I can no longer walk. The cabs whizz by, the music filling my brain, my lungs, until I need air. Choking, I yearn for a drop, only a snifter of air. I stop as the people are sliding by me, open my purse, pull out the inhaler. Taste the cool plastic. I need to sit down. Breathe. Breathe. But the music has already filled my lungs. I open my eyes to white. One day, I will have a garden like the one on the Cape, at my mother's house. Breathe. Whiteness and color. Daisies everywhere.

Joshua

In the end, I had no choice. Dad wouldn't or couldn't eat. He had become incontinent. He cried, now, all the time. Besides, Mrs. Ruiz could no longer take care of him. So what was I to do?

Only last week, he had broken one of the little musicians on the shelf, one of three he had saved from the old home. He had managed, somehow, to make his way to that high shelf to clean it. Can you imagine! And when it broke, of course, he cried like a baby. I tried talking to him, but what was the use anyway?

It wasn't easy. None of it was, not financially, logistically, certainly not emotionally. The Golden Years Hebrew Home for The Aged as they so euphemistically referred to the nursing home, was only about twenty miles from our house and had an impeccable reputation. None of that funny stuff about the seniors left in wheelchairs simmering in their own urine. The majority of the nurses, male and female, were there for the long haul, like the patients, considered "lifers," dedicated to compassionately supporting, cajoling, and singing lullabies to the elders, many of whom had begun to view death in the same way teenagers look forward to senior prom. And speaking of senior prom, it was only a few days before this social gala that we got the call.

"Mr. Goldman?"

"Yes?"

"It's Julius Lieberwald from the Golden Years. I have some good news for you."

"Some good news? Oh, my father."

"Yes, we've had an opening sooner than we had anticipated. After only two months. Wonderful, no?"

The truth was I couldn't exactly call it wonderful when the admission of my father could only mean that one of the residents had died. Besides, it also meant that my father would finally be leaving home. I would be alone with Adam until he too would leave me.

"Yes, certainly wonderful news."

It was only a matter of days until all the paperwork was in order. Since Dad, growing more confused and stubborn, had refused to provide substantial monetary gifts for me or Adam after Mom died, he was not eligible for Medicaid and would have to "pay down" the significant costs of the home until he had nothing, at which point the government would take over. Each time I remembered the mornings he would leave for work only to return home exhausted, spent of all energy, a lump would form in my throat. Thank God I didn't need to rely on him for Adam's tuition. The important thing was that Dad was physically in good health, at least for now.

Dom had promised to help that day, but was in the hospital again, this time with pneumonia as a result of the chemo which had compromised his immune system. Mrs. Ruiz would be at hand, but I couldn't rely only on her, so I was forced to ask Adam. I stopped him in the upstairs hall, as had become my habit, catching him on the stairs, coming out of the bathroom, on his way to one thing or another.

"Adam, I need your help."

He stops. The same exasperated look.

"Zayde's going into a home."

For the first time in many months, his eyes meet mine.

"Adam, he's not getting any better. He barely remembers us anymore. And, physically, well, he just needs more help than we can give him here."

His brow softens as he closes his eyes. When he opens them, I see a return of the old Adam. I can't help the hope I feel that maybe this one will stay awhile.

"Okay. Just let me know when you need me," he says, then turns away and rushes down the stairs. A door closes.

My father wakens early on the day he is to leave. This is unusual, since he has taken to sleeping as late as 10 PM these last few months. But by 8 o'clock when I come downstairs, Dad and Mrs. Ruiz are already seated at the kitchen table having oatmeal.

"Beautiful day, Dad, isn't it?" I hear myself say, trying my best, as always, to sound cheerful. Mrs. Ruiz takes the cue.

"Yes, a wonderful day. I think spring is really here at last."

Dad raises his head, oatmeal dribbling from the corner of his mouth as he looks from me to Mrs. Ruiz, as if we are speaking a foreign language that he does not understand. Then he looks down, taking another spoon of the milky cereal. Mrs. Ruiz reaches for a napkin and dabs his mouth.

As I prepare my own breakfast of scrambled eggs, toast, and hot tea, Mrs. Ruiz and I resume conversation as if Dad is not even in the room.

"Is all in order, sir?"

"Yes, they're expecting us at 2 o'clock."

"That is fine. I will make sure to have him ready."

"Good. I've packed most of his clothes already. I just need to get some pictures together for him. You know, of the family."

"Mr. Goldman?"

"Yes?"

"It is for the best."

"I know."

I stab the yellow curls of egg with my fork and take a couple of bites. I drink the tea too quickly, feeling the heat as it burns my tongue and heart. Then, I take the rest and throw it in the garbage.

Dad's room smells of urine, medicine, and the musky aftershave he still insists on wearing. The leather seat of the old desk chair is discolored and torn, with cotton tufts peeking between the seams. But the desk, as always, is clean and the mahogany still shimmers from numerous waxing. On its surface is the local paper which I diligently place in front of him each morning before I leave for work. Sometimes, at day's end, I will find the paper open to the sports or business section, the edges still wet with saliva. But in the last six months, as Dad's preoccupations have turned inward, the paper has remained on the desk just as I have left it, until the streaks of sunlight on the front page have faded, the night already clothing the newspaper in darkness before I take it out to the recycling bin.

There are only two other items on the desk. One is an old photo of my father and mother on their wedding day. The black and white photo shows Mom standing outdoors in front of a restaurant. She is wearing a suit and holding a bouquet. There is a startled, or maybe bemused, expression on her face. My father's hand is on her elbow.

The other photograph is more recent. It is of Dad lighting a candle at Adam's Bar Mitzvah celebration. The two are already the same height, with the glow of the candles illuminating their faces. Both are smiling for the camera, Dad's hand on Adam's as he holds the taper.

I separate the pages of the newspaper and begin to wrap each of the frames when I hear Dad and Mrs. Ruiz, who is humming softly, walk into the room.

"We did very well today, finished all of our breakfast," announces the caretaker, adopting the plural pronoun, a recent habit which I find somewhat disturbing.

She eases Dad into his chair.

"And we have just been to the bathroom," she adds. I clench my teeth as I fold what remains of the "community events" section and place it under my arm.

"How are you doing, Dad?" I say, turning to him. He does not say anything, but simply looks around the room, at the night table where the clock radio once stood, the desk.

"Do you remember what we talked about yesterday? That nice hotel that we visited with the stuffed cabbage you had for lunch that you said was so *batampte*, so tasty? And the music room where they played the old Jewish songs? I know you loved the piano music. You even sang a little. Do you remember?"

He does not answer, just looks at me as if I am a stranger. I keep on.

"You will have your very own room just like here at home, only much nicer. Plenty of people to talk to too. Some other survivors like yourself, Dad. And I will come visit you practically everyday, it's so close. Just around the corner really. I'll tell you about my shop and bring you the paper, and Adam will visit you too whenever he gets a chance. He'll be close by right here at Cornell. He's going to be a doctor to cure people. Aren't you proud of your grandson? Yes, we'll all be there; it'll be just like home."

"Won't that be nice?" says Mrs. Ruiz.

But Dad doesn't appear to be listening, until suddenly he turns his head and his lips move as if he is about to say something. The faintest smile.

Adam is standing at the door wearing shorts and a Knicks basketball jersey. He is on spring break this week and has just come from one of his pickup games at the high school, fresh beads of sweat still rolling off his brow.

"How you doin' Zayde?" he says, ignoring me and Mrs. Ruiz as he walks over to his grandfather, embracing him. Dad looks up at him, then licks his lips as if about to speak again, but instead only stretches his arm in front of him, toward the desk.

"Oh, your stuff," says Adam, then to me, "Where's his stuff?"

I point to the picture frames wrapped in newspaper, along with a sack filled with other mementos. Adam turns back to his grandfather, but not before sending me a quick scowl.

"It'll be okay, Zayde. No one's getting rid of your stuff. You'll still have it."

I turn back to my father.

"Dad?"

But his eyes are still on Adam. His eyelids begin to flutter.

"Dad, look at me."

He turns his head slightly as a lock of white hair falls over his right eye. Mrs. Ruiz quickly moves to push it back.

"Dad, up there. The musicians. Do you remember the musicians you brought back from the old country?"

His eyes fly up. He is hearing me.

"Dad, would you like me to wrap them too? To take with you?"

"Oh," he says, beginning to cry.

"No, Dad, please."

"Oh!"

"It's okay, Zayde." Adam moves toward the shelf and reaches up, not even needing the stepstool. Carefully, he removes the two remaining ceramic figurines, the violinist and the mandolin player, from the shelf. Cautiously, he steps down, one in each hand. Standing before Dad, he cups each in his hands, as if they are newborns. He knows their value.

Dad stops crying. He stares at the figurines for a moment, then at Adam.

"Zayde, do you want to take these with you?"

Dad says nothing, but reaches out with both his hands, placing them over Adam's.

"Zayde?"

"For you," he says simply then closes his eyes.

Adam goes back to the bookcase and places the little boys on the shelf where they had been.

"We'll hold them for you, Zayde," he says, then to me, "Let me know when you're ready." He walks out, shutting the door, leaving me with the papers still in my hand, Mrs. Ruiz leaning against the wall, arms folded, and Dad fast asleep.

As the four of us slowly approach the double doors of the nursing home, I can't shake the feeling that I am selling him out. Only Dad, perpetually cold, wears his heavy wool overcoat even though it is already April and the sweet smell of spring has already begun to cling to the shivering branches which frame the new brick building. Adam still wears the jersey he had come home in, and keeps close to Dad, his hand at his back, as the doors open automatically for us. Dad seems not to recognize the place and looks around at the well-groomed seniors conversing on the floral upholstered loveseats, the octogenarians navigating the lobby with their metal walkers. I feel a pang as I realize that Dad would not be among this group, but upstairs on the fourth floor in the Alzheimer's unit.

Julius Lieberwald, seated in an armchair facing the entrance, springs to his feet as soon as he sees us.

"Welcome, welcome!" he says, straightening his gold tie as he walks briskly toward us. But before I can extend my hand, I feel a strong force pulling me back. We all stop suddenly as if hitting a wall, and I am stunned momentarily by the power still left in my father's aging muscles.

"No, Joshua. No more."

It is the most I have heard him say in weeks.

"Dad, it's okay. We are not leaving."

"No, Joshua."

A delicate hand on my arm.

"It's fine, Mr. Goldman.   Nothing to worry about," says Lieberwald, oozing syrup then turning to my father, "We don't have to go right up, David. Dinner is not for another couple of hours, so we can have a look at the game room for a game of dominos or cards, if you like. Maybe the music room."

"No, Joshua," says Dad, straining back toward the doors. The strength in his arms both amazes me and breaks my heart.

Adam moves forward and takes Mrs. Ruiz's hand, which he places in Dad's. Then he plants himself in front of Dad so abruptly that even Lieberwald goes silent. Adam crouches down so that he is looking up at his grandfather. His voice is low, gentle.

"Zayde, how about let's listen to some music? Come on, I'd really like to listen to a few songs with you."

My father pauses from the pulling, looks down at Adam, and like a light flooding the darkness, smiles.

"Okay, Daniel," he says, "okay."

The music room is bright with colorful oil paintings and the show tunes of the musical *Forty-Second Street* which cheerfully envelope the room. A woman who seems no older than sixty is seated at the piano forcefully hitting the keys and singing soprano as some of the residents sing along, others clapping their hands and swaying in wheelchairs.

All four of us occupy a long sofa in front of a picture window as Lieberwald greets the residents by name.

"Bella, so glad to see you're better!" "Looking good, Max!"

The music is so upbeat, so contrary to the atmosphere in our own household, that for awhile we allow ourselves to float along with the notes until, finally, the music stops.

"David, may I introduce to you Mrs. Myerson, our pianist as well as our office manager downstairs in accounting."

"So pleased to meet you," she says. Extending her hand to my father, she has, I notice, the long delicate fingers of a pianist. Her complexion is fair, and her face is framed by an ash blond bouffant of waves which somehow resembles a halo.

It is a moment before Dad looks up and slowly gives her his hand, his elusive smile once again lighting up the gray features of his face.

We go upstairs and look at the room which will be my father's final home. For a moment I marvel at its size, contemplating how as we age, our dwellings grow more spacious to accommodate our needs, but by life's end we have been reduced to a bed, a couple of books and photos, our only lifelong possessions.

Mrs. Ruiz insists on unpacking, and arranges his clothes in the drawers and closet. Meanwhile, I unwrap the frames, place the photos on the night stand where he can see them, plug in the clock radio. Adam sits on the edge of the bed talking softly to Dad as Lieberwald and Mrs. Meyerson are engaged in conversation just outside the room. Dad's face is bland, emotionless, and I wonder if he is hearing Adam or still listening to the music echoing in his head. In any case, he is no longer agitated, and I suppose that is something after all.

We drop Mrs. Ruiz off at her apartment and the two of us head home with the rock music station, a concession, filling the vacuum between us. At the driveway, Adam sprints out of the car without a word, entering the house through the garage door. I park the car, click off the station, and remain for a minute or so contemplating whether or not I should go to the shop. I decide not to go since Tara, the young student going to night school who I hired last month, would have everything under control. Besides, it was already past 4. As I get out of the car, I realize that I am more exhausted than I thought.

When I come into the house I can already hear the rapid splash of the shower upstairs. I place the car keys on the console in the hall and, without thinking, head toward Dad's room. I sit down in his worn chair and take a deep breath. The smells that were so noxious to me hours before are bittersweet now as I gaze up at the shelf with its two solitary musicians, their music silenced. I recall how Dad's father had hid them behind a mirror, instructing his son to retrieve the figurines after the war, as he had instructed him to protect his younger brother. Dad had promised him he would, but could only keep one of those promises. He came back with Mom after the war and found them, some already broken, nestled in cobwebs, and eventually brought them here.

I think of their journey as I stare at the small violinist and mandolin player, the only survivors. And, as the sunlight ebbs, casting a gray shadow over the shelf, I arise from the chair and leave the room, trying to forget. But I can't help it. I feel like a traitor.

The two months before Adam's graduation seemed interminable. Both of us were alone together for the first time since my mother's death; we were both uneasy, trying to spend as little time at home as possible. I would leave early before he was awake, exiting the house with a thermos of tea in hand just as the stars were fading from an early morning sky. I was grateful for the work, which was therapeutic, as well as Tara who was both competent and wise enough not to ask any questions when my mood grew sullen or even forgettable at times. Dom would come in whenever he could, but kept up a steady stream of phone calls daily, as if the place couldn't function without him, an illusion which I encouraged whenever I could. I still couldn't bring myself to visit him those days he spent at the hospital, feeling that the thin thread of sanity which supported me would tear and I would—well, I just couldn't do it. He seemed to understand. I hope he did.

Visiting my father was easier, though, a task which I dutifully undertook each evening and on Sundays, when Adam would accompany me. Since I would usually arrive after dinner, Dad and I would often go to the music room and listen to Mrs. Meyerson play show tunes or to *Songs from Israel* on the DVD. Remembering his love of documentaries, I would bring him the occasional *Pearl Harbor* or *The Civil War Years* which we would watch together on the flat screen downstairs when it was available. I always brought the paper too.

Nights were worse than ever. With Adam returning home past midnight on most evenings, and the sounds of Dad's moaning (who would have thought that comforting) now gone, the house became more like a tomb with only my dreams of happier days to fill the spaces between the sorrow. I no longer cried at night, for Alicia had receded back into my mind. Instead, I tried to hold on to my hopes for the future, visions of Adam walking the tree-lined campus of Cornell, backpack in tow, Adam examining patients in medical school, stethoscope around his neck. It was these images I summoned each night as I gazed at the lit numbers of the alarm clock and waited for the garage door to crank open. And it worked, this forced optimism, at least for a couple of months, that is, until graduation.

I had forgotten how charming Adam could be when he wanted to be. And charming was just what he was on the day of his high school graduation when he and I forged an unspoken truce, even if it was for only a day.

I don't know what made me happier, seeing Adam in his graduation gown and cap with the special white tassel for "high honors," or having Dom there to accompany us for the event. I have to admit that when Adam went up for his diploma, a small gulp stuck in my throat and the tears sprang once again to my eyes. Immediately, I felt Dom's hand on my shoulder. He knew I was thinking of Alicia, my Dad, of them all. What he didn't know was that I was thinking of him too.

After the ceremony, outside Adam greets the two of us exuberantly. I hug him, tell him how proud I am. When he accepts my embrace, I can feel only the slightest bit of stiffness in his chest. Dom, though, is like his old self, marveling at how tall Adam has become, what a genius he has blossomed into. As they speak, I hang back watching Dom. He appears more gaunt, his face assuming a dull gray pallor, yet I can't help but think that here is a man who can overcome anything. After all, he is Dom—Dom the eternal.

After five minutes, Adam tears himself away from us, remarking that he needs to talk to one of his friends. My guess is soon confirmed, as he rushes past the crowd toward Meghan, the white gown floating behind him. Dom notices too and without hesitating, begins to engage me in a conversation about the Yankees' prospects for the season. Smiling, I offer my opinion, as my son and the girl continue to talk for, well, for a very long time.

Chinese food is Adam's favorite, so Chinese it is. Adam scoops up the vegetable lo mein, letting the noodles drop into his mouth, just the way he did when he was a kid. I pile spoonfuls of chicken and broccoli onto my plate, some fried rice along with a couple of egg rolls, with a generous dollop of duck sauce over all. As before, Dom initiates the conversation, interspersed with his trademark hearty guffaw, so that only I notice the two shrimps and noodles left on his plate uneaten.

We talk a great deal that day, continuing our discussion of the Yankees, and Adam's new endeavor, shadowing a local pediatrician as he goes about his duties, just to get a "feel" for things, the sudden early heat wave. It is a day for forgetting the past, anticipating the future, a day so joyous that it leaves me completely unprepared for what is to come.

"Dad, we need to talk."

Every parent, I believe, has a natural dread of these words, but as Adam stands in the doorway of my bedroom, with a look which I interpret to be remorse on his face, I have to admit I feel almost gleeful. My son's true spirit is back without a trace of that false bravado which had frozen the air between us, and I am more than eager to welcome him.

"Of course. Come in, Adam. Have a seat," I say, motioning to the chaise next to the bed. But he chooses to stand facing me awkwardly as I sit on the bed, one shoe off. I glance at the clock on the night table.

"You're home early. Is everything all right?"

He ignores the question, seeming to weigh his words. Words he had prepared.

"Dad, first of all I want to say that I love and respect you. I know who I am and where I come from, but I also believe I have earned the right to make up my own mind about things. I want to be a doctor, and that's not going to change. But I have fallen in love, couldn't help it. If I could, I would have chosen a Jewish girl, but it didn't turn out that way. Besides, she isn't that religious anyway. She doesn't care. I know it's ridiculous to talk about this now, but if and when we have kids, I'd make sure they grew up Jewish. I just wish you would give her a chance. Meghan's a great girl, Dad, and even though she knows you don't approve, she isn't angry at you or anything."

"Well, that's a relief. Adam, where is all this business leading about you and this girl?"

He shuffles his feet uneasily, and I can tell he is suppressing the anger.

"Not a girl. Her name is Meghan. Look, Dad, the point is Meghan and I want to be together. We want to get married. I'm sorry, but I'm going with her to Florida. It won't be a problem registering at the community college. After that, I can always go on to a four-year school. Who knows? We may even come back here at some point. That's why I want to defer my admission to Cornell. And don't worry; I fully intend to become a doctor, like I said. You know that's always been my dream."

"I don't know. I don't know anything about you anymore, Adam," I manage to say, feeling the heat rising to my head.

He is still shuffling, looking down, trying to find the words.

"Meghan and I are going to be together whether you like it or not. In fact, we're leaving tomorrow."

The words ignite a whirlwind of feelings inside of me, like a runaway elevator rapidly descending. I want to say something to him, but my mind is a jumble. I can't put my ideas together, can barely form a sentence. Finally, I just blurt out, "You've gone crazy."

The comment only serves to release a torrent of anger from my only son.

"You can't tell me what to do anymore! All my life I've been a good kid, doing what you said, making top grades, and now when I want something for me, you simply say no. You don't understand me at all. Do you really think that I'm going to listen to you?"

"If not to me, Adam, to the voices of your ancestors, Bubbe Sarah and Zayde. You are the light of Zayde's life, his joy. Did they go through everything just to have you betray who you are?"

"Don't give me that crap!" he lashes out, swiftly turning his back to me, his shoulders rising.

"Adam," I plead, "you are who you are. Yes, you are an adult now, can make your own decisions, that's true. But you are also a link in a chain which began many many years ago. I can't let you break that chain. We, *you*, have a responsibility."

Adam murmurs something under his breath.

"What?"

"It's a burden," he says quietly, turning to face me again.

"How can you say that, Adam? You never had to suffer starvation, beatings, murder of loved ones, and yet you think *you're* the one carrying a burden? Funny, I see my existence, yours, as a privilege. And another thing, Adam. I will never, *ever* condone this idiotic relationship with that *shiksa*."

"Her name is Meghan," he retorts, nostrils flaring.

"Oh, Adam, all these years alone with me, and how you helped care for your grandfather. How proud I have been of you. I know it hasn't been easy, living as an only child, without a mother. But you managed, giving me your strength when I thought I had none left. How you persevered, always getting good reports from school, being so tender with Zayde when he started failing. Adam, I have always counted on you, always been so proud of you. But today, today I am not proud. I'm disappointed. And something else, your mother would have been disappointed too."

At the mention of his mother, Adam suddenly advances toward me, fists clenched, eyes ablaze.

"Don't you ever, ever talk about my fucking mother!"

Looking back, I guess I couldn't help what came next, and neither could he.

Driven by a wind, something dark and irrational, I swing, catching Adam square in the jaw. He pauses for only a moment. And then, suddenly, I sense something, a vice squeezing so tightly, I feel I can no longer breathe. What is it, I think wildly as I gasp for air. And then, in an instant, I know. It is his hands. His lovely healing hands.

Christine

Only minutes after Ginny left, the phone rang. It was a surprising call, but now that I think back, not totally unexpected. I listened to the voice on the other end which rambled in its urgency for many minutes. But my answer was succinct, even calm, and when I hung up it was not with a sense of regret, but pride.

I got up and walked over to the dresser where she had placed five one-hundred dollar bills. I picked up the bills, feeling their weight in the palm of my hand, marveling at the feathery lightness of the paper, new and crackling stiff. Something inside of me wanted to burn them, not to destroy, but just so I could roll the gray ash in my hands, rub it against my skin, create another tattoo, making it a part of me forever. I turned back each bill slowly, feeling its shape and size. Five thin unremarkable sheets of paper that would change my life forever.

I was going over a list of the things I would need, clay, sculpting tools, paints—setting priorities. Thinking would I start with the little Chinese girl, or begin anew, when the phone rang again. This time, I didn't hesitate. After hanging up, I grabbed my blue striped sweater and flew out the door, leaving the clean unused bills scattered across the dresser.

The doctors had just stopped working on her when I arrived at the hospital.

"It's the daughter. Let her in," I heard someone say as if from a distance.

I caught sight of her just before they covered her up, blouse and bra ripped open, her breasts sagging, defeated, pushed to the sides. Her red curls so golden only an hour ago, turned dull, scattered around her face like fallen pennies. Her face was white and bloated like the casts of my art, her lips an ugly shade of purple. But it was her eyes just before they closed them, which scared me the most. The eyes I had witnessed so many times sparkling with indignation, shining with disappointment, burning in their love, were resigned. Tired, exhausted, nothing.

I throw myself on her.

"Mommy, no! Wake up! Wake up, Mommy!"

Meghan and Dad come rushing in and the room goes like a funhouse, with rapidly shifting colors and movement everywhere, and throughout it all, the worst, most horrible searing pain I have ever felt in my life. A knife to the heart.

Meghan is hysterical. She is screaming and crying all at once. Finally, I wrap her in my arms. She is screaming, "How, how, how, how, how, how, how?" "Ssh," I say, "ssh." Her screams eventually become murmurs. "How, how, how…" Dad's voice. "Meghan. Meghan, honey." But she just continues to cry. Her eyes have swelled into two red orbs. When someone asks, she even forgets her own name.

Later, they would tell us that it was her heart. A genetic abnormality, they said. Is there any history of early cardiac death? Yes, says Dad, her mother. Her mother died young too.

I thought of the grandmother I never knew. The one who painted. The one she said was just like me. But she had died so long ago. My mother was alive. She had just been in the apartment talking to me. She was telling me that whatever I wanted to do would be okay. That everything was going to be okay. And I knew it was, too. I knew it exactly at the moment Peter Krasdale called to apologize for leaving so abruptly, some financial issues now solved, and that he would be back next week and needed my help. I knew it when I said no, no I couldn't work for him anymore. I needed time to concentrate on my own work. To be an artist. I was going to tell her right after I decided exactly how to spend the money. I could almost picture her smiling into the phone.

I moved most of my things back home that evening. It wasn't a complete move, actually. I just took a couple of shorts and T-shirts, my glasses, grabbed the cash and pushed it deep into the pocket of my sweater.

Meghan, who had been sedated at the hospital, slept clinging against my shoulder, snoring and intermittently whimpering. Dad just talked, a lot, the whole ride home. I think he was trying to tell us something in the same reassuring tone he used when he would caution us to look both ways when crossing the street or warn us against going out on a date with someone who doesn't have enough money to at least pay for dinner. It was that kind of voice. Only I couldn't tell you what he was saying this time. It was just his tone that I listened to. The steady one-note monotony like the testing signal on the TV.

When we entered through the garage and stepped into the large foyer, the house, my mother's house really, seemed chilling, cavernous. My arm still around her, I felt Meghan shiver, sending an icy crawl up my spine. I wondered how my mother had felt this last year, what she thought coming into such a big house all alone. Did she rush upstairs to remove the trim, well-tailored suits she wore to work? Or did she instantly take off the high-heeled shoes which made her already tall frame seem more statuesque, and kick them into the corner? Or maybe she didn't bother with her clothes at all and headed straight for the kitchen where she made herself a mug of steaming Earl Gray tea and looked out on the backyard, sparse and cool, where the shadowy skies sealed the house and her inside in a cocoon of isolation. Or maybe she didn't do any of those things. Maybe she just sat down on the stairs and cried. About me? I didn't know. I didn't care.

Meghan's cell phone was ringing. She didn't bother to answer it as we held onto each other, taking the stairs slowly. At the top, she removed it from her back pocket, looked at the phone expressionless then clicked it off, tossing it on the carpet. Not bothering to change our clothes, we submerged ourselves under the covers in my room. We are floating in a cottony sleep, and then, from below we hear the sound of bells, my father's hushed voice. Still hugging each other tightly, we take deep breaths until the trembling stops, until the night settles over us like a shroud, and, finally, we fall asleep.

I look out at the silent row of people dressed in black. So many people. They shake our hands, some glancing askance at the floor, others murmuring a few words of comfort. I try to recall the play I was in when I was in high school. Was it *A Midsummer Night's Dream?* Was I a tree? A towering oak? A towering oak I am, sturdy with lusty green leaves that sway in the breeze.

"Hello...Thank you for coming. Hello."

Standing in line first is Dad looking very *Dadlike*, you would never have thought he and Mom had been separated at all. Next to him is Meghan all in black, short skirt, turtleneck even though it is already almost the end of June. Every so often I can feel her fingertips on my forearm, leaving a heat in their wake. Next to my sister is Aunt Isabel in an oversized black and silver floral print dress. Her feathery ash blonde hair hangs indiscriminately around her face which looks now red and swollen, and I can't figure out if it is from the realization that she had just lost the last member of her family or if it finally hit her that her time is limited too.

I emerge from my fog long enough to hear, "I worked with your mom, a wonderful lady. I don't just mean a knowledgeable, competent attorney. She was my friend. My best friend."

Through the haze of tears, I see a girl not much older than myself. So this is Sandy, I think, the one who reminded her of me. As I allow myself to be embraced by this stranger, I think how unlike me she really is. Maybe the height, the short reddish hair is the same, the powdery white complexion. But this person seems like a clone of every other attorney friend of hers I had met. Her touch, even her embrace, is workmanlike, and in her strained thin-lipped smile I can see just the smallest hint of reservation. Her hips, her breasts are more rounded than mine, and yet she lacks the requisite softness I had seen in Mom's older friends from home. What gives her the right to call my mother her best friend, anyway?

Sandy moves down the line to make room for some of her colleagues, all males in their thirties it seems, their names and faces instantly forgettable. Then there's Bart. Bart himself.

"A great loss," sighs the middle-aged man in the Giorgio Armani charcoal gray suit, "A great loss to us all." As he dabs at his eyes with a tissue, I can feel Meghan give my arm a little pinch. Mom's boss reminds me of a lit match, with his slender build atop which rested a well-tanned head and a glowing glob of white hair. Just as I am about to whisper the observation to my sister, Bart moves on and is replaced by a flurry of tight hugs and kisses as Emily and Mom's other friends surround us. Meghan and I are the "poor, poor girls" and yet "blessed, so blessed" to have had a mother so wonderful. I nod and smile the phony smile while Dad continues to thank everyone just like he had never left home, the marriage, at all. Aunt Isabel stands, her body slightly trembling, looking as if her knees could buckle at any moment, her chest visibly rising and falling so that I worry that she will lose it at any minute. And Meghan, well, the tears, these tiny well streams of water, spring to her eyes so quickly that it is astonishing, really, to think that now, a week later, the space behind her eyes could still hold enough water to fill a lake.

One time, though, she doesn't cry, and that's when the boy she is seeing walks over. He is so much taller than anyone else that Meghan can spot him when he is still standing, waiting in line in the lobby. As he approaches, though, I can sense her arms stiffen as her features harden into a stoic mask.

"Meghan," I whisper, "isn't that him? Adam?" She ignores me, and then he is in front of us, hesitating as he extends a cold limp hand.

"So very sorry," he says, then turning to my sister, "Meghan, I—"

"Thank you for coming." Meghan lifts her chin slightly as he faces her, indicating there is nothing more to say. He moves on.

I look at the crowd of people, glad that we had asked the priest alone to say the eulogy, along with the requisite prayers. No long sermons, simple burial, done. The priest is speaking of Mother's "fine attributes, loving wife, mother, sister," and other words. More words. I look at the people, pinpoints in black which fill every corner of the room. Meghan, sitting next to me now with her hand, as always, on my arm, moves restlessly in her seat. She tilts her head next to mine and whispers, "Who are you looking for?"

Had I been looking for someone? There were so many people, faces, perhaps a hundred of them, and yet it seemed that I didn't know any of them, not Laney or Ryan, or even my own father who sat to my left. I couldn't believe the room could hold so many people. So many still in the lobby, on the sidewalks outside, in the theaters, in restaurants and stadiums, so many people, billions, in the world. And yet among them all, one was missing. So many people and one I would never see again.

"I'm not looking for anyone," I say.

"Chrissie, can I tell you a secret?"

"Sure," I said as I lifted the soggy bed sheets and stuffed them into the dryer.

Meghan was standing in the doorway of the laundry room, still holding a heavy history book along with a copy of Shakespeare's *King Lear* and a couple of notebooks. Even though it had been two months since our mother's death, she still needed to see me, be close to me as soon as she came home from her classes at the community college each day. Although I knew of her plans to attend Florida State, neither Dad nor I questioned it when she decided to register at the local college in the fall. Almost immediately I had completed my move back home, the consequences of which, I am sure, certainly pleased both Laney and Ryan.

"I don't miss Adam, you know."

"You don't?" I say casually as I slam the dryer door shut.

"No. I'm not even sure I loved him to begin with. In fact, I don't think I ever really loved him at all." She stands leaning now against the door jamb, her straight black bangs barely concealing the questioning look in her eyes.

"Well," I say, switching on the dryer and raising my voice above the low rumble, "I suppose that's a good thing. I mean you're not sad about it or anything, right? So I guess that means you're becoming more mature." While my voice oozed confidence, truthfully the role of romantic advisor made me feel somewhat uneasy. That was one thing Mom was better at, at least. But I had no choice now. She was my sister.

"He used to be after me at first, you know. I know he felt bad about our plans, but well—I suppose it's for the best."

"Yes, I'm sure it is."

"Only, Chrissie, you won't tell anyone what I just said, I mean about never loving him. If it ever got back to Adam, well I—I wouldn't want to hurt him, you know?"

"I won't tell anyone, Meghan," I say, putting my arm around her as we walk into the kitchen, "It'll be our secret."

That night, Sandy called. After the funeral, she had taken to phoning me at least once a week. And after a while I came to believe she was not so bad after all. In the beginning, it was just some words, attempts to comfort those who needed no comforting, I thought. I am surprised that she knows so much about me, my sculptures, the year spent with Laney and Ryan in the city, the tattoo on my neck, even my love for the color purple. It was annoying at first to think Mom would confide such intimate details to a stranger, until I realized she hadn't divulged any of the messy stuff, the name calling and the interminable fights. She was telling her the good stuff because she was proud. She was being a Mom.

Sandy also began talking about herself. She had an interesting life, at least to me whose own life had always seemed anything but interesting. She had lost her Mom too when she was around the same age as Meghan, just at the time, as she explained "when a girl needs a mom the most." She quickly added, "But when is the best time to lose your mom, anyway?" Eventually, the two of us fell into easy conversation, and I found myself telling her stuff I hadn't even told Laney. I told her how I saw things differently from most other people, and how I could go to the park and just stare at an old man on a bench feeding pigeons, memorize the lines on his face, the slope of his jaw. It all seemed pretty fascinating to her, believe it or not. She confessed that she always wished she had a talent, like the ability to write or draw. But as a young girl growing up on a farm all she wanted really was to get out, be a part of a broader, more sophisticated world. Eventually, she did, although her Dad didn't like the idea of her going away much.

"Why?" I asked, not understanding, "it was what you wanted."

She quickly responded, "He's always been *old school*, excuse the expression, about these sorts of things. I was a girl. I was needed at home." I had plenty of things to say about that, but thought it best to remain silent.

"Anyway," Sandy continued, "this farm girl is finally going to work in the big city, and I don't mean Binghamton. I've accepted a job with Legal Aid, working with women's rights."

"How wonderful!"

"It's for the best. Besides, even the guys have found other jobs. Paul actually decided to go back to teaching. The only one left here will be Chad, besides Bart, of course. I guess things kind of fell apart after your mother—well, it was Ginny who convinced me to take the new job in the first place."

"Really?"

"Sure. I guess I was a little scared to be starting a new venture, moving to a new town, and all. But she told me I should do it, I needed to do it." Sandy paused.

"Does that surprise you?"

"No," I said, "no, not really."

I was never hungry anymore. I mean I ate three times a day, what Mom would have called "well-balanced" meals. I ate because I had to, but not in the same way as before. What I mean to say is the food, the mashed potatoes, pizza with the sloppy cheese running off of it, the creamy éclairs, none of it ever seemed to fill me up. There was never enough to fill the bottomless hole when I wasn't eating, and then, all of a sudden, there was too much—so much I couldn't hold it in anymore. Now, eating is just something I do to stay alive, like breathing, and Dad and Meghan are always telling me how much better I look these days. But I don't know, because I've ignored the scale in the bathroom ever since I got here and, truthfully, I don't even care to look at myself in the mirror. The only thing I do care about, the *only* thing, is Meghan.

I knew she was always attached to Mom, Mom's best little girl and all that, but I didn't know how much until after Mom was gone. Sometimes, when she doesn't even know that I'm around, I'll watch her sitting over some book at her desk, crying. Or just sitting by the window staring into the sky, whimpering as if the wind could hear her. Still, I envied her pain. Her grief was real, a solid thing inside of her that you could touch. Pure, unclouded by regret, it was a raw open wound that would heal with comfort and time. It wasn't some amorphous nameless thing circulating in the blood looking for its place. It wasn't the way I felt at all.

One morning, after Dad had driven off and Meghan had gone to school, I decided to fix up my closet, an early spring cleaning, by getting rid of the stuff I no longer wear or like, and, finally, unpacking the suitcase I brought home that day which lay near my bed, a half-filled repository. Close to the top lay my unfolded blue striped sweater, and as I picked it up, the hundred-dollar bills which I had shoved in the pocket came tumbling out like autumn leaves. I picked each one up off the carpet and held it in my hand, again feeling its weight. This time, though, the bills felt heavier than on the day she touched them, and, taking it as a sign, I realized that I had to get rid of them, get rid of them as soon as possible. So, without making any lists, that very afternoon, I crumpled the bills into my wallet, got into Mom's car, which was now mine, and drove the thirty minutes to the art supply store. By day's end I had begun work on my next piece—the little Chinese girl, reborn.

I hadn't realized how much I missed working with clay until I dug my fingers again into the cool putty, feeling the joy of the flat gray patches like tiny kisses against my skin, molding, cutting, shaping something into life. It was when I worked that my mind traveled sometimes to the pieces I would make, and plans for the future, the new bedspread, maybe some flowers for the garden. Sometimes, though, my mind would loiter in the past. As I pinched and pushed until I found the life within, I would think about my mother and all the times I hated her. During those first few dark weeks after her death, we had opened the old photo albums. That only made Meghan cry more, I think, because she remembered too much and needed to forget. But I would return late at night, untangling myself from sister's arms, walking barefoot into the den, opening the bottom drawer of the china closet, pulling out the albums. I would look at the photos of Virginia running along the shore as a newlywed, and as a young mother with her daughters posing for a formal photo, laughing over drinks with friends. Sitting cross-legged on the carpet, I tried to know her, figure out who she was. But I wasn't very successful.

And now, as I stood tracing the long straight hair of the Chinese girl, her face newly-etched, I could only remember the coldness whenever she entered my room, the condescending tone of her voice which remained like icicles suspended in the air even after she was gone, the disappointment in her eyes. I think sometimes she wanted to mold me in the same way I gave shape to blocks of clay, in the same way she was continually transforming herself. Perhaps she never knew who she was either, destroying past incarnations the way I did, just to create another. And yet, in the end, she did understand. In the end, there was the weight of the paper bills in my pocket.

Meghan comes into my bed, yawning. She has just taken her first college midterm and the flush of exhilaration is still in her cheeks. She speaks of the work that needs to be done, the classes she must take to transfer to another college so that she can become a teacher. Tonight she will not cry. And later, as I hold my sleeping sister in the darkness, I feel a sense of relief that her sadness is seeping away. But I feel something else too. I want my mother. I want her so bad.

Adam

I have killed my father. I know it because I squeezed his throat so hard until he began sputtering, the spit coming out of his mouth, his face as red as a beet. I know it because of his eyes turning from angry to pleading in seconds. I squeezed until my fingers hurt, but his eyes wouldn't close, so I pushed him away, down to the floor in one quick motion. And then I left.

I didn't have the keys to the car, so I just ran. I really didn't know where I was going until I found myself at Meghan's front door. It was only then that I stopped, having run over a mile, put my hands on my knees and bent down, trying to take a few deep breaths. But the air, already filled with dusky gray clouds, was warm and sour, and instead of feeling refreshed, I felt my stomach cramp. And before long I was puking right in front of Meghan's house.

After I was done, I sat on the top step figuring out what to do next. I looked up directly over the door to Meghan's bedroom window. The shades were drawn and the house seemed oddly quiet and empty. I took out my cell phone and held it in my hand for awhile. If I called her, what would I say? I would have to tell her what I had done. I would tell her that I wasn't thinking. It was my hands, as if they were a thing apart from me, and I had lost control. And suddenly they were around his neck, and wouldn't stop, and a part of my brain was watching it all take place like I was in bed at home watching an old movie. I just couldn't help it. But she wouldn't understand. She would know what I now knew, that it wasn't my hands at all, but me. I was the one trying to make him stop, trying to get him out of the way. I sat for a long time on the top step until the clouds eventually closed in, becoming black, and mercifully, hiding all from sight.

My hand was still trembling when I clicked on Meghan's number. But the phone rang only once, and then her recorded message came on: "Hey, it's Meghan—I can't get to the phone, but leave a message, and I'll catch you later. Bye!" I shut the phone off and sat staring at it for a few minutes, as if Meghan herself could come tumbling out of the speaker. Then I called her back, leaving a simple message—"Call me." My voice sounded strange, muffled, like it was wrapped in cotton, like the voice of someone who hadn't spoken for a very long time.

Where was she? Seven o'clock. Surely she couldn't be asleep already. I glance down the block and can't see any parked cars patiently waiting on the curb of the neat cul-de-sac, already awash in the brilliant light of street lamps. But, I reason, this didn't mean that no one was home, just that the cars were already parked in the garage for the night. I took a deep breath, inhaling the noxious smell of vomit still on my tongue, and rang the bell. I rang more than once, and it was a good three minutes before I could hear the heavy footsteps of someone moving toward the door. Instead of seeing Meghan, her arms extended, welcoming me home, it was her father, a man I recognized only from her pictures, who appeared at the door. He wore a plain white T-shirt over navy blue dress pants, his thick black hair disheveled, as if he had just woken from a deep sleep. He looked terrible.

"Yes?" he said, barely looking at me. I realized he didn't know who I was.

"Um...I'm Adam, a friend of Meghan's. Is she in?"

He thought for a moment.

"Meghan? No, she can't. She can't see you now."

"Oh. Okay. Well, could you tell her I was here? Tell her Adam was here."

"Yes," he says, more to himself than to me, then starts to close the door, but seems to remember something.

"Adam? Did you say that's your name?" He doesn't wait for me to answer.

"Meghan probably won't get back to you for awhile. She's upstairs with her sister now, sleeping. Ginny—her mother—passed away earlier today."

"What? How? Oh, my God, what happened?"

"She was in the city when it happened. Her heart. Her heart just stopped. So, Meghan won't—"

"Oh, my God, no, of course. Oh, Meghan. Please tell her, tell her—"

"I'll tell her you were here," he says, and slams the door shut.

I feel suspended in air suddenly as I turn away from the door, as if I am looking down on the earth watching someone else's life unfold. Meghan's mother dead? I had seen her in my house, my kitchen, sitting at the kitchen table. Or did I imagine it all? Meghan's mother. The tall woman with the red hair. The smiling woman in my kitchen. Meghan's mother. I walk out of the cul-de-sac, my head throbbing, following the light of the new moon. I decide not to call Meghan anymore, at least for now. I bounce the phone in the palm of my hand for awhile. Having no one to call, I click the power off and place it in the pocket of my jeans. I look up at the moon again, which is full, streaming a shower of light ahead of me. My body forms a long ragged line in the light. I continue walking, following the shadow ahead. And then I do the only thing I can do. I go home.

By the time I reach my house, my legs feel like straw ready to break beneath me. My block, like Meghan's, is eerily quiet at this hour, but the single yellow torch light casts a welcome glow on the path, and inside all the lights are still blazing. My hands shake as I key in the numbers on the pad next to the garage door, and when I open the door and see the staircase in the hall, my mind goes numb. I ascend the stairs. But when I am halfway up, I stop because to my left in the stark metal kitchen, I see something. He is there, sitting at the kitchen table, a mug of tea held between his hands. As always, he is waiting.

After the funeral, I stopped asking questions. I could tell by the cold look in Meghan's eyes that it was over. As I walked away from her and took my seat among the mourners, I felt as if I had been drained of all feeling, as if a gate had opened and all the pain inside of me had been finally flushed out. Maybe the happiness was too. All I knew is that I felt somehow too young to have all these feelings, feelings I could no longer carry. As I sat there and listened to the priest speak of Mrs. Womack (*was she really dead?*) all I felt was relief. So as I sat for awhile with a couple of Meghan's girlfriends, ignoring me for the most part, I felt my head become inflamed, consumed by what lay ahead.

What could I do? I had called Meghan probably a dozen times each day, but she never answered. At first, I thought that I had done something to hurt her, insulted her in some way. But I couldn't have. Well, she always said she had issues, and now with the sudden death of mother, I guess those issues had become magnified. I tried to reason that it wasn't my problem, and yet when I would place my blanket over my head, each night there would be the lingering scent of her strawberry-scented shampoo, or whenever my phone would ring, the second just before I looked at the number, I would feel a little quiver of anticipation inside me thinking it might be her. But, as I said, now I just feel a kind of relief. And as I walk out of my dorm, book bag slung over my shoulder, sometimes I can't even remember her face.

My father never said anything about that day, and neither did I. We kind of have this agreement about it now, except occasionally when I would walk into his bedroom to tell him about my day at work or problems with the car, he would turn his head and there would be that look. And I wonder.

That summer turned out to be not so bad. In fact, it was kind of exciting shadowing Dr. Lewis at the office and hospital. It made me think that I had been right all along in my desire to become a doctor. So now, I suppose, the real work begins.

We are in Mary Donlon Hall, and my father has beads of sweat on his forehead which is red with the effort of his trying to piece together the cable to my new laptop computer on a desk so low and small that I have to sit sideways to use it.

"There!" he announces finally, "I think I've got it," and rises, placing his hands against his lower back as he stretches to full height. He looks out the window at the line of cars with parents and students hauling everything from sandals to freezers through the double doors of the dormitory.

"Look at that," he says, reaching for a tissue and wiping his brow, "The leaves on those trees outside are already beginning to change color."

"Yup," I say, feeling helpless. I have already hung my shirts into my half of the closet, and my socks and boxer shorts are neatly lined up in the bottom dresser drawer.

He surveys the room once more, opens a pack of new ball point pens and stacks them in the pencil holder, which is really an old tin can covered with brown and yellow paisley fabric, something I made at camp I don't know how many years ago.

"Dad," I say gently, "I've got a freshman orientation meeting soon."

"I know, but not for another hour, though, right?" He glances around for something else that needs to be done, then remembering, "Hey, what happened to your roommate, what's his name, Les?"

"It's Lee. I'm meeting him later. His flight was delayed."

"Oh, yes. He's from Nevada, right? I never thought of people actually living there before, but that's good. It's good for you to meet all kinds of people from different places. That's the advantage to going to a school like this, don't you think?"

"Yeah. I guess so."

He pauses, looks around again. Lee's stuff, a TV set, some posters, and a tennis racket, all shipped early, takes up half the room.

"What about your books, Adam? Where do we get those?"

"I already ordered them. Online."

"You need to pick them up at the bookstore, then?"

I sit down on the bed, propping my head on the new navy blue headrest which goes with my new plaid navy blue comforter.

"I've got time for that. Dad, don't you think you should be going?"

He looks down at the carpet, picks up a stray piece of plastic, but says nothing.

"Dad?"

My father glances at me, smiles quickly, stretches again.

"Okay, yes. Well, I guess I had better be going now." He gets up, gathers the tools he brought to set up the air conditioner, and takes one step toward me.

"Dad?"

"What's up, Adam?"

"Are you going to visit Zayde now?"

He looks at his watch. When he turns from me, his profile catches the light which streams between the branches of the huge oak tree by the window. In that second, I realize, perhaps for the first time, how old he looks, how tired.

"No. He'll be eating dinner by the time I get there. I'll wait till tomorrow."

"Okay. But be sure to tell him that I'm at school now."

"Adam, you can tell him yourself. You did say you would try to visit him most weekends, right?"

"Yeah. Sure. But tell him I love him, anyway, okay?"

"Okay, but—yes, yes I'll tell him."

An awkward silence settles over the dorm room which seems smaller now with the two of us standing, the atmosphere dense with emotion. We listen to the grind of the rollers of the dollies in the hall, the excited convivial chatter of freshmen, the occasional blare of a horn outside. Finally, after what seems an eternity, Dad moves toward me.

"Adam—"

"Dad, I'm not that far away. You'll be seeing plenty of me."

"Yes, of course."

He gives me a quick bear hug and takes one long stride out of the room. I wait until I hear his footsteps fade down the hall, and then I sit down on my bed with the new plaid comforter. My heart clenches as I listen, alone now, to the rollers, the horns, the happy students just outside my door.

It is only the first week in November, but here in Ithaca, where the vast silvery skies are precocious for the season, the rooftops of the Baker Laboratory are already drizzled with snow. Shivering, I move through a shifting veil of white, my books pressed against my back. I have stayed late today after a full day of lectures and labs, to meet with one of my professors, Dr. Spiegel, who spent much of his seventy-one years working in a research lab out in California. He only began teaching fewer than ten years ago, and the profession suits him. Next to Zayde David, he is perhaps the smartest person I know. I don't mean that because he can expound on formulas, theories, and cognitive relationships just as well as a child recites the alphabet, but because he is wise, different from most people. When one of the students asks a question, you can tell he is really listening by the way his eyes focus directly on him from beneath his bushy gray eyebrows. And then he hesitates before speaking, considers, as if your question were the most important thing in the world, as if it had *value*. When he speaks, his voice is thick with the strains of Eastern Europe. He once explained that he was only a child when war broke out in Vienna, where he was born. He confided that by the time he arrived in America, he had no one, no parents nor his two older sisters, not even a wife. I think that is pretty remarkable, coming to a different country, going to school, and then even becoming a professor. I tell him about Zayde, and his bushy eyebrows jump up suddenly. "We must talk sometimes," he says.

Midterms begin tomorrow, but as I walk through the whirls of snowflakes, hunched over, heavy with the weight of the slick black book bag against my back, I am unable to focus on the three-part chemistry exam I am scheduled to take at 10 am. Instead, my imagination soars back to a time before I was born. Is it possible that Professor Spiegel and my Zayde knew one another? The world of a Holocaust survivor is a small one, and even if they were unable to recognize each other today, their shared memories would bond them in a sad kinship. I had seen this happen once before when one of my Zayde's friends from the war had come to visit. I was only five at the time, but I remember a large burly man with gray hair and an unusual smile, the kind of smile one has when glee is appropriate but you are feeling anything but on the inside. I remember his name because it wasn't American like Zayde's, but unusual, sounding like the light weapon used by the Star Wars figures I loved to play with—*laser*. This "laser," Zayde explained, was a friend from the old country, someone whom he called a righteous person or savior. I asked him what that meant, and he said "a person who saves a life." Then he told me how this fellow had saved him by taking him in after Zayde's younger brother was killed on the streets. This "laser" didn't talk much to me, but spent several hours in my grandparents' kitchen, reminiscing with them in Yiddish, over layers of honey cake and glasses of hot tea. Before long, he had to leave, to get back to his new wife in Miami where the couple lived. He patted me on the head just before exiting, leaving behind only a T-shirt from Florida which was one size too small for me to wear. Although I was too preoccupied playing with my model car collection and I wouldn't have understood their conversation anyway had I been interested, I recall standing transfixed as my usually loquacious grandfather remained seated at the kitchen table, his head in his hands, trying to hold back tears. Seeing my grandpa like this frightened me, and I asked him what was wrong. For the first time ever, he turned his back to me as my grandmother quickly led me out of the room to watch TV while we waited for my father to come pick me up.

The next time I saw Zayde I had forgotten the incident altogether. But now the memory came floating back to me like the white wisps of snow settling on my forehead. The impression made on me at that time, I now saw, was an indelible one because for once I was given not another story, but a tangible glimpse into Zayde's past. This old world, the time "before" had come colliding with the new one, reawakening all the sorrows and personal regrets, almost too much for Zayde to take. I remembered the incident again just as I had begun high school, when Zayde had to take a trip down to Miami when "laser," his savior, had died of a sudden heart attack.

I became increasingly frustrated with my daydreaming as I dropped my sack on the floor of my dorm and collapsed face up onto the bed. I never did study that evening as sleep stealthily entered the room, draping over me, rocking me into several hours of oblivion. Sometime, though, during the darkest hours of night, I awoke. Too tired to lift my head to look at the lit numbers of my alarm clock, I could only discern the huddled gray mass of my roommate sleeping beneath the covers of his bed. But then there was something else, standing at the door, waiting.

It had been many months since I last saw him, descending the hill outside my window, or standing at the foot of the bed. Somehow, he had found his way here, and though cold winds now rattled the panes and ice stuck petulantly to the window ledge, he remained calm, gray woollen coat open, cap askew, clenching a wooden flute tightly in his hand. Overpowered by sleep, I could not move as he placed the instrument to his lips. He no longer frightened me, this strange child who played a melancholy song, and as I listened, I felt myself pulled toward something, a magnetic merging of the past and future, hypnotizing me until I finally succumbed to exhaustion. Later, as the first streaks of light appear on the ceiling, I open my eyes again. Just before sleep washes over me once more, I lift up my head and look. He has disappeared. But when I close my eyes, I can still hear the strains of the flute calling me in the distance.

David

They think I don't know, but I do. They are trying to get rid of me, lock me away to meet a disastrous fate. I am doomed.

I like to sit in my chair and look out the window, watching the tint of early morning sky go from soft charcoal then, with a burst of sun, to violet and finally to the silky blue of a new day. In the camps I never saw the daylight, had forgotten what it was when the fires of Auschwitz lit the sky, so now as I sit on the soft brown leather seat cushion, I let the natural light fill my soul until, when I turn away, I can remember again.

Home was always where Sarah was. After Joshua was born, she took to housekeeping and motherhood as if she had been doing those things all her life. She seemed the consummate homemaker when I came through the door of our small abode each evening; there waiting would be a table neatly set with a hot stew of *flanken*, boiled potatoes, cabbage and carrots along with a cooling tall glass of water to be followed by a thick helping of homemade applesauce with cranberries blended in, my wife's very own recipe. Always too was the alluring aroma of baked goods which swiftly transported me to my adopted Prague, and as my fork would sink into the multicolored brick of marzipan still warm from the oven, I imagined the cousins noiselessly ascending the stairs and primly walking into the room, their white aprons still glistening with flour. Sarah herself looked the very American housewife, her hair lightened and teased just the smallest amount at the top, the deep crimson of her smile, her dainty ruffled red and white apron confidently tied at her waist, covering a belted button-down day dress. She didn't need to say a single word as I entered my home (my home— my *castle* really!), for the moment my eyes settled upon her dear smooth pale face, my heart opened like a flower, and I had only to embrace her to forget about the cooking aromas beckoning me from each corner of the kitchen. The drudgery of work and the oppressive feeling which grew around me like a stubborn fungus slowly slid off my body as Sarah watched me eat (she would eat later, she argued, claiming that to suck the meat from the bones was the greatest delicacy anyway), and filled the air with news of her female adventures during the day—how the butcher, Leo Rosen, had saved the best turkey leg for her, or how our next door neighbor complains because her colicky twin daughters keep her up all night and day, or how the spinster on the top floor had asked that she teach her to speak Yiddish—can you imagine that! My only response as I sat watching her animated narrative was simply the soft clink of the fork against my plate.

Sometimes, for novelty, Sarah would boil hotdogs and cut potatoes into strips for French fries, so we could have a real "American" meal, then she would invite me into the living room where we would click on the wondrous TV set which sat in front of the striped couch and watch the antics of Milton Berle, the formality of Ed Sullivan, or, for sheer excitement, a wrestling match between the champ, Bruno San Martino and powerhouse Haystack Calhoun. Sarah was the one to precipitate the biggest step toward becoming a real American when she presented me with two tickets to see the New York Yankees play, a present from our neighbor and her husband, whose twins both came down with the croup, making it impossible for them to attend the game. So Sarah and I leave Joshua with Mayer and Mina, and we get on the D line to the Bronx where we are pushed along with so many other Americans with blank faces whose proud shoulders and shouts to the players themselves wash away the bitter memories of the last time I found myself among so many others, when I had not even the boldness to lift my eyes to meet those of my captors.

But here in Yankee Stadium where Sarah and I have our own seats and stand to sing the anthem of our new country, I lift my voice until it blends with the others in a single note of honor. Then, ignoring Sarah's objections, I buy us both a bag of popcorn and later purchase Joshua his first Yankee cap. After all, I reason when Sarah laughs at my foolishness, our son being born on American soil claims more of a birth right to these items than we do. Besides, after a few years, he will surely grow into the new cap. Then Whitey Ford hits a homerun, and we rise as one with the others, screaming and waving with joy. "Wouldya lookat dat?" says the round-shouldered man with a mustache sitting next to me. "Yes," I respond, "such a wonderful thing!" Here even strangers talk to one another. In America, I think, everyone is on the same side.

Years later, I realize I was right to buy Joshua a Yankee camp, because when he turned three he wore it proudly to his first Yankee game, along with his Yankee T-shirt and, later, his own Yankee jacket! Holding my son's small hand in mine as we ascend the stairs of the Bronx stadium, or as I explain the fine points of the game, which I had long ago taught myself, I feel a warmth, a sense of pride radiate within me, for now Sarah and I are creating our own family traditions, just as my own parents had when Mama sat at the piano, Papa made the strings of the violin hum, and I sang when clouds threatened heavy with rain.

While I molded our son into a number one Yankee fan, who eventually had a collection of no less than 300 cards, Sarah imbued the child with a love of books. Although she was self-taught, never having learned English in school and urging me to take classes instead, she would read Joshua the funny pages when he was old enough to turn the pages himself. By the time he was six, he knew his way around the library as well as he did our own kitchen. She had befriended another young couple from the building, both

American-born school teachers who encouraged Sarah's questions and supplied her with books from time to time. So, when Joshua was in fifth grade, he had already read an entire book of Shakespeare's sonnets, owned several of the James Bond books by Ian Fleming, the entire set of the Hardy Boys series, and a bookshelf lined with twenty-four volumes of the latest version of the *World Book Encyclopedia,* which we paid off on the installment plan.

If truth be told, Sarah doted on the boy, paying equal attention to his Hebrew schooling and daily can of apple juice in his lunch box as she did to inspecting the dirt under his nails. When I joined the union and found steady work for an electric company, I quietly congratulated myself for the luxury of having a wife who could devote herself to homemaking and looking after our son. I found no greater pleasure than walking in the door on a Friday afternoon, knowing soon the Shabbat lights would be glowing on the silver candelabra, surrounded by the aroma of Sarah's home-baked *challah* and sweet chicken soup. But it was seeing the eager look in my son's eyes when I sat down with my family to say the *motzi,* the prayer of thanks for our food, which made me feel most like a king. I may have been the one who made the light shine for others, but it was Sarah who had brought the true light into my life.

If we had one regret in our tranquil lives, it was that Joshua had no brother or sister. While one happy letter followed by another from Israel announcing that Malka was again with child—she would have two girls and two boys in all—and our hearts shared their joy—disappointment would follow the two of us like a stray puppy. The problem was not becoming pregnant, for Sarah conceived from almost the moment I touched her, but holding the child proved an impossibility. After suffering four heartbreaking miscarriages, and months of saturating the pillow with hot tears, Sarah reconciled herself to the gift of our one child. She often said, "After all we have gone through, David, we are blessed." And, looking at the faces of my wife and son as they stood in the light of the Shabbat candles, I would have to agree.

In spite of the fact that I had become a number one Yankee fan and could support a wife who stayed home, I understood that I was still an outsider, and would probably continue to be one, for I could no more relinquish my past than scrub away the color of my skin. Each night when the shadows crept upon the wall, I would see the faces of my dear parents appear before me, and hear the sound of Daniel's flute chasing me into the old pickle shop, its melancholy tune torturing me until, burying my head under the covers, I finally fell asleep. But as the years in our small apartment went by, I would stare at Sarah's face, serene in sleep, and my parents' faces would again fade into the past. Listening for the sound of my son's measured breaths as he slept close by, I could hear no other sound, and even the flute became but a dimly remembered note.

When I was well into my fifties, a time when most men are sustained by memories of earlier years and fears of what is to come, I tucked the fading past into my heart and saw the future as only a bright blanket slowly unfolding its wonders to me. As my family grew, I had already reached a climax in my life, a goal at one point I had never dreamed of attaining. I was content. Who would ever have predicted that David Isaac Goldman, the young boy crying for his parents beneath the covers those cold nights during the war could have found such a thing as contentment? Truly, this was a wonderful land.

We forged our own world, a small world inside of a greater one, where our new American friends crossed paths with the friends from before the dark times, our *landsmen*, as we called them. On two occasions Malka, Igor, and their young ones came to visit, making our already small apartment seem even more cramped, and yet with the squeals of the little ones and playful arguments between the sisters over whether it is half or a quarter cup of sugar in the *kuchen,* or the problem of more butter than needed in the pound cake, our rooms on the sixth floor seemed more a home than ever before. When we visited Malka's family in Jerusalem, the feeling in our hearts was much the same.

Once, when our son Joshua had grown into manhood and had a son of his own, I thought I saw a ghost. Already retired, I was recovering from a bout with the flu, after Sarah, as always with her quiet confidence, had nursing me back to health with tall glasses of hot tea and menthol rubs beneath heavy fleece blankets. Finally free of fever, I lay delighting in watching my grandson play with his stock of action figures, when I heard the familiar jangle of the doorbell. Obscuring the light from the hallway was the wide figure of a man, his girth filling the narrow doorway. I rubbed my eyes. Had the fever consumed me once again? Had I become delusional?

No. For as soon as Sarah fell away from the open door, I saw him. More gaunt, grayer now than I remembered, but there he was with the sad eyes I will never forget. My voice found itself.

"Lazar!"

He lumbered toward me and, ignoring the intense odor of the menthol in which I had been swabbed, drew me to him. For many minutes we remained this way, ignorant to the eyes of Sarah and the young one riveted upon us.

During the days of my illness, Sarah and I had completely forgotten the letter written in Yiddish from Miami which questioned, "Could you perhaps be one and the same as the young David Goldman, the electrician whose brother had perished on the streets of Lodz?" More letters followed, and a date was set for a visit—a catching up on old times. But that had been months earlier, and then one week, a sweeping fever had captured the appointment from my mind. Poor Sarah, in spite of her stoic compassion, had been too distraught to remember. And yet, here he was as if from another universe, staring down at me just as he did on the first day we met.

Immediately, I arose, health fully restored; the words could not fly out of my mouth fast enough.

"How are you?" "How did you find your way here?" "A wife! Is she a *landsman* too?" "No young ones, my friend?" Within minutes, we had reviewed the past thirty years, but the time before that—well, those were more difficult pages to turn.

In the kitchen, Sarah brought out more tea along with slices of sponge cake, for there was always an abundance of sweets in a baker's house, and coaxed the boy into another room as Lazar and I resumed our conversation. The talk was more one-sided than I had anticipated, since with age Lazar had grown more introspective than ever.

And yet, with patience, I pulled the past slowly from him, ripping the bandage of time to reveal the still unhealed scar. He never did get over the loss of Sonya, and had married a fellow survivor whom he met in Miami, his first and only home after the war.

"Rose is a fine woman, and a good wife. She has a large family who had immigrated to America before the war," Lazar confided, "and of money she had plenty to keep me in an easy chair for all my days. Ah, but David, you know that is not my way.

"She too had lost many loved ones in the war, a husband, two daughters. When we met we were both only halves of one human. However, as you well know, sorrows unbearable when one is alone are somewhat lightened when shared with another."

"And has marriage lessened the load?" I ask.

Lazar takes another bite of his sponge cake, looks down.

"Lessened? Yes, I suppose it has lessened."

It was clear, though, as the hours progressed, that even though Lazar had begun a new life with another, the past, a morbid and angry companion, had not abandoned him. He still toiled daily as a carpenter and had no children of his own, only the memory of the child who would have been, and yet there was the hope within five years time, of making *aliyah*, setting up a home in Israel where at last he would find the peace which had eluded him.

After three hours, Lazar looked at his watch and rose. He had a meeting with a lawyer set for the next morning and then a plane to catch for Miami. After he left, and Joshua had picked up our grandson, I pulled Sarah to me and held her in my arms.

"How was your meeting with Lazar?" she asked.

"You know, my dear, I realize I should feel sympathy for the man, and a part of me does. But, somehow, I also feel good, good that my friend has returned to me, that I could speak again of those days, and good that I have you and Joshua and Adam in my life."

Sarah smiles and, resting her head against my chest, in that quiet way of hers, places my hand to her lips and kisses my fingers.

After Lazar's visit, Sarah had an idea. She had seen a change in me that day, as I spoke passionately about the old times. I too had felt it as my memories became released as words into the air, feeling a certain lightness of spirit when I spoke of my parents, the antiques shop, the songs. And there was something else. The dreams had now stopped. Daniel had finally left me.

Sarah told Joshua about her idea, and he mentioned it to the principal of Adam's Hebrew school, and soon I had become a regular speaker at the schools in the community, telling the children about my story. And each time I told the tale, my spirit lightened again, and my dreams were undisturbed.

This is not to say that life was perfect, no, it was far from that. For Sarah and me, life had become a patchwork existence, always pieced together after tragedy. Sometimes, in the dark hours of the night, we would lie next to each other and ask ourselves, how could we not have seen it coming? We were Holocaust survivors, wary and fearful, so busy looking over our shoulders that we could not see the terrors looming ahead. But could anyone have guessed what was to come? A lovely young girl having her first child in a peaceful time in a real hospital—a healthy child—a son, and then the unspeakable. My son is a widower, and once again Sarah and I patch a new life together, a life with our son, our grandson. A new life.

Could we say we were happy? At the time, the question would have given me pause. But, of course, in retrospect through the eyeglass of time, we tend to see things with a new clarity. So, yes, if anyone had asked me that question later, after that day in April, the day that once again changed my life forever, I would have said yes. Yes, we were happy. Deliriously happy.

Did I know it then? The joy of coming home to the wisps of flour and sugar arising from the oven; the cold pressing of cash in my hand after I had hooked up Mrs. Levinson's new TV; the smile on old Mr. Taveras's face each morning as he reached across the counter with one gloved hand and dropped change for the paper into my own; the warmth of the fleece blanket straight out of the dryer, reminding me of home. Was I to know then that Sarah's presence was responsible for all these things? No, only in the void left by her absence did I realize it. And, alas, I could do nothing but fill the void with endless tears.

I will never forget that day. The hovering gray clouds which opened suddenly to a deluge of rain, the shoes rushing, stepping into frozen puddles, the unexpected whoosh of cars, the chatter rising to a white noise, the blackness of the brim of my hat as I lifted my eyes to see. And then she was gone. My Sarah was gone.

Once again I had to piece a new life together. A life of three-- two men whose souls had literally been scooped out, and a mother- less boy. I gave up the apartment and moved into an empty home with my son and my grandson in a place—Ithaca, New York— which was as foreign to me as Brooklyn and Prague once were. A new life pieced together again. But this time was different. This time I couldn't do it. I didn't even want to try.

My world became smaller still. I had been reduced to a desk, an armchair, some shelves for the figurines, a bed. And while my Sarah had joined the specters which clouded my mind daily, and my tears continued to flow each night, I still had one glimmer of hope for the future. Adam held my dreams in his small hand, and when my eight-year-old grandson placed his tiny fingers in mine and we walked together down the avenue, stopping to purchase a new pack of baseball cards or another chocolate ice cream cone, I knew that, in spite of it all, I had a future. Gradually, I returned to my speaking engagements, driving Adam to his Little League games, lining up all-American hotdogs on the broiler for our dinner. It felt good to be of use to someone, even if I knew this too would end one day.

I love the little children, their incessant questions, their hope. When I speak to them, I talk freely, the colors of the past, the old streets, Mama's piano, Morgenstern's pickle shop, all come into focus again, and I am the young boy, the apple of my parents' eye. Adam is so proud of his Zayde, a hero now, and accompanies me whenever he can. But one morning when Adam is fifteen, something happens. I cannot get out of the bed. The pain in my back is great, and Joshua must drive me to a doctor. The doctor says I have sciatica and gives me some pills. I am confined to my room, the bed, the chair. When I do recover three months later, I lose the feeling to go anywhere. I never return to the classroom again.

My world is smaller than ever. To help pass the time, I read the newspaper, watch the documentaries on the TV, listen to my music. Sometimes, Adam comes in to read me something he has written for school. He wants to become a doctor and needs to go to a good college and work very, very hard if he is to succeed. When he leaves, I look in the bathroom mirror at the creases in my face. Can you believe it, I say to myself, a doctor! And I shake my head, disbelieving still.

My son comes in to talk to me, but I cannot understand what he is saying, for the skies are becoming cloudy again. Lately, the clouds fill my mind—large, rolling clouds just like the ones which obscured the sky that day. The clouds in my mind make everything fuzzy, and I cannot make out the people, the words; sometimes I do not even know who I am. A woman comes, a gentle woman like the cousins in Prague. She holds my hand and makes me tea and cookies, but not as good as the ones from the old bakery. Sometimes, the clouds part, and I see Adam—or is it Daniel—I do not know which. And, I listen to the sound of the flute, but this time I do not run away. He wants to be a doctor—how wonderful. This boy is my future. He is my hope.

The days are better than the nights when I can hear the sounds of my sobs echoing, seeming to come from every room in the house. The ghosts of them all haunt my dreams again, and I yearn for the wide-eyed exhaustion the sun will bring.

So now I know they want to rid themselves of me, for I have become a burden. I can't say that I blame them. They will put the old man who wets himself and no longer speaks, away. They will free themselves of me, and my world will be smaller still.

As we approach the gates of the camp, I look at my son, trying to implore him with my eyes. No, I say finally, for I am a survivor, I cannot go there. Please take me home. He does not listen. In his eyes is the cold Nazi stare. But on the other side, as we enter, is Daniel looking up at me. He wants me to stay. Okay, Daniel. I won't leave you, I say. I will stay.

And then a miracle happens. She is sitting at the piano playing music, the most glorious music. And when she turns and comes to me, I see it is Sarah—my Sarah! In her quiet way, she extends her soft hand, like a white dove. And I know it will change everything.

Joshua—Ten Years Later

The baby's legs feel like two soft baguettes beneath my hands. I remember reading somewhere that babies are born without knee-caps, and I soon find my thumb slowly inching over to the center, only to discover a gentle padding. He doesn't cry at all. Not even a peep.

I look up, hoping my hands will not shake. The *moyel* arranges his instruments over a white tablecloth and opens the child's diaper. I hold firm. Then I turn my head away.

"Thanks, Dad. I know that couldn't have been too easy for you."

"Piece of cake, Adam," I say, holding up one quivering hand, "I was honored to do it."

My son laughs, emitting a huge guffaw befitting a man of his stature, and pats me on the back. I smile up at him. At 6 feet 3 inches, he is a good three inches taller than I am, a realization which gives me a mild measure of paternal pleasure.

Melissa, his wife, enters the room tentatively, still holding tight to her mother's hand.

"Is it over?"

"Yes, it is. He only cried once," replies Adam, handing her the child, who is contentedly sucking on a swab of cotton dipped in red wine. With both her hands, she takes him from his father. The baby is being delivered over like a grand prize, I think, wrapped in blue silk blankets.

"You poor little thing," she murmurs.

"Wait a minute," I grab Adam's digital camera from a nearby table, "let me take a picture of this beautiful family."

Adam, standing tall, places his arm around his wife as the two look down at their treasure.

"Perfect," I say.

Later, Melissa, looking svelte and refreshed in a pink belted shift, not at all like a woman who has just had a baby, takes me by the arm and we head downstairs. The silver bangles at her wrist clang against each other as she offers me a "smear," a classic bagel and cream cheese, and a cup of green tea. The sound of her bracelets continues to echo in my brain, reminding me of Alicia. I look again at the sculptured curves of Melissa's cheekbones, the arched eyebrows, the soft waves of honey blonde hair framing her face. There is nothing about her which resembles my late wife, and yet today I can't seem to get Alicia out of my mind. This was to have been the day we shared together, the *bris*—the ritual circumcision ceremony of our new son, but instead, I stood alone, enduring a quick solemn ceremony under a veil of tears. Strangely, though, today the memories which press against me from all sides do not make me feel sad. Today, I feel only happiness.

I find a seat at the long glass table in the dining room, next to Adam and some of his friends. As the friends chat, I glance around the room, my eye finally falling on a mirrored wall unit. Behind the double doors in the center is a collection of crystal birds in miniature, and next to them, the two musicians of my father's home, shining in the light. I turn back to face my son. His face, narrow and dark with the beginnings of a receding hairline like my own, is still flushed with the excitement of becoming a father for the first time.

His friends, most of them doctors like Adam, make him the object of their good-natured ribbing.

"The thing to remember with boys," says a broad-faced rotund fellow who still sports a gold velvet yarmulke on his head, "is to close that diaper as quickly as possible before the air gets to—uh—well, let's just say it's not exactly fun getting hit in the eye by a stream of piss."

"Thanks for the advice, Al," says Adam, grinning, "I'll try to remember that." He turns to me. "Al's got two boys, five and one."

I nod. Our children are having children. I recall my parents and their friends always saying that, but I never thought I would be thinking it too, and yet now at age sixty-two, I was a grandfather.

I gaze around the room. There are at least forty people milling around the large open kitchen, dining and family rooms in my son's home on Sackett Street, only blocks from Long Island College Hospital where many of them, including Adam and Melissa, work. I sit back, slowly sipping my tea out of a Styrofoam cup. I feel my body relax as the liquid's warmth radiates within me. It felt good not to have to rush anywhere, not to have to be somewhere in ten minutes time, knowing you had to be somewhere else ten minutes after that. No, I had no regrets about selling the print shop five years ago. It had ceased to be profitable years before that, with PCs and other technology making it possible for our clients to do many of the jobs in their own homes. As for the projects which still could be done on site, well, I never could keep up with the technical expertise modern times demanded. Besides, without Dom around, it wasn't much fun anymore. Sometimes, I would forget that he was no longer there, and turn from the counter, seeking his advice about a car I wanted to buy or sharing my excitement when the Yankees moved to a new stadium. Even now, hearing someone laugh in the next room, I turn again, half-expecting to find the cherubic face of my old friend.

Adam takes a bite out of a bialy stuffed with whitefish salad, wipes his mouth, and stretches languorously. It may be strange to admit, but only now that he has a son of his own, do I see Adam as a man. As his friends continue their conversation about politics and the economy, he suddenly catches my eye, and in that instant, I think he realizes it too—the responsibilities of the future looming ahead, balanced by the weight of a distant past.

It wasn't going to be easy for Adam and his wife, but when is it ever? Both were doctors, she a pediatrician, and he an orthopedic surgeon. Like so many others, they would learn to juggle career and family obligations and, I thought as I reached for a chocolate glazed doughnut, they were bound to make it. After all, it was their destiny.

Adam had decided, finally, to become a bone healer. After choosing his specialty, he confided in me that it was his Zayde who had been the motivation behind his decision, for he recalled how a back problem had robbed him of the robust outgoing grandfather he remembered. Of course, I knew that his back was not the reason my father had changed; the change had begun to occur years earlier on that day on the streets of Brooklyn. And before that, when he was just a boy, when the world broke in two. Sometimes I wondered if I ever even knew my real father, if Adam ever knew the man his grandfather could have become.

Nevertheless, orthopedics was a good choice for my son. Physically and mentally, he seemed the man for it, the one who had always wanted to fix things with his able hands. A bone healer.

Gradually, the laughter and voices in the rooms began to diminish to whispered sounds, like a soft rain. A baby nurse wearing a white uniform and slippers padded into the kitchen and helped herself to a bagel and a cup of coffee.

"Your son is sleeping like an angel," she announces, much to the relief of his parents. Then, taking her food, she slowly climbs back up the stairs. I busy myself, helping Melissa's parents and younger sister dispose of the leftovers. Once all is put away, I look around the spacious kitchen with its tan speckled granite countertops and lush green plants hanging from every window.

Again, I promise myself to add some life to my colorless kitchen, maybe some floral curtains or a bright yellow tablecloth. But, as with all my other good intentions, I'm fairly certain I won't follow through. Instead, my mind will probably be occupied with the adult education courses in literature and world history I am taking at the community college, and now, of course, my new grandson.

I look at my watch and stand up.

"I'd better be going."

Adam, wiping the kitchen counter, looks at me quizzically.

"I thought you weren't going back home until tomorrow?"

"First train out in the morning. I meant I want to go out for a run before it gets dark."

"Oh, yes, I'd forgotten. You still run everyday. Your sneakers are in the closet, Dad."

"Thanks."

I remove my sports jacket which has begun to feel confining, fold it neatly, leaving it on the stairs, and lace up my pair of Nikes tightly, not bothering with a coat on this unseasonably warm April day. Before I leave, I am compelled to walk over to Adam and, smiling, I give him a hug.

"Thanks for the honor of letting me be *sandek* today, to be such an important part of the ceremony. It meant a lot to me."

"Of course. Whom else would I give it to?"

"You know, that baby is just about the best thing that ever happened to me."

Adam smiles, swallows back tears.

"I thought I was the best thing that happened to you."

"Well," I laugh, looking down at the floor, "maybe the second best thing."

I walk into the small vestibule, turn the doorknob, and feel my breath catch as a lilac-scented breeze brushes against my face. And then I remember something.

"Don't forget to give David Daniel a kiss from me when he wakes up," I call, heading out the door.

"I won't," my son says.

The neat brownstones of Carroll Gardens with their small well-manicured lawns sail quickly past me as I run, fueled by the light spring air. I turn the corner onto Court Street and, feeling a sudden peak of energy, decide to make the run to Prospect Park. The grimy pavement beneath my feet acts as a spring, lifting me higher with each step as I push on. The street opens up to a series of white-faced warehouses whose stoic facades are interrupted only by dump trucks and tractor trailers which sporadically punctuate the silence with thunderous clamor as they rumble by. I sprint across the small bridge suspended over the Gowanus Canal, and I am in Park Slope, where the scents of garlic and basil from a local Italian restaurant mingle with the breath of newly mown lawns. I avoid a collision with a man carrying a large blue comforter into a dry cleaning establishment. On the next corner, two Hispanic teenage girls, black hair in ponytails, V-necked T-shirts stretched tightly across their bosoms, are exchanging heated words, oblivious as I pass by. This is the Brooklyn of my youth, with its mosaic of street life, the vendors, the young professionals coming off the subway on their way home this late Wednesday afternoon. The sounds of the city blend in with a circle of starlings which glide on the cumulus clouds overhead. I have reached the park.

Prospect Park spreads before me like a welcome haven, and, as the tall grass crunches beneath the soles of my sneakers, I slow my pace. There is the lake meandering around some large oak trees which stand like sentinels awaiting my arrival. The park is deserted now save for a couple of dog walkers and their animals which yap excitedly as they run haphazardly along the grass, their earlaps flapping in the wind. It is much the same as I remember, so much so that for a moment I feel as if I had been transported through a glitch in time. Alicia and I had spend many of those early days under the trees here, strolling, taking pictures, or just sitting and talking in the shade of one majestic tree. I stop and look up at the sky. The sun is ripe and full like a split orange which hangs low in the afternoon sky.

Disregarding my clean dress pants, I find a clear spot beneath a sheltering oak where the dirt is still black and a few buds have already begun to sprout. A breeze stirs the new low-hanging leaves, creating a whistling sound, a melodic blend of voices, voices I recognize, voices I have loved. My father, my mother, the tender whispers of a family I had never known, the single cry of a new-born child. The breeze, the rippling notes of the nearby lake, the enduring voices all fill my ears and then my heart. Who knows what voices we have yet to hear, what music? I sit back, close my eyes, and listen.